Time for
the Wind

Time for the Wind

Dennis Waite

COSMIC
EGG
BOOKS

Winchester, UK
Washington, USA

First published by Cosmic Egg Books, 2015
Cosmic Egg Books is an imprint of John Hunt Publishing Ltd., Laurel House, Station Approach,
Alresford, Hants, SO24 9JH, UK
office1@jhpbooks.net
www.johnhuntpublishing.com

For distributor details and how to order please visit the 'Ordering' section on our website.

A CIP catalogue record for this book is available from the British Library.

Design: Stuart Davies

Printed in the USA by Edwards Brothers Malloy

We operate a distinctive and ethical publishing philosophy in all
areas of our business, from our global network of authors to
production and worldwide distribution.

...there is a time for building
And a time for living and for generation
And a time for the wind to break the loosened pane
And to shake the wainscot where the field-mouse trots
And to shake the tattered arras woven with a silent motto.

From 'East Coker'
T.S. Eliot – Four Quartets

Weston, near Runcorn, Cheshire, England, Jan. 2000

The knock at the door was totally unexpected. Albert Braithwaite looked at his wife questioningly but didn't yet feel the need to expend unnecessary energy in actually speaking. She shook her head. "I can't imagine who that could be at this time of the morning." She moved towards the window. Out of long habit she was going to pull back the net curtain, to vet the respectability of the visitor before opening the door. Then she remembered that her husband was home with her now, and she changed direction. She pulled open the new mahogany door with pride at its heavy, yet smooth movement and admired again, out of the corner of her eye, its natural, grained finish and leaded, double-glazed panel. Only the slightest tinge of guilt reminded her that one really ought not to be supporting the use of hardwood for this purpose. But the nice man from the firm that sold it to them had assured them that more trees were being planted than were cut down. And it did look so much smarter than this new UPVC stuff.

Three men were standing there, none of whom she recognized. Their demeanor might have resembled that of mourners at a funeral, she thought with amusement, had their front garden been a graveyard. The two older men were dressed in dark suits and she vaguely thought she had seen the one on the left somewhere before, in the local newspaper perhaps: earnest, thin graying hair and moustache. The other was also important-looking, used to responsibility and exercising authority but less reassuring, an air of condescension about him. The third was dressed in smart but casual trousers and sweatshirt, also wearing trainers as opposed to the polished black shoes of the others. His left hand rested on the handle of a trolley, similar to, but looking much more expensive than, the sort that was once used by railway porters for moving suitcases around: on it were two very

1

large and somehow foreboding, aluminum cases. It was also transporting a machine whose purpose she could not imagine. It had a protective plastic cover, although the weather hardly seemed to justify it, so that the details were obscured but a wealth of buttons and dials suggested something impressively technical.

"Mrs. Braithwaite?" asked the earnest looking one.

She nodded, curious but with a hint of nervous anticipation beginning to mar the experience.

"I'm Peter Greenfield, Runcorn Council." He turned the statement into a question, as though guessing that she might have already recognized him.

Although she was still unable to place where she had seen him before, the name, too, seemed familiar.

"This is Mr. Drew, Safety Executive Manager from ICI and Stuart Rolands, one of their science officers. I wonder if we might come in for a few minutes?"

Albert, who had been out of sight, but nevertheless eavesdropping on this interchange, moved into the doorway. "OK, Fran, I'll deal with this. What is it you want?" he asked, looking the visitors over with considerable suspicion. "We never buy anything from door-to-door salesmen."

"It's official business concerning the plant," said, Drew, clearly believing that the phrase conveyed all the necessary information and authorization. "It really would be better if you allowed us to come in and explain everything. Here's my identification." He handed a plastic coated photograph to Albert, who examined it carefully. It corroborated the details and the photo was a recognizable likeness of the man in front of him, albeit clearly taken quite a number of years earlier.

"Right, well that seems to be in order," said Albert handing back the pass, although the notion did pass fleetingly through his mind that anyone could have one of these made quite easily. "I suppose you'd better come in then."

Drew and the Councilor followed them into the house, leaving

Rolands to maneuver the trolley, with some difficulty, over the step.

Fran looked back with concern, worried that the door might be scratched. "Does that thing have to come in, too?" she asked. "What is it anyway?"

"We will explain, Mrs. Braithwaite," Greenfield attempted to reassure her. "Perhaps you would both like to sit down first."

The couple looked at each other with dawning trepidation. This was all beginning to sound too much like someone bearing bad news.

"I expect you knew that there were once quarries a couple of hundred yards beyond your back garden," began Drew, "and that ICI used these to bury factory waste until the early nineteen seventies?"

"Well, actually, no we didn't," answered Albert, clearly somewhat taken aback at this revelation. "We only moved into the village six months ago and no one told us anything about it when we bought the house. I mean, we knew there was a chemical factory here obviously – you can't really miss it can you – but what do you mean by 'factory waste' exactly?"

"It all began a long time ago. There's been a site here for the last eighty years. In the early days, they weren't very good at keeping records. It was mostly rubble, lime and general indus-trial waste but we know that some more dangerous chemicals were disposed of. Of course it was all covered up a long time ago so ought not to be a problem." He paused to clear his throat, as though he had only just realized that the very fact that they were here now implied that there might well be a problem. "It's just that we wanted to be absolutely sure so, about six months ago, we began taking some samples from around the area and analyzing them. We wanted to show that there was no danger from any leaks or contamination.

"Anyway, to come to the point, we've recently found traces of a gas that we hadn't expected and we want to check all of the houses in the area, just to reassure ourselves, and you of course," he added quickly, "that there's nothing to worry about."

"What gas? You mean like coal gas?" asked Fran. "I remember once, when I was little, there was a leak of coal gas in our street. New Years Eve, it was. Policemen came round in the middle of the night to wake everyone up and ask them to go and stay with relatives. It seems that all of the people in the two end houses had been found dead; been gassed in their beds, they had."

"No, nothing like that, Mrs. Braithwaite," Drew said quickly. "This is a gas that's been formed as a result of the decomposition of the material that was dumped in the quarry. It's called hexachloro-1,3-butadiene, HCBD for short. The quantities are only very tiny; nobody's going to be gassed in their beds I can assure you!"

"It's obviously something to worry about though, isn't it?" asked Albert. "Otherwise you wouldn't be coming round here without any warning, with that thing, whatever it is. So what is it?"

Drew seemed unsure whether he was being asked about the gas or the analyzing equipment so chose the latter as the easier option. "Well, we take some samples of air from the rooms on the ground floor, in the corners, away from the doors and drafts. Then we feed them into this machine, called a gas chromatograph. It analyses all of the gases in the sample and produces a graph on the screen. From that we can measure the amount of HCBD in the air."

"I suppose you'd better get on with it, then," said Albert, with obvious reluctance. Drew nodded to Rolands, who immediately set to work uncovering his machine and looking around for a suitable location and power socket.

"Would you like some tea?" asked Fran, being from the generation that was ever conscious of such social responsibilities and, equally, convinced of the restorative power of tea for any emotional or physical upset. In reality, it was simply something to do to take one's mind off the problem in hand, if only for a moment, and give providence an opportunity to bring forth a miraculous solution.

"No, that's quite all right," answered Greenfield, to Fran's obvious disappointment, "it won't take us very long. And we have to visit all of the other houses in the village too," he added, clearly without much enthusiasm.

Rolands opened one of the aluminum cases, somewhat deeper than a typical brief case, and took out two black plastic objects, each about six inches by four and two or three inches deep. Protruding from one end of each was a clear plastic tube that divided into two, each branch then terminating in rubber tubing sealed with a spring clip. He gave one of the boxes to Drew, who indicated he would go into the kitchen to take a sample there. Rolands bent down in the far corner of the room, unclipped the tubing and pressed a switch on the side of the box. A faint whirring ensued and, about ten seconds later, he placed the clip back on the rubber tube and returned to the machine. Having switched on the equipment and connected the rubber tubing to a brass inlet on the rear of the casing, he turned a small tap above the pipe and released the spring clip. He pressed a number of keys and the screen illuminated, showing a flat green line and a vertical scale.

"What happens then, if you find this ABCD stuff?" asked Fran, hesitantly.

"Well, if it's present at levels that could be detrimental to health, we'll have to ask you to leave the house. Naturally, we'd pay all your expenses at a good hotel, until other accommodation could be found," Drew answered with as much encouragement as he could inject into his voice, although he clearly realized that this idea would be unlikely to sound very attractive.

"How long for?" asked Albert, the rising incredulity in his voice showing that the potential seriousness of the situation was only just beginning to dawn.

"Shall we wait to see what the results are first, Mr. Braithwaite," interrupted Greenfield. "No use worrying unnecessarily."

"But you've already worried us just by coming here! We've put all our savings into this house; spent the past six months decorating and putting in a new kitchen and central heating. What happens if we have to move out?"

"As I say, we would reimburse you for everything. We would even buy the house for above its current selling price, if that were necessary. I assure you, you would not lose out – the company would make sure of that."

"But where would we go? We couldn't live in a hotel for ever, could we?" Fran's voice was becoming clearly emotional as the possible repercussions grew more significant in her imagination. She raised her hands to her mouth to stifle an involuntary cry of alarm.

Albert moved quickly to her side and put an arm around her shoulders. "Don't worry, love. We'd be sure to manage, and anyway, it hasn't come to that yet, has it?"

Rolands had meanwhile been taking readings from the digital scale and jotting down figures in a notebook. He looked up and waited for the others' attention. "I'm afraid it's rather high," he announced apologetically.

"Just how high is 'rather?'" asked Drew, impatiently. "Let's not keep the Braithwaites in suspense any longer than necessary."

"Well, we need to check back at the labs to be absolutely sure but I reckon it's between ten and fifty times higher than our agreed limit."

"Oh!" was the response to this, the significance lost on no one.

"Oh, God!" wailed Fran.

"We can arrange to have you in a hotel by tonight," said Greenfield. "Someone will call round in an hour or two to make arrangements with you and sort out any problems." He tried to sound conciliatory but the enormity of what was happening could not escape him.

"Look," said Albert, trying desperately to avert the increasing inevitability of the outcome. "I thought you said there wasn't any real danger of explosions or anything; that the quantities of gas were very small. We've been here six months without any problems. Why the sudden urgency? What does this stuff do?"

"Well we know that it can be very toxic. We don't know an awful lot about it. It's possible we may be over-reacting but we must err on the side of safety."

"But what does it do?"

In significant quantities, HCBD has caused reproductive problems in animals and reduced fertility and it can concentrate in the kidneys and cause problems there."

"Cancer, you mean?"

"Yes, it's probably carcinogenic. The company will arrange to give you both full medical examinations to make sure that everything's all right so please try not to worry."

Fran suddenly looked up and stopped her silent weeping, the implications of the recent announcement filtering through the other worries. "Reproductive problems? You mean birth defects and that sort of thing?"

"That's a possibility, yes, but nothing for you to worry about." Drew slightly regretted the inadvertent comment on the obvious fact that Fran was well past childbearing age.

"But what about Helen? Albert, what about Helen?" Her hands returned to her mouth again and the sounds of alarm and despair broke forth with renewed vigor.

"Helen's our daughter," explained Albert in subdued tones. "We moved into the village to be close to her. They've been here a couple of years." He looked up desperately. "Helen's three months pregnant."

Just as moths rush headlong into the blazing fire, so does this world plunge to destruction into your mouths. XI.29

Oldham, Greater Manchester, England, Apr. 2015

Frank Bradley lingered over the opening screen, with the three-dimensional skull slowly pulsating with phosphorescent blue and green, rotating first to the left, then back to the right. The rear of the skull was missing so that, as each eye-socket moved to centre screen, a different part of the previously hidden landscape became visible. At the left was the silhouette of a factory chimney against a foreboding red and violet sunset; at the right foreground a 'Keep Out!' sign, replete with obligatory skull and crossbones, partly obscured by what was obviously a graveyard.

He knew he ought not to but he couldn't help feeling just a little self-satisfied each time he saw the image. It had taken him weeks to produce and he had told himself practically each day that he was spending far too much time on it. Once, it would take so long to download that everyone would simply click on the 'Skip Introduction' banner before it completed and his artistic imagination and web-coding expertise would not be appreciated. Nowadays, however, most people had fast broadband connections so that aspect was no longer a problem. The danger that had to be avoided was that visitors might simply find it irritating, and a distraction from the information that they were seeking, so that they would look elsewhere. Any animated intros had to be *really* good these days.

But he had given in to vanity, telling himself that potential clients for his architectural design services would be browsing not because they were in the slightest bit interested in toxic waste but because they wanted to see how he had put his skills to use in the production of a web-site. Accordingly, he decided, it was important that the overall appearance of the site was professional and showed off his skills to advantage, irrespective of content.

The name had posed great problems, too. He had racked his

brains for weeks looking for clever acronyms or plays on words. Above all he had not wanted it to sound remotely like some right-wing fringe element. He would be getting emails galore from nutters whatever happened, without positively encouraging it. The best acronym he had been able to come up with was WASTED – 'War Against Systematic Toxic Environmental Destruction.' But it sounded far too contrived and the word 'war' was more emotive than he liked. In the end he had settled for 'Toxicaria,' a word that conjured up both the idea of nature, as in the species of a plant, and of poison and the admixture of the two. As a watermark to his web pages, he used the picture of a mythical tree called the Bohun Upas – the tree of poisons, rumored to have been used by Malaysians for executing prisoners, by tying them to the trunk. The legend was thought to have been based on an actual tree called the Bausor Tree, (Antiaris toxicaria), the sap of which is used by natives to coat the tips of their arrows. It suited his purpose admirably, although he had a lingering worry that many people these days might confuse it with the disease caused by dog excrement.

The site had been active for several months now but he had still not finalized the format. Virtually all of the source data was available elsewhere on the net, of course, but he wanted to pull together several themes and also, importantly, divest much of the material of its emotional content. This was sometimes appropriate (and many sites specifically catered for that taste!) but his own view was that a point argued coolly and logically carried far more weight than one that played upon fear or resorted to hyperbole and doom-laden warnings. Many of the facts seemed sufficiently able to disturb on their own account without the need for help from activists.

Accordingly, much of the information that was presented consisted of almost clinical summaries of the current major sites of contamination around the world. In addition to the Internet itself, input was gleaned from the relevant local and national papers, along with information from science journals where relevant and, of course, from the key organizations such as Greenpeace and Friends of the Earth.

One of the major elements that he intended to introduce, which had not yet been implemented, was a database of the common toxic materials and poisons that were dumped, spilled and leaked from domestic, industrial and military sources. This would grow only very slowly because he wanted to introduce them one a time as a highlighted 'Flavor of the Month.' There were thousands overall so that, in a sense, his task was hopeless but he intended to concentrate initially on those that were commonly encountered or well known. He even vaguely thought that, once it reached a critical size, others might see it as a valuable resource and offer to contribute entries.

The number of people potentially at risk was staggering. There had simply been no control over what was dumped and no records kept until the late twentieth century. Over time, toxic material leaked out into groundwater and from there into wells and streams, forming what they euphemistically referred to as a 'completed exposure pathway,' meaning that it was only a matter of time before people started developing cancers and dying.

Bradley had decided to begin with Dioxin as 'Flavor of the Month,' this being the substance that seemed to occur most frequently in news reports and probably – ever since Seveso and Times Creek, Missouri – the one most likely to spring to peoples' minds if anyone mentioned toxic leaks. It was incredible how prevalent this had become in the environment, considering that no one wanted or used the stuff in the first place – it was only produced as the byproduct of other processes. Incinerators were the worst offenders – ironic really when these had been advocated as the means for saving the land from being overrun by waste from the ever-spreading landfill sites. Municipal garbage and hospital incinerators belched out loads of the stuff.

He had really wanted to put a 3-D image of the molecular

structure of "This month's Poison" on the opening page of the section but had to concede that the effort probably wasn't worth it. Unless, of course, he thought again, he used the structure for Dioxin, regardless of which substance was actually being dealt with. After all it was probably more toxic than most of the others.

Bradley tipped back on his chair and stretched his back. The material of his shirt stuck to his skin. It was surprisingly warm for early spring but he had resisted opening the window because of the damned smell. His thought turned briefly to his real job. Strictly only a part-time campaigner for personal and public rights in the arena of toxic hazards, he would soon be an out-of-work architect if he didn't get back to the Arts Centre design very soon. It was frustrating that he found this 'spare time' pursuit so much more interesting and fulfilling. He allowed the chair to return to a more stable position and gave his attention once more to the screen... and immediately sat up straight and more than a little startled.

The web page that he had been viewing, together with the browser window behind it had disappeared. But his first immediate thought – that the system had crashed, since the background was indeed the dreaded blue color – was just as immediately dispelled, because the centre of the screen was filled with the following message, not in simple, sans serif text but in simulated three-dimensions, with glowing, ever-shifting colors.

This is the way the world ends;
This is the way the world ends;
This is the way the world ends;
Not with a bang but a whimper.

His reaction was fast but not altogether motivated by considered logic. His left arm reached quickly down to the PC unit beneath his desk and his forefinger contacted the 'Off' switch. But then his rational brain kicked in and he attempted to halt his movement before completing the action. But the speed of his reactions defeated reason and the screen lost its image.

Damn! Perhaps that had not been the most sensible thing to do, after all. He had to assume that he had downloaded a virus of some sort that had not been detected by his protection software. Perhaps he should have tried to clean up any problems whilst it was still in memory. But no, if the virus had not been detected in the first place, then it was unlikely that the software could correct anything that had been corrupted. God, having to re-install all of his software and data was the last thing he needed! It had taken him several weeks to get back to a fully operational status the last time he had had to do this, when an untraceable fault had been causing him lots of problems.

After further thought he was still undecided as to the best course of action. Still, whatever he did necessitated that he at least switch the computer back on first. It might be that there would be no virus after all. Perhaps the message had actually been a web page or a Java-produced image or something. It was clearly relevant to the topic. No virus, surely, could generate an original message that was entirely appropriate to the task being performed by the user at precisely that moment. He reached out again and pressed the switch.

Instead of the normal boot-up sequence, there was a period in which the operating system checked out the condition of the hard drive. He had known this would happen obviously, since he had failed to log out in the approved manner, but the delay provided additional frustration. The opening screen appeared normally. With somewhat reduced trepidation he ran Windows Explorer to display the contents of the hard drive. He checked out key direc-tories to reassure himself that his latest designs and the drafts for his updated web pages were still there. He loaded the most recent files and scanned them. Relief! First indications were that nothing was amiss. So, what had happened? He couldn't even guess. He loaded the virus-checking package and checked the date. He had last downloaded virus data earlier that day so any known virus ought to have been picked up. The message must have been generated by the web page he was viewing in some way. After all, although he was familiar with the basics, he was no expert and had not used any of the very latest tools or programming languages so who knew what you could do these days?

He needed some fresh air! He rose from the chair, suddenly conscious of limbs aching from sitting for far too long and walked to the door. He picked up a light anorak from the hanger – it was dry outdoors and there was very little wind so he should be adequately warm for a brief, brisk walk. Checking that he had his door key, he let himself out and set off towards the nearest area of anything resembling greenery.

Bradley's walk was indeed brief. He had set out, at a brisk pace, in the direction of the nearby landfill site, a little over half a mile away. Since he was unable to avoid the smell, he thought he would see if it worsened noticeably as he got nearer. It did, so he was not inclined to linger longer than necessary. He had had some exercise at least so, as soon as he came within sight of the main entrance, he turned around and began a speedy retreat.

He was fit and healthy enough for his thirty-six years. He felt the benefit of his brief walk but would have appreciated it much more had he been able to fill his lungs with some fresh cool air. Instead, he would be more than a little relieved to get out of it, back into the slightly stuffy but odor-free interior of the house. It was not possible to escape this damned smell any other way and, the more he thought about it, the more he resolved that it should not be tolerated. There had been occasions in the past when a transient whiff of putrefying food or burning refuse had drifted by, caught and transported by an unhelpful gust of wind but rarely did anything persist. It would have been unreasonable to expect otherwise in the vicinity of any such place – sewage disposal, chemical factory, landfill, all entailed similar problems. Since the prices of housing in the area reflected this, it had to be acceptable. But anything more than this was not. Anyone with overly sensitive smell had to avoid such locations!

It was only April but it was unseasonably warm. If this were a foretaste of the summer, Bradley would not be very happy. Never one for holidays abroad in Mediterranean or tropical climates, he disliked temperatures above 20°C, flies, prickly sweat and related summery inconveniences (such as lawns, which forever needed mowing). He had promised himself a holiday in Iceland one year, if it became too hot but perhaps, he thought, that was going a bit too far. The temperature could certainly explain the smell. The weather conditions had been stable for the past week or more with a gentle southeasterly breeze blowing directly over the landfill site towards their estate – an explanation but not an excuse, he thought! The prevailing westerly wind would have taken any smells away to the Summerton area and it would, as they say, have been someone else's problem but Bradley had never liked this sort of attitude. There was something wrong and it ought to be rectified.

Neither he, nor any of the neighbors to whom he had spoken, was able to describe the precise nature of the smell, let alone hazard a guess as to its source. It was certainly beyond any simple description. It wasn't particularly acrid – it did not seem to be particulate in nature, adhering to one's clothes; nor was it redolent of decaying organic matter. It was not industrial – it seemed inconceivable that anyone could manufacture such a stench. It was not agricultural – the various fertilizers and slurries might sometimes come close to stimulating retching but even they seemed natural and acceptable compared to this. There was a hint of sweetness, though in its sickly sense; a throat-catching bleach overtone, varying from quite subtle to sufficiently strong to cause one to cover one's nose with a handkerchief (for all the good that achieved). And there was a heavy, stomach-turning base note, reminiscent of the lees from home-brewed wine, tainted by contamination and left for far too long. And... Bradley could have gone on, trying to define the indefinable but he was dwelling on this for far too long. He had decided to act!

He entered the house and quickly closed the door behind him, taking off his jacket and hanging it on the coat rack on the wall. His mind was already racing ahead, anticipating some background research on the web to bolster a letter to the council and the local paper on the subject of the tip. Perhaps he ought to back this up with some sort of petition as well? Everyone within the Waverly area, and probably much further afield, should be happy to sign up to any complaint. He was sure he would be able to recruit some others to help obtain the actual signatures, while he put the material together and coordinated everything.

He scribbled down a few key words to use as search strings before switching on the computer to bring it out of standby mode. He poured himself a generous measure of gin and walked to the kitchen to get a slice of lemon, ice and tonic from the fridge. Unfortunately, he knew virtually nothing about the rubbish tip at Crow Field. Clearly all the local household waste was taken there and it was all landfill, no incineration, but he had no idea from how far afield waste was collected. He didn't know what, if any, industrial waste was dumped there or even, he realized guiltily, if any toxic materials were involved. He hadn't noticed any particularly high security anywhere around the place, so he guessed the answer was almost certainly 'no' on the last point.

He looked in the main food cupboard under the stairs and managed to find a bag of peanuts still unfinished. He took these, together with his drink, to the study and sat down in front of the computer. He positioned the piece of paper on the desk to the left of the monitor. Perhaps some music would not go amiss either, he thought, something uplifting but not too obtrusive: Chopin

Nocturnes. He took an initial sip of the drink, the cold sweet bubbles in his mouth and the bitter aftertaste in his throat occupying his full attention for a moment. Before sitting down, he returned to the living room to locate the CD in the rack.

He loaded the disc into the DVD tray and sat down, adjusting the volume when it began. He checked his email first, as always, but, apart from the latest missives from several Egroups (to which he subscribed but which he scarcely ever read these days) there was nothing. He opened the web browser and used a simple search string of 'waste landfill gas' in Google to begin with. Despite the fact that his research had caused him to find out a great deal about toxic waste, of which some was connected with landfill, he had never specifically had reason to look into nuisance caused by smells particularly. He guessed that those who often suffered such a problem just learned to live with it and took it for granted. In fact, he remembered, whenever he drove past the chemical plant en route to the city, he nearly always switched the car's outside air ventilator onto 'recycle' to avoid the smell of naphthalene that was nearly always present. He had often wondered how residents could put up with it day in and day out.

Just the odd 405,830 hits! He tried refining the search by adding additional key words and soon began to identify some articles that looked promising. He tried one of them at random.

"Landfills are a source of PCB's to the air; thousands of pound of potentially toxic substances are released (Jackson). The US EPA says that landfills pose more threat to the air than to groundwater." Yes, yes, we know all about that!

"Non-methane ground level ozone producers are 10 times greater from landfill than from incinerators. Companies that manufacture incinerators say that if landfill sites meet incinerator emission standards, then…

"…Gas emissions come from meat scraps and other organic material/putrescibles deep within the landfill where there is no air." What a superb word – 'putrescibles', could it possibly be real? Surely it was one of those new American pseudo words, which amused readers in England for a few years but then found its way into the OED. Of course, most of these entries did still relate to the USA. Despite the fact that the Internet was now in worldwide use, the fact that they had such a head start meant that their information far outweighed that from any other country.

He couldn't restrain himself from clicking on the word and launching his dictionary tool. Amazing – it really was a word! "Adjective: liable to decay; subject to putrefaction: putrescible domestic waste. noun (usu. putrescibles) something that is liable to decay." Well, there you go!

And so he continued. One thing could not be denied – the World Wide Web was a great time waster! Virtually everything one might ever want to know was out there somewhere; there was just the small problem of locating it and of maintaining sight of the objective when there was so much in the way of interesting diversions.

He was already half way through his second gin and tonic (having postponed preparation of his evening meal in order to continue his research) when his browsing was rudely interrupted. Several windows appeared in the middle of the screen in front of the material he was reading in the browser, the uppermost indicating the title of a program he had never seen before: 'mIRC'.

He had completely forgotten about the possible virus scare he had had a few hours earlier. As before, in the short time that the program took to load, there flashed through his mind considerations as to whether he should try to close the new program, before it completed initialization and started to do whatever was intended or if he should physically switch off the computer. Having already had some opportunity to consider the factors, he decided, on balance, that it would be best to hold tight and see what happened next, difficult though this was to bear. Accordingly, he just sat back and watched, albeit with some amazement, as the computer appeared to proceed to do things with a mind of its own. Of course he was slightly familiar with the remote operation facilities. He seemed to recall that British Telecom had installed one, to find out why his broadband wasn't working at the advertized speed. But the key difference was that he had actively participated in the download and installation of the software. In this case, he knew nothing at all about it.

The introductory screen gave some information about the program, together with several buttons for such things as obtaining introductory information and for registering the software. This was all that Bradley managed to take in as, briefly, once his initial astonishment had receded slightly but long before he could make anything more of it, this disappeared too, to be replaced by what seemed to be a 'Joining Details' form. There were boxes for his name and email address and several others. Again, however, even as he was struggling to read the data, the fields were filled in for him automatically. There was an entry for 'Nickname', which he watched being completed with something he could not instantly make sense of in the brief time before this window closed.

Another window opened briefly but, out of a long list of options, one was selected before he had time to read it and the window disappeared, to be replaced by another containing the heading of "#mIRC", together with various meaningless acronyms, round and square brackets, and numbers.

There was text in two adjacent panes, together with scroll bars, but he was not going to be allowed to read this. A menu was clicked for him and an arrow selected a 'Channels List' option from a 'Tools' menu. Lots more information then appeared and, again, something was selected and a final blank window opened.

He was, at least, now able to catch up with his thoughts sufficiently to guess that this program must be an Internet Relay Chat client. As far as he knew, these were mostly used by those web addicts who liked to indulge in live meaningless discussions with similar sad people around the world.

He was still wondering what he should do but was increasingly tempted to re-boot the computer. He no longer feared that the system had been infected by a serious virus but now realized that he was in what was possibly a far worse scenario, namely that some external source had taken control of his computer. While still inwardly debating the consequences of such action, and weighing this against the intense curiosity that had been aroused by this display of technical wizardry, the text "/join #Kurukshetra" appeared at the top of the screen. This was quickly followed by:

{Krish} Good evening, Mr. Bradley! Thank you for your patience; you are well I trust?

{RJ} Bradley was dumbfounded and, for the first time in his life, aware of exactly what that word meant. Not only had someone managed to take over control of his computer, to the extent of stopping currently running programs and installing new software, but also this action had been targeted at him personally. How was it possible to do something so sophisticated? Why should someone want to? What was he supposed to do now?

His mind was still in turmoil when more text appeared.

{Krish} I imagine you might be feeling surprise, possibly even anger. Please suppress this for the time being. We are connected by a private channel using IRC. Feel free to type anything you wish and I will then respond.

{RJ} The cursor was flashing against the name 'RJ', clearly

waiting for Bradley to enter some text. Several options occurred to him but he rejected each as either rude, childish or both. He wanted to be rude but mature, to respond appropriately to this clear invasion of his privacy, however impressively clever it might be. In the end, he gave up and simply typed 'Why?' He recalled with a flicker of amusement that this was the classic question that one asked (in old SF or James Bond films) of super-intelligent computers in order to cause them to crash and, more often than not, subsequently explode.

{Krish} Let's say that I just wanted the opportunity to answer some of your questions, whether about toxic waste disposal, T. S. Eliot or even philosophy.

{RJ} Why should I wish to ask you any questions? I don't even know who you are.

{Krish} But you have just asked two in the space of only three short sentences. I'm sure you also wish to ask whether 'Krish' is my real name and why I have chosen to call you 'RJ'.

{RJ} Yes, who are you? How did you know my middle names were Ralph James? I never use them.

{Krish} It amuses me to think of you as R. J. Una; 'una' standing for 'one', of course. There is only One, you know. My own name is just an abbreviation of Krishna – not my real name but it suits our purpose in this discussion as you will discover later.

{RJ} I have no idea what you are talking about. OK, I'll allow you to try to explain what this is all about but then you must allow me to tell you where to go, if I see fit. Why all this technical display anyway? Why couldn't you simply have sent an email if you just wanted to communicate?

{Krish} I apologize sincerely for any concern I have caused. You must indulge my eccentricities. I confess to being fascinated by the Internet and its potential. It is still very fragile though and extremely insecure!

I listen in to quite a few of the more intelligent email lists and your article on allusions to Eliot's 'Four Quartets' in Alan Watts' 'Wisdom of Insecurity' particularly impressed me. I also noted that you had visited a number of different religious and mystical sites and groups. Clearly you have a serious interest in spiritual matters and a genuine wish to find a system, shall we say, to which you can relate? I felt I might be able to offer you some guidance. There are so many false paths and blind alleys for those without any training in discrimination. The Net is a wonderful source of information but, on the subject of spirituality, the amount of rubbish outweighs the serious and worthwhile thousands of times over. Whether traditional or so-called 'New Age', there is so much pseudo-mystical mumbo-jumbo, you could rapidly come to the conclusion that it is all nonsense and become an atheist or nihilist. And that would be a great pity.

{RJ} But you haven't explained how you come to know this. Unless you were... hold on a minute will you...

Sorry, I just had to get up and close the window. In fact, I could do with lighting some aromatic candles or something. There's the most terrible smell outside; I would sooner have the stuffy atmosphere inside.

{Krish} I can give you some useful information on the topics of domestic refuse and associated smells too if you are interested.

{RJ} How did you know I was looking for that? Are you actually monitoring everything I do on the Internet in some way? Why are you doing this?

{Krish} I am not doing anything. Appropriate knowledge is arising to meet the need.

{RJ} Did you not type the answer to my question then?

{Krish} The fingers may have typed and I may have watched them but I was not involved.

{RJ} So the fingers are not yours? You are not responsible for your actions?

{Krish} Where there is an embodiment, the fingers are merely tools. I would not think of them as MY fingers, in the sense of 'I am doing something'. As for responsibility, this is more difficult for the mind to understand. Let us say that there appears to be freedom of choice. Perhaps we can discuss this later.

{RJ} What do you mean – 'there is an embodiment?' Are you not a human being, a body? Perhaps this is a Turin Test, is it; a clever computer program, testing my ability to differentiate real from artificial intelligence?

{Krish} There is a fundamental misunderstanding here. Our bodies are merely food, nothing else. Every cell in your body has developed entirely from what you have eaten. I read that Sophia Loren once said 'Everything you see, I owe to spaghetti.' Beautifully put, though whether she realized the full import of what she was saying, I do not know.

We traditionally believe that we are discrete bodies, containing individual souls. As with many traditional beliefs however, this is quite the opposite of what is actually the case. In fact, we are a single Consciousness which, for the moment, in most so-called 'people,' happens to be identified with a mind or body.

{RJ} And the thoughts that your fingers typed – where did they come from?

{Krish} They simply arose in the mind. Where do your thoughts come from?

{RJ} I think them, of course.

{Krish} Really? Look at the process very carefully. You will find that the 'thinking' part of the mind may well play with thoughts, once they have arisen. It will bring in memory and try to match it with other thoughts. It may indulge in special games like 'logical analysis,' 'reasoned criticism' and others with fancier titles. But what did it actually do to bring about the initial thought? Be very careful with the mind. It is a useful servant but, when we allow it to become master, it soon grows tyrannical!

{RJ} Look, I'm going to stop here. I really don't know what to make of any of this. It's been very interesting but I resent this intrusion. I'll consider your offer and perhaps I can come back to you if I wish to continue this conversation?

{Krish} Certainly. Please do give this some serious thought. You and I both know that you are looking for some sort of meaning to your life. I can provide you with answers to questions that you have been asking for many years but for which you have never received satisfactory replies.

Whenever you decide to proceed, just run this IRC program and link to the 'Kurukshetra' channel. I'm always here, day or night. I'll look forward to hearing from you. Goodbye for now.

I will tell you about that which has to be known in order to attain immortality. It is Brahman – supreme and beginningless, neither existent nor non-existent. XIII.12

Bradley continued looking at the screen, now inactive, for what must have been a couple of minutes before forcing himself to drop the semi-daydreaming state and return to the present. He put the computer into standby mode and stood up. He felt in need of a break, mentally to digest what had just happened and consider what, if anything, he ought to do about it.

Looking at the clock on the wall, he saw that he had now left it rather late for preparing a meal, unless it were something instant. He was supposed to be going round to watch a video with Brenda later. Impulsively, he decided to go out to buy some fish and chips and, quickly collecting the wallet from his jacket, left the house.

He had almost reached the parade of shops at the top of the estate before he realized what it was that, until now, he had only sub-consciously registered. The smell from the tip had, in the short time since he had been forced to close his windows, completely and mysteriously disappeared.

"And now, ladies and gentlemen, we come to the final item on the agenda for today. I have purposely taken the liberty of leaving this until the end in order to get the more routine matters out of the way. In light of the prevailing concerns about environmental questions, I've no doubt this is likely to provoke some dissension amongst you. However I hope we'll all keep our opinions to the point and not get carried away. I'll hand over to Julius now as it is more specifically his concern."

Councilor Mathers eased his corpulent posterior into his chair at the head of the table, his albeit brief speech seeming to have caused him a degree of breathlessness out of all proportion to his apparent effort. Obviously, he had some strong opinions of his own on the matter about to be raised. Or he really was in need of some basic exercise... or probably both. He was one of those people whose strong attraction to ritual endears them to the democratic conventions of meetings of this type, indeed an ideal choice for chairman. He was quite happy to wait before making his own comments, puffing almost contentedly at his pipe which, perforce, was empty, since the council chambers had been a smoke-free zone for many years. He was thoroughly enjoying the proceedings though did not normally allow his expression to betray that fact.

Doctor Julius Sanderson had stood at the mention of his name and now raised his spectacles, with a forefinger as lean as the rest of his frame, allowing him to scan the rest of the room and ascertain that everyone's attention was held. Replacing them, he brushed a hand through his thinning grey hair while, with the other, he selected a sheet of paper from amongst those on the table in front of him.

"I'll come straight to the point and not keep you in this unjustified suspense any longer. We've received a petition complaining about the refuse tip down at Crow Field. We've had the odd personal complaint in the past, of course, and found no reasonable cause for action of any kind, but this time it looks as if every adult occupant of the Waverly estate has signed the damned thing. They demand that we do something about it."

He looked round significantly as he emphasized the word 'demand,' as if registering disbelief at such audacity.

"It quotes from some 1975 EU Directive to the effect that the waste process must be carried out 'without causing nuisance through noise or odors' and says that, in contravention of this, for the past fortnight, there's been 'a most obnoxious and repugnant odor obviously arising from some animal or chemical decomposition on the refuse disposal site.'"

As he said this, his voice altered to indicate he was quoting from the letter, which he now held between the extremities of his thumb and forefinger, at arm's length, as though the paper itself were reproducing the stench for corroboration.

"It seems more than likely that this is an extreme exaggeration – after all, the estate is half a mile away from the actual site

– but it's the first time we've had such concerted action. They also claim to have sent a copy of the petition to the local papers.

"However, what is much more worrying is that the originator – some of you may have heard of Mr. Frank Bradley in connection with other, non-local environmental issues – has obviously researched his topic most thoroughly. I must also be the first to admit that he raises a number of worrying questions to which I would like some answers. Accordingly, I have asked both Mr. Bradley and a Mr. Cleveland Struthers," he glanced down at a paper on the table, as if to confirm this somewhat unlikely sounding name, "to attend this afternoon. Mr. Struthers, an American," he added by way of extenuation, "is employed by United Waste Disposal Ltd., and is an expert on landfill technology. As you know, our tip at Crow Field was privatized nearly five years ago and the contract is due for renewal. I don't think anyone has had any complaints, up until now of course," he added, looking around the table, daring anyone to contradict him. "We put out the request for tender several months ago and UWD are the only ones so far to submit a fully compliant response.

"I've asked them both to join us at 3.30. So that gives us about twenty minutes for you to have a look at the petition and make any general points which you might not wish these outsiders to hear. Perhaps we could have tea now, George?"

From the sheaf of pages in front of him, he counted out the copies that he had made of the text of the petition, retaining the signature sheets, and handed them to the person on his right, motioning with his hand that he should take one and pass them round to the others. Having said this, he sat down abruptly, and, with another vague gesture of his arms, indicated that he was throwing the matter open for discussion.

"Well, I think the whole thing's been blown up out of all proportion," came a booming voice with strong northern overtones from his neighbor, and its owner flung the petition contemptuously down on the table, having glanced briefly through its contents. "It's obviously the weather that's to blame. It's been so bloomin' 'ot this last two weeks, tips all over t' country'll be smellin'. It's unfortunate o' course for them 'at live near 'em but I don't see what we can be expected to do about it."

Harry was something of an anachronism amongst the elected councilors. His family had lived in the area for generations and, amongst the elderly members of the community who had also live here for their entire lives, there was much respect for him. The number of people who fell into this category was continually reducing however and it was increasingly likely that, either Harry himself would retire or die, or insufficient numbers would remain to vote him into office. Whichever was the case, most of the other council members would not be too unhappy to see him go. Neither his rotund exterior nor his blustering manner endeared him to those who espoused a modern, efficient approach with a swift and appropriate response to problems as they arose.

"I'm inclined to agree," claimed another, in what seemed, by comparison, a very meek, well-mannered voice. "A gentle, south-easterly wind constitutes precisely those circumstances which will always cause the maximum inconvenience."

"But surely that's not the point at all," spoke up a new voice, the assured and persuasive tones of Myra Hardwyke. She could always be relied upon to steer the arguments into a reasonably well defined and salient area, and also to inject some succinct and relevant ideas of her own, with that air of conviction which always resulted in nods and grunts of approval from those assembled.

"We know perfectly well that the weather has brought the problem to a head but the wind direction is quite irrelevant. If it hadn't been blowing down to the Waverly Estate, somewhere else would have been affected and someone else would have been complaining."

"At least Bradley wouldn't have been involved," mumbled Doctor Sanderson miserably.

Hardwyke looked across at him disapprovingly. "It would have been someone else complaining," she repeated, with the added emphasis of impatience. "You have to concede that something at the tip is causing a smell which, at the very least, must be unpleasant and persistent to have caused such an impassioned response. As George says, our first concern is to discover whether or not it constitutes a health hazard. Then we find the source and eliminate it. Now I don't really see that there is much to be gained by prolonged discussion. I presume someone has already obtained a list of all of the non-domestic users of the site. She turned the sentence into a question at the end and, raising her eyebrows, looked around expectantly.

No one answered immediately and, eventually, Mathers coughed somewhat apologetically and muttered something inaudible, perhaps hoping that the rest would treat the question as rhetorical.

"I agree," said Sanderson, "the best thing to do would be to find out from these people precisely what wastes are disposed of there and for us to pay the tip a visit personally to see, or perhaps 'smell,'" he added, with a quick glance around, "what the estate has to put up with."

This sensible prosaic approach communicated itself to the others and elicited a murmur of agreement.

"But surely we must already have lists of all materials disposed of," commented Hardwyke, a rising note of incredulity in her voice, anticipating an answer in the negative.

'Well, hmm, yes, that's true I suppose," agreed Mathers, sounding a little unsure of himself and as though stalling for time to think. He had, after all, only held the position of chairman for two months and, as yet, did not know his way around all the various departments. Indeed his lack of assurance in the face of Hardwyke's complete self-confidence indicated that perhaps their positions might be reversed before very long. In an attempt to retain his appearance of authority he went on to say, "I agree with Myra. I presume that UWD will keep the records on our behalf. I would hope that Struthers will bring that sort of information with him this afternoon. Irrespective of whether or not he does, though, I suggest we try to borrow one of the forensic experts from the University. We must have retained authority to carry out periodic inspections of the site and it sounds as though the time is ripe for us to do just that. We'll go out there tomorrow, have a look around, take some samples and so on."

He took out a handkerchief from the pocket of his waistcoat, which he insisted on wearing even in these scorching, early summer conditions, and wiped his perspiring brow, which was even more flushed after his momentary lapse of control. He clearly did not appreciate that any positive impression he might make from being dressed in a smart, three-piece suit was more than negated by his consequent over-heated condition; strands of hair slicked down by sweat and finger vainly attempting to create space for movement of air around his shirt collar. He started to raise the still half-full glass of water in front of him, but realizing that it had now grown warm, returned it to the table with a faint grimace. It really was far too hot for comfort. Perhaps he should investigate the possibility of appropriating some money for air-conditioning.

"Where's that tea?" he asked impatiently, to draw attention away from his embarrassment.

Myra, who was nearest the door and always preferred to do things herself rather than wait indefinitely for someone else, rose from her seat and went to chase up the kitchen staff. The others rose and the meeting broke up as the participants dispersed to exercise their limbs, visit the toilet or merely escape from Mather's foul-smelling pipe which, though lacking combustion, nevertheless seemed to permeate the surroundings.

The noise in the Council Chambers lacked its usual enthusiasm and decibels. All knew each other well and their breaks were usually animated by numerous, simultaneous conversations as diverse as fishing and photography, golf and amateur dramatics; topics far more interesting than those with which they had to deal in the formal parts of their meetings. However, the few conversations were subdued, and most simply waited expectantly, glancing surreptitiously at their visitors, as they waited for proceedings to begin.

Both newcomers looked at ease and confident. The American had that additional air of superiority shared by many of his nationality and especially by those who are acknowledged experts in their field, risking and often succumbing to the sin of condescension. Bradley, by contrast, simply appeared completely at rest, without expectation or demand, ready for whatever might arise and in no way intimidated by the likely opposition from the other. He sipped quietly from the cup of tea he had brought with him from the other room, clearly unconcerned by his role of protagonist in the coming debate. He had a folder of material on the desk in front of him but paid it no attention, apparently giving all of his attention to the taste of the tea and none to the matter ahead. Struthers had brought no papers with him. As an 'expert,' no doubt any required fact or statistic would be available from memory.

Mathers rose to his feet, pushing with his hands on the edge of the table to provide additional assistance, as if there were some doubt as to whether his leg muscles would manage unaided. The already minimal conversation quickly subsided. "I would like to welcome Mr. Frank Bradley, who's come along to put his views on the matter of the refuse site in person, and Mr. Cleveland Struthers, who's kindly agreed to provide some expert guidance on the subject. With his help, I hope we'll be able to put Mr. Bradley's mind at rest on some of the points that were raised in the petition. First of all, I'd like to ask Mr. Struthers to give us an overview of the general principles of using landfill sites for waste disposal. As Julius mentioned earlier, the company for whom he works – UWD – is currently operating the site. Mr. Struthers is, I assume, familiar with the Crow Field facilities..." his raised eyebrows elicited a curt nod from the American, "...and will, I hope, be able to put Mr. Bradley..." He paused, realizing that he had already expressed his desire regarding Bradley's mind and concluded instead, "He should be able to answer any questions we may have."

He lowered himself once again, the muscles in his forearms bulging beneath rolled-up shirt sleeves as they took the strain, hands gripping the arms of the chair. He reached over for the water jug and re-filled his glass. Cleveland Struthers waited until this was finished before beginning to speak. He did not stand, preferring simply to push his chair back slightly to give himself more room for any gesticulations that might prove necessary.

"Thanks, Councilor. Pleased to meet you all. Just a bit of background about myself – I majored in Biology at UMIST back in the mid-seventies and then went on to specialize in Waste Management at Texas A&M with Brown and Donnelly. Got my feet wet working with the EPA – that's the Government's Environmental Protection Agency – during the time of Love Canal, which you may have heard of?" He looked around the table but only Bradley and Hardwyke gave nods of recognition. Sanderson screwed up his face as he strove to whip his memory into obeying his demands, aware that he should remember the details but unable to recall them on the instant.

"That all caused lots of buck-passing and ass-kicking and changed the face of waste disposal forever. The outcome was the setting up of Superfund to start cleaning up all the shit left by the military and industry over the years. Anyway, about this time I set up on my own as a consultant – government or private sector, didn't mind, as long as someone was paying!" He started to laugh but, realizing that no one was joining in, stopped almost immediately, but without embarrassment, and continued. "Been working with UWD for the past three years; in particular, helping them bid for a number of municipal disposal contracts in the UK at the moment, yours being one of these of course."

"Sorry, Mr. Struthers," interrupted Sanderson, "before you move on, could you remind us about this er… Love Canal, which you say was so significant?"

"Sure, glad to. It's an area in Niagara Falls, New York State; named after this guy, Love. He wanted to build a canal for a hydroelectric scheme at the end of the last century but it was hardly even started. Effectively it stayed as just a big hole in the ground – filled with water of course because of the clay – until '42 when Hooker Chemical Company bought up the land. They then used it for the next ten years to get rid of all the crap from their factories. And boy, did they get rid of some stuff! Lindane pesticide, benzene and chlorobenzenes, PCBs, even neat dioxin – just threw it all into this hole, an estimated twenty thousand tons of assorted chemicals. Do you know they reckoned there was about 130 pounds of dioxin? That's enough to kill around seven hundred million people." He paused, and seemed for a moment to drift into a reverie, as if considering the enormity of this, or perhaps trying to think of a country which had a population of this size, so as better to illustrate his point.

"Dioxin – isn't that the stuff that killed all those people in Pakistan in the eighties; Union Carbide was it?" asked Sanderson, his memory having been triggered now.

"Well, no, there was a major and widely reported leak of dioxin at Seveso, in Italy, in the eighties, I think, but no one was killed; they managed to evacuate everyone in time. You're thinking of Bhopal, in India, where about two and a half thousand people died when methyl isocyanate escaped from a Union Carbide pesticide plant."

"Oh, right yes, that was it," murmured Sanderson, somewhat subdued again.

"So this chemical dump in the canal started leaking I suppose?" asked one of the other council members.

"You're damn right it did!" answered Struthers, enthusiastically.

"But not until after they'd built a school on top of it," added Bradley quietly, speaking for the first time, and causing everyone to turn towards him. He wasn't really looking at anyone; it was as though he had just voiced the thought aloud and had not intended to communicate it. He appeared to be almost idly looking through some of the papers he had brought with him and it was clear to everyone that he did not intend to pursue his comment at that time.

Struthers picked up on it, however, and continued in his vein of vilification of the chemical company, for its irresponsibility in dumping so many toxic substances, in apparent disregard of the well being of the future residents of the area. "They were perfectly well aware of what they were doing. Do you know they actually sold it to the local Board of Education for just $1, on the understanding that they would be absolved of any liability? That didn't stop them from taking a tax deduction for 'charitable contribution,' though!"

He paused for effect but Bradley put down the pen he had been toying with and spoke again. "You're not being entirely fair are you? I think the government has to shoulder a good portion of the blame. Hooker tried everything he could think of to dissuade them from using the land. They refused to sell at first; it was only when they were told that, if they didn't agree, the government would force them, that they gave in. They told the authorities that there were dangerous chemicals there and showed them. When they finally handed it over, they insisted it should only be used for car parking or playing fields at the worst.

"When they eventually started building, they had to move the location because of chemical pits that they found. And even after that, they went back later and started adding sewers, rupturing the clay liners that kept the chemicals contained. It seems to me that at least the company was open about it all – after all dumping toxic waste was legal then. It was the officials who were secretive and corrupt.

"Is it not also the case that the army had already used it for getting rid of chemical warfare material, and God knows what, from the Manhattan Project, long before Hooker came onto the scene?"

Struthers seemed momentarily at a loss for what to say. Or perhaps that would be a somewhat unreasonable conclusion. Perhaps, more likely, he was debating inwardly about whether he should continue to dispute this aspect, since one guessed that he was used to winning arguments. Certainly it seemed clear he had not expected to find anyone at this meeting sufficiently knowledgeable as to be able to disagree with him. "Well, Mr. Bradley, I guess you just might have something there," he eventually conceded. "You've obviously done your homework." It seemed as though he had graciously agreed to leave it there but, at the last minute, his nature obviously got the worse of him since he was unable to resist adding, "Still, Occidental Chemical Corporation had to pay over $100 million into Superfund in '96 to help refund the government for the cost of clearing up."

"Excuse me, gentlemen, but would someone mind telling the rest of us what actually happened?" asked Mathers, impatiently, "and what's this 'Superfund' thing that you keep referring to?"

"Sure thing," Struthers continued. "As someone said, the inevitable happened – it started leaking. Chemicals escaped into the soil and the water, even the air. Cancer rates and miscarriages went up. There were fires, explosions and subsidence. By 1977, the chemicals were everywhere; in the basements of homes and puddles outside; you could smell them in the air. People fell ill after eating vegetables grown in their gardens; children even got burned through playing in the stuff. The community started fighting for an investigation and eventually the government had to listen. This all went on for several years but, in the end the place was declared a disaster area and over 200 homes were evacuated with a further 700 plus relocating later as the pollution continued to spread.

"Superfund was a government law set up with the idea of making companies who pollute the land pay for the costs of clearing up subsequently. A tax was placed on oil producers and chemical manufacturers. So they spent the next twelve years and $275 million clearing up the mess so that, by 1990, the EPA said it was OK to start moving people back in. Part of the site is still sealed off but a new residential area – Black Creek Village was built in the mid-nineties."

"Yes, it all sounds fine doesn't it," commented Bradley, with just a faint note of clearly intended cynicism. "Love Canal was actually not a particularly big site as far as toxic waste problems are concerned; it just happened to be the one which benefited from the media attention. Superfund has spent, what, about twenty billion dollars or more so far and achieved hardly anything, given the magnitude of the problem." He had been leafing through the folder and quickly found what he was looking for.

"In 1989, one of Congress' research organizations, the Office of Technology Assessment, reckoned that, if you included military sites, mine wastes, underground storage tanks etc., there were probably more like 439,000 chemically contaminated sites. More are being discovered all the time, since most were never officially registered. The estimate even then was that the cost of cleaning them all up would be in the region of $750 billion through to 2020, possibly as much as $1 trillion. Based on demographic data in the 1980s, there were approximately 41 million people in the US living within a four-mile radius of just the top 1200 sites. This problem affects everyone."

"You make it all sound very gloomy, Mr. Bradley. Are you

thinking we might have another Love Canal here at Crow Field by any chance?" asked Mathers.

"I sincerely hope not, Councilor. Perhaps Mr. Struthers could tell us just what we have got and how UWD propose to keep it where it is. It's quite clear that something is amiss; I only hope it's nothing more than a bit of gas escaping."

"OK, then! Let's go," Struthers enthused, pushing back his chair and striding up to the end of the room behind Mathers, where a white board was propped up on an old-fashioned easel, which would not have looked out of place in a nineteenth century school. He took up a dry-marker from the chalk tray at the base of the board and, removing the cap, took a deep breath. "Just love these things; sure can understand how kids get hooked on sniffing solvents, can't you?

"OK. What we have at Crow Field is a basic, non-hazardous, landfill site. The intention is that the waste material – which is mainly what we call MSW or Municipal Solid Waste but there's also some non-hazardous industrial waste – is contained for an indefinite period while it biodegrades. This can take decades but we monitor it throughout this period and extract any liquid or gaseous byproducts before they endanger the environment.

"First of all, you should know that facilities such as these are very tightly regulated now, since the Integrated Pollution Prevention and Control Directive of 1996 and the subsequent Waste Landfill Directive in 1999. All landfill sites have to have an operating permit, which means proving that we meet all the requirements for emission limits of pollutants and that we follow the guidelines for monitoring them. We have to show that we utilize 'best available techniques' to minimize any impact on the environment and so on – otherwise, the EU won't give us a license. And, since 1999, there have been stringent requirements for minimizing all the potential risks from pollution. So you can be certain that we are not knowingly doing anything that might be causing your problems.

"So, let's look at what actually goes on at Crow Field." He began making a crude drawing on the board. "As I said, this is a non-hazardous site. That means that we can't take anything at all that falls into the hazardous categories of the European Waste Catalogue.

"Anyway," he continued, turning back to the white board, "the basic landfill site is one of two types. Either you start off with a hole in the ground or you build up from the ground like a football stadium. Whichever, the main problem is to keep water out of the system and to stop any of the stuff you put in there from getting out into the groundwater. Once water gets in, any toxic material in the waste has a vehicle for escaping; the poisons don't necessarily have to be water-soluble. What's called a 'leachate' forms and sinks down to the bottom under gravity." He rapidly scribbled in a series of arrows making their way through the mass he had drawn to represent the garbage.

"So, the basic designs for landfill sites are aimed at somehow keeping out the rain with a 'cover' or 'cap' and at stopping the leachate escaping from the bottom, with a 'liner.' Since you can never completely stop leachate from forming – even if there's no rain, lots of the garbage we dump contains water to start with – we also incorporate some sort of 'leachate collection system.' Usually, this is a series of pipes with holes. We slope the site and lay the pipes along the bottom. We can then pump out the leachate and treat this elsewhere; any solids extracted are then returned to the landfill.

"We also have a pumping extraction system to pump the gas out of the landfill. Normally the volumes are quite low here so that we discharge this to the atmosphere. But the volumes are closely monitored and whenever this increases, we flare it. We monitor both within and outside the site boundary. We normally do this on a quarterly basis but are always ready to step this up if necessary. We use sub-surface probes as well as portable devices for carrying out the tests."

"We can see the results of the samples over the past year, can we?" asked Bradley.

"Yes. I've brought them with me. Now, each stage of the process of land filling has its own problems. I'm sure you've already thought of some as I've been talking. No doubt Mr. Bradley here has a whole long list of them." He smiled across at Bradley but the latter's face remained straight. "Let's start with the liner. No, on second thoughts, let's start with the geology. You wouldn't want to go dumping waste somewhere where you had frequent earthquakes for example, would you? But, anticipating some leakage, you have to avoid anywhere with fractured bedrock. You want the rocks as tight as possible. Then if leaks do occur, you can just pump the liquid out and all's hunky dory. And, whereas you might have thought at first that a mine or quarry would be a good place because the hole is already there, that's not always true. These frequently contact the groundwater and that's exactly what we have to stop the leachate from doing.

"Traditionally, the best natural liner has been clay but that's not held up too well under close study. One report reckoned that a three-foot thick compacted clay liner would be breached in fifteen years by three inches of water standing on the bottom. Thereafter, it would leak at the rate of about ninety gallons per acre. That's classed as a 'large' leakage incidentally," he added. "Organic chemicals like benzene can get through even quicker by diffusion. The normal flow is what's called 'advective' and since that's caused by pressure, we can slow it down by pumping out the leachate. Stop me, if I'm getting too technical." He looked round and someone stifled a yawn, turning it adroitly into an attention gathering, throat-clearing exercise, which at least had the effect of waking him up again. The ploy had not escaped the keen eyed attention of Myra Hardwyke however and she ostentatiously rose to take him over a glass of water.

"The reason I'm telling you all of this is not just to give you an overall background – though of course I want to do that as well –

but to show you that we actually use a combination of techniques at Crow Field. So let's move on to plastic liners. I'll ignore early attempts at these. The material that's mainly used now is what's called HDPE." He wrote this up carefully on the board and underlined it. "That's High Density Polyethylene. This has good resistance to most chemicals; it's quite tough and forms clean seams. You just have to be careful not to puncture it. Now some parts of your site were set up with this technology back in the nineteen eighties, though the more recent cells use composite liners, which I'll talk about later."

Bradley let out a sigh at this point and said, "I was afraid of that. Are those areas still in use and, if so, what sort of waste is disposed of?"

"Indeed they are, yes, but we don't allow any industrial waste there; domestic only."

"But that's no guarantee of safety," continued Bradley. "It's been shown that all polymers synthesized from oil derivatives – HDPE included – deteriorate naturally and eventually decompose. After a few decades at the most, they fall apart and what was inside is then outside. Apart from that, there are loads of ordinary household chemicals that have been shown either to soften HDPE or make it become brittle and crack." He turned to another page of his notes. "Things like alcohol from spirits, vinegar or even margarine will cause it to develop stress cracks. Aromatic chemicals like mothballs or chlorinated aliphatic ones like dry-cleaning fluid are deadly. With them, failure can occur in as little as two years.

"It's extremely likely that a large amount of 'domestic only' waste would contain some of those chemicals," he added, looking up. "And, another point I would like to make now, before we go any further." Bradley was now sitting forward in his chair, palms down on the table as though to launch himself to his feet, if anyone objected. He did not refer to any of his notes for these comments, having clearly remembered the details from interest and enthusiasm rather than any dry task of memory. "There's a great danger of us spending an inordinate amount of time talking about so-called 'hazardous' waste and looking for an industrial culprit. But studies have shown – and I have some of the details here," he added, tapping the folder on his right, "that the leachate from everyday domestic waste can be every bit as toxic as that from industrial. It's not all that surprising when you think about it. Typical items that lots of households still put in the dustbin include things like batteries, old paint cans, aerosol pesticides, household cleaners, cosmetics and garden chemicals. It's only really in the past 5 – 10 years that recycling has become prevalent. With a cocktail of all of those, who knows what will result down amongst the tin cans and decaying food?

"In recent history, this problem has been made worse by the attempts to make food and medicine supposedly safer; by marking everything under the sun with these 'sell by' and 'best before' dates. Just think how much more is thrown away now. People used to keep medicines like eardrops, laxatives, cough medicine and so on for years. After all, they probably only used a little before the symptoms had cleared – whether or not this was due to the medicine is beside the point. Then they would keep what was left until the next time someone in the family needed it. And this was usually fine. Many of those sorts of medicines do keep for years before real deterioration presents a danger. But now, companies put these dates on the bottles, with additional warnings about lifetimes once the bottle has been opened. People are taken in – as they have to be to be on the safe side – and they throw the stuff away after perhaps three months. Chemists ask for unused medicines to be returned to them for proper disposal but let's face it, ninety per cent or more ends up down on the tip.

"Incidentally, since we've been talking about Love Canal, one of the studies actually compared the leachate from several municipal dumps with that from Love Canal and found them just as carcinogenic. In fact I'll give you an actual quote, if you'll just hold on a minute." He placed his thumb on one of a number of 'sticky note' tabs protruding at the right of his sheaf of papers, and opened it to the relevant page. After only a few seconds searching, he found what he was looking for and announced, "This is from your people at Texas A&M, coincidentally," he said, though without any animosity, looking over to Struthers. "They say, 'There is ample evidence that the municipal waste landfill leachates contain toxic chemicals in sufficient concentration to be potentially as harmful as leachates from industrial waste landfills.' So," he concluded, "I don't think we need spend too much effort looking specifically for a scapegoat. What should be concerning us is whether the cells are leaking or not, rather than what's actually being put in them."

Frank Bradley sat back in his chair once again and, almost as a single body, the audience looked over to Struthers to see how he would react to this impressive attack on his last statement.

He did not immediately speak, clearly being somewhat taken aback. He had already acknowledged Bradley's 'homework,' as he had put it but it seemed he might have under-estimated the extent of it. "I'm impressed," he finally conceded, "and of course you're right about the toxicity of domestic leachate. If the councilors are happy to consider the question of industrial waste as secondary, then so am I." He looked round the table and, since a number of the listeners nodded or mumbled their agreement and no one dissented, he continued. "OK, so let's move on to the leachate collection system. Mr. Bradley's told us that the liners are very likely to soften or become brittle. In either case, they'll leak, sooner or later. In order to avoid this we have to prevent the buildup of pressure by removing the leachate as it forms at the bottom of the cell. We do this by collection through pipes, as I mentioned earlier and pumping it up to the surface for treatment. We also analyze the composition periodically, Mr. Bradley, and ensure that there are no unexpected or dangerous chemicals forming."

It was clear that Struthers was now aiming to convince Bradley of the integrity of the landfill, rather than the council, and Mathers, intuiting this, was not particularly happy. "You'll let us have records of these analyses, will you, Mr. Struthers?" he asked, as much to remind Struthers that he was here at the Council's request as because he really wanted to know. He had, in any case, done rather badly in Chemistry when at school and had avoided all scientific subjects as soon as he was able to exercise some choice in the matter.

"And you won't object, presumably, if we bring an independent analyst onto the site to take some samples?" asked Doctor Sanderson before Struthers had had an opportunity to reply.

"Yes and no to those questions," answered Struthers. "I actually have some of the results here with me now." He handed these to Sanderson, having already guessed that they would mean little to Mathers. "As to the independent analyst, of course you're welcome to bring one in at any time. I rather think it's in the contract that you can do that, actually, whether we like it or not." He grinned.

"Now, I think I was telling you about the leachate collection system..."

These madmen do not know when to act and when not to act. There is no integrity, nor morality, nor sincerity to be found in them. XVI.7

{Krish} You obviously worry a lot about 'responsibility'.

{RJ} Should I not then? I have taken on board a 'responsibility' for finding out what's going on down at this tip. I want to know who is 'responsible' for allowing the leak to occur; if someone was 'responsible' for dumping toxic waste and so on. Are these not reasonable concerns?

{Krish} There are a number of presumptions here. The most basic ones are that there is freedom of will and that one is able to 'do' something in the first place. You use the word 'reasonable' but this is a glib colloquialism. Is true 'reason' being exercised in this process or is it just a matter of how your attitudes and outlook have been colored by your upbringing?

{RJ} I must confess I find it very difficult to discuss things with you. We are apparently talking about something simple, which everyone would understand, and suddenly you remove the very foundation of the discussion and I begin to question even the basic words we are using.

{Krish} Good! I don't know if you remember but someone in one of the email groups to which you once belonged on the Internet used this excellent signature file in his communications: – "To gain knowledge, add URLs every day; to gain wisdom, remove URLs every day." We all seem to believe without question that to become wise, one must read and travel and gather more and more information and knowledge. In fact the reverse is rather the case – everything must be dropped and only when our minds are still and empty is there the possibility of true wisdom being received and assimilated.

To return to the question of the use of words like 'responsibility,' this is a big part of the so-called problems in this world. If you describe a perceived problem clearly and unambiguously, rather than in the casual language of everyday speech, you can sometimes find that the problem has disappeared.

Indeed, the dichotomy of cause and effect can be dissolved in many cases. As the Scottish philosopher David Hume explained, saying that something is the 'cause' of something else is not really telling us what we think it is. It is simply going into more detail about what we observe. Although we say that A 'causes' B, if we describe what is happening in more detail, the need to resort to this pseudo-explanation may disappear. For example, we say that lack of food 'causes' death. But, as we discussed last time, the body IS food. As Alan Watts put it, eating is simply the process of converting the pattern of the food that is eaten into the pattern of the food that is eating. Death is a word we give to the cessation of this particular process of pattern changing. Another process takes over subsequently. If the food is not eaten, it will eventually decay and become food for worms or fungi. Indeed, if this body-food stops eating, exactly the same thing happens. There is no mystery and no need to resort to causality.

In fact, there is another philosopher called Gaudapada, who lived around the 6th or 7th century CE, who shows that the very notion of cause and effect makes no sense when you analyze it. Perhaps we can talk about that another time.

{RJ} That is all very interesting but, when I've had time to reflect on it, I rather think I'll be getting back to you with some questions – it all sounds a bit farfetched! Isn't it avoiding the topic that you started about responsibility, though?

{Krish} Let's return to the idea of 'doing' then. You asked me last time if I typed the answers to your questions and I replied that, though I may watch the fingers typing, I am not involved. This is difficult for the mind to understand but easy to see in practice. Have you ever watched yourself doing something, for example making a cup of coffee? If not, get up and do it now – I know you'd like one! Don't interfere; just watch it happening. Legs walking, arm raising, hand moving etc. Incredible complexity even at this level but, below that, there are impulses moving along nerves, blood vessels contracting muscles and, at an even lower level, synapses triggering in the brain and enzymes and proteins interacting etc. Are 'you' *doing* any of this? Would you indeed have the slightest idea of where to begin?

You are the observer of all of this, which, in a very real sense, just 'happens.' You, the 'Self,' *do* nothing. As a metaphor, think of the petrol in a car. Without the petrol, the car can do nothing but in no sense could the petrol be said to be acting. Similarly, electricity enables a refrigerator to become cold but the electricity is not cold; it can just as readily enable a cooker to become hot. In an analogous manner, no-**body** can act without the support of the 'Self' – it is after all just a lump of food – but the 'Self' does not act. The 'Self' will support the actions of a murderer just as much as those of a doctor, in the same way as the petrol will enable both tank and ambulance to perform their respective functions. You are simply the equivalent of the petrol in the car – without it the car cannot move but the petrol is in no real sense 'responsible' for how the car behaves. This is deter-mined by the 'nature' of the car – whether it is a tuned racing car or a rusty heap.

{RJ} This is incredible! I'm afraid it's all rather too much to take in at once. I certainly see what you mean about not doing though. I just made a coffee as you suggested and it really was most strange. It was as though some mechanism were functioning quite independently; legs taking the body to the sink, hand turning on tap, unscrewing coffee jar and so on. There were a tremendous number of things going on simultaneously. Actions started without my being conscious of initiating them in any way whatsoever. But isn't this just habit? Like when you start to drive a car, you have to think about each movement – foot down on clutch, change into second etc. – but after a while they become second nature?

{Krish} That's exactly it. There is the body at the gross level and there is mind at a subtle level. But they are both mechanical and subject to law. At the most basic level of inanimate matter, Consciousness is not reflected – rocks can do little in response to their environment; there is no motor to utilize the electricity if you like! Plants are much more complex and can respond in a limited way – growing towards the light for example. Animals can do many things but, nevertheless, they are unable to change their own nature. A tiger can never choose to act like a cow. Man has the unique ability to change his nature, difficult though he may find this and it is possible for him to transcend it. Consciousness is reflected by the mind and exhibits the autonomous nature that we call 'ego'.

{RJ} You keep referring to 'man' and 'he'. You have also said what 'he' is not, namely the body or nature. I take it, from what you have just said, that he is not the mind either.

{Krish} Indeed not! I assume you are now happy to accept that you are not the body? If you are still not absolutely sure, let me ask you a couple of other questions. Presumably, having done some science at school, you know that the body replaces all of its cells completely about every seven years? So that, even if you can look at a photograph of yourself when you were two or three years old and say 'that is me', you will readily acknowledge that your appearance is now radically different? In fact, you have incorporated, presumably, at least seven or eight stone more food into your system since then. And yet, is there an event from childhood which you can remember clearly – ideally, a Maslow 'peak experience' type incident? Can you recall how 'you,' the observer of this incident felt at that time? Is the observer now, at this moment, different from the observer then? (Note I am not referring to the body, which is clearly different, or the mind, which will have new thoughts and memories, or even the personality, which may well have changed slightly, but to the observer of all of these things.)

{RJ} Yes, I see what you mean. That which I somehow think of as 'myself' doesn't seem to have changed at all.

{Krish} Yet the body has changed drastically. As for the mind, I expect the way you view some topics is completely different now. You can change your mind in an instant if someone presents an argument that you hadn't previously thought of. And your personality can change too but at a much slower rate. Were you not once very shy, unable to stand up and talk in front of people? And yet now you can do this without any concern?

{RJ} That's right. How did you know that? So are you referring to some sort of 'soul' then, which is unchanging?

{Krish} Not exactly, no. I would prefer not to use that term at present, until we have agreed some basic definitions. There is always a very real danger in these sorts of conversations that we can use the same terms in what we say to each other yet understand something quite different. I would like first of all to draw a distinction between what I would call the 'true Self' and the ego.

When we say 'I' as in 'I think such and such' we are really referring to the ego. This is the first problem, and a major one, because the ego is not a 'thing', it is a 'process'. It is the process by which the 'real Self' (if I may continue to use that phrase) 'identifies' itself with something in creation. In fact a much better term for it exists in Sanskrit – अहंकार (ahaMkAra), which literally means the making – कार (kAra) – of the utterance 'I' – अहं (ahaM). It is the identification of this 'universal feeling of existence,' which is completely unlimited, with something limited in creation. As, for example, when you say "I am an architect" or "I am miserable." Suddenly your world closes right down to something very small and you completely forget that your 'real Self' is infinite.

{RJ} How the hell did you do that? And how did you know I was an architect? I haven't told you.

{Krish} Yes, sorry about that. You may remember you received an empty document by email a few days ago? Well, it wasn't entirely empty. When you attempted to read it in WORD, a macro installed a Sanskrit font onto your PC so that it would be able to interpret these messages. You really ought to update your virus protection software you know!

As to your being an architect, I know far more about you than that!

Anyway, to get back to the point, there is a fundamental principle at play here: namely that, if you can see something (and I don't necessarily mean literally 'see' it) then you cannot *be* it. That which is 'doing the seeing' must be something 'higher.' Thus, seeing the body, you cannot be it; seeing the thoughts in the mind, you cannot be them. Unfortunately, it follows that you can never see the 'real' I that is doing this seeing because that is what you really are. Nor can you 'understand' it as such. Since it can see the mind at play, it must be much subtler than the mind. How could the mind ever really understand it? The most it can do is to 'realize' the truth of the situation.

This is one of our basic problems – always trying to 'understand' things with the discursive mind. The Self is beyond the mind and cannot be understood. Coming back to the 'ego,' this has been described as being like an onion. One can remove the successive layers of complexity to try to get to an understanding of what it is but on peeling away the last layer it is found that there is actually nothing there at all.

The true Self is quite other than this. It is the only reality, always the same and everywhere the same; Consciousness providing the motive energy for every seemingly separate thing, but itself doing nothing (as I said before, rather like the petrol in a car).

{RJ} So how does one come to appreciate what this 'real Self' as you call it is, if you can't comprehend it with the mind?

{Krish} Although the Self cannot be objectified by the mind, the mind can nevertheless apprehend the truth, once all of the 'self-ignorance' has been dispelled; once all of the identification with 'things' has ceased; once all of the obscuring ideas have been removed.

You could say that, in a sense, it is thinking which causes all of the problems. Thoughts arise and we find some of them attractive and identify with them. They become 'opinions' or worse still beliefs. We are then in danger of mistakenly thinking of them as 'knowledge.'

Believing that it is merely the senses surrounding the objects of sense, though seeing, hearing, touching, smelling, eating, going, sleeping, breathing, talking, mentally grabbing or letting go, even just opening or closing the eyes, the Sage, knowing the true nature of (the Self) should think 'I do nothing at all'. V.8-9

It was raining. It poured down unceasingly from an even grey sky, bouncing up again from streets and car roofs with an almost tropical intensity. The parched soil in gardens and fields thirstily attempted to drink the water as fast as it fell but the earth was so hard-baked that much of it ran off into gutters and ditches. The atmosphere was one of intense relief after the weeks of dry heat, so uncommon in this temperate climate, and everyone seemed to breathe again, the dust having been washed away and the pollen laid to rest. Unfortunately, it was with mixed feelings that the party of councilors re-assembled at the town hall, trailing streams of water from umbrellas through the corridors. The more conscientious of them were somewhat dismayed by the change, and not because of personal discomfort. The conditions that had given rise to the complaints, which they were duty bound to investigate, were now no longer present. Others, however, were rather relieved that they would not now have to subject their nostrils to the 'obnoxious and repugnant' to anywhere near the same degree as might have been the case, even if they were likely to get extremely wet instead.

As they were discussing this new development and its implications, a secretary ushered in a new arrival. He was slim and of medium height but round shouldered and with a slightly stooped posture. He carried an unfurled umbrella but the lank brown hair dripping over his domed forehead, together with the blurred appearance of his spectacles, suggested he had not been using it. He looked about fifty but could have been younger, as the general impression was that he was not over scrupulous about either his appearance or level of fitness. He did, in fact, fulfill most of the requirements of the stereotyped absent-minded professor and it was no surprise to anyone when he introduced himself as Doctor Andrews, a research chemist from the university. As Hardwyke shook his hand, she couldn't help thinking how amazing it was that external physical characteristics so often corresponded with particular vocations. The limp handshake fitted in with the overall aspect of his clothes and stance, but the penetrating eyes revealed a quite different level of order behind the disarray of the facade. As he continued wiping the spectacles he had removed with a somewhat soiled looking handkerchief, Andrews explained that the city medical officer, with whom Sanderson had got in touch, had enlisted his help previously, not least because of his access to the extensive facilities of the university laboratories.

With the formalities of introductions and explanations over, the ambivalence of feelings manifested itself in a general unrest and impatience. On the one hand, the opportunity to get away from the offices for a while was distinctly attractive to the majority and there was the vague suggestion of a childish anticipation of a day's outing to the seaside. Indeed a school minibus, out of commission because of holidays, had been commandeered and this heightened the illusion. On the other hand though, the unexpected turn in the weather had, metaphorically if not literally, dampened the enthusiasm to no small degree. There could be no hope that it might not be raining at their destination, which was only about three and a half miles away. There were numerous comments as they boarded the bus, to the effect that it would now be a wasted journey, except for the fact that they would probably all get soaking wet. Long before the grumbles had died down, however, they were on their way and it was a mere five minutes journey down to the south eastern edge of the town, about half a mile past the last visible habitation.

There was little to be seen when the bus drew up by the side of what appeared to be the entrance. The cloud layer was so low and the rain falling so heavily that visibility was down to less than a hundred yards. A green, plastic-covered, chain-link fence stretched into the mist on either side of a double iron gate. Neither was in particularly good repair. Although no breaches could be seen in the fence in the immediate vicinity, some of the concrete posts which supported it were cracked and leaning, as if nearly uprooted and the fence around these caved inwards or outwards, looking in danger of imminent collapse. The gate itself was constructed of lateral and diagonal iron bars covered with netting. It was topped with the inevitable strand of barbed wire, in a corresponding state of decay, red with rust and bristling with sharp rusty prongs of wire where the netting had been worn through by the combined attack of weather and time.

They were held up at the gate while the worker there waved through a drab yellow, UWD, rubbish disposal truck. Apparently no one in authority was present or, if there was such a person, he or she had not been informed of the distinguished official visit. A third possibility, suggested by Hardwyke, was that whoever was responsible had been told and had chosen not to be impressed. Mathers had been remonstrating with the man by the gate for some minutes, and was striving to keep his temper. He appeared to succeed in convincing the laborer that the whole council really had come to look around and that they should be allowed through the gate. He had expected Struthers to be there, waiting for them. Bradley, too, had wheedled himself an invitation but there was no sign of either.

A few hundred yards beyond, the minibus halted again and the occupants, quickly raising umbrellas or pulling anorak hoods over their heads, gathered outside. Nearby, the truck that had held them up a few minutes ago was still disgorging its contents, sitting atop a small incline with its body upended over the edge. Despite the rain, dust and other debris disturbed by the torrent from the truck rose about the pile and drifted in the direction of the crowd. All the larger particles were soon brought back to earth, however, to join the rest of the sodden waste, leaving only the stench of partly decayed food to reach the nostrils of the bystanders, who flinched and turned away, screwing up their faces.

"Let's 'urry up then and get this o'er with," complained their Northern member. "What's your plan of action, Doctor Andrews?"

"I can only suggest we have a general look around," he replied, and select some places to take samples. We shall need specimens of soil and of any waste that looks or smells suspicious. If anyone sees anything unusual or has any ideas, I'd naturally be glad to hear from them."

"Shouldn't we wait for Struthers?" asked Sanderson. "I'd assumed he'd want to give us a guided tour and explain what was what."

"I'm sure he does," Mathers retorted, "but I think we should decide what we want to see; he isn't likely to be completely impartial about any of this."

They agreed that they should first of all make a complete circuit of the main area of the tip and accordingly set off, with the perimeter fence on their right. Afterwards, they would try to arrange for the attendant in charge to take them on a guided tour through the central areas and point out to them where the various types of waste were disposed of, unless Struthers had turned up by this time. They had been warned to keep away from particularly muddy ground, as this could be some of the sludge from the electrochemical or light engineering plants, on the industrial estate north of town. Hardwyke had considered asking how one was to distinguish 'particularly' muddy from, presumably, 'ordinarily' muddy, since the entire place seemed a virtual quagmire. The man, however, emitted a distinctly unfriendly aura and one gained the impression that he would not prove amenable to such a sarcastically phrased question. She therefore simply resolved that they must be extra careful. Certainly they were not really dressed appropriately; even had the weather remained dry. They should have wellington boots at the very least. She glanced briefly at the attire of the others, idly wondering who would be likely to suffer from this little expedition. She always seemed to have a wardrobe of old clothes and had had the foresight to choose something appropriate to the weather and the anticipated conditions, whilst still appearing reasonably smart. Someone, of course, had gone to the extreme and was wearing what looked like old gardening trousers under a ragged and stained raincoat. Most, though, had on their usual business suits and their faces were only just beginning to register a realization that they might have made an error of judgment here.

"If you don't feel you're suitably dressed for these conditions, I'm sure no one would object if you stayed behind in the bus," she finally addressed them. "There's no need for us all to get wet and mud stained."

Only one of them made an immediate move towards the shelter of the waiting bus. The rest looked guiltily around, each waiting for another to take the initiative. Mathers cast a slightly envious glance after the man who had taken up Hardwyke's offer but managed to convert it to a contemptuous one before the others caught it. Being nominally in charge, he could not reasonably exclude himself.

"Shall we get on with it then?" he asked impatiently, turning and setting off without waiting for the rest. After a few further exchanges of disgruntled expressions and mumbled expletives, they resigned themselves to the situation and followed.

Their first impressions were of disappointment. The surroundings appeared distinctly uninteresting, consisting of gentle hills of various dull hues, whose slopes were mostly covered by a sparse wiry grass. The hollows contained pools of dirty water, collected from the past few hours rain, the surface often striated by rainbow bands of color, the diffraction patterns from thin films of oil or other immiscible liquids. Where puddles had not formed, however, there was often to be seen quantities of sludgy material, surrounding the mounds and interconnecting like a series of drained dykes. Mostly this was the usual black, muddy color but occasional variations of browns and dark dull reds indicated that nature alone had not been involved in their construction.

They wandered for some time around what they presumed to be the extremities of the dump itself. Some areas seemed to have been out of active use for a considerable time for they had almost reverted to the natural state and had the appearance of bleak moorland, with short stumpy grass and black peaty earth.

Myra Hardwyke finally broke the silence and, addressing no one in particular, commented, "Odd but there seems to be something missing. Where are all the old prams, rubber tires and milk bottles? It hardly looks like a rubbish dump at all."

"Stuff like that has to be separated out for recycling these days. I'm fairly sure that used tires are not even allowed to be land-filled any longer," answered Sanderson. "You'll probably find the larger items like bedsteads and washing machines in the stream by the railway viaduct," he added, cynically. "The council charges for removing them and not everyone can be bothered to take them to the official disposal sites."

"Noticed any smells anyone?" asked Mathers, avoiding the jibe. Sanderson had always been an advocate for making every conceivable service free, as if unlimited supplies of money were available. He didn't want to embark upon an argument to point out the realities of the situation.

"The rotting food we smelled back there isn't likely to cause any concern half a mile away," answered Andrews. "This industrial waste, which we haven't seen yet, must somehow be at the root of the problem. Chemical decomposition, possibly reacting with the food matter, must have produced a rather potent gaseous by-product. At any rate, it's probably water soluble so don't expect to catch the scent of it now."

"Damn nuisance," someone commented, though he was probably alluding to the discomfort caused him by the rain, rather than to the fact that it had taken away the pleasure to be afforded him by sampling the smell personally.

"Struthers hasn't yet told us how they cope with toxic gases," Hardwyke reminded them for Andrews' sake. "He mentioned briefly about collecting and burning off the methane but he was going to show us where it all takes place today, along with a number of other aspects we didn't get around to."

They had been pressing persistently onwards, threading their way ever more carefully between the puddles, which were now growing in number and individual diameter, but it soon became apparent that it would take them some significant time to walk all around the perimeter – it was, after all, about three miles. Although this might have been quite acceptable in the weather of the previous day and with the ground dry under foot, in these conditions it seemed distinctly unattractive. Nor, argued Mathers, was it likely to be productive. The heavy rain and low-lying cloud made it quite likely that they would miss anything relevant. Accordingly they returned to their starting point without encountering anything unusual or noteworthy.

The man at the gate was processing another domestic refuse

truck and they had to wait while he checked the paperwork and typed details into the terminal on his desk. He put on his coat and walked over to the vehicle, which had parked on a weighing platform after arrival, so that the weight might be automatically recorded. He inspected the contents somewhat cursorily and, eventually, the truck moved off. Asked whether he was now free to conduct them through the central areas of the tip, he replied that he was, but couldn't go out of sight of the gate as he was expecting a tanker of waste from the industrial estate shortly. He led them up the track, now like a swamp in places, after the passage of the dustcarts. On rounding the corner at the top of the incline, they observed that the track continued more or less in a straight line for about two hundred yards before reaching a sudden drop. At this point there was barely sufficient room for the trucks to execute a turn on full lock. The area to the left had been practically filled with domestic refuse and the cart, about fifty yards away, was tipping over the drop to the right.

"How many loads do you have each day?" asked Sanderson. Having observed two trucks in the half-hour or so since they had arrived, he was wondering how, if that rate were maintained every weekday of the year, there could still be room for more. Actually though, on looking down at where the truck ahead had just deposited its contents, there hadn't been much impression made.

"Well, we got four trucks and they each make two or three trips a day," answered the attendant, grudgingly, more intent on wiping some mud off his boot on a clump of grass at the edge of the path.

"Hmm. That's about two thousand cubic feet per day, I suppose, said Sanderson, tapping away on his mobile, now doubling as a calculator. "But then, most of that stuff will compress down to considerably less when it's been out in the weather for a day or two. So, call it five hundred cubic feet and, considering an area of a hundred by fifty yards down there, that's... around forty-five thousand square feet. To cover that to a depth of one foot would take about eighteen weeks, which sounds about right," he concluded with an air of satisfaction.

"'Course, at the end of each day, we also tip a couple of inches of soil over everything and then the compactors move in and pack it all down, like."

Ah, yes," Sanderson began again. "Well, yes, you would have to do that, of course." This was a minor detail that had not been mentioned the previous day. Clearly such a procedure would be needed on a regular basis, to prevent the area becoming dangerously unstable, as well as to make the most use of each 'cell,' as Struthers had called the separately sectioned-off areas used for dumping. It did somewhat throw his calculations though.

"Doesn't seem to be anything to worry about here anyway," said Mathers without the least trace of irony, scanning the vista of tin cans, broken glass and other amorphous excreta of civilized, suburban existence. He stepped back as he spoke to avoid a cloud of smoke and flying ashes from a small bonfire of cardboard boxes and other paper waste. This had been set alight by two of the workers below, who were wandering around, selecting combustible materials from the debris of the recently dumped loads.

"I suggest we take a look at the industrial sites," he spluttered, coughing into his handkerchief as billows of grey smoke blew in their direction and sparks from the conflagration spewed skywards.

"I'll just collect a few samples over here," said Andrews, waving towards the filled in area to the left and setting off in that direction.

"You'd better watch your step mate," cautioned the attendant, "it hasn't been completely covered yet."

"How long since you stopped tipping there, then?" This was the voice of Bradley, much to most people's surprise, scarcely anyone having seen him arrive. He looked very much at ease in a Gore-Tex anorak and waterproof trousers over wellington boots.

"Oh, er." The attendant's face screwed in concentration as he endeavored to remember. "Only a few weeks; I don't remember exactly."

"That's bad," said Bradley, turning to the others. "The whole point of the cap is to prevent surface water from filtering down through the waste and forming the toxic leachate at the bottom. It needs to be done almost immediately and obviously before any serious rainfall such as we are getting now. What's the point in capping after several inches of rain have fallen?" He turned back to the attendant. "Is this area set up for leachate extraction?"

"What? You mean pumping out the liquid from the bottom of the cell? No. This was mainly solid domestic. We didn't put no poisonous stuff in there."

Bradley groaned but said nothing. The others walked back towards the gate. Andrews, undeterred but stepping gingerly among the rubble, set off across the old tip. Various grasses and dandelions had already taken hold, lessening the impact of the desolation and he was suspicious that it had been 'only a few weeks' since tipping ceased. There were many puddle-filled hollows and it was still raining quite heavily but most of the surface seemed reasonably solid with a gravel-like consistency. A slope nearby showing a cross-section of old bricks, pieces of metal and loose stones warned him not to become too confident, however. A sizeable area of smooth, grey red, earthy material, about three yards long and one across, attracted his attention to the left. It was probably the milk bottle, apparently leaning out of the middle at an angle, as though half sucked under, which land-marked the scene. He moved towards it and stopped at the edge noting the odd purplish tide mark around the circumference. He abandoned his umbrella, folding it up and sticking the point into the ground to avoid dirtying the nylon, leaving his hands free to unfasten the case he carried with him and take out a specimen bottle.

Taking a spatula from his inside pocket, he spooned a little of the colored material into the bottle and replaced the stopper, wiping the spatula on a tissue extracted from the case. He looked around for a moment, wondering what to do with the spent tissue. Then, with a short, self-conscious laugh, realizing where he was, tossed it to one side, nevertheless experiencing a slight twinge of guilt as he did so. He glanced quickly around to ensure that no one had observed his foolishness. He was one of those people who, having forgotten something while walking along in one direction, will loudly snap their fingers or utter some resounding expletive before making an about turn, to illustrate to bystanders that he is not completely mad, but who only succeeds in drawing attention to himself. Using the lid of the case to keep off most of the rain, he activated the Global Positioning switch on the mobile phone he had loaned from the college, and located a sheet of labels from a pocket inside the case. With great difficulty under the adverse conditions, he copied the figures from the display onto one of the labels, peeled it from the protective backing-sheet and attached it to the sample.

He slotted the sample tube into another pocket in the case and prepared to move on. On impulse, however, he reached out to lift the milk bottle from its swampy death. He was expecting to have to exert some degree of force to release it from the grip of the mud, which had already half engulfed it. It was with considerable surprise therefore, to the extent that he almost fell over backwards, that he found the bottle shifted with scarcely any effort whatsoever. Momentarily amazed, he stood gazing at the object, whose lower end terminated at the point where it had been apparently embedded in the soil. It was, in fact, only half a bottle, cut cleanly through, slightly diagonally, below centre. On closer examination, though, the edge was not sharp as though cut with a saw, but soft, as though melted.

How very curious, he thought. I suppose someone must have used one of those bottle cutters on it and thrown it away when they found they hadn't made a very good job of it. Funny how the edge has worn down though – must be weathered over a period of time. Almost looked as if it had been placed there deliberately with the intention of deceiving one. Why, I can't imagine.

He took another sample tube from his bag and scraped some of the material still clinging to the bottle down into it, labeling it as before.

On his way back, by a different route, a similar looking area, containing the remains of various bits of rubbish, called for closer examination. A piece of tubular metal, red with rust, possibly from an old bicycle, made him wonder if that, too, ended where it entered the ground. On inspection, he discovered that it was indeed part of a bike. He could distinguish the 'Raleigh' badge on the crosspiece joining two half immersed sections. He leaned over and firmly clasped his hands round the bar, resigning himself to the fact that he was going to get his hands dirty. Actually, this time, he didn't expect to be able to budge the cycle if the rest – at least seventy per cent – were below ground but, almost losing his balance for a second time, he found that the remains came loose with surprising ease. The buried metal, the lower crossbar and part of the upper, terminated prematurely. It was clear that they had not broken because of oxidation, as he would have expected, for the ends were quite clean, with no sign of rust. Indeed, they literally gleamed like new steel and the edges were not jagged but smooth and worn, as the milk bottle had been. He examined the ground as best he could without kneeling down and excavating the soil but could see no signs of the remainder of the frame.

This was unusual and no mistake. Taking another specimen bottle, he quickly collected another sample of soil. He then took a small test tube and a bulb pipette and, sucking up a little water from a nearby puddle, transferred it to the tube. Locating a bottle of universal indicator in his case, he added two drops and shook the contents.

"Good grief!" he exclaimed aloud. "The pH is less than one. Ridiculous!" He threw the tube and pipette aside, this time without a second thought. He established the position of the new site; wrote and attached the label to the specimen and placed the sample in the bag.

Refastening the case, he stood up and retrieved his umbrella, preparing to set off to return to the others. Having a sudden thought, however, he stopped again and held up the umbrella to examine the brass ferrule at its tip. Sure enough he saw, and drew in his breath sharply at the confirmation of his suspicion, that, in the short time that it had been sticking there, the discolored metal had gained a renewed sheen of brilliance. There was a distinct mark indicating the depth to which it had been inserted. Continuing on his way, he couldn't help wondering further about the bottle. "If that wasn't a natural phenomenon, erosion over a long period, the only chemical I can think of which might have caused it is hydrofluoric acid and that's so unstable it couldn't exist under normal conditions for very long. In any case no one could possibly be stupid enough to dump the stuff in the first place."

On reaching the gate, still musing over his findings, he found that the others had already set off to view one of the sites for the disposal of non-domestic waste. One of the laborers, who appeared not to be doing anything in particular, directed him and he followed the main road away to the left from the entrance. This soon dwindled to a muddy track, bounded on either side by steep gravel covered slopes. It wound gradually up and round to the right until, ahead, he saw the group of council officials, standing by a tanker at the side of a large pit, which stretched away for some tens of yards. As he drew near, it gained the appearance of a peat bog surrounded by grass and gravel banks, or a mill reservoir which has dried up, leaving the mud and waste of generations at the bottom.

A rubber hose had been connected to the lower rear of the tanker and, from its other end, pulsed a flow of viscous reddish-brown liquid. It slurped slowly and malevolently down the incline onto the surface, where it spread and was very gradually absorbed into the sludge already present.

"What's this then?" he asked as he caught up with the group, preferring for the present to withhold his findings. "I thought that you weren't allowed to dispose of liquid material at landfill sites."

"Load of waste from the photographic plant, guv'," answered the man at the tap of the tanker. "Hypo, soda and stuff," he added knowledgeably. "And it won't be liquid once it's cooled down. This is under pressure at around 70°C."

"I'm surprised they're still in business," muttered Andrews.

"Last film processor in the country," replied the man proudly. "Still quite a lot o' professionals that frown on digital cameras. There are even some young 'uns taking it up – you can't get the same quality as films, not even with those cameras costing thousands of pounds."

"We have a list here," Mathers began. "It's probably more meaningful to you than it is to me. Chapter 4, sub-chapter 02 – wastes from the textile industry; 14-02 – wastes from textile cleaning and degreasing. What about this: 09-01, wastes from the photographic industry – thiosulphates and... what's this ferro-cyanide stuff? Isn't that dangerous?"

"No, it's fairly innocuous as far as industrial waste goes," answered Andrews, reaching for the list and glancing down the contents. "I don't see anything here to worry about unduly. No acids ever?" he asked, turning to the driver.

"Oh no, guv'. Leastwise, not to my knowledge," he said, scratching his head.

He seemed to share the general layman's attitude that any acid was, by that sole fact, an exceedingly dangerous substance.

"No, I wouldn't really expect anything from there. They've more than enough alkaline waste to neutralize any acids they might use," Andrews commented, more to himself than to any of the others. "I'll just collect some samples."

"Could I have a look at the list please?" asked Bradley, as Andrews was about to depart.

Andrews looked up distractedly, failed to recognize the person who had addressed him, but handed over the list anyway and moved off.

He proceeded to extract a number of his empty sample tubes and some tissues and, spatula in hand, he carefully eased himself down the slope and set off round the edge, stopping here and there to examine the surface or collect some of the material.

Bradley scanned the list and then the field of chemical mud in front of him. His face revealed feelings of anger and helplessness. "Where's Struthers?" he demanded loudly, with pent-up frustration. "He should be here to explain all of this. Who exactly is in charge?" he asked of the laborer who had accompanied them but clearly knew little of what was going on in any technical sense.

"Archie Booth's the gaffer but he's off sick this week. Somebody came in to see us on Monday afternoon but they told us to just carry on as usual 'till 'e gets back."

They all wandered around aimlessly for a few minutes, while Andrews' figure continued to move further away along the eastern edge of the cell.

"We still haven't noticed any smells at all," complained Sanderson, breaking the silence. "I think we're wasting our time here."

"Look," said Myra Hardwyke suddenly, addressing the attendant, who was still playing with his boots, trying vainly to relieve them of the accumulated mud and dirt. "Surely you would know if there was anything in the way of fumes or smoke to complain about. Has there been anything exceptional recently?"

"Not especially," he answered. "'Course, it's been hot. Always stinks a bit more when it's hot. Most people that works 'ere, though, don't bother much about it. Them that's sensitive that way don't last long at this job. And it has been hot," he repeated, "rain'll dampen it down now all right."

"Yes, I suppose so," agreed Hardwyke. "I expect all the workers here are quite inured to it. Probably wouldn't notice if you threw a bad egg at them. No offence intended, of course," she added quickly with a glance at the man with the boots, who hadn't seemed too friendly to begin with, she recalled.

The rain had now stopped but the sky, which remained ominously overcast, suggested that only a brief respite would probably be allowed. The group shuffled their feet impatiently, awaiting the return of Andrews, who could now be seen on the opposite side of the bog, still intent on his studies, stooping occasionally to examine something more closely. The man with the Lady Macbeth complex pursued his obsessive pastime to one side.

The noise of the pumps on the tanker changed tone; the steaming, gurgling ooze from the pipe became a sputter and finally stopped. The driver unlocked clamps and released the pipe from the tanker. Lifting the end above his head, he then made his way elaborately down the length of the tubing, lowering it to the ground behind him as he went, so that none of the contents should escape but be driven by gravity out into the morass below.

He is both inside and outside of all creatures, whether moving or unmoving. He is both near and far away. This is so subtle that it is not easily understood. XIII.15

{Krish} So, are you prepared for your battle with the Chemical companies in your war against toxic pollution of landfill sites?

{RJ} I must confess that I am wondering if it is all rather hopeless. What can one man do against huge companies with almost limitless funds and the most skilful lawyers? I really do sometimes wonder why I bother.

{Krish} Aren't you trying to avoid having what happened to you happen to someone else?

(RJ} What do you mean? What do you know? How can you claim to understand my motives?

{Krish} In this world we have to act. At the most basic level, breathing and pumping of blood etc. takes place. We must feed ourselves to keep the body healthy. We have fundamental obligations such as bringing up our children etc. and occasional ones such as telephoning for an ambulance if we encounter someone who is injured. But to act only at this level would only maintain us at this level. If we are to purify the mind and try to uncover the ignorance preventing the realization of our true nature, we need to cultivate characteristics such as discrimination, dispassion and discipline.

But, in all of this, we should allow our own particular nature to suggest the general direction which our life should take e.g. if our natural inclination is toward leading men, we should not shy away from such a course. If we have always been interested in ecology and pollution, then by all means act appropriately in response to environmental problems. You cannot deny the facts of your own particular background. You are uniquely positioned to be able to take action against those who have wronged your family and possibly prevent a similar occurrence in the future. But beware the ego! If your interest is motivated by anger or revenge, any consequent action is unlikely to be beneficial.

{RJ} What on earth do you mean? What are you talking about?

{Krish} Do I need to spell it out? I'm talking about your wife having a miscarriage and your marriage breaking up after the events in Cheshire. Everything that happens does so because it has to, because it needs to. There is no choice except in respect of how we respond to it. Everything should be seen as an opportunity to re-evaluate what we are.

{RJ} Who the hell are you? How do you know all of this? No one around here knows my background. Have you been following me, prying into my life history? You've got a damned nerve!

{Krish} Please do not take offence. I have no morbid curiosity to 'pry into' your past, as you put it. I simply wish to help. I may be idiosyncratic in my philanthropy but I am in no way malevolent. Unfortunately, the world is in that era of its development when ignorance is on the increase! There is almost universal misunderstanding about the true nature of things.

In all of this it must be remembered that this world around us is just like a play. It isn't real. There will always be heroes and villains and, at the end of the performance, both get paid equally (assuming that the play is not so bad that the producer has to close it down of course). In each and every moment, everything is perfect in reality. It is only the ego that gets stuck in the appearance and wants things to be different.

The Self is not born, neither does it ever die; nor, having been, will it again come not to be. Unborn, beginningless and endless, it is not killed when the body is killed. II.20

He showed no sign of reluctance upon receiving instructions that he was to lead the next scouting party into the Northern Wastes. Indeed, this emotion was far beneath him, who, after all, was revered throughout the Army as the finest scout in the land. Not that he had any choice – the royal command was absolute and, while he stood little chance of survival if he undertook the mission, he stood none at all if he refused. Inwardly, though, for the first time in his life, he felt fear. He knew that five previous forays into the north had failed and no one had returned alive to provide an explanation. Only one twisted corpse had been found, presumably having somehow dragged itself, or been dragged, almost back to camp. One of the workers had discovered the remains and relayed a message back to the hill. He had been one of those summoned to investigate. He still recalled the expression on that face and the horribly contorted limbs. He failed to repress a shudder at the startling vividness of the memory. With an effort of will, he forced himself to consider the importance of the task and his concomitant responsibility, and succeeded in bringing his muscles under control.

The position at home was worsening. The rain of the past few days had been of unprecedented magnitude and they had been forced to abandon the lower levels probably forever, many of the tunnel walls having been washed away by the raging floods. As yet, the upper levels were not in danger but there was, nevertheless, good reason to fear that the whole structure of the hill had been undermined.

This extremely serious problem was not their most immediate, however. Most of their food supplies had been destroyed when the main stores had been inundated the previous day. Only a bare subsistence had been salvaged and severe rationing was now in force. There were ample supplies to the southeast, or had been, but, since the rain, new torrents had sprung up where, before, there had been mere trickles or dry beds. Any slight hollow that had existed previously was now an impassable lake. Many had been killed by the storms already – the numbers were not yet known but could be estimated to be upwards of a thousand. Others were missing who, out on food parties, had been cut off by the sudden downpours and had not returned. The way things were going they would not see any survivors for some days to come. Moreover, he had to admit that chances for these, too, were slim unless they had found a well-protected cave or similar shelter.

The skies had now cleared but it could still be days before the floods subsided and they desperately needed food and possibly a new home if this one should collapse. Hence, the queen herself took the decision to instigate the sixth mission to the North. It was an indication of the extreme seriousness of the situation that she had chosen her best scout to lead it – this one must not fail.

He had grasped all of this immediately and he put his fears and doubts aside, forcing those unworthy emotions to drain away, leaving the unconditional courage and determination which he had learnt to cultivate, or which had been inculcated in him, by his lifetime's service in the army. Resolutely, with no further thoughts of personal danger, he set about making preparations for the venture.

He had been given complete authority in the matter, able to choose whomsoever he wished to accompany him and make whatever plans he thought necessary for a successful outcome. The choice was easy – there were no bad soldiers in this army – but he naturally tended to take those with whom he had had dealings in the past, whom he knew personally and with whom he could therefore communicate easily. It was probable that situations would arise where it would be essential to think and act together, with the shortest possible delay, to avert a crisis.

The briefing he gave to them, when assembled, was minimal – they had so little information to go on. They knew that the terrain presented more difficulty than most and that the recent rains would have considerably aggravated this. Apparently the ground became very uneven with loose rocks and rubble and a very fine dust, though this latter should now cause little hardship. Further on, however, there were rumors of flatter land with dangerous swamps and invisible slimes, which could trap one without warning. It was these that would prove most hazardous.

The purpose was quite straightforward. It was thought that on the other side of these inhospitable lands could be an ideal location for a new settlement. The scent of food in abundance was unmistakable and the general appearance, from a distance, was distinctly favorable. Unfortunately, there was no alternative method of approach. On the western side, there was a permanent lake at the best of times and, to the Northeast, the land fell away steeply to a vast, poisonous swamp.

The general atmosphere of unease could not be dispelled by rational discourse. The others knew, as well as he, that there lay an unknown factor out there. Something had destroyed without trace, apart from the single returning soldier, five previous groups of scouts and this they could not easily cast from their minds. Actually, the fact of the survivor, if that he could be called since he had died before reaching camp, had never been reported generally. Orders from above had censored the information to all but those already involved and these had been warned, under threat of execution, not to speak of it to others for fear of causing panic. The rumors rife among the soldiers were already sufficient to cause more than a little unease, however.

They were to set off immediately, taking minimal supplies, it being envisaged that they should find something to eat along the way. The weather reports were fair and it was expected that, barring unforeseen eventualities, they should return well within twenty four hours.

They left the hill by the northern gate and, marching in single file, crossed the distance to the far perimeter with little trouble, the waters having been dispersed some time ago by a trench constructed by the workers. After a brief communication with the guard on the watchtower, he led them on a slow winding ascent of the boulder strewn southern aspect of The Wastes. The going was difficult but presented no insurmountable problems. They were all supremely fit and rested only occasionally and for the briefest of intervals.

As scout for the party, he led the way and, some distance ahead of the others, selected the best of the many routes available to them. The most rigorous discipline was to be maintained and they followed almost precisely in his steps to avoid any misadventure. Continuing in this way, they finally reached the plateau without any difficulty. Here, he ordered them to rest for a while, though they were all eager to continue. It was ahead that their dangers were likely to begin and they would need all their wits about them.

He knew that he, too, should pause for a while and not give the others the impression that he thought himself superior in terms of stamina. But someone had to determine the lie of the land ahead and, without any false modesty, he knew himself to be the most experienced for that job. Accordingly, he set off to climb to the top of a huge outcrop of rock nearby. It was a stiff climb with the face almost vertical in places and it was some minutes before he was recovering his breath at the summit.

On the other side, the rock gave way to a sheer drop and, not incidentally, to a spectacular view. Impressive, that is, but by no means attractive. Admittedly, much flatter ground replaced the rubble but he could discern the beginning of what looked like swamps in the region between where he stood and the hills of their destination. A dense, tropical growth of vegetation also began a short way ahead of them, with tall grasses lying in clumps around and often partially submerged by pools of unknown depths. Giant weeds, supporting enormous yellow heads, climbed hundreds of feet into the air. In only a few places could he actually see bare earth through the tangled growth of plants and this would no doubt prove to be muddy on closer examination. He fought off an almost overwhelming feeling of pessimism, reminding himself yet again that this was perhaps the last chance his community had for survival. He must execute his task completely dispassionately, with no emotions. He would pretend this was another training test with, maybe, a promotion if successful. He paused a moment to try to reinforce this fantasy, then he turned back to the prospect before him with his peace of mind somewhat restored.

There was no easy passage – that much was certain. The sun was now high in the sky and reflections off the various tracts of water, discernible through the green, indicated that there might be a continuous stretch of lake between them and their objective. If that should prove to be the case, they would have to turn back defeated but, if that happened, they would return with ignominy and, having failed, they could expect no mercy from their doomed colony. No, at all costs, they would succeed. The thought of shame, a feeling so alien to his character, more than anything else brought about his resolve and, without further deliberation, he made his way back down to the ground and waved them on.

At first, the going was easy after their long hill climb, and they made good progress. They had now lost sight of the hills in the distance but had no difficulty maintaining a steady pace in the right direction. As they had anticipated however, as they entered the jungle, the firm, sandy earth became a damp and then a soggy soil. The forest seemed to have collected all the water; indeed, huge drops still fell from overhanging fronds. Possibly the ground here lay slightly below that of the surrounding areas, which compounded the problem. At all events, they were now forced to start making detours to avoid impassable bogs.

The ravages of the storm were apparent here too. The stalks of grass no longer stood up tall and slender but had been bent and battered into hanging, sodden clumps, tangled with the mud and debris washed through by the deluge. Many were broken and washed away, while the stronger ones were merely bent and now rose up, curved across the sky and bowed down again, laying their tops, still heavy with rain, upon the path in front of them. These worst excesses of the storm also provided them with insurmountable obstacles and they were forced to backtrack and search out an alternative route. Under normal weather conditions, forests like this were pleasant places to travel, with plentiful food sources. Now, neither was the case. Conditions were distinctly disagreeable, if not positively insufferable, and most of their food was under many feet of water.

Eventually, their worst fears were realized when, upon breaking through one of the seemingly more impenetrable growths, they came face to face with a wide expanse of mud, broken here and there by lakes of varying sizes, still sprouting the tops of grasses drowned by the floods. He reacted quickly. Not wishing to allow them to lose hope or begin to feel despondent, he immediately set about assigning them tasks. Ostensibly, they would make use of this convenient halting point to look for something to eat and to rest before continuing their arduous trek. His main concern was treated as of secondary importance. He selected four of them, split them into two pairs and sent them in opposite directions along the side of the bog to look for a way across. The remainder was not fooled by this naive attempt to persuade them that the situation was not now extremely desperate but, in order to serve him to the best of their ability, they did not show it. Indeed, everyone knew the seriousness of their position and knew that the others also knew it. But the fact that they all maintained a facade of enthusiasm and optimism achieved its purpose and spirits still ran reasonably high, considering the circumstances.

Their morale was soon to suffer another blow, however, when the scouts returned with negative results. They would probably be able to get around it if they travelled far enough in one direction but how far was open to question and there was no guarantee. Furthermore, their time was limited – they couldn't afford to experiment. They would have to attempt a crossing and, since from the reports the nature of the bog was reasonably uniform everywhere, here was as good a place as any.

They set off cautiously, tentatively picking their way over the mud and avoiding wetter patches and pools without too much difficulty. The storm, though the cause of all their problems, had, in fact, indirectly assisted their passage. In places were what would normally have been impassable stretches of water but the intensity of the rains had been such that grasses had been completely flattened and now provided natural bridges and safe crossings.

Not all was smooth going though, by any means. They had to retrace their steps from many a dead end and some of the grass bridges gave directly onto the water. They also lost two of their number, drowned when a tendril of some lesser plant, with which they had constructed their own bridge, was washed away. There was no hope of saving them – the current was far too swift. They could only stand and watch helplessly and then despairingly, as the bodies of their companions disappeared from view over a waterfall.

The sun was now past its highest point and they had to push on regardless. They could not even afford time to mourn the passing of their comrades. Fortunately, their leader did not have to order them to carry on. He had not been wrong in his choice of soldiers; no courage was lacking. They set off again with almost renewed vigor and determination.

It was when they seemed to have crossed the worst of the swamp that they saw the mist ahead and halted for a moment. It hung, like a grey wall, a short distance before them, extending but thinning to the left and right. The sun still shone brightly above it, so it was obviously not very thick but it was rolling straight towards them. Already, in the brief moments since they had first noticed it, trees a few hundred feet ahead had been obscured.

He thought it a little strange but gave orders to move off to the left to bypass it, there being no point in hampering their progress even further by trying to march through a fog. Before they had travelled very far, however, the mist began to appear there too. It could be seen rising like steam from the ground ahead and streaming towards them as if on a faint breeze, veiling vegetation and pools as it drifted nearer. There was no time for retreat; even had it occurred to them – the original patch was, in any case, now to their rear – the mist was upon them in an instant.

It was immediately obvious that this was no ordinary weather phenomenon. Vapor does not suddenly condense in the middle of a hot summer's day. Moreover there was something not quite normal about its texture and it exuded a faintly aromatic odor, not damp and slightly acrid as expected. It was too late to warn the others not to move for risk of stumbling into water or becoming bogged down in the mud – he was cut off and unable to see more than a few feet in front of him. Fear was, for the moment, in the background but it had already occurred to him that here was the 'unknown' that had brought about the downfall of the previous expeditions. They must have lost their way back and drowned. Then came the memory of the one who did return and he realized that the explanation could not be so simple and the fear hit him.

Whether he really had become very cold or not, he could not tell but he began to shake uncontrollably. He found he could no longer think logically. He knew he should formulate a plan of action but his ability to concentrate had gone completely. Ideas and impressions totally unrelated to the circumstances stumbled over each other, unchecked. Visions appeared before his eyes, and sounds crashed through his hearing. Again and again, the image of the corpse he had seen, together with the real or imagined sound of hideous screaming punctuated the sensory illusions.

He lost his footing and fell off the stone from which he had been observing the encroaching mist, collapsing in a heap upon the mud below. He no longer had control over any of his muscles; his limbs began to twitch convulsively and his back arched and writhed, twisting his head over and around, backwards and forwards. A final inner atom of mind attempted in vain to command his body to obey but the remainder of his mind failed to back it up, now itself involved in convolutions and convulsions of its own. Ultimately, he lost consciousness, while his body continued for a time to dance and gyrate with a will of its own until it, too, eventually became still and lifeless.

Some short time later the mist dispersed as suddenly as it had appeared, to reveal the miniature battlefield, and the mud gradually took the bodies of the ants unto itself.

I give heat; I hold back and release the rain; I am immortality and I am death, what is and what is not. IX.19

Later that day, a hurriedly organized gathering met at the Council Chambers to follow up the morning visit. Mathers had decided that the full council was not required and had called on just those he felt either essential, like Sanderson, or those who would complain bitterly if not invited, such as Hardwyke. Bradley and Andrews were also there, already being considered key to the investigation and, though Mathers probably would not have admitted it, sufficiently knowledgeable to ensure that Struthers did not try to 'blind them with science.'

Tea having been poured, Mathers opened the discussions. "Thank you all for coming at such short notice. I thought we should move this business along as quickly as possible. I want to ensure that, if anything is amiss, we rectify it as soon as we can and, if not, we reassure everyone that there is no cause for concern."

"And cover your ass," thought Struthers. He had offered his apologies to Mathers for not turning up that morning. His actual excuse was that he was having urgent consultations by videoconference with his head office in Ohio, but what he actually said aloud was, "Yeah, sorry I couldn't make it this morning but perhaps it was better that you look round yourselves anyway, without me breathing down your necks. I'll be happy to try to answer any questions that came up."

"If I might begin," continued Mathers, "I was somewhat concerned at the general state of disrepair of the place, at the shortage of facilities and at the significant lack of expertise. No one seemed to be able to tell us much about anything."

"Well, it is a dump, you know," joked Struthers, with a smile, but it was apparent that the mood of the others was one of seriousness. "In the first place, it's not a 'Special' site – that is, there are no hazardous or toxic wastes – so there's no need for high security. It covers a large area so the perimeter fence is a couple of miles long. And it's been there some time – since long before we took over. Still, we acknowledge responsibility for its maintenance and I'll get someone to look at it if you feel it's not adequate.

"There are storage buildings for the earth moving equipment and compactors in the north west corner. You can't see them from the main gate, so you probably missed them this morning. They also house a kitchen plus shower and toilet facilities, so the men can wash up before they go home. The cabin by the main gate is a bit basic I admit but there's a toilet in there and a phone.

"What else was it? Oh yeah, expertise. You only saw the guys who push the shovels around, I'm afraid. The supervisor's sick and his deputy was already on holiday, so we couldn't get anyone in to cover at short notice."

"Thank you. That sounds reasonably satisfactory. Mr. Bradley, I believe you had some concerns?"

"Yes, a couple of things. We were told that a completed cell we saw was still uncapped after two weeks. Also I'd like some details on the lagoon we saw being used for disposal of photographic waste."

"I think you got hold of the wrong end of the stick there, Bradley. The cell isn't complete in the sense of ready for capping. Perhaps I'd better just run through the basic procedure, as it applies at Crow Field.

"The site's about half a square mile in area. That's about 130 hectares. Not sure how we came to use those units historically, something to do with fields and agriculture I guess. Anyway, it's convenient because our cell unit in this case is about 1 hectare. So we have, or rather aim to have, eventually, 120 cells. These will be split about 40 – 80, with the larger number dedicated to municipal waste and the smaller for industrial. Some of those will be built as lagoons, like the one you refer to.

"The cells aren't all used at once. There are several phases ongoing at any one time. One phase will be preparing cells for use by lining, laying collection pipes and so on. A second phase will actually be in use for tipping and a third phase will be covered, or eventually capped of course. The logistics can become quite complicated, I can tell you!

"As far as the domestic cells are concerned, the way we work is to cover a cell to a depth of around ten feet – that's about forty thousand cubic yards which, at present rate, takes up to twenty weeks to complete. Then we top it off with nine inches or so of earth and move on to the next cell. We use earth excavated from future cells for this incidentally, as well as bringing in topsoil from outside. We'll probably use around forty of the cells in this way before we return to the first and start a second layer in the same way. Each cell will have up to five layers before we cap it and landscape for building or whatever. You can see that'll be quite some time in the future. The total lifetime of the site could be up to 250 years. If landfill isn't banned altogether before then of course," he concluded with another of his weak grins.

"There are some problems with the cell you saw but nothing to do with not capping – we've nowhere near completed a single layer yet over the thirty cells we've established. That particular cell is on higher ground, so will probably only take three layers but the thing is, we have some voids in the layer and the situation's been made worse by one of the workers using a tracked vehicle, instead of the steel-wheeled machines for compacting. The net result is we've got uneven settlement and we may have to do some re-evacuation. But it was covered with its layer of nearly a foot of earth within twenty-four hours of completion, so there should be no vermin or insect problem."

Bradley did not look completely appeased. "But what about all this rain? I gathered from your man that there's no leachate collection system."

"That's only partially true. As I said, he's not particularly knowledgeable about procedures. I've recommended that the company undertake a significant program of education incidentally. I believe that safety and efficiency would both be enhanced if the men understood the basic principles. It'd also increase their own interest and give them more job satisfaction. Anyway – sorry to digress – the cell itself has no collection system but, as I said, it's on higher ground. So it's designed to drain into one of the adjacent cells, which does have pipes, a sump and an extraction pump."

Bradley did not immediately respond. His initial assessment of Struthers, as far as his integrity was concerned, was being revised by the thoroughness of his answers. "Thank you," he said eventually and sincerely. "Could you tell us a bit about the industrial cells now, then?"

"Surely. The other forty cells I mentioned are designated for co-disposal – that means we mix liquid waste with solid to absorb it. We have two lagoons active at the moment, with another two being prepared. They're really just big holes excavated in the ground or, in this case, the ones we have started with are in naturally low-lying ground. In fact we're generating the next two by tipping layers around the areas marked out for the lagoons. This has the benefit of being able to create drainage holes as we build up the walls, to help soak up the liquid when the lagoon comes on line."

"But what about preventing leakage into the environment?" asked Hardwyke, anxious to get to the crux of the matter since Bradley did not seem to be pushing Struthers for this key information. "What about liners and so forth?"

"Well, we do use liners but, in fact, these are there only as a backup. The idea is to control what's called the field capacity of the infill. We never actually have free liquid in the lagoon, though it may have looked like that when you saw it this morning. In fact, liquid wastes are specifically banned from land filling under the EC Waste Landfill Directive. We add solid absorbent material at such a rate that any liquid is taken up and the resultant mix always has spare capacity. Only if this is exceeded do we get leachate percolation. It's all a matter of careful management."

"I'd like to know what you do about gases generated at the site, since it was smells which started all of this off," asked Sanderson.

"We're in the process of setting up a collection system so we can use it as a resource. I believe you're planning a new estate over at New Malden? We had it in mind that perhaps we might set up a methane plant, for partially centrally heating some of the houses. You know, government and industry working together for the environment – that sort of thing."

Bradley sniffed, wondering if perhaps he had been premature in revising his estimate of Struthers' character upwards. This smacked of a sycophantic ploy, he thought, to get the council to take off the pressure.

"However," continued Struthers, "we do monitor the gas migration on a regular basis and, should it exceed a specified level, we would drill diagonal bore holes from the edges and burn off the excess."

Throughout all of this, Doctor Andrews had been sitting silently, only the occasional shifting of his position in his seat betraying some possible frustration at the topic of discussion. With the pause after Struthers' last comment lengthening fractionally, beyond the point at which that particular discussion might naturally have continued, Andrews thought it would not appear rude to change the subject. "I believe you were bringing with you the lists of industrial wastes and the results of your leachate sampling? Do you think we could go through them now please? There was evidence at the tip this morning of chemical activity of an unexpectedly corrosive nature. Do you have any idea what that might have been?"

Struthers looked up, suddenly alert and with an expression of genuine concern on his face. "Indeed no, Doctor. I'm certainly not aware of anything that could be classified in that way. Could you be a bit more specific about what you saw?"

Andrews briefly recounted his experience with the bottle and cycle frame, noting that the effect on the tip of his umbrella ruled out any physical cause or the remote possibility of a deliberate prank. Struthers retrieved his briefcase from under the table and began searching for papers. "Actually, Doctor Sanderson, I believe I gave you one of the lists yesterday. Do you have it with you?"

They spread the various papers out on the desk and, with the exception of Mathers, who went away to make himself a coffee, began to sift through the lists of chemicals involved...

Know that 'That' by which all this is permeated is indestructible. No one can bring about the destruction of that which is eternal. II.17

Doctor Andrews was bemused. It was almost unthinkable that one of his students should play such a stupid and pointless practical joke but there wasn't really a plausible alternative. He tapped his fingers impatiently on the desk. He had sent out a call for Johansson, asking him to report immediately, missing a lecture if necessary. This matter was far too serious to delay clarification.

He looked briefly through the report on his desk. He almost knew the contents by heart now, having re-read it countless times. It was what should have been a straightforward, preliminary inorganic analysis of the samples he had collected. The results from most of them were uninteresting, providing nothing out of the ordinary: iron oxides, common alkali and alkaline earth salts, lead, traces of copper and, here, a fairly high silver content – that would be the photographic processing plant – zinc, manganese and so on. Anions also as expected: chlorides, nitrates; he scanned down the list.

The results from two of the samples, though, were totally anomalous. Johansson claimed to have received positive results to every single test, for virtually every element in the periodic table, in so far as he had been able to ascertain, by this admittedly, fairly crude, qualitative semi-micro technique. The material acted as acid or alkali, depending on the reagent, and the report added, almost as an afterthought, that it had corroded the glass sample tube in which he had brought it. Furthermore, it appeared to attack all metals and even rubber and some plastics. It was outrageous!

A knock on the door finally signified the arrival of the student and an end to Andrews' impatience.

"Come in!" commanded Andrews, somewhat more loudly than he had intended.

A young man of about twenty-two years entered, of tidy appearance, despite the roll neck pullover and jeans and shoulder-length blonde hair, which indicated that casual dress was quite in order in his line of work. He also had an air of frankness about him, likely to engender immediate confidence and trust in anyone with whom he had to deal. Andrews was reluctant to adopt the attitude he had resolved to take but continued nevertheless.

"I presume you wanted to see me about the report, sir," ventured the student.

"You're damn right I do, what's the idea?"

"Well, actually, I was going to ask you the same thing. I presumed you'd know more about it." He looked questioningly at the doctor's grave face for a moment but, when no comment was forthcoming, felt obliged to continue. "I carried out the analyses as you asked and there was nothing out of the ordinary apart from two of the samples. I thought at first that someone must be playing a very clever practical joke and had somehow substituted the reagents on the shelves but I couldn't imagine why and still less figure out how it could have been done. Anyway, I repeated the whole sequence using chemicals from another lab and got the same results. By this time, I was beginning to think I must be going mad, so I managed to persuade Barry Davies to carry out the tests separately. That confirmed it – he reached the same conclusions or rather lack of conclusion, if you see what I mean. Where on earth did you get that stuff?"

"Oh!" was all Andrews could manage to reply. He was dumbfounded, his mind in a turmoil. So, it wasn't a joke – unless Johansson was acting. The last logical explanation, however improbable it had been, had now to be discarded. He had known about the corrosive effect from his experience with the bicycle and then his umbrella and he had suspected that the milk bottle must have suffered a similar fate, though he couldn't explain how. Nothing made any sense. Nothing in the list that Struthers had provided was particularly dangerous. What could this possibly be? He looked up and realized Johansson was still waiting for a reply.

"Sit down a minute and explain to me exactly what happened," he said, in a more normal voice. "I know you've made a full report but I'd still like to hear it in your own words."

"Well, sir, he began hesitantly, "I followed the standard procedure for isolating the metal ions of the various groups. The material was fairly soluble in water, so I made the assumption that it was probably inorganic. As I carried out each test, I got an initial positive result but by the time I'd attempted to filter off any precipitate to analyze further or use the filtrate in another test, it had disappeared. That is, the precipitate had dissolved again," he added in a less excited tone of voice, realizing that his last remark had not been too scientific.

"I tried taking the original solution and adding a variety of reagents to it. Sodium hydroxide gave a precipitate. So did sulphuric acid and ammonium sulphide. But each time, if I left it to stand for a minute or two, it dissolved again. I then tried adding a few things to it out of curiosity, although that's rather an understatement – by this time I was completely baffled – lead sulphate, barium hydroxide and so on. I tried a range of insoluble salts, just adding them at random without any thought of a systematic test. They all dissolved. I even tried chucking some charcoal in – I was beginning to feel pretty desperate, I suppose – and that disappeared too! It appears to be a universal solvent as far as I can make out but I don't see how such a thing can exist. I mean it doesn't fit in with theory, as I understand it."

He looked questioningly at Andrews as though hoping for some contradiction, as if some new theory, as yet unpublished, might explain all. Indeed, though he hadn't voiced the opinion, he secretly thought that Andrews, himself researching in advanced inorganic chemistry, had synthesized the material and knew the theoretical background to explain it. Andrews, however, retained a blank expression and seemed to be expecting him to continue.

He did so, though obviously with considerable reluctance. "If it's essentially ionic in structure, how can it act as a solvent for something like charcoal? If it's mainly covalent, how can it contain all those metal and salt radicals?"

Those two questions seemed to impose a degree of finality on the conversation. Johansson was obviously at a loss to provide any explanation and it was soon apparent to him that Andrews too was in a similar position of complete ignorance. It was some minutes before Andrews broke the silence.

"Have you got any left?" he asked finally, having apparently reached a conclusion.

"Yes. I put some inside a beaker which I'd sprayed with PTFE, though I don't suppose that will hold it for long."

"Well, take some over to the organic labs and have them run some spectroscopy tests: IR, UV, mass, the lot, over the whole range of frequencies. I'm going to send a sample over to the reactor lab for neutron activation analysis. Meanwhile, do some physical tests on it if you can – molecular weight, conductivity, anything you can think of. Let's collect all the information we can and then I'll call a meeting of experts from all of the scientific disciplines and we'll try to make some sense of it.

{RJ} Who exactly are you anyway? You said that 'Krish' stands for 'Krishna' – are you Indian, then?

{Krish} Krishna, yes. I am not Indian, though. Why do you consider nationality to be important or sex, come to that?

{RJ} You seem to be avoiding the question. I simply want to know to whom I am talking. Is that so unreasonable?

{Krish} But why does it matter? If I told you my name was Abraham Lincoln (no relation), currently living in Wisconsin, what would this tell you? You wouldn't even be able to verify it. I had hoped that our discussions would have persuaded you that we are not this body, mind and intellect and that, ultimately, these things are unimportant. To what is it that we give a name? As far as most people are concerned, it is the body only.

{RJ} Are you American, then?

{Krish} I am not.

{RJ} You live in England?

{Krish} Much closer than you think! Now, I must insist that we terminate this discussion. I assure you it is not helpful. I believe you have a saying about curiosity and cats?

{RJ} Could I just ask one last question? Are you in any way involved with the events here at the tip?

Meanwhile, Myra Hardwyke had been pursuing her own line of investigation, based upon Struthers' statement about the amount of rubbish disposed of annually at the tip. It might well be that the place had a lifetime of up to 250 years but it had been there in one form or another since her childhood and she couldn't help wondering how long it had been in existence before that. She knew that it was not particularly relevant but it interested her nevertheless. She also felt that she ought to do some background reading on the subject of waste disposal in general, not being happy with her present inability to contribute significantly to the proceedings, owing to lack of knowledge.

She had been half-heartedly concerned for some time about the environmental problems created by the disposal of refuse and, since the petition had been received, she had become determined to investigate workable alternatives to what seemed to be the current, exceedingly crude techniques. She vaguely recalled having seen some television program about the subject. Solid refuse was burnt in huge, specially adapted furnaces and turned into fertilizer, or was it bricks for building? She couldn't quite remember. Also liquid waste could be chemically treated to neutralize any toxicity, possibly even producing commercially marketable by-products or, at least, rendering it sufficiently safe for direct disposal into the sewage system. She would very much like to show that it was both desirable, and economically viable, to replace such dumps as theirs with the latest methods now available to science. Rationally, she acknowledged that it was unrealistic to expect to be able to acquire sufficient under-standing to be able to argue such a case against the likes of Struthers. He had after all been working in the field for many years and would presumably be aware of all the advantages and disadvantages, so that he could take either stance depending on the desired outcome. Nevertheless, such realities had never deterred her before from reading up on a subject, and this one was particularly interesting.

It was with this in mind that she set out for the public library, to try to procure some books on the matter, not that she held out a great deal of hope of finding the latest books in the local library. She would have to search the abstracts of the technical journals down at the university library. Nevertheless, there was another, far less useful but more intriguing question which had stimu-lated her curiosity, namely the history of the site. She had already searched the council records but they were not terribly infor-mative. Certainly the tip had been in existence in its current location since the war but she had expected that. Unfortunately, earlier records had been destroyed when the old council buildings had been bombed.

Upon making initial enquiries over the counter at the library, the woman in charge pointed out an ancient gentleman in raincoat and hat, apparently asleep at a table in the study section. She said that he was something of a specialist in local history and spent most of his time here. He would undoubtedly be very pleased to be able to give someone the benefit of his knowledge and would be certain to prove more helpful than she could be.

Hardwyke thanked her and walked over to where the old man was sitting. From behind, it was still difficult to ascertain whether or not he was actually asleep. He was hunched over an encyclopedic book, with his arm on the table as though resting his head on it. On rounding the table though, it became apparent that he was merely in a state of intense concentration with his finger carefully tracing the line of small print as he read.

"Excuse me," said Hardwyke hesitantly, and she waited for a moment thinking that he must be finishing his sentence. There was no response however; the man seemed to be completely ignoring her. She sat down opposite and again attempted to interrupt him verbally but the man did not seem to be aware of her presence. Hardwyke glanced at the librarian who had been observing her progress and shrugged her shoulders. The woman gestured with her finger pointing at her head and Myra interpreted this as a rather impolite indication that the old man was a little mad.

"I'm sorry miss, were you addressing me?" asked a mellifluous, cultured voice suddenly and Hardwyke realized that the man had looked up at last. "Excuse me a moment," he added before Hardwyke had time to reply. He proceeded to fumble in his jacket pocket, eventually extracting a cord and inserting a hearing aid. "I take it out when I'm reading you understand. It's quite convenient to be able to cut out all the distractions but it can prove a bit awkward at times."

Hardwyke felt distinctly embarrassed and rather stupid at her mistake. Some of the other regulars had watched the proceedings with obvious amusement. The other chose to ignore her discomfort. Indeed, he probably failed to notice it, being now quite used to such errors and soon his open and friendly manner put Hardwyke quite at ease.

Having explained her problem, she received an immediately

enthusiastic response; his expression and bearing became at once more animated, in obvious anticipation of putting his funds of dormant knowledge to use. He eagerly quizzed Hardwyke for more specific details of the information she was seeking.

"Certainly an unusual request," he muttered eventually, "not the sort of thing that people are normally interested in – refuse dumps. Still, I think we ought to be able to find some references for you."

Soon, a pile of slightly musty books, of indeterminate age, lay on the table, unearthed from some remote room at the rear of the library for which he appeared to have his own personal key. He had even managed to find several maps of the area as it had existed at various times in the past. Together they studied the books, though, Mr. Bailey, as the man introduced himself, was seemingly already quite familiar with them and quickly skipped through to any potentially useful references.

The picture that gradually emerged was that, although the site of the current council tip had only existed as such for some sixty odd years, yet the area itself had always been regarded as something of a dump, so to speak. It had never actually been farmed or cultivated and was shown on the maps as 'wastes' or 'rough ground.' It was, in fact, as though it had presented a natural tip, if that were possible; nature's own rubbish dump, ready prepared for use by civilization.

The name 'Crow Field' was a corruption of its original name, and was shown in the oldest map of the area as 'Krew Field.' Bailey seemed particularly interested in this. "The word 'Krew' is not a meaningful word in any language that I'm aware of," he said. "I rather think that the word was actually 'kuru.' 'Kuru' was a country in what's now the northern part of India. There was once supposed to be an epic battle there – you know, it was described in the Hindu poem, the 'Mahabharata.' Hundreds of thousands of pilgrims and tourists visit the archaeological sites there every year. Yes, I rather suspect that our field was named after that for some reason: 'Kurukshetra' the place was called – 'Kuru Field;' field of the Kurus. Kshetra is the Sanskrit for 'field,' you know."

Nothing more specific could be found which might help to explain this curious feature. Writers seemed to prefer to devote more prose to the beauties of nature and the surrounding countryside rather than its harsher, more unpleasant aspects. Still, Hardwyke's initial curiosity had been somewhat assuaged and, grateful though she was for Bailey's help, she was now anxious to continue to her slightly more official business of searching out the technical books. She soon realized that she was going to have some difficulty in extricating herself. It looked as though Bailey had such infrequent opportunity for conversing about his subject that he was making the most of this one. Eventually, during one of the other's brief pauses to draw breath, Hardwyke managed to say that she really must go, indebted though she was.

"You've heard about the myths associated with the place, have you?" he asked, changing the slant of the conversation and trying to stimulate curiosity in a last desperate attempt to hold his visitor's attention.

"No," answered Hardwyke, in a tone intended to suggest that she didn't really want to either.

"Oh, yes. People once believed that demons or spirits of the dead used to live out there. It's only superstition of course but it's said that something strange happened back in the Middle Ages; fierce storms with colored lights in the sky. People are supposed to have been killed, though no records were kept of what exactly happened. No one would live anywhere near for a long time after. Naturally, with stories like that, the details become more and more embroidered as they're passed on from generation to generation and it becomes impossible to tell where fact ends and fiction begins. I suppose one must disregard all of it. Still, I just thought you might be interested," his voice tailed off at the end of the sentence. He seemed, at last, to have got the message that Hardwyke really did intend to depart and to have resigned himself to the fact.

Hardwyke left without looking for her other books – she didn't want to be collared by old Bailey again that day, her face breaking into a grin as she realized the unintentional pun.

"Lights and things in the sky indeed!" she said as she went down the old stone steps to the street. "Seems they had flying saucers in those days as well!"

I am the source of everything. All evolves from me. Intelligent people who understand this worship me. X.8

Mark Houldsworth was eight years old and very bored. It was Sunday too, which didn't help. He didn't understand quite what it was that seemed to happen to everyone on Sundays, the grownups that is; they all appeared to sit around reading enormous newspapers or got up late, only to go back to sleep again in armchairs. They didn't want to be disturbed. What was he supposed to do? 'Go and play quietly somewhere,' he was told by his mother. He wished he had a father to play football with or something, as he imagined his friends doing. Perhaps Mr. Bradley would come and live here; he'd been round quite a lot recently and he was all right, though he seemed more interested in Mummy.

It was dry outside now. Maybe he would be allowed to go out to play at last. What had made it so much more boring this last week was that it had been raining nearly all the time and he had been forced to stay indoors. It wouldn't have been so bad had he been able to have his best friend, David, round to play but he was on holiday at Alton Towers. Peter, too, had gone yesterday – it wasn't fair. Mark wasn't going until September; that was nearly three whole months. Oh, what could he do?

He lifted down the box of toys from the cupboard in his

bedroom and began to sift through them for inspiration. His most recent acquisition, which he had specially asked Mr. Bradley to buy for his birthday, caught his eye immediately; its dark yellow paintwork gleaming with reflected light from the bedroom window. He lifted it out carefully and fondled it lovingly – a true to scale model of a rubbish dumper truck.

He had always watched with fascination, from his bedroom, early on Monday mornings, awakened by the noise of the plastic bags of refuse being piled up in the street outside, as the dustmen arrived to conduct their weekly ritual. He would wait impatiently as the truck moved slowly up the avenue and eventually came into view outside the house. And then one of the men, with his fluorescent orange jacket and baseball cap, would come into view. With scarcely the slightest effort, he would grab the bags, one after the other, with his gloved hand and casually throw them up into the hopper of the waiting truck.

The best part was still to come though, and it was disappointing indeed if the truck moved on out of sight before he had seen it happen. That was when the driver started the mechanism for grinding and churning all the rubbish, tearing and crushing, flattening and mangling the waste as if it were paper. One day, he would drive one of these and operate the levers that controlled all of this power.

The most exciting function of the truck, of course, was only performed at its ultimate destination. Living close to the tip itself, he had naturally visited there frequently with a friend or even, occasionally, by himself. He would watch from afar, through the fence, as the trucks on top of a hill raised their loads again, the narrow columns of steel seeming to expand and force the backs almost vertically into the air. Then the doors would swing wide and a torrent of garbage would pour forth and slide down into the valley, leaving a trail of litter and debris.

He had attempted to recreate the excitement with his model up in his bedroom, filling the container with bits of screwed up paper and rice, which his mum had given him from the kitchen. But it wasn't realistic enough to satisfy his imagination. On the spur of the moment, it occurred to him to take it out to the real tip and play with it there. He knew where he could get through the fence, down by the old railway line, where it was almost completely fallen down. Yes, that's what he would do to liven up this boring day.

Quickly, lest he should lose his resolve and change his mind, for he knew that he had been forbidden to play near the tip or to go so far from home by himself, he picked up his toy and ran downstairs. He stopped briefly to call in the kitchen and stuff a few biscuits into his pocket and then looked into the sitting room where his mother was falling asleep over her paper.

"Just going out to play for a bit, Mum," he shouted, in case she actually was asleep.

"All right," she mumbled, "don't go far and be back for dinner," the volume of her voice increasing at the end, for he had already disappeared.

He ran all the way down the avenue, across the road at the bottom and on down to where the bridge crossed the railway, turning right into a dirt track bordered by hedges almost double his height. Here he slowed to a walk, free at last, out in the open air, away from the house where he had been seemingly imprisoned for a whole week. Soon the hedge grew lower and he could see down to where the railway lines had once been in the steep cutting to the right.

As he continued, the path veered to the left and opened out onto the side of a small valley with the tip on the opposite hillside. Already there were signs of the desolation of what was left of the urban countryside, with an old iron bedstead and various less conspicuous litter down in the polluted creek at the bottom. He made his way cautiously down the side of the hill, holding on to clumps of weeds here and there, where his footing was less secure. At the bottom, he jumped across the stream which, though normally quite dry, now ran quickly with a murky grey liquid.

Along the base of the valley ran a much wider track, leading back to the main road at the left and down to the canal about a half-mile further on to the right. He crossed over and clambered to the top of the hillock opposite where the green fence separated him from his objective. He knew that a short distance would bring him to the place where he could gain access and, without resting from his exertions, hurried towards the spot.

At last he was inside. Initially, though, he saw little of interest, the main tipping area being over to the west. Indeed, it looked very much the same as it did on the other side of the fence but the fact that he was on the inside, in forbidden territory, made all the difference. He knew he wouldn't meet anyone of course, it being Sunday, but pretending he might be caught added even more to the excitement. Accordingly, he made his way across the ground at a furtive run, zigzagging his way in spurts as though being fired upon by snipers, stopping at the slightest cover provided by a growth of nettles or clump of weeds and crouching behind them, looking carefully back to ensure that he wasn't being followed.

About half way across, he realized that the ground was becoming damper, with puddles showing here and there, still sprouting strands of half drowned grass like a jungle swamp. Here, he began to be on the lookout for crocodiles and poisonous snakes, wishing he had brought his rifle with him. He was forced to backtrack. He couldn't afford to get his trainers all covered with mud; he would be sure to be found out if that happened and he'd probably be made to stop indoors for days as punishment. Accordingly, he changed direction, now heading back parallel to the fence, looking in vain for a safe path across. He decided eventually that things didn't look too hopeful. It had rained so much it was probably like this everywhere. Still, having come this far, he couldn't be put off by a bit of water. That hilly ground now opposite should be fairly dry; it was just a matter of treading carefully and avoiding the puddles; once over he'd be safe. The hill where they dumped must be over there, just out of sight.

Having made up his mind, he resolutely, though tentatively, stepped out onto the marshy ground, holding his arms outstretched as though walking a tightrope. All went well for a few yards and then, almost inevitably, he lost his footing on a slippery clump of grass and his foot went right in, the water seeping into his shoe and soaking his sock. He could have cried out of annoyance and frustration – indeed only very great restraint, and the fact that there was no one within hearing anyway, prevented him. It was not because of the wet foot – that was incidental and almost part of the fun – but because his mother would now ask awkward questions and require some explanation. Still, perhaps if he stopped for a while on the hill he could take off the sock and dry it in the sun, since it was quite warm. But wouldn't that take ages? If he wrung it out with his hands first it might not. What about his trainer, though? It was all muddy. He could clean it with some grass and clean water; it would be all right when it dried.

Engaged in these deliberations, he was unaware that his foot was becoming firmly embedded in the mud. He succeeded in taking a step forwards with his right foot as he set off again but then discovered, too late, that his other foot was staying where it was. Balance being what it is, he lost it and fell headlong onto his face. This time he really did break down and cry. He was now covered in mud and he'd really be for it when he returned home. He wished now he'd never seen that toy earlier on. He lay there sobbing and utterly miserable, unaware of the strange odor that assailed his nostrils.

After a while, his tears ceased, although his body was still shaking slightly. He realized he had to set off back and take what was coming to him. Anyway, he felt rather cold now, even though the sun was still beating down above, or was it? He made an effort to rise to his feet and, with a shock, discovered that he could not. His foot couldn't be that stuck surely but he didn't think he could move it, indeed he couldn't actually feel it. He raised his body on his arms and twisted slightly in order to see his leg but everything was rather hazy. He felt very odd; dizzy and tired but something else too, and he was shivering. He looked up and noted without much concern that the sky, if sky it was, was now a deep violet and the sun a bright glaring ball of emerald green. Funny that he hadn't noticed earlier; obviously a magnetic storm was brewing; he would have to look for shelter.

The light faded very quickly as it always did so close to the equator. He must have fallen asleep; he could have sworn it had been bright daylight only a moment ago. He would be caught unprotected, out in the open at night time, if he didn't find somewhere to hide soon. The noises of the animals were much closer already; unearthly screams and ominous grunts which chilled his blood and made him shiver even more than the effect of the cool air on his lightly clad body had already done. He must set about lighting a fire straight away to keep them at bay. He felt some relief as he realized he still had his rifle with him. He clasped the butt firmly and quickly checked that it was fully loaded.

It was then that he saw the spaceship landing. It was a fairly ordinary ship descending vertically on a sheet of crimson and orange flame, the base of the silver cylinder glowing from the heat of the discharge. It hovered for a few moments, while the pilot waited for the smoke and fires of the blasted vegetation to clear so that he could see a suitable place to land. Then it touched down without mishap about fifty yards away. The high pitched whine of the atomic engines descended through the octaves to a deep throbbing hum and then ceased altogether. The dust thrown up by the jets gradually drifted away and all was silent.

After a short pause, there was the hiss of an airlock opening and a ladder lowered itself automatically to the ground. Immediately, a huge rubbery creature emerged and began to descend. It had three double-jointed legs and a number of tentacle-like arms, which it waved about as if using them to test the air. It moved swiftly in a curious fashion so that it appeared, at any one time, to be standing on one leg while moving one down to the next rung and maintaining its balance with the third, held like an arm above its head. Having reached the ground, it turned and began to advance towards him.

He could now clearly see the shapeless mass of the head and it was the single, unblinking eye which gave away its Tellurian origin. What could it possibly be doing so far from home? The last episode he had seen, it had been engaged in an intergalactic war with the Aldebarans. It was much nearer now; the ear receptors on the sides and rear of the head waved about in time with the long tentacles, which were reaching out towards Mark. He screamed, now in terror, completely forgetting his discomfort. It was one thing seeing these things on the television and quite another meeting them face to face.

"What do you want?" he tried to shout, but only a strangled gurgling seemed to emerge. The Tellurians, of course, are telepathic so he heard the answer in his own head.

"You. I've come to exterminate you. You're a danger to our existence," and, without further warning it pulled a plaser gun from one of its folds of grey-blue flesh and pointed it at him.

"No!" he started to cry desperately but it was too late. He saw the bright scarlet flash from the gun and then the pain and shock of instant, complete annihilation enveloped him and the violet curtain faded to black.

I am all-destroying death... and the source of all that is yet to be. X.34

Brenda Houldsworth was on her feet the instant the front door bell rang, as though it were connected electrically to her rather than simply sounding the bell. The severe tension of the past two days was plainly visible on her face as she rushed to open the door.

"They've found him," she gasped, "please God, let them have found him."

She pulled the door violently open to reveal the gaunt, strangely portentous figure of a man in the shadows. He moved forward, out of line of the tree, revealing his pale features in the orange glow of the sodium lamp.

"Mrs. Houldsworth?" he queried in a quiet voice, nullifying to a large extent his seemingly diabolic appearance.

"You've found him," she began, midway between a question and a statement but, observing that he was alone, the hope faded from her voice even before the first three words had been spoken.

"Who are you? What's happening? Why hasn't..." she continued but was interrupted before she could finish.

"You are Mrs. Houldsworth? May I come in please? Inspector Harris," he said, showing her his identification.

"Yes, of course. You have found him then?" Her hopes rising swiftly and uncontrollably again at this confirmation of his officialdom. She turned and led the way into the interior, thoughts and emotions falling over themselves as she strove to deduce all she could from this minimal exchange. Eventually, one gained dominance – fear – though she fought to repress it.

"Is he down at the police station, then?" she asked, attempting to introduce a note of optimism into her voice but then, on the spur of the moment, continued with the question she really wanted to ask but almost dared not. "He isn't hurt, is he? He's not in hospital or anything, is he?"

She turned slowly, as they were now in the living room, but kept her eyes averted, looking down at the floor. She would be able to see the expression on his face if she glanced up but couldn't bring herself to do so for fear of reading there that which she inwardly dreaded. He didn't speak for a moment, however, and, unable to restrain herself through what, to her seemed an eternity, she lifted her gaze, beginning to say in a flat voice, "Is he—" but not having the courage to put her fears into words.

"I'm afraid..." he began but was not allowed to finish. She had seen his face, heard his opening words. She raised her hands to her face, uttered a despairing cry, and ran from the room.

Harris stood for a moment, attempting to recover his composure. This sort of task affected him far more than any other aspect of his job. Corpses he could usually bear; at best they merely looked like placid marble statues, at worst like unrecognizable lumps of meat, but relatives were quite a different prospect. Even the most strong willed of people would betray something unpleasant in their expressions, caught off guard at the moment of breaking the news. The fleeting glimpse of pain as the information was given, as if surgically implanted to gnaw its way to full realization in the brain, later to break out as the patient broke down, alone with her torment. Much worse were the cases like this young woman here, who was totally unable to contain her emotions and suffered a breakdown right before him. One particular case in the past, quite unlike the others, still held the most unpleasant memories however. Then, a young man, upon being told of the death of his wife had, quite unmistakably, allowed an expression of malicious glee and exultation to flash across his features before he recovered himself and put on an exaggerated act of dismay and horror. In all instances, though, the fact remained that he was, in that unguarded moment, seeing past the superficial facade of their persona, direct to the innermost, and most private, recesses of their souls. That was a dubious pleasure, which should be reserved for their closest confidants.

As he was musing on the problem and wondering whether to leave or to wait for the woman to return, a man appeared from the other side of the room. It was a startling indication of his own emotional turmoil that he hadn't noticed there was someone else there and it immediately brought him back to the present.

"Sorry, sir, I didn't see you before. You're the boy's father, I take it?" he apologized.

"No, Mr. Houldsworth is dead. I'm a friend of his mother, Frank Bradley. Perhaps you'd like to explain to me what's happened and I'll tell her when she's recovered." He waited expectantly but received no immediate response. "Well, inspector?" he prompted.

"Yes, of course, sir. It's a bit difficult. We have found a boy and, as you have probably gathered, I'm afraid he's dead. Obviously we need a formal identification before we can say anything definite but..." Again the faint nausea hit him, tightness of throat, increased heartbeat and respiration. He would be glad when this was over. He'd call at the pub on the way back he decided, and have a stiff drink.

"Yes, but where did you find him and how did he die?" persisted Bradley.

"We found him a couple of hours ago, down on the tip," he began.

"The tip!" almost shouted Bradley and he too now, in turn, fought to stop the thoughts and emotions evoked by this single word. He had feared, from the start, that one day something would happen to bring that situation to a head. But he had never envisaged anything so drastic, nor had he thought that it might involve him personally. "Well, what happened?" he managed to utter eventually, his mind still racing.

"There had apparently been some kind of accident," answered the inspector evasively. "We don't suspect any foul play, at least, not in the conventional sense," he added as an afterthought.

"But what, for God's sake? Where's the mystery?"

"We're not entirely sure. We found him partly drowned in

some sort of a bog. Only it wasn't just mud. There must have been some chemicals present. We're having some of the material analyzed now. And there will have to be an autopsy of course," he added.

"How do you mean, 'chemicals'? Did he die by drowning or what?"

"As I said, we don't yet know the precise cause of death. As for the chemicals, I wouldn't know about those things, possibly acid. Anyway," he paused to take a deep breath, "his body wasn't... He was..." He paused again, vainly striving for a suitable way of phrasing the information but eventually deciding on the straight facts. "The whole of the right leg and part of the left were missing," he succeeded in stating.

"Good God!" ejaculated Bradley.

"Also part of the arms and the right side of the face, where he had been lying."

Bradley sat down, stunned and speechless. How could he convey something like this to Brenda? She wouldn't be able to cope with something so unbelievably terrible. He felt faint himself from the shock. It was much worse than anything he could have imagined. He had expected, perhaps, that Mark had fallen and cut himself on a piece of glass and bled to death. That would have been horrible enough. He forced his mind to turn away from personal aspects and consider the wider implications.

What on earth could it have been? Andrews had raised the issue of corrosive waste at that last meeting but one didn't somehow think of people in the same context as milk bottles or bicycle frames. Someone would pay for this all right. How typical and yet how appalling it was that authorities always had to wait for an incident of this nature before being forced to take action. The same story time and time again in the local newspapers; installing traffic lights at busy pedestrian crossing points after half a dozen old people and children have been knocked down; imposing speed limits on roads which have been causing accidents for years. Safety measures in industry followed the same pattern; obvious precautions only enforced after employees had been maimed or killed. It was human nature extrapolated to an exaggerated, impersonal, organizational level. It was also a tragedy.

"Excuse me, sir, are you all right? Can I get you a drink or something?" asked Harris of Bradley, who sat drained and motionless on the chair despite the profusion of thoughts which currently assailed him.

"Oh, er, yes, thanks." Bradley looked up and pointed a shaking hand in the direction of the cabinet on the far side of the room.

Harris walked over, selected two glasses and a bottle of Scotch whisky and took them back to the table. He poured one and handed it to Bradley. "Do you mind if I...?" he asked, holding the empty glass towards Bradley.

"Yes, go ahead," he answered, taking a gulp of the liquid and coughing as it caught on the back of his throat.

Harris readily complied, pouring himself a substantial measure before continuing. "I'm afraid someone will have to identify the body. Perhaps it would be better if you could, yourself, rather than the mother.

"Yes, of course, but what am I going to tell her?" he asked desperately. "She's sure to want all the details, however bad. I've no right to lie about it. And even knowing the worst, she'll almost certainly want to see him herself for the last time." He looked imploringly at the inspector as though, since he had obviously been through similar experiences before, he must be aware of a solution to the impasse.

"I suppose you're right, sir. Perhaps you should call in the doctor to prescribe something for her until all this is over."

"Good Lord, yes, I'd better go and see if she's all right," said Bradley, jumping to his feet as he realized she had been left alone for some time now.

"I'll be going then," began Harris but Bradley was already on his way out of the room. He drained his glass and replaced it carefully on the table, shaking his head slowly and gravely from side to side, as if to indicate to any invisible bystander that he considered the ways of God and Nature to be beyond the understanding of mere mortals. He opened the front door and stood for a moment taking deep breaths of the fresh and cool summer night air, to clear away the unpleasantness of the recent events symbolically if not actually. Then he left, extremely thankful that the confrontation was over, though unable to suppress a twinge of guilt that he had been spared the ordeal of breaking the gory details to the mother and that that unenviable lot now fell to another.

The embodied Self can never be destroyed, Arjuna, so you should not mourn for anyone. II.30

Doctor Robert Andrews awoke to the sound of fire engines, which only gradually resolved itself into the ringing of the doorbell. He rubbed his eyes, eased himself out of the armchair and glanced at his wristwatch before realizing that the bell was still calling for him to answer the door. Yawning widely, he stumbled across the room, still groggy from his interrupted snooze. The bell, silent for a few seconds, had resumed its infuriating monotone. Someone was very persistent. He pulled open the door with quite unnecessary force, preparing to register extreme annoyance at such unsociable behavior, should the intrusion prove to be of anything less than life or death importance. What reasonable excuse could anyone have for calling at this time of night?

The face of the man standing there gave an immediate impression of strength of character, intelligence and reliability but the features were tired and strained and his generally untidy appearance seemed at variance with what one might have expected, suggesting a high level of emotional stress. Andrews modified his anger slightly.

"Mr. Bradley, isn't it? What on earth is the matter at this time of night?" he asked, unable, and unwilling to keep the irritation out of his voice.

"I'm sorry, Doctor," began Bradley, "do you mind if I come in? I've something important to discuss."

"Would you mind telling me exactly what it is that you want to discuss before I ask you in?" retorted Andrews, unwilling to invite this unruly young man in without solid justification.

"It's regarding your analysis of the samples you took down at the tip. I have some further information that should prove relevant."

This last sentence was muttered through almost clenched teeth and Andrews' curiosity and unease were increased still further.

"All right, I suppose you'd better come in," he condescended. The subject of the landfill site had, inevitably, been on his mind too before he had fallen asleep, and all the incongruities and insoluble problems now came flooding back, wearying him with their implications and ramifications. "It'd better be important," he added, holding the door open for Bradley to pass through.

"It is," shouted Bradley, "a boy has been killed out there. Killed, I say, not 'had an unfortunate accident' as some will no doubt try to imply. I intend to make sure that something is done about it. It's unbelievable: outrageous; there are just no suitable words…"

The man was obviously in a very distressed state, indeed he seemed almost at the point of collapse. Andrews drew him to an armchair and made him sit.

"Look, sit down here a minute and try to calm yourself. I'll get you a drink and then you can tell me the facts with a bit less of the emotional outburst eh?" said Andrews, in an almost fatherly fashion and crossed the room to pour drinks. He, himself, had had a considerable shock at the news, but his outward composure was unchanged. This horrifying development suddenly brought everything out of the realms of scientific research and intellectual exercise into a harsh and frighteningly immediate reality. His mind was totally alert as he handed Bradley the glass. What would happen now? The results of their investigations were far from complete but the authorities would require some answers. What would their reactions be if he were to put forward some of his fantastic theories with insufficient evidence to back them up? Still, even the results they did have, without any explanations, were more than enough to startle anyone.

Quickly, Bradley related the facts as known to him so far. He hadn't yet seen the body himself – that awful task still awaited him in the morning – but Harris' description was graphic enough, without the additional data that first hand observation would bring. Andrews listened in silence, only his face registering horror as the facts were revealed. Afterwards, he remained without speaking for some minutes, unable to decide how best to respond.

"Well?" queried Bradley eventually, still retaining some of that belligerent attitude not altogether foreign to his nature.

Andrews stared intently at the other for a long moment, wondering if he could entirely trust him. Still, he could do with talking to someone about it himself and Bradley was not going to be put off until he had found out what Andrews had discovered.

"All right, Mr. Bradley, I'll tell you what we've found but only on one condition. That is, for the time being at least, you do not go to the newspapers or tell anyone else what I'm going to divulge. Do I have your word?"

"Look, Doctor, there's no need to be so melodramatic. I presume you're going to tell me our tip has been used for the disposal of toxic wastes without the public's being aware of it. Well, I can promise to keep quiet until I've collected all the damning evidence I can. Thereafter, I'm going to do my best to ensure that everyone who reads a newspaper or watches television is going to know about it and some of those bureaucratic bastards are going to feel mighty sick before I'm finished with them."

"You look here, Bradley, this is far more serious than even you would like to imagine. I want your word not to release my findings until we are surer of what exactly we're up against, and it's not bureaucratic officials, of that much I am sure."

Bradley was taken aback at this sudden change in Andrews' hitherto placid temperament and the ploy succeeded in subduing any further outburst. That the man was very much in earnest was now evident and he could only accede to the request.

"Very well," continued the doctor. Have you any chemistry background at all?"

"Not especially; I took a general science course at school and I've done some structures of materials and so on, from the architectural viewpoint."

"Never mind; I'll try to keep it simple though, goodness knows, it's anything but. We've found this substance..." Andrews paused, as if turning the word over carefully with tweezers while he examined it, "which is quite alien to our knowledge of chemistry to date. It's extremely reactive but in a curiously selective fashion which follows no known laws. It reacts with metals, for instance, but not in the order of the Electro-chemical series. It seems to form some sort of co-ordinated inorganic complex, which is reasonably stable but which can become quite unstable if another, more favorable, metal is introduced. It appears to consist of a long chain-like molecule with tentacles, if you like, which can sequester a metal ion at one end and then pass it on down the chain by making and remaking chemical bonds. It's quite unbelievable."

He glanced at Bradley to see if he was still following and, choosing to read the expression as one of disbelief rather than incomprehension, continued. "Somehow, this molecule seems to incorporate most standard radicals, as though it were a sort of packaged laboratory, capable of synthesizing practically any chemical compound."

Again he paused, pondering the implications of what he had just said. The last phrase had just slipped out quite unintentionally but seemed almost to follow logically. "It's almost like a... well, like an inorganic organism, if that's not a contradiction in terms. There's more, too.

"We've run some mass spectroscopy tests and it looks as though some of the isotopes present are not those which commonly occur in nature. Certainly, the ratios are markedly different. It's all unbelievably odd," he concluded, looking at Bradley as if hoping for some enlightenment.

"Well, where the hell has it come from then? Surely it must somehow have resulted from chemical decomposition and interaction of all the waste products dumped by those industrial plants?"

"No, that's extremely unlikely; in fact, I'll state categorically that it's impossible! I think that there are only two possible explanations, however preposterous they may seem. The first is that it evolved. Of course, the fact that it is essentially inorganic disqualifies it as living in the usually accepted sense. All living things are carbon-based, with units of amino acids and nucleotides. But it doesn't obey chemical laws and it appears to exhibit an almost intelligent selectivity over its environment. Also, we haven't established that it can in any way reproduce itself, God forbid! So, we'll have to leave aside the question of whether it's alive or not for the time being, until we've done a lot more investigation. In any case, two points arise out of this assumption. Firstly, considering its complexity, it would have taken millions of years to evolve, and no one's ever encountered it before. Secondly, if it had evolved, it would have done so with its isotopes in their natural ratios. Both these factors would appear to rule out this theory. The second explanation is that it isn't natural at all."

"What, you mean biological warfare?" interrupted Bradley, explosively. This was more familiar territory and something he could understand and was prepared to fight.

"No, I've just explained," said Andrews, with a tone of exasperation in his voice. "This stuff is so complex, we can't even determine its structure, let alone manufacture the damn thing."
"If you'll reflect a minute on the points I've just made, you'll see that, whichever the explanation, they all indicate the same conclusion. If it evolved, it couldn't have done so *here* and if it was made, *we* didn't make it.

"It must have come from another planet," he finished in a subdued, almost apologetic tone.

It was some time before Bradley found himself able to speak. He was out of his depth. He had no lack of imagination; indeed some of his architectural designs had been rejected as too adventurous. Science fiction had always interested him, he was quite open-minded about ghosts or God or life on other planets but he still felt strongly tempted to close his mind completely to Andrews' fantastic suggestion. On the other hand, he was always prepared to accept the conclusions of science, even when he himself was unable to follow the reasoning. Unless he had grossly misjudged, he could find no reason to question Andrews' sincerity or integrity. Moreover – the deciding factor – the logic of his arguments, assuming the validity of the postulates, was incontrovertible. But, things from outer space! He couldn't think of anything to say, his thoughts spinning again without finding a solid concept to grasp hold of.

"As yet, there's no suggestion of what we can do to neutralize or counteract it," continued Andrews, following his own thoughts aloud. "We could, for example, pour a load of chalk or something onto it and that would tie up all the chelating ligands with calcium. But if it came into contact with, say, silver or potassium, or anything else it took a fancy to if it comes to that, it would just spit all the calcium out again and start bonding to the new metal. That's an interesting thought actually. If we had enough of it and could control it, it would revolutionize methods of extracting metals from ores." He paused a moment at this thought and Bradley glanced at him doubtfully. "You see, we haven't found anything yet capable of actually rupturing the system. It's even stable to high temperatures, so far as we've tested it."

"I'm afraid I don't entirely follow," said Bradley, finally beginning to think logically again and attempting to take in what was being suggested. "Surely, even if it can form complexes with lots of different metals and make substitutions if circumstances present the opportunity, there must come a point in time when all these arms or whatever you call them…"

"Ligands," prompted Andrews.

"…ligands are all tied up with something and then it won't react any more. I mean it can't go on reacting forever, can it? I thought there was some chemical or physical law about it; entropy is it?"

"Well, yes, all the reactive substances with which we are familiar don't hang around for very long in the free state. They react almost instantaneously with virtually anything that happens to be around, eventually resulting in products that are themselves usually very stable. Take sodium and chlorine, for example. Both these are extremely reactive but, once they have found each other, the resulting common salt is very stable. To begin with, this material acts similarly and, since we must assume it's been out there for some time, it must have attained some sort of equilibrium. But, as I tried to explain, it appears to have this mechanism whereby it can disrupt the bonds of what is essentially a stable structure, thereby giving rise to an intermediate of much higher energy. It can then combine with different atoms which, according to our version of scientific laws, should give a less favorable structure than it had originally. And all this occurs without the input of any external energy. Course, we didn't try carrying out the experiments in the dark. I suppose it's conceivable that some sort of radical reaction stimulated by sunshine is taking place, I don't know, I've spent days thinking about it.

"Anyway, as for entropy, if this stuff's alive in some sense or has some external source of energy that isn't a problem, is it? We're not living in a vacuum, you know. There's more than enough disorder in the universe to compensate for the small degree of order we have in our lives."

Bradley was trying desperately to absorb this lecture and Andrews had apparently had a further idea for he sat quite still, his face rapt with concentration. It was some time before either spoke again. Finally, Andrews began again, hesitantly. "Yes, that would be much more reasonable."

Bradley looked up, expectantly.

"Perhaps it needn't be alive at all," continued Andrews, almost as if speaking to himself. An external energy source would explain it. What if there were something out on the tip which is producing this substance and using it to provide itself with raw materials, almost like food?"

"But you carried out these tests in the laboratory, didn't you? Surely you're not suggesting communication at a distance are you? Why, it's like cutting off one of your arms and telling it to go and get something from the other room!" This last suggestion had proven too much for Bradley and he was forced to give in to his skepticism. He rose to his feet and began to pace up and down.

"I'm not so sure," Andrews persisted. "I'm no biologist, but there are lots of things which go on in the body at a sub cellular level which are almost comparable. If there were some sort of genetic coding, it could perform selectively without itself being intelligent. In a sense, doesn't a dandelion 'tell' its seeds to separate, get blown away by the wind and start a new plant when they finally land? Is that 'communication at a distance?'"

"Hmm, good point I suppose. Anyway, all this theorizing is a bit too fantastic for me. What are we actually going to do?"

"Yes, I must admit we haven't really got sufficient facts, as yet, to put forward any ideas like this."

"Quite; I can just see the headlines: 'Invaders from space claim their first victim,'" interrupted Bradley, grimly.

Andrews nodded vigorously. "Definitely! We can't afford to let the papers get hold of anything like that. It would cause chaos if it were taken seriously. And it might turn out to be not so far from the truth," he added with a meaningful, yet almost theatrical, glance over the top of his spectacles.

Bradley recollected the primary purpose of his visit. "Nevertheless, if I may remind you, Doctor, a child's been killed. We have to do something; not only to discover who or what is responsible but also to avert any possible danger of another accident."

"I assure you, Mr., er… Bradley, I never intended to suggest that we let the matter slide. The police will be making independent enquiries now, anyway. We'll have to try to get them off the job. I'll have to go to see Mathers first thing in the morning and see what can be done about closing the tip down for the time being and ensuring that the surrounding fence is secured."

"I'm coming too, then," said Bradley, rising from his chair.

"I don't know that there's any need for that," complained Andrews doubtfully.

"I instigated the petition if you recall; I'll see you at the town hall at nine o'clock," replied Bradley, leaving the other no opportunity for further argument and heading for the door. "Goodnight, Doctor."

The deluded world does not recognize me, birthless and changeless. I am not visible to everyone, being covered by the veil of illusion. VII.25

Bradley did not go straight back to Brenda. He could not leave her on her own tonight and would sleep on the sofa downstairs but she was heavily sedated and it was unlikely she would awaken before morning. He was exhausted too but didn't think it likely that he could sleep, even in the comfort of his own bed, let alone in a makeshift one. He wandered aimlessly for a while, musing on what Andrews had been suggesting – preposterous of course. What seemed likely must have happened was that something had been dumped there by mistake; something so new and so secret that Andrews had no inkling of its nature. Either a government department, of which the government would deny all knowledge, or one of the new biotechnology companies that had sprung up in the last ten years, altering genes in totally unnatural ways to introduce supposed 'improvements' – one of these must be responsible. Something had gone wrong and they had tried to get rid of the evidence, not suspecting the consequences of their action.

He found himself back at his own house, the doorway shrouded in darkness, and the chill of the night air now suddenly making itself felt through his thin anorak. He let himself in and switched on the light. His initial thought was to make a coffee and then, in perhaps an hour or so, go back to Brenda's house. He caught sight of his unshaven chin as he passed the hall mirror, the rest of his face, too, giving the general impression of someone in need of sleep, refreshment and a good wash. Perhaps he could have a shower before he went out again.

As he filled the kettle and located a clean mug in the cupboard to the left of the sink, he suddenly recalled the exercise given to him by Krish about making a cup of coffee. 'Krish The Enigmatic,' real identity and location still a complete mystery, technical wizard yet communicating an intriguing, almost sublime philosophy. He possessed the skills necessary to break into Bradley's computer, disdainfully bypassing the security checks. Also, he recalled, as the idea gradually took shape in his mind, Krish had said that Bradley could contact him any time. 'I'm always here,' he had said, or something of the sort. He wondered if that meant at three o'clock in the morning.

The events of the evening had undermined his usual sensibilities and, having stirred more than the usual amount of sugar into his coffee, he went into his study and switched on the computer. Now he had, somehow, to remember how to do this. It had previously always been Krish that had contacted him. He ran the IRC program – that bit, at least, was easy…

Eventually, after much examination of the menu options and racking his slightly befuddled brain for some reasoned intuition, he succeeded in logging on to the London chat line that Krish had used. Responding to the introductory dialogue was fairly straightforward – over the years, web service providers had migrated towards reasonably common standards for this – and he was soon looking down the list for the 'Kurukshetra' connection.

The response was almost immediate. Clearly there had been no ringing telephone or other mechanical device awakening Krish from his sleep and the inevitable delay of someone 'booting himself up' for the day.

{Krish} Mr. Bradley! I'm pleased that you have called. I was very sorry to hear about your sad loss and thought it might help to talk about it. I did try to contact you earlier but of course you must have been out.

The black cloud carries the sun away.

{RJ} As you say, "The black cloud carries the son away." How the hell could you possibly have known? We were only told ourselves about seven hours ago. There haven't been any newspapers. I suppose it must have been on the late television or radio news then? It really is the most awful tragedy. I don't know whether to feel terribly angry or unbearably sad. It just seems so unfair that someone so young should have to die, especially like that. Where's the justice? Is there an explanation for how your God can behave in this way?

{Krish} What is it that dies? Grief is a valuable process for coming to terms with the death of a loved one but let us be dispassionate for a moment. Difficult though it is to accept, the only real problem is your coping with the attachments you had for the perceived 'other person.' It is your association with various ideas, thoughts and emotions in the mind that is the cause of your confusion. The Self (of yourself and of the 'other person') is totally unaffected by any of this – call it a 'play' or a 'dream.'

{RJ} How can you talk like that? Mark is dead. He will not be here anymore. We have to learn to live without him.

{Krish} These are all misconceptions. Think of a cupboard containing shelves stacked with various jars and bottles. If the space inside one of these jars could think, it might well look at the other jars on the shelf and conclude, "Here I am, quite separate from all other jars, with a fragile glass body. And when the glass breaks, that will be the end." It might well feel very isolated and vulnerable. But when, one day, the jar falls off the shelf and breaks, suddenly the space finds, not just that it is still there but that it always was there, before, as well as after the glass was formed. Moreover it is continuous with and in no way separate from the entire universal space, which is, was, and always will be single and undifferentiated.

Or think of a wave on the sea. If it were able to look around and think, it would see all of the other waves and might well conclude "Here I am, one insignificant little wave amongst all of these thousands of waves; doomed to a perilously short existence fraught with danger. Even if I should grow to a giant tidal wave, though my life might be dramatic and go down in history, it will be over all too quickly and my existence will be no more." And inevitably the wave will die but when it does so it finds that it is nothing less than a part of the vast ocean. And you can take this even further to see that the essence of the wave is literally the same as the essence of the ocean – both are water. Thus, the wave's imagined separate existence was only an illusion; its apparent birth and death was just a temporary changing form on the surface.

It is only in our imagination that we are confined to that glass jar we call the body and mind; we need to recognize that we are unlimited. (And remember that re-cognize means to know again – we have merely forgotten.) It is ignorance of this truth that causes all our perceived problems. Our own particular wave is only transitory. When the form breaks up, there is no death; we remain the same H_2O that we always were.

We are not our bodies. We do not live in the walls of our houses; we live in the space. If the house is knocked down it no longer functions as a house, but this is only because the space is no longer defined by the walls. The space itself is totally unaffected. Similarly, when the body is destroyed it no longer functions as a person but the Self is totally unaffected.

But Mr. Bradley – in fact, perhaps I could call you Frank now, could I? – *You* contacted *me* this morning. I hope what I have said has been of some small consolation but what was it that you wanted to ask?

{RJ} It occurred to me that you might be able and willing to help me find out what is happening down at the tip. You obviously have a very high level of technical expertise when it comes to computers. I was hoping I might persuade you to hack into the

UWD database to find out what toxic materials they have been dumping without telling anyone...

He who sees that the Self is the same in all beings, undying when they die, truly understands. XIII.27

It was misty and still quite cool that Monday morning as Bill Maitland walked into the yard at the Council's Highways Department. But it was only 7.25 a.m. and there were distinct signs that this would be another scorching hot day like those of the week before last, before the storms had provided such an unusually welcome interruption. It would be shirts off and adding to his St. Moritz tan again later on. He could only hope that the work would not be too strenuous. Not that he didn't enjoy hard work – this, his first summer on the roads, was the best job he'd had so far; good, healthy, outdoor life – but sweating under a sweltering sun did tend to take some of the spice out of it. Still, it was infinitely preferable to the cotton mills in which he had spent a number of years, where one sweated all day and never even saw the sun.

Most of the men had been idle during the previous week, being prevented by the heavy rain from continuing their scheduled work. There had been the occasional outing to erect urgent road signs for flash floods and associated traffic diversions, but all the big jobs had been postponed and it was simply impractical to fill in pot holes under those conditions. Bill himself had been on an extensive tarmac-laying job, with four other men, in the centre of town when the rains came down. He fervently hoped that he'd get something easier today. That was hard work in this weather, whether one was shoveling the damn stuff into a wheelbarrow, pushing this to the actual site of laying (the lorries always seemed to unload a huge pile of it about fifty yards from where it was actually required) or spreading it out with heated rakes at the other end. Unfortunately, the town had many locations where access for the automatic machine-laying equipment was just not possible and they had to resort to the old, traditional and arduous, manual methods.

He entered the staff canteen and grunted his good mornings (taking care not to sound too enthusiastic) and glanced at his watch to see if there was time for a quick pot of tea. He decided that there was, just, but then discovered to his mild annoyance that the water was not yet boiling, the big immersion-heated kettle not having been switched on for a sufficient length of time. He went outside to wait with the others until the gangers came back from the supervisor's office with their assignments.

"Morning, Stu," he called out when he saw Stuart Brent sauntering out of the office, scrutinizing a paper in his hand. "What's on, mate?"

"Hi, Bill! There's some bloody crack opened up in Honeywell Lane, down on the estate. I reckon it ought to be a job for the gas board or water board but it seems they can't pin it on either of 'em yet, so we've got to go and look into it. We're taking that young lad, Scott whatever-his-name-is. Where is he, anyway?" he asked, suddenly, looking around.

"Not in, yet, I don't think."

"Lazy bugger," commented Stuart, laconically. "Look, we'll get over to the stores and collect the stuff anyway. Ben's taking us down, so dump the things on his wagon – spades, picks, usual rubbish. Afraid we can't take a van down – we don't expect to be there very long – so we won't be able to make a brew. We'll have to get one from one of the houses. Luckily, I do know a couple of pieces on the estate," he added, with a knowing look in his eye.

He always does to hear him talk, thought Bill, slightly envious but not fully believing him anyway. He wandered off towards the stores, glancing over to the line of lorries to identify the position of Ben Hogan's, the one with the slightly mangled tailgate, where the big mechanical shovel had misjudged its tipping angle. Stuart went off in the other direction to look for Scott. If he wasn't coming in today, he needed to know fairly quickly so that he could negotiate a replacement.

Bill collected all the gear and loaded it into two wheelbarrows ready for transferring to the truck. He was just wheeling one of them over when Stuart returned, in animated conversation with Scott.

"How about a hand?" he shouted to attract their attention, none too pleased at having to do all the work himself.

Stuart broke off and came across to take the handles of the other barrow, motioning for Scott to climb onto the back of the lorry, to receive the tools as they handed them up.

Soon, they were on their way, trying to maintain a comfortable position; leaning against the sides of the open truck as it bounced and jolted along the uneven road.

"We won't have anything to do for a short while," shouted Stuart, against the wind, "we'll have to wait for Paul and the compressor." Having offered this small consolation, however, he remained quiet, his breath having been taken away by the rush of air.

It sounded like a very typical job; one gang or another was out most days, digging up the road somewhere. Bill wondered if some of the work was really worth the effort. They were often sent in after the gas board. The gasmen would dig a bloody great hole to repair a minor gas leak, fill it in again, and then, before the week was out, the council would be out to dig it up again and do the job properly. Why they couldn't co-operate in the first place, Bill would never know. Most of the work, though, consisted of re-surfacing, where constant movement of heavy traffic had loosened the tarmac and subsequent weathering had caused potholes. Subsidence was worse. In these cases, they had to dig a hole and dump concrete at the bottom before topping it up again. It looked as though this might be one of those jobs, if cracks had been reported.

So, they would have to sit around and wait for Paul to arrive with his pneumatic drill. That could take hours – Paul was often in demand, also operating one of the little steamrollers, which were used to finish off the surface after small tarmac jobs. Bill was distinctly glad he didn't have to operate one of those drills; he had heard somewhere that the vibrations were supposed to cause impotence. Didn't seem to affect Paul, though; he was another one always talking about women. Only been married about six months too, he recalled.

His train of thoughts was soon broken by their arrival however, and Stuart jumped nimbly down to the ground and began to unfasten the bolts holding the tailgate. Most of the lorry drivers always seemed to be in a hurry, never standing around for long chatting as the others so frequently did. Possibly because of their relatively solitary jobs they never got to know any of the other men very well or perhaps they had restrictive schedules to keep to. Whichever the case might have been, Ben was no exception. A surly character with decidedly brutal features, he glanced repeatedly, with obvious impatience, from his cab until they had unloaded the tools. Eventually the wheelbarrows and the piles of rubber cones with their white and orange plastic sleeves lay on the roadside, the lorry moved off and the grey cloud of diesel fumes cleared allowing them to survey the extent of the damage.

There had been numerous times when Stuart had been sent out on a repair job, after a complaint had been made to the council, in which he had been quite unable initially to determine the problem. Often it turned out to be a cracked paving stone, which seemingly could scarcely have presented a hazard even to a blind person. There was no such difficulty here. The crack was in the side of the road near the bottom of the hill, about twenty yards before the point where the main road forked to the left by the side of the park. A brief strip of tarmacked road continued ahead, but soon degenerated into a dirt track leading up to the tip. Fortunately more than half the road remained undamaged leaving ample, single-track, passage for vehicles.

Their initial impression was unanimous. The open-mouthed expression upon Scott's face was quite adequate to express the general feeling but he felt obliged to comment nevertheless.

"We're not supposed to handle this all by ourselves are we?" he asked incredulously. "It'll take us weeks."

Indeed, the damage was far more serious than they had been led to expect, although presumably, it might have worsened since the council had been informed. There were a number of minor fissures at one point near the crown of the road but these drew together about two feet from the pavement. The rift then advanced parallel to the curb, widening considerably to a gap of about eighteen inches at its central point, the whole being some twenty feet in length. Other subsidiary cracks lay to either side where some of the road surface had started to fall into the chasm. The maximum depth of the cleft measured about three feet.

"Better set the cones up anyway," said Stuart eventually, realizing that one of the supervisors would be driving around shortly to survey the situation himself. The extent of the damage was cause for dismay rather than wonder as far as he was concerned.

They removed the temporary danger signs left there by the police and set up their own triangular 'men at work' signs. Next, they spaced out the cones along the middle of the road, blocking off traffic for a distance of some fifteen yards. It was fortunate that this particular route around the town was little used now, since the construction of the new bypass. They would not be burdened by the additional inconvenience of having to set up traffic lights or, worse still, operate 'Stop' signs manually. Still, thought Stuart, they would need some lamps before dark. He'd have to order them when the super' arrived. Having finished the initial preparations, there was nothing further with which they could usefully occupy themselves until the drill arrived. Hence their thoughts inevitably turned to speculation about possible causes.

"No culverts round here, are there?" asked Bill knowledgeably, thinking that the recent heavy rains must have been the primary factor in precipitating the damage.

"No, I don't think so," answered Stuart, scratching his head thoughtfully. "Anyway, if that were the cause, it would have happened last week in the rain wouldn't it, not now, three days later."

"Oh, I suppose so," conceded Bill, somewhat nonplussed.

"I must admit though, it is very odd," Stuart continued. "Can't think what it could be. A burst water pipe would have explained it but where's the water?"

"Can't smell any gas," added Scott, not wishing to be left out.

"No, it definitely seems to me that part of the foundations must have gone," commented Stuart, after a pause. "Look." He pointed, by way of confirmation. "If you look from the right angle, you can actually see that there's been some subsidence."

At this, they all proceeded to march around, bending and kneeling here and there, gauging the level of the ground. Upon this close inspection, it was indeed apparent that the whole side of the road, wherein lay the crack, was noticeably lower than the rest and was itself sinking slightly to the edge of the actual chasm.

"You sure there aren't any old mines or wells down there? I don't want to fall down any holes," said Scott, obviously quite worried now.

"I'd hardly think so," retorted Stuart, patronizingly. "They wouldn't be likely to go building roads on top if there were now, would they?"

The apparently unassailable logic of this remark seemed to satisfy Scott, who had seemingly never acquired the cynicism and distrust of authority that came naturally for most of his contemporaries. Without further deliberation he sat down and began to unwrap and consume a packet of sandwiches. Bill, however, remained contemplative for a while and slowly and methodically unwrapped a new pack of cigarettes. He withdrew one and ritually tapped the filter end on the side of the box. In the same thoughtful manner, he opened a box of matches, took one out and carefully drew it along the striking surface, cupping the flame in his heavy workman's hands as he held it up to the cigarette now between his lips. He inhaled deeply as he flicked the still burning match out into the road, watching the streaming arc of smoke trail out behind it. Pressing his lips tightly together he produced a fine prolonged jet of grey smoke, fanning this up and down by slight movement of his mouth. All this was a sign, to those who knew him, that he was thinking and about to say something. It was an annoying habit of his, however, that by this technique he managed to trap the attention of his companions, leading them to suspect some revelatory profundity before stating some fairly obvious conclusion. Yet, at the same time, and which was even more annoying, it was usually a very relevant observation, which no one else had seen fit to make. Whether he was merely slow-witted and took much longer to assimilate and analyze information or whether it was his natural caution and thoroughness, no one had been able to ascertain. At any rate, it was by no means unlikely that he additionally derived some perverse pleasure from the obvious annoyance that this pantomime caused to other people.

"OK," said Stuart wearily, "what obvious point have we overlooked this time?"

"Well," said Bill slowly, "I was just thinking that what Scott said wasn't so stupid after all. I mean it's not impossible that the road was built on top of a mineshaft is it? There used to be coal mines not far from here. Of course, I don't suppose they would have deliberately done it if they'd known about it but happen there is and happen they didn't.

"Anyway, Stuart, you said you could see that there had been some subsidence so it doesn't really matter what's caused it, does it?" He glanced around at the others and, upon receiving a glance of perplexity from Scott, ignoring the look of annoyance on Stuart's face, added, "The point being that there's every reason to suspect that we might fall down a hole."

Scott paused in mid-bite and leapt to his feet, backing away from the side of the hole where he had been sitting. A mischievous grin broke out upon Bill's face and Stuart, finally realizing that all of this had been a winding-up of Scott, failed to suppress a brief smile though still half angry that he too had been taken in. Scott, seeing the expressions on the other men's faces, cautiously returned, an embarrassed flush rising to his cheeks.

"Well, it is possible isn't it?" he asked desperately.

"Aye, stranger things have happened," conceded Stuart. "Look," he said, anxious to change the subject, "how about finding somewhere to get a brew?"

The others nodded in agreement but just then, to their immediate dismay, a van appeared around the corner with the compressor unit in tow.

"Damn!" said Bill, with feeling. "Not wasting any bloody time, are they?"

The van drew up past their cordoned off area and Paul Bates and Cliff Hall climbed out. Paul paid scant notice to the scene, straightway setting to work to uncouple the trailer. The supervisor came over, nodded briefly at them and began immediately to inspect the damage.

"Looks quite serious, doesn't it?" he said after a moment. "Any ideas, Stuart?" he asked, condescending to the greater experience of the older man.

"Not really. Possibly a cracked sewer or water main – washed away foundation somehow," he answered.

"Hmm, well, get to it. I'll call back later this afternoon to see how it's going." And, without further comment, he climbed back into the van and set off up the road.

"Not very talkative, is he?" commented Scott, rhetorically.

"He's a busy man, isn't he," replied Bill, somewhat

sarcastically.

Meanwhile, Paul had extracted his drill and attachments from a recessed cupboard in the body of the machine and now connected up the pressure tubing.

"How about a brew before we start, then?" he asked, echoing their previous sentiments.

Bill laughed aloud at this comment. When he had worked in the mills, some grudging worker had told him that the blokes on the roads had it too easy and did scarcely anything but drink tea all day. Although this had proved to be some way off the mark, it was nevertheless true to say that they spent considerable time thinking about that activity. At any rate, Scott, being much the youngest present, was sent off to knock on the doors of the nearby Victorian terraced houses in quest of boiling water. The others produced their tea bags or jars of instant coffee and sugar and got their mugs ready.

It was much later, nearly an hour and a half after they had clocked-in at the depot, that they eventually got down to work, with Paul triggering the starter motor of the powerful compressor as the signal to begin. The surface yielded readily to the intense vibration of the chiseled head of the pneumatic drill and he soon had squares outlined over the first quarter of the area and proceeded to prize them up for the others to drag to one side. With the under-surface laid bare, their work finally began in earnest as the sun climbed up towards its zenith in the cloudless sky and beat down relentlessly on their already perspiring forms.

Robert Andrews and Frank Bradley waited impatiently in an anteroom for the appearance of Councilor Mathers. They knew perfectly well that he was in his office, having heard snatches of his raised voice, apparently on the telephone. Bradley was all for going in without awaiting a formal summons, considering the matter far too serious to be put off until Mathers had a free moment, but Andrews persuaded him that such an approach was unwise. Not only would it be discourteous but more important from their point of view, it would put the councilor into an unreceptive frame of mind. He assured him that Mathers knew they were here and would put in an appearance within minutes. He didn't and was, in fact, making further phone calls. Bradley, unable to restrain himself any longer, banged loudly on the door to the adjoining room, much to the dismay of Andrews, who didn't wish to associate himself with such unmannerly conduct.

"One minute, please!" came a shout from inside, in a tone that indicated its owner was in no mood for such effrontery. Very shortly afterwards, the door did in fact open and Mathers appeared in the entrance. "Come in," he ordered, in a voice only slightly moderated from its previous annoyance, and he stood aside to allow them through.

"Morning, Andrews," he conceded the pleasantry but scowled at Bradley as he passed by. "What can I do for you, Mr. Bradley?"

"Quite a lot I hope, councilor, if you want to stay in your job," answered Bradley, preparing to embark on an impassioned harangue.

"Hold on, Bradley," intervened Andrews, "no point in getting overexcited. Let's sit down and discuss this calmly."

"Yes, I think you better had," said Mathers. "What's going on?"

They sat down and Bradley recounted his visit to Andrews the previous night, while Andrews himself took over to repeat the story of his discoveries concerning the tip. As the information was revealed, Mathers looked increasingly worried, shifting uncomfortably in his chair and puffing furiously at his empty pipe. He allowed them both to finish with only an occasional "Good God!" or other muttered expletive. Then, they sat in silence for a moment until Bradley spoke up with an expectant, "Well?"

"This explains quite a lot, I suppose," he conceded eventually and continued, "I think I'd better tell you what happened while you were waiting."

The ominous note in his voice was apparent to the heightened awareness of his two listeners. The lines of worry, which had recently become marked upon Andrews' face with the burden of his discoveries, increased in depth and clarity, drawing his features into the mask of tension and overburdened responsibility which was to become his habitual expression. Bradley merely gripped the arms of his chair more tightly and pushed his torso more erect in anticipation of yet more doom laden revelations.

"First thing this morning, I had a phone call from UWD. It seems that one of their drivers, having finished his early collection round, arrived at the tip to find no one there to let him in. The company had had a call from the wife of one of the men, saying that he wasn't feeling too well and would have to take the day off. But there are normally five workers there, so clearly, none of the other four had turned up either."

His sense of the dramatic forced him to stop here and look to the others for some appropriate response. Though the expression of concern deepened still further on Andrews' face, however, he found himself, somewhat disconcertingly, slightly disappointed to see no look of surprise on either of their faces. They waited for him to continue.

"Naturally, I had to try to help them out; make alternative arrangements – borrowed some men from Highway's; can't afford to have five trucks and twenty men sitting around idle because there's nowhere for them to dump their rubbish. But that's beside the point. Since UWD hadn't bothered to try to find out what was wrong with the men, I thought I'd make some investigations of my own. Most of the men there used to work for us and we still had their records, so I called one of them at home myself. I was talking to his wife while you were waiting outside. She tells me he's been in bed all weekend, half-delirious with a high fever. Doctor's trying to get him into hospital so it must be quite serious. What do you make of that, Andrews?"

"I really don't know. I could imagine one of them accidentally getting some of the stuff into his system via a cut or something. But five of them... perhaps there's some gaseous manifestation, though the material itself is far too heavy to exist as a gas at normal temperatures. Possibly a reaction with some of the industrial waste has produced a toxic gas or maybe it got into their drinking water, how should I know? Good Grief," he began again, as the thought hit home, "I hope there's no way it could get into the water supply, if this is the effect it has."

Mathers jumped to his feet. "I think we'd better have some action," he said, picking up the phone. "I'll get UWD to suspend all operations at the tip indefinitely. They'll have to take the rubbish elsewhere. And they had better ensure that the fence is secure all around the perimeter. Then we'll have to have a think about what to do next."

At that moment, there was a knock at the door and his secretary looked nervously in.

"Sorry to disturb you, sir, but there's a group of newspaper men outside. They insist on seeing you about some boy who died on the tip yesterday."

A glimmer of satisfaction lit Bradley's face momentarily, the sight of the councilor with his mouth partly open, telephone still in his hand, now hanging limply by his side, in no way detracting from his enjoyment of the moment. A sharp look of disapproval from Andrews soon quenched his enthusiasm, however; no doubt he was of the opinion that Bradley was to blame for leaking the story to the press. Nevertheless, thought Bradley, ignoring his personal dislike of Mathers, the lack of decisiveness and general ineptitude made him an extremely unsuitable man to have in charge of the handling of a crisis such as this. He must endeavor to persuade Andrews to help him take it out of this fellow's hands as soon as possible.

Mathers eventually put down the phone and attempted to regain his composure but it was still some time before he could reach a decision.

"I can't keep them in the dark indefinitely," he said to Andrews, desperately. "They're going to find out about these new developments sooner or later and, if we don't give them some reasonable explanation, they'll be printing any number of wild rumors." He turned to the secretary. "Tell them to come back at two this afternoon and we'll have an announcement then."

By early afternoon, they had begun to make some impression on the hole. The actual surface had quickly been cut away with the help of the drill, and had laid bare the rather more resistant foundations. They had chosen to work first on a small section, concentrating on digging to a depth of some four or five feet, to try to ascertain the cause before excavating the entire area. After clearing a square of about six feet to a couple of feet depth, they had conquered the most difficult part and a pile of broken stone and loose rubble lay at the side. Below the foundations, the loose clay and soil allowed relatively swift progress though it was hardly light work, as the shirtless and perspiring bodies of the three laborers testified. The day had proven as hot as its dawning had promised and numerous spent bottles of mineral water and empty coke cans lay alongside their tools.

It was Scott who was down the hole when they uncovered the 24" diameter pipe of the sewer. There was no apparent fracture at this point, though the mud around indicated that there was seepage of water from some source. It seemed even hotter down in the trench, with the sun beating down from directly above and no movement of air to evaporate the sweat pouring down his body. It was to this that Scott attributed the slight dizziness each time he rose to throw a spadeful of earth up and over his shoulder, to the side. He felt decidedly weak, though his stint down the hole still had some ten minutes to run. He couldn't bring himself to complain, however, valuing too highly his esteem in the eyes of the others. He mustn't allow them to think him unable to pull his weight alongside them. So he continued, pausing ever more frequently to wipe the perspiration out of his eyes. His breathing became increasingly erratic – he felt he couldn't gulp in sufficient air to provide, via his blood, the energy his aching muscles needed.

"What's up lad? Hard work?" shouted Stuart from above, though he had to repeat it before the meaning was grasped.

"OK!" he managed to gasp. "Just hot."

"You come on up, I'll take over for a bit," said Bill. His experience in the ring rooms of cotton mills had better prepared him for working in these conditions.

"No,'s all right," insisted Scott, though he knew he would not be able to continue for much longer. The spade seemed to be growing heavier, or the soil itself. He was having difficulty actually removing earth to throw out and a large proportion of it was falling back into the hole as he lifted it. The men above were speaking again but, whether to him or not, he couldn't decide, being unable to make out the words, which seemed so far away. The feeling in his hands was strange, similar to pins and needles but more a sort of numbness. He had better get out, he decided. It would make it look even worse if he fainted or something – he'd never live it down. Accordingly, he dropped the spade not noticing the clatter it made as it struck the pipe. He succeeded only with difficulty in standing, the odd tingling sensation now seeming to suffuse his whole body. He attempted to raise his arms to pull himself out of the pit but his muscles would not obey his commands and he realized he would have to ask the others to give him a hand. He looked up and the glare of the sun struck back, nearly blinding him; all else shrank into a dazzled haze at the edge. Two faces suddenly appeared partially blocking the searing beam but it was impossible to recognize them. He tried to shout for help but only a hoarse choking gurgle arose in his throat. The outlines of the images above blurred still further and the whole began to rotate about the centre of that fierce burning light. He suddenly felt violently sick but, as he tried to bend down to obey the instinctive urge to vomit, his vision faded and he collapsed into unconsciousness.

The buzz of voices in the adjacent room was growing distinctly louder. The assembly of newspaper reporters was obviously becoming impatient. Mathers' discomfort appeared to increase proportionately as he mechanically wiped his brow every few minutes with an already sodden handkerchief. Andrews shuffled the pile of papers in front of him, finally selecting one and pointing out some of the figures to Doctor Sanderson. The latter looked on over his shoulder, the spectacles almost falling from the end of his nose, where they were precariously perched. Bradley and Hardwyke conversed in low tones in the corner of the room. Struthers was standing at the side of the room, looking out of the window. At a cursory glance he appeared at ease, almost disinterested in the events going on around him, but the nervous drumming of his fingers on the windowsill betrayed him to the careful onlooker.

The two senior council officials had now been brought up to date on the latest developments and the group had been attempting for the last hour to devise the best method of presenting the facts to the public. It was decidedly no easy matter. Clearly they could not disclose Andrews' opinion that the material was extra-terrestrial in origin. The unscientific members of the group would require far more concrete evidence before even considering such an outrageous notion. On the other hand, as they could hardly presume to claim that it was, in any sense, a natural phenomenon, they were therefore forced to admit that the accidents had arisen directly or indirectly from substances dumped at the tip with the council's full knowledge and approval. Undesirable though this was – virtually admitting responsibility for a child's death and the workers' illness – there seemed to be no alternative.

Word appeared to have spread remarkably quickly in the space of such a short time and they now had not only the local newspapers to deal with but also the national press. Mathers, aware of Bradley's previous involvement with environmental issues, suspected that the latter had tipped them off, but was unwilling actually to accuse him of such complicity. He noticed that Bradley seemed to be getting on very well with Hardwyke; it was difficult to believe they had only just met. He wouldn't be surprised if Hardwyke hadn't put him up to that petition in the first place. He had always suspected the woman's loyalty; she was clearly after his job.

"I think everyone's here now, sir," said the voice of Mathers' secretary from the door.

"Very well. Are we all ready to go in?" asked Mathers, nervously adjusting his tie.

The conversations ceased abruptly; Andrews carefully gathered his papers together and followed the others into the next room. The board room had been temporarily converted for the press conference, the large oak table having been somehow removed and rows of chairs set out facing a long, narrow, collapsible table erected at the front, behind which the group now seated themselves. The chairs were all occupied and a number of people were even standing at the rear of the room, though most of these appeared to be photographers, cameras at the ready, most with external, electronic flash. In all, there were about forty people present. Apart from the journalists from the local and county press, Bradley recognized several of his acquaintances from the big nationals. Obviously someone had let it be known that there could be a major story around.

Mathers stood and waited for the room to become quiet, clearing his throat self-consciously. His short spell of office had not previously presented him with the unpleasant experience of facing the press and he was desperately afraid that he would be unable to control the situation if the meeting should start to get out of hand.

"I'm sorry for all this, ladies and gentlemen," he began, realizing immediately that he had not meant to begin like that at all. "I didn't want to speak to any of you this morning and have you going off in possession of only half the facts and blowing things up out of perspective. Above all, let's keep calm and not get all dramatic, shall we?"

He glanced around at the faces in the room. It had been his intention to begin by attempting to dispel the general air of expectancy, the feeling that some exciting earth shattering news was about to be revealed, for that had been his impression of the atmosphere upon first entering. It was apparent immediately, however, that, whether correct or not in that initial assessment, his preliminary speech had had precisely the opposite effect. They may have been slightly curious about the rumored circumstances surrounding the tragic accident but now, since it was obvious that the chairman himself was extremely worried, they began to think that there must be much more to it than they had previously thought. Now, all faces were upon him, alert and eagerly awaiting the forthcoming announcement.

Mathers was feeling more uncomfortable by the minute and paused to take a sip from the glass of water before him. He genuinely needed to relieve the dryness at the back of his throat. He also needed as much time as possible to consider his next words and also the mildly dramatic effect to reinforce his position of authority as the current speaker.

"First of all, I regret to have to announce that a young boy met with a fatal accident at the Crow Field refuse tip on Sunday. Mr. Struthers here," he gestured vaguely in the direction of the American, who partly raised his arm in identification, "represents United Waste Disposal, which operates the facility. He'll be able to answer any technical queries you might have."

There were renewed murmurings at this, the key phrase being 'first of all.' What else, then, had happened? As yet, however, no one asked the question, all being content, for the first few sentences at least, to let the man talk without interruption.

"After breaking into the area, the boy was—"

"Excuse me, sir. He actually 'broke in,' did he?" interrupted a loud voice, obviously one of the more discourteous of those present.

"Well, he was trespassing, certainly, and he must have entered illegally, via the perimeter fence, since the main gate was locked," answered Mathers, uncomfortably.

"How old was the child?" a new voice asked.

"Umm, eight years old, I believe."

"And this eight-year-old child broke down the outside fence, did he?" insisted the original voice, the sarcasm undisguised.

"Well, part of the fencing may be in some disrepair," Mathers was forced to concede.

"We'd already started a process of upgrading all of the old sections of fencing. This began last week and should be completed by the end of the month," added Struthers.

"I see. Thank you," said the voice, maliciously, and its owner, a well dressed man in his thirties, sat down again and began writing in a small notebook.

"The boy then made his way towards the centre of the tip, where he became bogged down in an area of waste material of some toxic nature," continued Mathers. He looked up, obviously hoping at this juncture for the prompting of further questions, but this time, to his dismay, there was silence and everyone waited for him to carry on. "Here, he was overcome, possibly by fumes, and died," he ended lamely.

"Were there not any marks on the body?" asked another man, obviously knowing perfectly well that there were.

"The waste was corrosive and the body was mutilated, yes,"

answered Mathers, savagely.

"Isn't it true that the limbs were... dissolved?" asked the well dressed man again, after searching for a moment for a more satisfactory word and finding none.

"That is true, yes." Mathers breathed a sigh of relief that this at least was out in the open now.

"What were the chemicals involved?" asked the elderly representative from the county press.

"I'm afraid we don't know that," began Mathers.

"But surely you've had them analyzed, haven't you?" he pressed.

"Samples have been taken from the body and sent for forensic tests," Doctor Sanderson answered. "We will not know the results of these until later today."

"Look," began a new voice, that of the local journalist, "before we continue, I think it should be made clear to everyone that a petition was sent to the council about two weeks ago, complaining about the smell from the tip. I have a copy of that petition here." He held aloft a sheet of paper. "Furthermore, I happen to know that a chemist was enlisted to take samples from the tip for analysis." He sat down again, his feeling of self-importance in the presence of these higher echelons of journalism evident, although he had not followed his announcement by any of the more obviously pertinent questions. Nevertheless, his disclosures had created the effect he had intended and a minor uproar was in progress.

"That's done it now," whispered Hardwyke to Bradley.

Doctor Andrews stood, motioning Mathers to be seated. The latter readily complied, immediately taking a gulp of water and almost choking.

"Could I have your attention, please!' he called and waited for the din to subside. "That is quite true. My name is Andrews, from the Chemistry department at the university and I was asked to take some samples for analysis, which I did about ten days ago. The results of the analysis are still being prepared in detail but are, I'm afraid, somewhat indefinite or, that is, inconclusive. We'll have to make further investigations and carry out a number of additional tests before any statements can be made. What we can say is that it can in no way reflect direct blame on to the council for what has happened."

"You'll have to be more specific than that, Doctor," the belligerent voice of the well dressed man spoke out.

Doctor Andrews breathed heavily. "I can't be too specific. As I say, the results are inconclusive. But the toxic substances were not dumped directly, with or without the knowledge of the council."

"How can you possibly be sure it wasn't dumped without their knowledge?" the man continued, not allowing this unintentional slip to go unnoticed, and glanced around triumphantly at his associates.

"Because such a chemical is not produced by any industrial or other known process."

There was astounded silence at this reply and none was more surprised than the gentleman who had posed the question. Considering it unanswerable and intending it to be purely rhetorical, he had expected no reply at all. Andrews himself was unable to suppress a mild feeling of satisfaction at the reaction, reluctant though he had been to divulge such information.

"But what was the chemical?" asked the county pressman, for the second time.

"As Councilor Mathers has already said, we don't know," Andrews was forced to concede. "The initial structural and chemical analyses reveal something which," he struggled for words, "doesn't fall into any known category of compounds."

Mathers looked over at him, obviously considerably annoyed. They had wanted to avoid any revelations of this nature. He hoped Andrews would at least leave it at that. Still, the drift of the questions had, more or less, forced the admission.

Fortunately, the meeting was interrupted at this moment,

giving those at the front a brief respite to recover their composure. The secretary entered, looking nervously at the gathered newsmen, and handed Mathers a folded note. He took it but paused for a while before opening it, his expression registering initial disapproval at the interruption but swiftly transforming into one of worry as he strove to imagine what had made it necessary. He dismissed his secretary and then, noticing that a majority of the audience was watching him, attempted to assume an air of nonchalance as he opened the note and began to read it. At this point, growing impatient with the delay, the ill-mannered man chose to continue the interrogation so that few noticed that, now staring intently at the note, Mathers' face paled as he registered its contents.

"Can we get this straight, Doctor, I'm afraid I don't understand. You say this stuff couldn't have been dumped there. Then has it been there all the time? I mean, are we likely to find this liquid or whatever it is, which dissolves people, lying around anywhere in the countryside?"

Andrews floundered helplessly, unable to answer in the face of this reductio ad absurdum argument.

Bradley attempted to rescue him. "As the doctor has stated, this material has apparently not resulted directly from waste disposal. I haven't known the doctor long but our short acquaintance has convinced me of his integrity. I, for one, am happy to believe he's giving us his best scientific opinion. As you must appreciate, however, this does not exclude the possibility that it is the indirect result of processes not yet understood."

"Thank you, and who are you, sir?"

"That's Frank Bradley, the amateur ecologist," commented his neighbor, a young man in a light green sports jacket. "What's your angle in this matter, Mr. Bradley?" he asked aloud. "You're normally on the offensive," he added suspiciously.

"Believe me, I am on the offensive," exclaimed Bradley, in a clearly belligerent tone. "I organized the petition and I'm also a friend of the dead boy's mother so I am quite determined to get to the bottom of it. At present, however, we don't have any facts to pursue any plausibly guilty party. I believe it's important not to start speculating and taking action on the basis of insufficient information." He stopped at this point, before any further waffling led him into a more defensive attitude, one he was not accustomed to take. Still, it was clear that, as yet, the blame could not be placed on any particular body, whether private or public and he didn't believe in fighting without a concrete justification, nor without a clear target in mind. The flash from a camera caught him off guard before he had time to sit down again. A picture of a worried Bradley would add substance to the story.

"When you began speaking, councilor, you used the words 'first of all,'" someone said. "Might I ask what else you were going to tell us?"

Mathers climbed, somewhat shakily, to his feet once again. The note had obviously shocked him considerably and his confidence, lacking to begin with, had now deserted him completely. He had drunk the water and now toyed nervously with the empty glass as he addressed the audience.

"There's been a second er... incident concerning the workers at the tip. They became ill over the weekend and are now in hospital."

This was news. There was renewed hubbub from all parts of the room and Mathers looked desperately for help from his associates. "The MO will give you the details," he said aloud, looking helplessly across at Sanderson, who calmly stood and waited authoritatively for silence.

"There's no immediate cause for concern," he began, automatically adopting that particular mode of hospital vernacular, whose clichés give away almost nothing at all, often even implying the reverse of what they appear to say. "Their condition is not thought to be serious. They're all feverish and, for the moment, unable to communicate intelligibly."

"He means raving," muttered one man on the front row to his neighbor.

"They're expected to recover in a day or so."

"And what, precisely, is wrong with them, sir?" asked a new voice.

"Again, I'm afraid the hospital doesn't know *precisely*. There are many minor viruses insufficiently common or serious to have been categorized," he answered, attempting to sound unconcerned but not succeeding convincingly. He took a quick glance around the room and, no immediate questions being forthcoming, sat down again.

Hardwyke, observing that Mathers seemed to be entirely lost in his own thoughts, his eyes slightly glazed and staring into infinity from his pale face, rose at this point and announced in a clear authoritative tone, "Well, gentlemen, thank you for coming. We'll keep you informed of any developments. I don't believe there's anything more to be said at the present time."

"But there is, if you don't mind my saying so," said the ill-mannered voice again. "Just what are you proposing to do about all this?"

Hardwyke strove to keep her patience in the face of this bellicose individual. "Naturally, we're closing down the site temporarily and there will be a full investigation. You may be assured that there will be no further occurrence of this nature."

At this point, Mathers leaned over and tapped Hardwyke lightly on the arm, motioning her to be seated.

"I'm afraid you're going to find out soon enough, so you might as well know now. Another man has been taken into the hospital with the same symptoms, a laborer who was working on a road down near the tip."

This time, it was not only the newsmen who reacted with surprise to this latest development and everyone began to speak at once. Andrews looked with concern over at Mathers, who had collapsed back into his chair.

"What work was he involved in?" The voice arose over the din and the noise subsided sufficiently to allow most to at least hear the response.

"I believe there was some subsidence in the road, large crack or something," mumbled Mathers, only just coherently.

"There wouldn't be any connection, would there, with that house wall which collapsed this morning out on the edge of the Waverly estate?" asked the knowledgeable local reporter. "That's down near the tip."

For a moment, there was a complete silence and then pandemonium broke loose. The reporters did not want any more sobering facts or theories attempting to refute any relationship. The sketchy details as they stood would enable them to fabricate a sensational story and they were all itching to phone in the details to their respective editors. They had to be in time for the evening editions, if possible.

"Gentlemen, please," shouted Hardwyke, and she slapped her hand hard on the desk in front of her. The combined decibels succeeded in bringing the audience once more to attention – occasional comparisons with Baroness Thatcher in her prime ministerial days had not been entirely without foundation. "I'm afraid we really cannot allow you to attempt to postulate any connection between this house collapse and the other details. There is no evidence and no reason to suppose that any will be forthcoming. I urge very strongly that, for the present at least, you confine your articles to the facts alone – that is, to the boy's death and the mens' illness. If you wish to mention the house, do so in a separate article. I cannot emphasize enough that we do not wish to create panic; there is no reason, no justification at all to connect these events. If you were all to act as irresponsibly as a certain member present," she gave a withering glance in the direction of the representative of the local paper, "giving quite unwarranted significance to totally unrelated items, you could have all the inhabitants of that estate out on the streets, looking for somewhere else to live, thinking they're in some kind of danger. I assure you that you'll be kept up to date. We'll hold a further conference here tomorrow at the same time and if there should be anything to connect these incidents, you'll be told then. I trust we can rely on your sense of proportion and public responsibility."

Understand that all creatures have their birth in this. Thus, I am the origin and the dissolution of the entire universe. VII.6

{Krish} You say that what is happening does not seem 'real.' Well, of course, it isn't. It only 'seems' to be real.

{RJ} Surreal, perhaps – it is almost like a dream, or rather, a nightmare. The whole situation just seems to be escalating out of control. It started with the smells and the petition just a couple of months ago – that seemed so important at the time. Then the council meeting and the visit to the tip. Next, in only just over a week, Mark is dead, the road has subsided and I don't know how many council workers in hospital. How can there be any doubt as to whether or not it is real?

{Krish} Ultimately, I would want to define reality as that which is unchanging. Anything that does change would be, by that definition, transitory and unreal. If A becomes B, then A cannot have been real. However, even looking at the world from the empirical standpoint, you must admit that we do not perceive things as they 'really' are. Indeed we cannot.

{RJ} I'm afraid you'll have to expand a little, or am I going to regret having suggested that?!

{Krish} Well, think of particle physics – the search for the building blocks of matter. From the initial discovery that atoms were not, in fact, 'atomic' or irreducible as the Greeks had thought, science has broken down even the protons and neutrons into first mesons and then quarks and so on; ever smaller and yet ever more inaccessible. Not only can we not see them because they are too small and exist for too short a time, even their nature is indeterminate. They are neither particles nor waves and any attempt to pin them down in one aspect results in some other aspect sliding out of our reach. The observer and the observed are somehow inseparable. Thus science has been forced to incorporate indeterminism into its descriptions of things at the microscopic level.

At the other extreme we also encounter problems. The big-bang theory is still the most widely accepted 'explanation' of the origin of the universe. But we cannot ask the question what it was that exploded, what existed 'before' this event, since time itself also began with the bang. Similarly, if we suppose that eventually the universe will begin to contract and continue to do so until there is a 'big crunch' (though this is a questionable theory), we cannot ask what will exist 'after' since time will then end.

'Transient' is, of course, a relative term – our lifetime might seem to be an eternity to a mayfly; continental drift seems inconceivably slow to a man but the life of the earth or even the sun is but an instant on a universal scale. But that is the point – the relative reality of the universe is not *absolutely* real.

Another way of looking at it is that we could never be aware of how things 'really are' anyway, because of the limited nature of our sense organs. Our eyes only operate in a very restricted range of the electromagnetic spectrum – we cannot see X-rays or radio waves. Our sense of smell is very poor compared to that of a dog or snake. We cannot sense sub-atomic particles or use echo-location and so on. Accordingly, there is much information associated with 'things' in the outside world about which we have no direct knowledge.

In any case, everything we sense about an object is actually only an attribute. It might be 'big' or 'round' or 'red' or have any number of other aspects but none of these in isolation could in any sense 'define' it. You could write a book about an apple but still not know its 'reality.'

{RJ} I'm beginning to think I need a rest in order to try to assimilate all of this. All these ideas are going round in my head and I still can't quite grasp the essence of what you are saying. Can I just get one thing straight before we sign off – is the world real or isn't it?

{Krish} Yes and no! While we remain ignorant there is no question that we experience it and, to that extent, it exists. Once we fully realize the truth however (I'll use the term 'enlightenment' in future), we know that it is not something separate from ourselves and, in that sense, it 'ceases' to exist. But, of course, we still continue to 'interact' with people and objects *as though* they were separate. You also have to differentiate between illusory, in the sense of a private dream, and the illusion (experienced by practically everyone for his or her entire life) that the world exists. In a sense then, the world is unreal and yet not non-existent. It is a paradox but a fact. It is called *mithyA* in Sanskrit.

There is a very famous metaphor that helps one to understand this. In a darkened room one may see dimly the outline of a rope and mistakenly think it to be a snake. (At least one presumes this can happen easily in India – less likely in England!) Clearly there is in actuality only the rope 'reality' but, because of our ignorance, we see a snake (the plurality of the phenomenal world).

We superimpose the apparent universe upon the reality in the same way that we superimpose the snake on the rope. As long as we remain in ignorance, we will continue to believe that the world is separate and real. Once the ignorance is removed, we know everything to be one non-dual reality, just taking on different name and form. Just like gold takes on many forms according to the skill of the goldsmith but, no matter how intricate the shape might be, it remains nothing other than gold.

The Sanskrit word for 'truth' is *satyam* and this is also the word for reality. The only reality is called *brahman* in Sanskrit. Everything else, including concepts, is *mithyA*. There is no English equivalent for this word.

Another metaphor that is often used is that of clay and pot. The clay exists before the pot is made. Even while the pot is in use to hold something, it is still clay. And after the pot has been broken, the clay is still there. I defined 'real' as being that which exists in all three periods of time (past, present and future), so that it is only actually the clay that is real by this definition. Yet whilst the clay is in the form of the pot, it would not be true to say that the pot does not exist. Clearly it has some reality but it cannot be described as real according to the definition. But neither is it false, since we can use it to carry water. Its reality is entirely dependent upon the clay and, moreover, it is always clay and nothing but clay whether it is in the form of the pot or not. The pot has a 'dependent reality' – this is *mithyA*.

Similarly, the world did not exist a few billion years ago and will be swallowed up by the sun in a few more. The reality upon which it depends is *brahman*. *Brahman* exists before, during and after the world. The world, whilst it exists is nothing but *brahman*. *Brahman* is the only reality; the world is *mithyA*. And the same applies to concepts, emotions etc.

{RJ} Does this also apply to the *ahaMkAra* you were talking about earlier? Our 'real Self' identifies with something in creation and the nature of that 'real Self' is forgotten. We have superimposed the limitation on the unlimited reality. Like 'I am an architect' superimposes the limited idea 'architect' on the unlimited 'I' just as the snake is superimposed on the rope.

{Krish} Excellent! I couldn't have put it better myself. In fact, once the initial identification of oneself as a separate individual has occurred, the rest follows. We believe that the creation and everything in it is separate, that we have choice and act, and so on. We effectively create our own world as a direct result of our ignorance.

{RJ} So, to bring this discussion back to where we began, you are effectively saying that all of this that is happening here is an illusion, imaginary, brought about because of a conceptual error on our part? I don't somehow think that Brenda would appreciate that! What is the point, anyway? It doesn't make any sense.

{Krish} Well now, that is another question altogether isn't it? To whom does it not make any sense? I've already explained that the nature of reality is not something that can be apprehended by the mind or intellect – it is far too subtle for them. You can only find pointers to the truth – *'hints and guesses'* as T. S. Eliot put it: *'The hint half guessed, the gift half understood, is Incarnation.'*

Know this, Arjuna: I am the knower of the field in all fields. I maintain that true knowledge consists in knowing both field and the knower of the field. XIII.2

This was the second night in succession that Frank Bradley had been unable to sleep. The events of the past few days, the strange facts that had come to light and the even stranger theories to explain them circled endlessly, imprinting themselves on the circuits of his mind. No new connections were made, however, and the futile exercise provoked intense frustration. Presumably a relationship must exist between these isolated incidents but it was beyond his powers of reasoning to find any. Certainly, he could not conceive of a fundamental cause. Over everything, loomed the tip itself, now wreathed with overtones of foreboding. The image conjured up by the word was quickly coming to assume a very real sense of evil, such is the effect brought about by a dread of the unknown, when it impinges upon everyday human existence with such devastating effect. Had the cause been known to be some particular form of industrial waste, for example, with some person or persons responsible, the reaction would have been quite different. A few people would experience concern, perhaps even horror that such a thing could be allowed to happen but no one would experience fear. Here, in the face of the inexplicable, man was still at the mercy of those same mysterious forces which had ruled him since primitive times when, perhaps, the bravest hunter would cower in his cave when the sky was rent with lightning and the thunder rolled. If Krish didn't offer something soon, he would have to prompt him again about providing some help in looking for information.

He turned over restlessly and adjusted his pillow again, hoping to find a comfortable position such that he might drift off to sleep. He had tried in vain that evening to turn his mind to work. The plans for the proposed arts centre had been progressing very favorably – he held high hopes for his design being accepted – but, now, the development of his ideas eluded him, driven into the background against his will.

The evening papers hadn't been too sensational about the events. Obviously Hardwyke's last minute speech had had the desired effect and possibly averted a panic. Nevertheless, Mark's death had been given front-page coverage and the headline of 'Unknown Horror Kills Local Boy' was quite sufficient to provoke more than a little concern. Though not actually stating it as such, and despite the exoneration of blame on the council insisted upon by Andrews, all the stories tended to imply that industrial waste was at the root of the cause and that any ultimate responsibility must rest with the council. This was much as he had expected and was probably for the best at this time. The implication was that the particular corrosive substance which had caused Mark's death, and presumably the illness of the workers as well, had resulted from a reaction between two or more waste products, which should never have been dumped in the same place. If this were the case then someone, somewhere, was directly responsible for such an error of judgment and should be held criminally responsible. Despite Andrews' insistence, Bradley still believed some such explanation would prevail in the end; the alternative was simply ridiculous and he had always subscribed to the principle that the simplest explanation for problems was usually the correct one.

The local paper had placed the piece about the collapse of the house wall on the front page also, next to the main article, but, other than that, no connection was implied. A small article on the back page had attracted his attention and given him as much cause for concern as this other incident. Indeed, he was very much surprised that the knowledgeable local man at the conference had not known about it and imputed some connection – he would tomorrow, no doubt. The story concerned yet another council worker, responsible for the maintenance of the drains. He had been on his routine weekly visit to clear the bars at the exit of the pipe in the valley near Park Bridge. Leaves and paper and other detritus, swept into the drainage system during heavy rain, would accumulate around the metal grating at the exit and had to be periodically scraped away and shoveled to one side to prevent any danger of blockage to the flow of water. Bradley, himself knew that it was not uncommon to see the occasional dead rat in the vicinity – no doubt the various channels and culverts in the system were infested with them. Apparently, that morning, the man had found scores of them washed up against the bars, causing a build-up of several feet of water.

The writer had made no attempt to provide an explanation or even to suggest that one ought to be sought. The facts were merely stated as one finds in those 'strange but true' articles, common to popular magazines and Reader's Digest. Bradley's hostile attitude to the offhand style of the writer was understandable, however, for what he knew, which the other didn't or had no reason to consider important, was that the path of that particular drainage pipe lay directly beneath the tip.

Having read this, Bradley began wondering whether in fact, the tip itself was the prime cause of the troubles. The laborer who had collapsed that afternoon and been taken to hospital, apparently with the same symptoms as the refuse workers, had been a few hundred yards away from the tip. There had, of course, been a drain in the road on which he had been working at the time, and this would be part of the same system as the outlet with the rats. Possibly that was the common factor. Perhaps the original source of the pollution was elsewhere; some obnoxious mixture of chemical effluents entering the system at some remote point and emerging through a fracture beneath the tip to combine with other waste to produce the effects observed. But no, it didn't fit all the known facts. Andrews had said that he was certain no known substances were involved and if it were a chance combination of drainage or sewage and industrial waste, the foundations of the road would have to contain the same materials as the tip. And where did the collapsing house wall fit in? As yet, there were too many unknowns.

The really frightening aspect of the situation in retrospect was the rapidity with which these events had succeeded each other. It was only a couple of months ago that the residents of the estate had begun to worry about the peculiar smell drifting across from the tip. Never before, to his knowledge, had there been any serious problem of this nature, certainly nothing to warrant the drafting of a petition to the council. Then, within just a few days, Mark had died, the workers at the refuse tip had fallen ill, the hole had appeared in the road, the laborer had collapsed whilst working in it, the house front had fallen down and the dead rats had been washed up. Of course, there was no guarantee that they were all related but it would be more than odd if there should be no connection at all, when all of them occurred within a quarter mile radius of the tip. And why was all this happening now? And if, against hope, it were not coincidence, then the inevitable conclusion would have to be that the Tip, with a capital 'T,' was radiating its malign properties ever outwards and, one would have to ask, with considerable trepidation; 'What next?'

And so the events and arguments, questions and feeble attempts to answer them, pursued their own tails into the night, while the full moon beamed radiantly through the open window onto the wakeful and restless features of the troubled man. The atmosphere was hot and humid, following on from yet another glaring summer's day. The heat wave had resumed after the respite of the previous week's heavy rains, the pressure systems in the Atlantic having returned to a very stable, high-pressure equilibrium. There was no cooling breeze even to ruffle the curtain and Bradley lay on top of the sheets to avoid the additional heat generated by his own body. Still, the nights were quiet around here, there being no major roads or pubs in the vicinity, and, despite all other inhibiting factors, this, together with his bodily and mental fatigue, combined to lull his consciousness, at last, into a welcome oblivion.

Explain to me who you are with such wrathful form. I bow to you, supreme one; have mercy! Truly, I do not understand what you are doing. XI.31

Subjectively, it seemed to have been only minutes since he had fallen asleep before something brought him suddenly back to confused awareness. He fumbled momentarily to regain his grasp of reality, the initial vivid memory of some weird dream rapidly fading as he succeeded in bringing his conscious mind into focus. He glanced briefly at the illuminated face of the alarm clock on the bedside table – two thirty. He had actually slept for over an hour. He turned over, intending to continue where he had left off; he was sure that dream had been very interesting, if he could only recall the thread…

He was just beginning to drift out again, away from the land of the conscious, the waves of drowsiness gently washing over him and promising shortly to submerge him in a welcome deep slumber, when, again, he ran aground. He became aware of raised voices in the street below; the disembodied sounds floated in through the open window and challenged his attention. He was tempted to ignore them but, very soon, the novelty of the situation struck him and he became wide-awake once more.

Muttering his annoyance to himself under his breath, he swung himself off the bed and strode over to the window to ascertain the cause of the disturbance. Before he got there, however, a loud knocking at the front door stopped him short. He retraced his steps and tugged his dressing gown down from its position on the knob of the wardrobe door. He quickly put it on and rushed back to the window to see what was going on before answering the door.

It was a moment before he could make anything out. Though the moonlight illuminated the road outside without the help of the street lamps, the figure at the door was standing in the shadow of a tree in the garden. There was also something odd about the scene in general, of which he was intuitively aware but whose precise nature did not immediately register. Then, as he recognized the shape of the policeman's peaked cap from above, he realized that, in fact, the moon was the only source of light – the lamps were out. Reflecting upon this and wondering what on earth the police could want at this time of the morning, he walked back across the room and switched on the light as he opened the door. No light – the electricity was off completely then. The knocking resumed at the door, louder this time, signifying urgency or impatience. He wasted no further time in contemplation; now fully alert, he rushed down the stairs, oblivious of any danger of stumbling in the dark, unbolted the front door and pulled it open.

"Sorry, sir," apologized the constable, sounding almost sincere, before Bradley had time to speak. "I'm afraid we're evacuating the estate. There's been some subsidence; a couple of houses have disappeared down a hole and everybody'll have to clear out until we find out how extensive the damage is and whether any more buildings are liable to be affected. If you'll just pack a few clothes and belongings into a case and leave as soon as possible please. Do you have any friends or relatives who you could go and stay with nearby but away from the estate?"

Bradley did not immediately answer. Indeed, he had scarcely even heard the question he had been asked and he was far from thinking of a reply at this instant. His mind was in a veritable turmoil at this latest development. So, his fears were being realized. Whatever was happening seemed to be increasing its sphere of activity... exponentially. The situation was completely out of control now all right.

"Sir?" prompted the policeman, interrupting Bradley's thoughts.

"Oh, sorry, er... yes, I'll be able to find someone to take me in." The thought occurred to him that he ought to go and wake up Andrews. He'd be sure to want to know about this straight away.

Suddenly he thought of Brenda but then remembered, with a sigh of relief, that she had gone up to Scotland to stay with her mother for a while. Still, her house could have been involved. What a tragedy that would be.

"Which houses were involved? I have friends living nearby."

"Lindsey Road, forty-three and forty-five. Two adjacent semi's they were; just disappeared – at least, most of 'em."

That was a relief, he thought, but then experienced a twinge of guilt as he realized that, though he might not know them personally, people would have been killed or seriously injured; innocent people struck down without warning in the middle of their sleep. He shivered involuntarily at this chilling thought. Had he lived nearer the tip, it could so easily have been himself, now lying crushed at the bottom of some suddenly opened chasm in the road.

"I suppose there were casualties," he asked, though he knew it to be extremely unlikely that both houses had been unoccupied.

"I'm afraid so, yes. As far as we know, there were people asleep in both houses at the time. By some miracle, a couple of children were unharmed. The rear of one of the houses was left standing and they were still asleep in their beds when we arrived. There's not much hope for any of the others though; we don't even know, yet, how many are involved."

"Do you need any help?"

"No, thanks all the same. We've got all the professionals on the scene now with floodlights and rescue equipment. There's nothing you or I could do to help. If you'll just leave as soon as possible. Lock up behind you and call by Rupert Street as you go and give your name and address to the officer there so we'll know when everyone's out of the area."

Bradley nodded absentmindedly in reply. He scarcely noticed what the man was saying, though, paradoxically, he reflected on the odd habit he seemed to have of trying to turn his orders into conditional statements but leaving each one hanging unfinished without completing the predicate – an occupational quirk, he supposed. The constable, deciding that Bradley had nothing further to ask, raised his arm in a brief parting gesture, turned and walked back down the garden path and on to the next house.

Bradley stood for a long minute, his mind fixed on nothing in particular. He was vaguely aware of the knocking further up the street and of raised voices, no doubt discussing the crisis, in the other direction, but he was not really listening to either. Then he realized he must make an effort to clear his mind of all the confusing thoughts and conflicting ideas circulating therein. Action was called for. Accordingly, he forced his attention to open wide, allowing his senses to freely take in anything without selection. He stood silently for a while longer, feeling the revitalizing effect afforded by this simple exercise of coming into the present. Krish would have been proud of him!

Eventually, now alert and accepting the situation, he went back inside and quickly dressed. He considered whether to pack a small suitcase with a few of his more valuable possessions but decided against it. If his house were to disappear, it might as well take his belongings with it – they were all insured. He couldn't imagine how the insurance companies would classify it though: probably 'act of God,' he thought with a grim smile. Finally, pausing only to collect the traditional toothbrush and, after a brief hesitation, a battery shaver he had hidden away in a little used drawer, he put on his jacket, checking that he had his wallet and mobile phone, and left the house, locking the door behind him.

Immediately, he set off towards the edge of the estate nearest the tip. He intended to go to see Andrews, to discuss what should be done about informing the Authorities of all that they knew and suspected but, first, he wished to see the extent of the damage for himself, so that he would be in a better position to relate this new incident to him. Even had he not asked the policeman which houses had been affected, he would have known where to look. He allowed himself a brief feeling of self-importance at the thought that he was one of few that would make the association with the tip. Not that it would be the case for long – this would be national, if not world, news tomorrow.

He reached the end of the avenue and turned left along the road, which formed the boundary of the estate. To the right now was open land. Across the valley, on the far hillside, the silhouettes of another housing estate could be discerned against the lightening sky. Between, lay the old railway cutting, the faint indentations left by the tracks still visible, leading south to the viaduct. The lines and sleepers had long since been removed. No more could one see steam engines laboring up the incline, pulling their load of goods wagons into the town. He remembered how, many years ago, soon after he had moved to the area with his father, he had waited for hours for a train to come so he could take a photograph of the scene near the viaduct. He had just needed the added element of a steam engine, with a long plume of smoke, to complete the perfect picture, balanced by the ruins of the steel mill nestled by the stream, down in the valley bottom. Of course, steam trains had long been obsolete, even then, and the train, when it eventually came, had been pulled by a diesel locomotive. He had taken the picture anyway and, of course, the result was a complete disappointment. If he could locate the original negative, he would now be able to add a steam train digitally without too much effort, he thought. Realistically, though, it was most unlikely that this would be possible in an effective and undetectable manner.

The novelty of seeing the scene at this early time of the day, just before dawn, seemed to bring the childhood memories flooding back. He passed this way every few days, when out for an exercise walk, without giving the landscape a glance but now all seemed imbued with an indefinable supra-reality, as if the ghosts of past events, collected over the ages, were freed to re-enact their former lives. To the Northeast lay the humps of the tip, still in darkness, showing ominously as darker indefinite shapes against the dark of the sky. Though there were really no hills to speak of, he couldn't help feeling that a sudden eruption of fire and sparks from the peaks of the mounds would not be out of place. The image of the tip as a long dormant, now suddenly violently active, volcano seemed strikingly appropriate. Would it were something so natural, though. The unknown hell of the reality was, in a way, even more frightening than his imagined picture.

He walked on, oblivious to the many bustling scenes of evacuation outside virtually every house, as their occupants strove to load up cars with essential belongings, while simultaneously trying to keep over-excited children under control. As he rounded a slight turn in the road, the brilliant beams of floodlights became visible about two hundred yards ahead. He slowed his pace and tried to take in the fantastic scene before him. The incongruous illumination gave a theatrical appearance to the action, as if the stage were set for the rehearsal of some dramatic rescue scene from a melodramatic soap opera. But more than that; there was something outlandish about the quality of the light itself. Possibly some of the men were wearing helmets of the type used by miners, with powerful lamps mounted on them. The huge flood lamps were mounted on poles and operated by other men who swung them to direct the beams on to the wreck of the houses. Figures moved around and through the moving rays of light, the bizarreness of the total picture giving them the appearance of dancers acting out some grotesque satanic rite.

As he approached, the scene became clearer but, to his heightened sensitivity, the meaning of what was happening seemed to diminish in proportion. He could make out a barrier erected across the road and a second some way further down. In between, a blacker area obscured what must have been a large hole in the ground. The gap in the line of semi-detached houses was now clearly visible, a jagged line of bricks – part of the nearest wall still standing – demarcating the discontinuity. Apart from this single wall, the whole of the first house was missing, a thin line of sky visible through the back even at this angle. Only the front half of the other house had gone but the sight of the interior laid open to public view lent far more to the impression of devastation. The spectacle was not uncommon amongst houses undergoing demolition but the startling difference here was that the remaining rooms were still furnished. All the floors were carpeted, though the one in the upper room partly overhung the floor, where there was a sudden drastic termination to its support. A bed stood untouched by the fallen debris from the roof at the rear of the room – this must be where the children the constable had spoken of had been. It certainly was a miracle that they had escaped injury. A chest of drawers nearer the front lay half crushed under a section of wall and the entire surrounding area was littered with roof slates.

Splinters of broken glass glinted here and there, where they intercepted and reflected and refracted the beams from the searchlights. A pile of smashed furniture, curtains and kitchen hardware had been made on the far side of the road and some of the figures were throwing still more on to the top of it. Three fire engines, a couple of ambulances and numerous police cars were positioned along the road, their blue lights flashing, each regularly but together randomly. The tinny voices of their radios could be clearly heard.

He still found it difficult to accept that it was really happening; the air of unreality remained, partially induced by the hour, when normally all is silent and sleeps, and partly by the fantastic nature of the cause which he thought must lie behind it. Perhaps, he tried to tell himself, it really was a scene from a film, very realistically staged but, when he reached the barrier, the producer would ask him to move along and keep out of range of the cameras. But there was an element of strangeness that excluded even this possibility. It was sharp but surrealistic, like some paranoid nightmare of a crazed psychotic mind. No doubt when daylight came, all would be revealed in its documentary reality. The news cameras would relay it to the nation. People would look up from their meals, forks poised in transit, and utter gasps of horror or expressive expletives, depending on whether or not there were others present in the same room. It would mean rather more to people in the town itself and infinitely more to those who had been evicted from their homes in the middle of the night; a cone of involvement drawing to a sharp deathly point at the scene of destruction itself.

He continued to observe for a short while but moved no closer. As the policeman had said, he could not help; he could only hinder those far more proficient at this sort of job than himself. A further thought had also occurred to him that deterred him from becoming involved. Serious though this was – and death was always a serious matter, not only to those now past caring – it was necessary to maintain the incident in perspective. Compared to what might yet happen, considering the acceleration of events, this might have to be relegated to only minor significance. Someone had to get things moving, and quickly. It might transpire that they would have to evacuate the whole town, not merely the estate. The highest authorities must somehow be made aware of the scale of this thing; they must start planning ahead. The top brains in the country must begin immediate work to try to understand what was going on and to find a solution before it was too late. If this thing were to be neutralized, it should be done while its sphere of influence extended only a few hundred yards. If it were to grow to miles, as it now seemed it might be within its powers to do, how could they begin to combat it?

His mind raced and he had to make a conscious effort to rein in his imagination. He had been reading too many old science fiction novels recently and, now that a plausible opportunity presented itself, with a classic 'unknown' essence about it, all the fantastic themes were competing in his mind for the chance to become reality. Not that this was altogether a bad thing. At least he had the type of mentality that would be flexible enough to consider out-of-the-ordinary explanations and not keep hammering away at the problem with traditional commonplace logic, as many would. Unfortunately, with his architect's background, he lacked the scientific method that would ultimately be necessary to get at the truth. This would need a battery of experts, if Andrews' speculations proved to be accurate.

At this point in his train of thoughts, he was reminded of his original intention to go to see Andrews and present him with a first-hand account of the latest developments. Andrews would also know whom to approach on the scientific side to speed the investigation. Mathers too, or probably Hardwyke, should be told. He took one last cool look at the scene up the road, where the floodlights were now losing their appearance of brilliance as the early dawn lit the sky behind them. Then he turned and, with a calm but determined stride, set off in the direction of town.

There was, for a time, as Bradley walked purposefully away from the scene of the subsidence, a vague hesitancy, an uncertain and elusive doubt worrying away at the back of his mind. His main stream of thoughts flowed swiftly as he marched along, with plans of action formulating themselves and speculations being made as to the development of the situation, but an almost imperceptible faltering forewarned of some forgotten pitfall ahead. His pace slowed as his mind backtracked temporarily, striving to discover the impediment and regain his mental balance. Had he overlooked some obvious and important fact or was he merely overwrought after the tenseness of recent events? He struggled momentarily against the feeling of frustration at his inability to identify the source of his unease but the mass of his main thoughts recovered its impetus and he continued on his way.

That inconceivably involved process of problem solving had been initiated, however, and its functions continued subconsciously while his rational mind was preoccupied with other things. Synapses triggered and transmitter chemicals transmitted and, some millions of reaction steps later, out of that incomprehensible complexity, a result was synthesized. On a conscious level, Bradley stopped suddenly in his tracks when a thought broke unbidden into his awareness, as a new connection was made between previously unconnected ideas. It came as a shock and, for a long moment, Bradley stood paralyzed with indecision. He was now some ten minutes walk away from the accident. He might be being alarmist in thinking that anything serious could have happened since he left. He could simply return and warn them of the danger. On the other hand, if the worst of his fears had already befallen them, it would clearly be best to telephone the police or ambulance service. They would in any case be able to get in touch more quickly, by radio. Also to consider, however, was the fact that he was one of only three people who realized the potential extent of the problem. He could not take it upon himself to reveal that knowledge out of hand to just anyone. They might choose to disbelieve him completely, leaking the information in advance as a joke. Certainly it would in all probability hinder, rather than speed any help, should it be needed.

He reached a decision. He turned and set off at speed back the way he had come. In the time it would take for him to convince anyone of his sincerity over the phone and for them to contact those involved in the rescue operation, he could be back there himself and explaining in person. His anxiety increased as he rushed along and slowly recollected and consciously analyzed those details that had been involved in his sub-conscious conclusion. Firstly, Mark; the circumstances of his death were horrific enough but how had he come to be so incapacitated as to prevent him from escaping before the corrosive chemicals had had such drastic effect? Then there were the men at the tip. They were still alive, as far as he knew, and perhaps that fact had tended to relegate them to minor news value, compared to the more dramatic and sensational incident of the child – certainly the facts had not, as yet, been made available. But, again, something connected with the tip had presumably put them into hospital. Finally, the worker on the road; no connections had yet been made between this and the other incidents but the fabric of coincidence was wearing thin. In all cases, people had apparently been overcome by something, be it gas, virus or whatever. And now this latest incident had occurred.

The twilight of dawn had lifted to reveal a dull, grey, overcast sky by the time he came again within sight of the convoy of vehicles. The spot lamps still illuminated the scene but the fact that the area no longer stood out from its surroundings to anywhere near the same degree, made the overall effect less dramatic. Instead, there was an air of anti-climax, almost disappointment, as though the floodlights illuminated a football stadium after the crowd has dispersed, following an exciting match for which one has arrived too late. Indeed, it looked very much as if the operation had been completed, the casualties rescued and taken away, leaving the participants to take a well-earned cup of tea somewhere before beginning to clear up the debris.

As Bradley came closer, however, it became more and more apparent that this could not be the explanation – there were too many incongruities. Previously, and it had only been about twenty minutes ago, there had been frantic activity with many silhouetted figures dashing to and fro in the glare of the lamps. Now no one could be seen at all. Yet there seemed to be about the same number of emergency vehicles present, their blue lights rotating feebly and the occasional words of a police message drifting over from a radio. Of their occupants, though, there was no sign. As he came within a couple of hundred yards he finally saw why. He had naturally been expecting people walking or standing around the area. What he had not prepared himself for was the sight of prone bodies.

He stopped abruptly. He could see three bodies from where he was now standing. Two were slumped near the gaping hole in the pavement, into which the garden and front part of the house had disappeared. A third lay prostrate near a police car, hand outstretched towards the door, his hard hat lying some feet away. Possibly another two figures were present inside one of the ambulances but he could not see clearly as another vehicle was partially blocking his line of sight.

Bradley found himself in a most curious psychological state, observing the details in an almost detached way. He thought how appalled and even frightened he ought to be, yet felt almost a complete lack of emotion, as though drained of the capacity for reacting to events such as this, so far outside his experience. He did not know, afterwards, how long he had stood there, his mind failing to superimpose any sort of will over his motor activity. Eventually, though, the wailing of an approaching siren succeeded in breaking through into his awareness and restoring his control. As if waking suddenly, under those unusual circumstances when one is immediately alert, he assessed the situation and decided what he must do.

Fortunately, the police car was coming from the direction behind him. Had it been the other side of the fissure, he would have been powerless to stop it. As it rounded the corner, he stood in the middle of the road and waved his arms wildly up and down. It seemed, for a moment, as though the driver intended to swerve around this unexpected obstacle of an apparent lunatic in the car's path. At the last moment, though, possibly when it became obvious that the man had no intention of getting out of the way, he jammed his foot on the brake and the car screeched to a halt, mounting the curb as it did so. The doors opened immediately and two large, very irate policemen descended upon him.

Much later, Bradley found himself once again outside Andrews' house in the early hours of the morning. Even less than before, however, did he concern himself with the desirability of calling on someone at such an unsociable time. His mind was a jostling mass of thoughts, worries, imaginings and reflections upon what had happened over the last couple of hours. Time seemed to be running out and it was necessary that Andrews be informed immediately about these latest developments. Perhaps the two of them could make some sense out of the totality of the data and plan a course of action. He rang the bell and left his finger there just a little longer than was strictly necessary.

"Damn!" exclaimed Bradley, as he sat in Andrews' sparsely decorated kitchen, waiting for him to cook them an early breakfast. They had talked and talked, revisited all of the recent events at length if not ad nauseam – and got precisely nowhere. They had concluded that the entire situation was almost certainly out of their hands now anyway, after the latest horrors. Bradley had gone back to thinking about who might be responsible rather than what was actually happening. Then he had recalled asking Krish to help track down information. This then led him to the realization that his computer, and only link to Krish, was back at the house, to which he would almost certainly not now be allowed to return in the foreseeable future.

Not one to over-indulge in self-criticism, especially when there was no opportunity for remedying the situation, he had fallen to musing over the circumstances under which Krish had first made contact and how, subsequently, he had seemed to be aware of everything before Bradley mentioned it. He seemed to know all that *had* happened as well as all that was happening now. As far as he could tell, Krish might even have a good idea of what was *going* to happen as well!

I wonder… he thought to himself and then aloud, "Robert! Have you got a PC with Internet access here?"

"Yes, it's in the lounge. Go and use it if you like; the router is on permanently so you won't have to log in."

Bradley did not wait for further discussion and immediately sought out the machine and powered it up. His idea was simple but optimistic to say the least. Had he explained everything to Andrews, the other would surely have though he was mad. As promised, the connection was swift and his first action was to link to 'Google,' the search tool that he had been using before Krish had interrupted and introduced himself. He set up a simple search that was doomed, unlike most, to find zero relevant matches – "Krish RJ Kurukshetra."

The response was immediate, finding nothing useful, though suggesting several links to personal sites of people with the unlikely name of 'Kurukshetra' and a number relating to the Bhagavad Gita. He noted with interest that the name 'Krishna' was also associated with these – so the chosen venue for the meeting place in the chat room was not coincidental. While he was waiting, he idly read through some of the links and looked up 'Bhagavad Gita' in Wikipedia.

He assumed that Krish (did he really think of himself as some kind of avatar?) had chosen to cast Bradley in the role of Arjuna – a warrior prince about to fight an epic battle against relatives and former friends, who had seriously wronged his immediate family. The finer detail of the overt story seemed incidental however and the main purport of the Gita, as it was called, appeared to be Hindu philosophy. The battle itself seemed to be a metaphor for life itself, in which every action has its inevitable consequence.

His mind was far too trapped into current events however, for him to give any of this his serious attention and, after several minutes had elapsed, he realized that he was being very stupid. Did he really imagine that Krish, whoever he was, had nothing better to do than continually sift the billions of pieces of infor- mation that were flooding the Internet worldwide every second? In any case, there was nothing special about his own machine other than that the necessary software was already installed and configured. All that he needed to do was download the IRC software from somewhere – it ought not to be too difficult to find

– and install it on this machine.

He stood up and walked through to the kitchen, where the smell of frying, smoked bacon momentarily took his mind completely away from the task. "Nearly ready?" he asked.

"Just another couple of minutes to do some eggs," answered Andrews.

"Look, I don't suppose you have any Internet Chat software on your machine do you?"

"Afraid not."

"You don't mind if I download some? There's someone I need to contact and it's the only mechanism I have, believe it or not," he ended apologetically, realizing how ridiculous this probably sounded.

"Go ahead, as long as you virus check it first and promise me you won't corrupt anything; I have some important research work on there."

Bradley returned to the lounge and sat down in front of the computer. He had been away from the screen for perhaps a minute at the outside. His jaw dropped as he read the message displayed there.

{Krish} Good morning Frank! And Doctor Andrews, unless I am very much mistaken. That was very enterprising of you – I would have missed our little conversations. I hope you are not too tired after recent events?

{RJ} Bradley was temporarily at a complete loss for words. Krishna's abilities (if that was, indeed, his actual name) were simply incredible. To begin with, he must be using a supercomputer rather than a PC. Had he already pre-loaded the relevant software on Andrews' machine, just in case it might be used for this purpose? It seemed exceedingly unlikely. This was a relatively fast processor, probably paid for by the university, he guessed. But even so, the download, installation, configuration and connection would surely take much longer than the time he had been out of the room – and that was assuming that his detection of the search was practically instantaneous.

Why was he doing this, anyway? What could possibly be so important about the discussions that they had been having, to cause Krish to go to such lengths to maintain contact? It didn't make any sense. Still, he had wanted to speak to him and now the link was there, awaiting his input.

{RJ} Good morning! Can I start using your real name incidentally? I hope I haven't disturbed you. Were you not sleeping either?

{Krish} Krish will do very well. No, I was just doing a little research on the Internet. I have some information for you, incidentally. I surmise that this was the reason for your wishing to contact me?

{RJ} Yes. You had agreed to see if you could discover anything suspicious.

{Krish} The word is yours, not mine. Some data relate to definite facts, others provide positive indications and still others can suggest inferences. Most, of course, are irrelevant. By 'suspicious,' I assume you refer to data that might implicate companies or persons, who may be directly or indirectly responsible for polluting the Crow Field Landfill with hazardous material?

The organization 'United Waste Disposal' has been effectively controlling incoming waste since 1997. It seems unlikely that the contamination has been present since before that date, so I have restricted my search to the time since they became responsible. Their main database is located in Ohio and is uploaded on Friday evening of each week. I didn't expect to discover anything untoward there. The email exchanges, between Crow Field and their head office, indicate that recent developments are quite inexplicable to both sides. Their board is expressing serious concern and urging Mr. Struthers and the site managers to find some answers very quickly. They are anxious lest adverse publicity affect several large contracts for which they are bidding at present.

No, if any person or company is to blame, I believe we need to look to at least the next level down. Examination of UWD's data provided a list of all of the registered suppliers of industrial waste. Obviously there exists no electronic data that would enable me to investigate domestic users but then it is clearly unlikely that the source lies in that direction anyway. I can state categorically that nothing that has been legitimately dumped could be to blame, but then you will have presumably assumed this already. Fortunately, the database is comprehensive, both with respect to chemicals involved and to the suppliers, so that it has been possible to make an inventory of all of the source companies and all the definite and potential chemicals that could be present.

None of this has been of any help, however. I had been working on the premise that I would discover a company for which the list of chemicals recorded appeared deficient, considering the nature of work in which they are involved. This meant tapping into the computers of quite a number of organizations and examining their accounts and material movements. Often, information about their suppliers had to be traced as well. As you can imagine the volume of data increases dramatically as this chain is followed. This in itself did not pose a problem but accessing the relevant computers becomes very difficult unless those machines are networked and, at least periodically, connected to the outside world. Fortunately most are. However, it is still possible that some key data is being held on a secure local computer, in which case even I would be unable to track it down.

The next step was to target those companies, the nature of whose business makes them potential sources of hazardous waste. Needless to say, the quantities involved need not be large. In fact, in the worst possible scenario, someone totally unrelated to any of the official sources might have simply wandered past the tip and thrown a test tube over the fence. This would obviously be quite untraceable. There are only two companies in the North of England that produce sufficiently toxic materials. Both, however, also have contracts with another landfill site in Yorkshire that is authorized to handle this. I have examined all of the data to which I could obtain access and there is no reason to suppose that either was to blame. Naturally it is conceivable that substances that should have gone to Yorkshire accidentally contaminated the ordinary waste, destined for Crow Field, but it does not seem likely. The procedures that each has in place would guard against this in all but the most unlikely situation. In any case, it does not seem possible that either could have produced chemicals responsible for the effects that have been observed.

Accordingly, I have now begun a different approach. I am looking, as far as possible, into the personal circumstances of everyone involved, from managers in UWD, down to relatives of employees of the various 'in-feed' companies. I will look at everything I am able to access, from bank accounts (for unexplained deposits) through to personal emails and use of the web. Naturally, this could be considered a gross invasion of privacy but I will not pass any information on to you unless it appears to be directly relevant. Needless to say, I assume that you will keep the details of this investigation to yourself. Do you find this satisfactory?

{RJ} I'm at a loss for words. How are you able to do this? You must work for the intelligence service or some other secret government department at the very least to be able to organize all of this. Do you, too, consider it sufficiently important to devote all of this time?

{Krish} I assure you it is only a passing diversion. I thought I had explained to you that none of this is really real. I am happy to participate in your dream if you find it worthwhile.

But of what value to you, Arjuna, is all this knowledge? I maintain the entire universe with a minute part of myself. X.42

Private Daniels saluted smartly as the official jeep containing the dreaded Brigadier Trowbridge arrived at the barbed wire barrier. The brigadier glared at him with that peculiarly derisive and withering look for which he was noted, his sharp eyes, pin-points of hard blackness in their slightly sunken sockets, scanning the soldier's dress and bearing for the most minute fault. Rare was it indeed that he failed to find some biting comment to fling scathingly at the subject of that fearful, piercing gaze but possibly the novelty of the situation had had the welcome effect of diverting his attention and thoughts to more serious matters. At any rate, with a last up-and-down glance and a sudden expelling of air, as though he had stored it in preparation for an onslaught of reproof and, finding none, had to let it out unused, he briefly returned the salute and signaled the driver to continue through the barricade.

Daniels let out his own sigh when the vehicle had passed; though this was one of relief. He was far more afraid of this man than of any of the other officers, though he had never even spoken to him. The rumors relating to Trowbridge preceded his presence by considerable distance and time. Daniels lowered his rifle to the ground and inserted a finger between his neck and collar, moving it as far as he could in both directions, to relieve the feeling of stickiness and tightness caused by his perspiration in this baking heat. He turned to his immediate superior, Corporal McQueen who, though several years older and more experienced than him, showed similar relief that they had avoided any altercation with the brigadier.

"Do you think we should have asked to see his pass?" asked Daniels.

"You joking? That would have been really asking for it, wouldn't it? Most officers of his type are real sticklers for the rules but he's happy just as long as everyone's afraid of him. He doesn't even mind if you hate him. No, he's not one of your run-of-the-mill bastards, who's only a bastard 'cause it's 'is job to be one; he's a genuine bastard."

Daniels had not really had much opportunity to talk to McQueen before this assignment. Obviously it was attitudes such as this which had held him to his corporal status for so long. He himself might fear his superior officers but, in the majority of cases, he respected them and wished to become one of them himself some day if he were able. Perhaps Trowbridge was the exception. At any rate, Daniels hoped he was not destined to fall foul of him.

He shifted his stance. It was extremely uncomfortable standing in one position for so long. How pleasant it would be to sit down and take off his boots. Even his jacket and shirt, he added to himself as an afterthought. Indeed, why not imagine himself plunging naked into a cool mountain pool; it was just as unattainable. Actually though, surely it wouldn't be unreasonable to sit down for a while... as long as no one saw them. The only trouble was, he didn't know McQueen well enough to know how he would consider such a breach of discipline. If McQueen were to sit down first, it would be all right but, at present, he was almost at attention and had been so since they had arrived on duty over an hour ago. He would have to try to chat him up to create a friendlier atmosphere between them.

Certainly, McQueen himself seemed none too eager to initiate any conversation.

"What do you reckon to all this then, Corp?" he asked genially.

"Right bloody lark, ain't it? Worse than Quatermass and the bleedin' pit. In fact, we got Quatermass 'imself comin' round this afternoon, 'cept he's called Andrews, I think, Doctor Andrews."

Daniels smiled at the response. He had not been born when the original serialization of this play appeared on television but he had watched the old black and white film with his father in his early teens and remembered going to bed terrified.

"Christ!" he exclaimed, as the plot of the story came back to him. You don't really think there's something from outer space down there, do you?"

"Don't be stupid, Daniels. It's bleedin' poison, ain't it? All them factories dumpin' their waste and chemical crap. Bloody pollution. Don't you read the papers?"

"Well, you never know, do you? I mean there might be more to it than that mightn't there?" said Daniels, defensively.

"Oh Gawd!" commented McQueen, raising his eyes expressively to the sky for the benefit of his imagined, rapt audience.

The sound of a car interrupted the conversation and saved Daniels' further embarrassment. The registration plates indicated that this was another army-owned vehicle and, as it drew up to the barrier, they automatically saluted. McQueen reached out to take and examine the proffered pass and then waved them through.

"Those'll be the engineering wallahs," McQueen informed the other knowledgeably. "You know what they're going to try and do, don't you?" he asked.

Daniels shook his head. He had probably heard precisely the same rumors as McQueen and didn't expect to learn anything new. Still, there was no harm in feigning ignorance. Taking the submissive role to McQueen's patronizing one might serve to commend him to the other's favor.

"They're only going to try and dam the whole valley aren't they, and shift the whole bloody tip down into it."

"Trying to unearth that Martian spacecraft then are they Corp?" he risked the jibe.

"Very bloody funny, Daniels. Shut up and let's sit down for a bit."

Inside the Portakabin, newly erected inside the cordon but outside the perimeter fence of the tip, the atmosphere was somewhat more serious. Contrary to the imaginative story so readily voiced by Corporal McQueen, no decisions had been made as to what actions to take regarding the tip. Indeed, few ideas had, as yet, been put forward and the mood of the men gathered together in the confined area of the portable office could be summed up as 'pessimistic' to say the least.

Bradley and Andrews had only been invited by virtue of their prior involvement, though their initiative and effort had not gone unrecognized. Hardwyke and Sanderson represented the council and health authorities, respectively, Mathers having excused himself on the grounds of illness. Inspector Harris was present for the local police force and Struthers represented UWD as still being nominally responsible for the site. Of those remaining, most were army officials: officers in charge of security, engineering and scientific experts, and several who were introduced as 'observers,' whatever that might mean.

One other, present at the request of Doctor Andrews, was professor of psychology at the university; an elderly gentleman by the name of Bull (his presence, however, belying his name and suppressing any temptation to smile upon introduction.) Small in stature and of an indeterminate age between sixty and a hundred, he retained a full head of overly long black hair and bushy eyebrows. Walking with the sprightly gait of a much younger man, he also had the disconcerting habit of looking directly into the eyes of the person he was addressing. This had the effect on the recipient of making him sure that his innermost reactions were being gauged, while his superficial and vocalized responses were being totally ignored. Why he was here, no one seemed quite sure, though presumably Andrews had had some reason for inviting him and the authorities for admitting him.

The initial excitement and eager anticipation, as each voiced his own pet ideas and solutions to his neighbor, had died down as each discovered their lack of originality or received objections to their feasibility. The buzz of voices had now dropped to a few isolated conversations, to the extent that the low hum of the generator outside became audible to those not involved.

Bradley was just refilling his cup from the vacuum jug of coffee on the table at the head of the cabin, when the door opened behind him and the conversation ceased abruptly. He turned in time to see the military personnel rising deferentially to their feet at the entrance of an obvious VIP, who carried the air of someone who is aware of, and relishes the fact of, his importance. Bradley, never one to stand on ceremony in the presence of superiors, added sugar to his coffee and proceeded to stir it, somewhat noisily as it turned out. No disrespect was intended and he considered his action relatively innocent but, upon looking up again, he discovered himself the object of the most ferocious glare from the new arrival. He half expected to be commanded to stand to attention, despite his obvious civilian status, but the searing look completed its assessment, concluded him as being beneath contempt, and released him from its hold.

"Good morning, brigadier," ventured one of the senior officers, boldly.

"I hadn't noticed," replied the other loudly and with an unpleasantness and vehemence totally uncalled for. The nasal whine of his cultured accent grated on Bradley's sensitivity (he was still attempting to suppress the flush of embarrassment and resentment from his having been judged and apparently found guilty.)

The door opened again revealing three younger officers, who saluted upon seeing the senior man standing there looking so angrily at them.

"Are you the last ones?" he asked them, as though they could have had the slightest idea as to the answer, having just arrived and not even entered the cabin.

The one nearest the door looked guiltily at his watch. "Well, sir, I guess we are a little late; I expect everyone else must be here already."

"Come in then. Don't just stand there looking like idiots." He pushed his way through to the desk and seated himself authoritatively behind it as the newcomers found themselves seats at the rear. He banged his baton loudly on the desktop and called for silence, although Bradley hadn't been aware of anyone's speaking.

"Thank you," he said, unable to exclude the suggestion of sarcasm from his tone as he glanced contemptuously around. "Now, perhaps we may begin, major. Would you like to review the situation for these gentlemen?"

One of the officers nearby stood and cleared his throat, drawing the attention towards himself. "I think we're all reasonably well acquainted with the circumstantial aspects by now. What we hope to achieve by this initial meeting is a rationalization; a setting down of the facts of the matter as opposed to speculation. We require suggestions for plans of action and priorities. But, first of all, I'd like us to establish precisely what the problems are, not explanations for what's happened mind you – that may come later, it may not – but we must clarify the problems before we can find solutions. Now I understand it was Mr. Bradley here who first notified the authorities of the likely inter-connected nature of the various incidents, having been involved to varying degrees with most of them. So, perhaps I could call upon him to go over the details again before we commence."

He looked expectantly over towards Bradley, who, not having anticipated being asked to address anyone, was modestly surprised at the request. Nevertheless, Bradley quickly obliged by standing and, as accurately as he was able, presented a résumé of the events of the previous weeks, from the unpleasant smells at the tip up to the rescue workers' falling ill a few days ago. He resolutely adhered to the facts and succeeded, to his own satisfaction, in not tainting them in any way with his own theories. He pointed out, literally, that Doctor Andrews must be consulted for the scientific aspects and for the results of the various analyses which had been attempted on the substance itself.

As he sat back down, conversation began again immediately at various points of the room but a sharp rap from the brigadier called the meeting back to order. Andrews was asked to speak next and, following Bradley's style, he attempted to outline the findings, in layman's terms, in as unambiguous and unbiased a way as he could and made no mention of his hypothesis of an extraterrestrial origin for the material.

"Thank you, Doctor," said the major, when Andrews had finished. "Are there any definite explanations for these results?" he asked, emphasizing the word 'definite.'

"No."

This time, there was silence as Andrews re-seated himself but two hands were raised for questions. Allen obviously saw them but appeared reluctant, for a moment, to acknowledge them. He leaned over to one side and rustled through a sheaf of papers, presumably hoping that, when he raised his eyes again, the hands would have been lowered. They hadn't.

"Yes?" he inquired his voice a mixture of impatience and trepidation.

The man in whose direction the major was looking half stood, awkwardly. "Could we not ask the doctor to elucidate on his last answer?" he asked, his voice, too, slightly embarrassed.

Major Allen was obviously somewhat uncomfortable and looked across half imploringly to the brigadier.

"As was said at the beginning, we wish to establish the known facts first of all. We're not indulging in supposition or speculation," answered Trowbridge, banging his baton again, quite unnecessarily, on the table.

The major cleared his throat again and nodded briefly in appreciation of the brigadier's authority. "Now that we have reviewed the situation, I'd like to outline the principal considerations as I see them. Firstly, we must prevent any possibility of this contamination – call it what you like – spreading. The area must remain isolated.

"Secondly, we must attempt to find the source of the pollutant and neutralize or destroy it, as appropriate.

"Finally, we will try to render the area reasonably safe and, if possible, fit for habitation again, though the last seems unlikely in the foreseeable future.

"We thought it would provide a useful introduction to the problems we face if Mr. Struthers here gave us a brief description of the methods traditionally used for decontamination of hazardous waste sites and an indication of why they are unsuitable for use in this case. Over to you, Mr. Struthers." Major Allen waited for the other to come to the front of the group and then sat down.

"OK, I'll be as brief as I can and not go into any of the technical details since those won't concern us here. There are five main categories for cleaning up toxic waste from sites, what we call 'remediation.'

"First of all, the most obvious thing to do is excavate; dig out all of the contaminated material and dispose of it elsewhere. This involves finding out exactly where it is, how to remove it, where to move it to and what to do when you get it there. A whole host of problems here, of course. We haven't yet mapped the site. We believe it to be extremely hazardous and don't know how to handle it. Worse still, we don't know how to neutralize it.

"Next, there's what's called capping. This means we leave all of the material where it is, without attempting to sort out the good from the bad, and cover it with something to keep it there. We normally use clay or concrete. What we're trying to do in essence is stop it spreading. A particular problem in this case is the apparent reactivity. We don't have a suitable candidate for the cap material.

"A combination of these two is used in what's called 'entombment.' Here, we make what's effectively a 'tomb' to contain the material for all time. This involves lining a suitable hole with one or more of clay, concrete and selected artificial materials, with sufficient thickness to ensure nothing can ever get through. You put all of the hazardous material into it and then cap it. As before, this wouldn't work if the waste were able to corrode whatever lining was used.

"Incineration might have been an obvious choice. Unfortunately, the tests so far carried out suggest that even very high temperatures don't destroy it. So that looks a non-starter.

"If the contaminant itself were leached from the surrounding soil by rainwater, we could use a process called air stripping to isolate it. This is sometimes used for VOC's – sorry, that's volatile organic compounds. Anyway, I won't go into the details since all indications are that the material doesn't separate out, instead remaining in the soil, at least for most of the time – I gather from Doctor Andrews that it seems almost to have a mind of its own!

"The final method also relates principally to situations where the groundwater is contaminated, usually by heavy metals. It's called 'precipitation' and, as you'll gather, involves causing the contaminant to precipitate out from the water, so that it can be filtered off. Again, not appropriate to our situation, I'm afraid.

"So, as you see, the methods that we normally use don't seem particularly relevant here, I'm afraid, which is why we've come here to try to brainstorm a novel solution."

Struthers returned to his chair, not altogether his usual ebullient self, clearly feeling almost a personal failure because he was unable to suggest any way forward. Major Allen stood as soon as Struthers had finished and was already speaking before the latter had had time to sit down.

"Now, Lieutenant Sinclair here, has been looking at the problem with a group of our young engineering graduates. Perhaps I could ask him first if they came up with any suggestions?"

"I'm afraid we didn't have any brilliant ideas, sir," spoke up a young man at the rear of the seated group. "Although we haven't previously looked at this sort of problem, we reached pretty much the same conclusions as Mr. Struthers. Straight excavation would pose a fairly massive problem. I reckon we'd have to clear the area to a depth of about fifty feet to be sure of removing the dangerous material. Supposing the tip to be about half a square mile in area, this would involve shifting about twenty-five million cubic yards of earth and it would all have to be handled as if it were lethal. That would mean protective clothing, decontamination areas, stringent precautions at all times."

"And where the hell would we move it to?" interposed the brigadier, scathingly. "Can't you come up with anything better than that?"

"Well, the only other reasonable alternative we've thought of so far, and actually it doesn't sound very reasonable either I'm afraid," he added despondently, "is to surround it with concrete, isolating it, like Mr. Struthers said." He addressed his answer to the brigadier, somewhat in the manner of a small boy seeking the least sign of praise from a strict and uncompromising father.

"We could dig a trench around the danger zone, about fifty feet deep and ten feet wide, and fill it with concrete." He was beginning to sound totally unconvinced of the ideas by now, even desperate, to the extent that he almost seemed to wish to point out the futility of them himself. "Unfortunately, this would require about," he glanced down at a paper, "about six and half million cubic feet of concrete. And we still couldn't be sure that there would be no leakage through the bottom, he finished, hopelessly.

"Or that the material wouldn't eat its way through the concrete," muttered Andrews, but fortunately the brigadier appeared not to hear him.

The major's previous optimism appeared to have been somewhat quenched by the lieutenant's cold facts and the overall effect was numbing rather than refreshing. At this point, however, Andrews raised his hand and, receiving no acknowledgement, the major being intent upon looking down at the floor, announced, "Perhaps it would be a good idea to introduce Professor Bull at this juncture, do you think?"

"Oh, yes, by all means," responded Major Allen. Brigadier Trowbridge frowned his disapproval, though he said nothing. He had naturally been informed prior to the meeting that this gentleman was to be asked to conduct part of it but had strongly disagreed with what he considered a civilian intrusion.

The professor rose and stepped carefully over the outstretched legs and between the closely packed chairs into the relatively clear space at the front end of the Portakabin, where the brigadier sat stiffly behind his desk. The major, who had been standing there, moved to one side, pulled up one of the two spare chairs, and sat down. The professor endured Trowbridge's look for a moment, presumably hoping vainly for some sign of permission to begin. Then, visibly shrugging his shoulders and obviously quite unafraid of this eminently unlikeable character, he turned to address the audience.

"What I would like for us to do is to have a 'brainstorming' session. I'm sure most of you will have already taken part in one of these at some time but, in case anyone has not, I'll just review the salient points to begin with. The ideas immediately suggested are not, in themselves intended to be workable solutions.

Subsequent analysis of them may, however, lead to other ideas that are.

"Now, this is what de Bono called a 'lateral' approach to problem solving and, as such I would like you to completely suspend logical thinking, which is the so-called 'vertical' method. The nature of the problem has been explained and I want you all to think of silly solutions. Don't worry how ridiculous they are. I want you to be totally non-serious for a few minutes and throw out as many suggestions as possible and treat it all as a game if you can. Try to forget it's about a real problem.

"I'll endeavor to summarize them on this whiteboard as we go and later we'll see if we can't extract something sensible from them. Could we spread the chairs out first, please? Get rid of these formal rows and make it more like a semicircle. I want everyone to join in; don't be put off by the brigadier here!" He looked across to this personage with a vaguely questioning look as if daring him to object to this taunt, joking though it might (at least superficially) seem to be. The latter appeared to redden slightly and visibly pursed his lips as if to prevent an explosion but he said nothing.

"Now, as many ideas as possible please. Initially we want quantity rather than quality. Would someone like to begin?"

There was a silence, which began to show signs of becoming prolonged. The soldiers appeared to be unused to such procedures, a situation that Bradley found surprising. Or perhaps, on second thoughts, they were merely intimidated by the brigadier. Eventually, the young engineer raised his hand.

"Don't put your hand up, man. Speak out," commanded Bull, encouragingly.

"Could we find some chemical to neutralize it where it is – just pour it over?"

"Yes, I dare say we could, but this is a vertical solution. Try not to be serious! Can someone start us off with an original, silly suggestion?"

"How about putting the whole lot into a rocket and sending it to the moon?" suggested Bradley, realizing what was required.

"Good," said Bull, writing on the board.

"Or wrap it in a big plastic bag and put it in the deep freeze," said Hardwyke anxious to get the others going.

"Send it to the North Pole?" suggested the major, beginning to enter into the spirit of things.

"Perhaps we should evacuate the earth's population in a rocket, instead of the tip," put in Struthers from the front row.

By now, the initial tension had gone and grins were breaking out across the room as others waited eagerly to express their ideas. Professor Bull was writing furiously.

"Set fire to it," suggested the young engineer, now more confident.

"Dig a hole and let it fall in. Better still, dig a hole from the opposite side of the earth until the tip collapses into it. Then fill it in, trapping it at the center of the earth." This was Sanderson's enthusiastic contribution.

"Dissolve it; freeze the solution and tow it to the North Pole as an iceberg."

"Could I direct your suggestions towards another approach?" asked Bull, when the initial rush of ideas had died down. "We can reckon that, of the – what was it? – twenty-five million cubic yards of earth, only a small proportion of it is actually contaminated, say, maybe one million, probably much less. Could we have some ideas as to how to find and separate the bad parts? We'd then have much less of a problem, relatively speaking, in disposing of it.

"Paint the contaminated areas red, to make them stand out?" asked Bradley.

"Very good!" encouraged Bull, writing again.

"Stage a play," thundered the brigadier from behind the professor, who turned to look with some surprise at Trowbridge, whom he had considered unwilling to indulge in this frivolous pursuit.

"Stage a play," Trowbridge repeated, "and fill the entire area with an audience of people, each having his own area of a few square yards." He paused and seeing everyone attentively waiting for further explanation, finished with a gruff laugh. "Well, when everyone's finished dropping dead, you'll be able to draw up a map of the contaminated sections."

"Excellent, brigadier. Thank you," acknowledged the professor, not a trace of disgust in his voice at this bizarre suggestion. Bradley suspected that the man had been being sarcastic, still disagreeing with the technique, but had to concede that the idea had potential.

"Breed animals to eat it," shouted a new voice from the audience.

"Build a computerized sorting system, like the ones they have for picking out bad potatoes."

Soon, however, the spring of original ideas dried up and, apart from a final fling from Doctor Andrews, who had been deep in thought for the last few minutes, no further suggestions were forthcoming.

"This stuff," he said thoughtfully, "has a remarkable proclivity for attacking other substances, virtually anything. Perhaps we could persuade it to attack and destroy itself."

Professor Bull nodded appreciatively, jotted the idea down and then stood once again. "Right. Thank you very much. I suggest we break for coffee now. Have a look through these during the break, while I group them into categories and we'll continue in about ten minutes."

{Krish} For all practical purposes, the world is obviously real. But then, when we are dreaming, we firmly believe that the dream world is real. From the absolute perspective neither is truly real, but perhaps the least arguable adjective we could apply would be to say that these worlds are 'relatively' real. The dream world is real relative to the dreamer and the waking world is real relative to the waker.

You probably have no problem with agreeing that our dreams are not real. All the objects in a dream are, as it were, 'located' in the mind. This might include entire cities and even worlds beyond the earth; they clearly cannot be real since there is insufficient space in the body to contain them!

And we may dream of events which, in the dream, last for days or even years, only to wake up and find that mere minutes have passed. We may travel to distant countries (which travel may take many hours or days) but awake to find ourselves still on the same bed; we never awake to find ourselves at the place to which we travelled in the dream. Clearly the time units of the dream do not correspond with waking time, which we believe to be the 'real' time, and distance units of dream do not correspond with those of waking.

We might meet a friend in the dream and discuss some topic or other. But if, after waking, we contact this person and ask them about the meeting, they will have no recollection of it. (The friend may even have been dead for many years!) And if we were given something in the dream, we find that we no longer have it on waking.

But you will also agree that we have a body in the dream, which may eat, drink and perform many other activities. Clearly this is not the same body as the one which is lying asleep on the bed; on waking, we realize that the dream body was unreal. Indeed, we acknowledge that everything that we perceived in the dream was equally unreal.

But, in an entirely analogous manner, those things perceived by the mind in the waking state are also unreal. This waking body and world disappear again when we go back to sleep. The waking body is supplanted by a dream body again.

Only Consciousness is absolutely real. It cannot be an object of experience because we are That. Therefore, anything that we do experience cannot be Consciousness; cannot be absolutely real. Consequently, we can regard both waking and dream states equally as *mithyA*.

{RJ} But waking and dreams are not quite the same are they? Everyone else experiences the same waking world, so that must be real. No one else experiences my dream, so that isn't real.

{Krish} Everyone in your dream world experiences the same world, also, and calls it a waking world. It is only when you wake up that your waking mind calls it a dream world.

{RJ} Things in the dream are hardly very useful, though, are they? I need a new drill, for example, to put up a shelf. I might come across one in a dream and buy it or take it, but it is of no use to me at all when I wake up.

{Krish} True, but supposing you do buy one, it would be of no help to you for putting up a shelf in your dream! Things have utility only in their own relative world.

{RJ} Surely the dream world is only subjective, while the waking world has objective reality. It is experienced as external to ourselves, whereas the dream takes place in our mind.

{Krish} I'm afraid that this notion suffers from the same confusion as before. We only recognize that the dream world is 'in our mind' when we are awake; at the time of the dream, it is just as much 'external' as is the waking world when we are awake. We might as well say that the waking world is really non-existent since it disappears when we are in the dream or deep sleep state. At the time of the dream, I experience external objects and events in just the same manner. Their illogicality or even impossibility only becomes apparent on awakening.

From a 'detached' point of view, both waking and dream are similar experiences. Within the dream, there are 'others' who validate my dream experience. I have conversations with them and I assume (as a dreamer) that they see the same external (dream) world as I do. It is only from the vantage point of having woken up that I am able to see that this world was internally generated and (no longer) has any objective existence.

Of course, I feel that I am unable to take a position from outside of this waking world to look at the situation in a similar fashion. And so I call the waking world 'real' and the dream world 'false.' But in fact I do take such a stand every time I go to sleep. In the dream, the waking world is negated and in deep-sleep, both waking and dream are negated.

If we imagine a dream A, in which we go to sleep and have a dream B, when we 'wake up' (from dream B into the dream A), we will say that the dreamt dream was 'only a dream in the mind,' and that we are now (in dream A) in the real world. Of course, when we 'really' wake up into the waking world, we realize that both A and B were dreams and think that we are now in reality. Except that we are now effectively in dream C!

So long as we continue to believe in the objective reality of a separate world, we have not really woken up! The bottom line is that the experience of an external world does not mean that the world is real. Of course, we assume that it does, but an assumption is no proof at all.

{RJ} There's a fallacy here somewhere! If objects of both waking and dream worlds are unreal, that must include the people who inhabit them also, including the waker and the dreamer! If this is the case, it is denying the reality of the knower as well as the known. But this makes no sense as there has to be someone who is doing the denying! So who is it who sees or imagines these two worlds?

{Krish} Good! I'm pleased to see you are alert and critical! But I didn't say that this world is 'unreal.' The word we should use to describe it is *mithyA*, as I explained before. The objects of the world are not unreal. Try walking in front of an oncoming car to demonstrate this! The objects (of both states) have reality relative to that state. What they do not have is absolute reality. Their reality depends upon I, the observer. That is I, the ultimate observer – Consciousness – not I, the separate person, which is equally *mithyA*. I, the waking person, cannot have absolute reality because I disappear, to be replaced by the dreamer or sleeper, when I go to sleep. I, the ego, also has only relative reality...

Fresh coffee was brought in from the adjacent Portakabin, which served as both canteen and general stores on the encampment, and the participants busied themselves with obtaining refreshments. Professor Bull had asked them to refrain from discussing any aspects of the business amongst themselves lest a chance comment, which might spark off a useful idea from someone else, failed to do so because that other person was outside hearing range or involved in a conversation of his own. Accordingly, there was little talk of any description. It was difficult for any of them to concentrate on any other topic and attempts to start up conversations on unrelated subjects soon died owing to lack of enthusiasm.

It was with some impatience, then, that they all watched as the psychologist summarized the suggestions on the whiteboard. Even the brigadier had begun to take an active interest since he had made his contribution, and he now left his seat and moved out amongst the others so he could watch as the ideas were marked up.

Bull was rewriting the various suggestions under four categories, erasing each of the original scribbled comments as he carefully wrote it out anew under the appropriate heading. Eventually, he replaced the marker pen in the aluminum shelf beneath the board and crossed to the table to pour a cup of coffee. Everyone took this as a sign to return to his seat and prepare for the second half of the session.

The assortment of ideas had been listed as follows:

Category 1 – Sorting out the contaminated material (if necessary)

a) Paint it red (stand out)
b) Stage a play (map from people who die)
c) Computerized sorting (c.f. potatoes)
d) Plant flowers/vegetables (contaminated where don't grow)
e) Find chemical which changes color

Category 2 – Getting rid of it unchanged

a) Send it to moon or N. Pole
b) Bury it (centre of earth) / cause earthquake to swallow it up
c) Dissolve and freeze it
d) Teleport to another dimension
e) Declare American territory (and let them sort it out)
f) Create black hole in middle of it
g) Tell whoever put it there to take it away again

Category 3 – Destroying it altogether

a) Set fire to it
b) Build a reactor on site and let it go critical/use for nuclear testing
c) Breed animals to eat it
d) Make it destroy itself

Category 4 – Others

a) Evacuate earth's population to moon
b) Pretend it's not there

c) Set up factory to harness ability for synthesizing chemicals

d) Study to find out how it works – scientific research

e) Population overflow area/penal settlement

Sensing the impatience, Professor Bull quickly drained his cup and returned to his seat. "Right then; let's continue. We'll take each point in turn to begin with, and see if we can derive anything useful. You should revert to using vertical thinking now, of course. The more analytical judgment you can bring to bear on the feasibility of solutions, the better. As I understand it, the main factors you should bear in mind in your critical analysis are that, while *cost* is not an issue, *time* is. Right major?"

"Up to a point, yes. Solutions like evacuating the entire population to the moon might over-stretch our budget, though," responded the major.

"If any other 'silly' ideas should be triggered, however, feel free to mention them at the appropriate time," concluded Bull.

"OK! Anything suggested by 1 a)?" He stood up again and, choosing a different color marker pen held it in readiness.

"Is it already painted red?" asked Lieutenant Tarrant, a young physics post-graduate. "I mean is it radioactive or anything?"

"We know that the proportions of isotopes present in some of the elements are abnormal," volunteered Andrews, "but, unfortunately, that's not such an easy thing to detect, is it?"

"Any unusual elements or compounds present, which could be detected chemically rather than physically?" inquired Doctor Sanderson.

"Well, yes, the whole thing's one hell of an unusual compound; reacts with virtually everything, as I said earlier, but I don't know that there's any one unique test which we could be sure that no other of the possible chemicals present out there wouldn't also satisfy. And then again, we'd probably need to be able to automate it, using a computerized technique as someone has already suggested. How many samples would we need anyway, and how would we take them? Anyone got a calculator?"

Andrews borrowed a proffered calculator and rapidly punched out some figures. "Even sampling only ten by ten foot squares, which would be very risky to say the least, we'd need nearly one hundred and forty thousand samples and at what depth do we take our material, whereabouts within the squares? No, I'm not at all optimistic about this line of approach."

"We could take core samples, as they do in geological surveys," suggested Tarrant, "down to a depth of about fifty feet easily. Then we could have them analyzed for these odd isotopes, using neutron activation, for example."

"Hmm. Slight problem transporting one hundred thousand, fifty-foot long tubes to the nearest reactor and processing them," commented Struthers.

"No material to be removed from the site, I'm afraid. That's definite," interposed Major Allen. "And I don't think that building a reactor on site is very practicable, so you can cross off 2 b)."

"Hold on major; we haven't got there yet," objected Bull, still busily adding notes to his board.

"That is a very important factor, though," insisted Andrews. "If we're compelled to keep all material within the cordon, then any method of analysis we propose will have to be fairly simple. Anything requiring the facilities of a fully equipped analytical laboratory, let alone a nuclear reactor, must be ruled out immediately."

"No," interrupted Allen. "I think we could provide most facilities immediately adjacent to the site, if necessary, even if we had to extend the boundaries to enclose it. Something like that would take time though."

"Hold on!" called out Bull. "Before we get too bogged-down on this one point, let's move on. We're still on essentially the same topic but perhaps some of these other ideas may help us to clear our thinking. Now, what about the brigadier's idea about having a play?"

"Perhaps mice or rats in pens might be a slightly more acceptable solution," suggested Sanderson. "I rather think the Health Authorities would clamp down on the original idea."

"Doesn't that still present similar problems, though, as far as thoroughness of sampling is concerned?" asked Bradley. "I mean, you'd only be testing the surface for contamination, wouldn't you. Presumably the surface might appear to be clear in some places, where rain has washed away any chemicals or deposited silt on top of them, for example, while the sub-layers still contain all of the contamination."

"Yes, I suppose most sampling techniques are going to run into this problem," conceded Sanderson, with a sigh.

"Next point?" asked Bull, sensing that the atmosphere would turn pessimistic if he didn't push on to avert it.

"We've got to find a method of sorting before we can start thinking about how to computerize it, haven't we," commented Major Allen, quickly dispensing with that next point.

"Very sensible. Next?"

Andrews had been punching away on his borrowed calculator again for the last few moments. Before anyone else could answer, he pointed out that, even supposing a technique could be found, which could be carried out by an untrained man in ten minutes, it would still take twenty men, working three eight-hour shifts, nearly seven weeks to complete the tests. During this time, the concentrations might have shifted again.

"Or a hundred and forty men one week or even... 980 men 24 hours. What do you think the army was brought in for?" asked Trowbridge with a snort.

Professor Bull, too, was glaring at his friend with some apparent annoyance, as if convinced Andrews were trying to prove the enterprise impossible. "Yes, let's not concern ourselves too much with the practical difficulties at this stage," he said encouragingly. "Has anyone any ideas about planting flowers?"

"Hey, wait a minute," said Bradley. "What about the plants which are there already? They have roots, which will be taking in chemical nourishment from a wide area. Not down to fifty feet, I suppose, but they'll be doing much more than just sampling the topsoil. Could it be that there's already been some visible change in them, where they're growing on contaminated ground? Perhaps a trained botanist could spot the bad areas at a glance."

"Excellent," congratulated the professor and there was a hum of excited murmuring from the rest of the group. Even the brigadier looked at him with a new expression which, for him, might have been approaching as near as it was possible for him to come to respect.

"Right. Well, I don't think we'll bother considering the chemical indicator now. It could easily be the case that nothing will come of this suggestion but let's press on to the next category while we're all feeling optimistic."

"I must point out again, before we continue, that we will not allow material to be removed from the site," insisted Major Allen. "I think we should pass over category two for the time being and start thinking of ways of destroying it where it is."

"Very well," conceded Bull. "I don't really think many practical ideas would have arisen out of black holes and fourth dimensions anyway," he added, with a laugh.

A hand was raised on the front row before they could continue and one of the officers who hadn't previously taken part rose uncertainly to his feet, drawing everyone's attention.

"Sorry, sir," he said, looking at the major, "but shouldn't we consider point 2 g)? I mean, if we could find out who was responsible for putting it there, mightn't they have a better idea of how to get rid of it? Presumably they must, at least, know what it is."

"Doctor Andrews, would you like to answer that one," asked Allen, in a weary tone of voice. It was time they had this one out, he decided.

Choosing his words carefully, Andrews explained how the chemistry of the material was not understood at all. The best scientists in the country had been quite bewildered by the mechanism of its reactivity. He pointed out how the additional peculiarity of its isotope distribution suggested that it could not have been formed naturally.

"Someone did put it there then and it must have been made artificially. Are you suggesting chemical warfare?"

Major Allen rose to his feet and Trowbridge banged his baton repeatedly on the table as everyone tried to speak at once. Allen didn't know whether to feel relieved or dismayed that this was out in the open at last.

"There's no evidence to support that conclusion," he said emphatically. "However", he continued less confidently, "since we've been unable to find any apparent use for this material and since it is just lying around like this, without our having any notion of how it got there... well, the possibility mustn't be ruled out.

"This must not go outside this room," he shouted above the noise that had again arisen. "You civilians," he added, when the conversations had died sufficiently for him to make himself heard without raising his voice, pointing at Bradley, Andrews and the others, "will have to sign the Official Secrets Act before you leave. Everything you've heard or will hear in this room must be considered top secret. Do you understand?"

Having been duly sobered by this authoritative statement, the group remained silent for some time, until Bull ventured to suggest that they continue.

"Er, could I say something please?" asked Hardwyke at this point. "Professor Bull did say that silly ideas were still permissible and there's something which has been worrying me."

Hardwyke went on to explain how she had visited the library to investigate the tip's history and how the old gentleman there had told her about the stories that had been passed down from the Middle Ages. Before she could finish, though, there was another loud snort from the brigadier. "Rubbish, Madam," he expostulated. "Where on earth is all this talk about Martians going to lead us?"

"If you'll pardon me, sir "interjected Andrews, "I'm not at all sure it's so stupid. As a matter of fact, I'd reached the same conclusion myself, though I was afraid to admit it before now. After all, if our best scientists can't understand it, why should we presume that anyone else's scientists should be able to make it?"

"That's a very interesting point, Doctor," conceded Major Allen. "Perhaps we mustn't disregard the theory after all."

"Rubbish, I say. Why, if this fellow reckons the spacecraft landed in the Middle Ages, should this pollution only appear today?"

"Perhaps it's started leaking, sir. Corroded through the fuel tank or something," suggested Lieutenant Sinclair, finding the romantic theory more attractive than the sober and more realistic one.

"Hold on a minute," said Struthers. "One of your writers – Hoyle wasn't it? – theorized that viruses such as influenza were carried here by meteorites? It's one of the few ideas that explained how epidemics could break out in several parts of the world simultaneously. Before rapid worldwide travel was commonplace," he added as the brigadier shuffled noisily in his chair, almost exuding skepticism.

"Well," he continued, "isn't it possible that this chemical or organism, whatever it is, could have arrived in a meteor storm and been buried underground all this time, until disturbed by recent excavations for landfill? There's no reason to start talking about intelligent aliens in flying saucers after all, is there?"

"That's an extremely good idea, Mr. Struthers," responded Andrews. "I'd been trying to see how I could rationalize the idea of an extraterrestrial source without bringing in UFOs. It does seem to be the only reasonable conclusion, far more plausible than biological warfare."

"If I may interrupt, this conversation isn't helping us to solve the problem, is it?" asked Bull, rhetorically. "Major Allen, you said at the beginning that our concern was to find out how to contain it, eradicate it or destroy it, depending on its nature. How it came to be there was not one of your principal considerations."

Allen nodded reluctantly in agreement.

"Very well then, shall we proceed to examine category three?"

This entire universe is pervaded by me in my unmanifest form. All beings exist in me; I do not exist in them. IX.4

{RJ} Right, I'm finally convinced that this is worth pursuing. What exactly do I have to do to become 'enlightened'?

{Krish} Excellent! I'm pleased and relieved that you are finding the material worthwhile.

Unfortunately, the way you have phrased your question is part of the problem and it is a paradoxical one. It is the person that wants enlightenment and yet, as we saw earlier, the 'person' is a misconception. Who we 'really are' is already free and therefore does not need to be liberated. It is the self-ignorance in the mind that obscures the knowledge of this fact. Accordingly, what you call 'enlightenment' is actually an effective event in the mind, namely the dawning of self-knowledge. Subsequently, it is known that there never was a 'person' to be liberated.

{RJ} Having been encouraging me to start learning, and presumably embark upon some sort of 'path,' you seem to be painting a pretty bleak picture. What should we actually do, then?

{Krish} The scriptures specify a threefold discipline of *shravaNa*, *manana* and *nididhyAsana*. Since you know practically nothing about the true nature of the Self at present, you must first be informed. This requires *shravaNa*, listening to a spiritual teacher. What we are doing here is a good start and you can do further reading on your own but, as I said earlier, it is far more beneficial to learn in the physical presence of someone who knows the truth. Secondly, you must spend time clarifying any doubts – this is *manana*. Merely hearing is not usually sufficient to bring understanding. Finally, having understood intellectually, you then need to completely absorb what has been said until it is all obvious. This might be further reading, writing, discussing or just thinking about what you have now learned; this is called *nididhyAsana*.

Prior to any of this, the mind usually needs some degree of preparation. This is partly so that it is receptive to these ideas and able to apply reason and discrimination optimally and partly so that, once everything is understood, you may enjoy the 'fruits of enlightenment' – tranquility, equanimity, fearlessness etc.

Ideally (and possible essentially) we should put ourselves under the discipline of a teacher or school. Without the unquestioning submission to a teacher in whom we have trust, it is going to be very difficult to get rid of the ego, which wants to question and authorize *everything*.

It is said that pursuing a path such as this is like taking poison in the beginning but that, on attainment of Self-realization, it is like nectar. Conversely, though the everyday pleasures of life may seem like nectar in the beginning, in the end they become like poison.

{RJ} I know you have pointed out how many aspects of these ideas seem paradoxical, that there is actually no 'person' to become enlightened to begin with, so that the idea of 'doing something' to achieve this is a misconception of the ego. But, having acknowledged this, you are nevertheless advocating certain things for me to do. What is the point, given what you have already said? And what is the purpose of a system, religion or whatever, if everyone is already one God anyway? I haven't put this very well but I think you know what I mean.

{Krish} On the contrary, that is very well expressed. The problem is, as I have mentioned several times now, one of ignorance. Once this is removed, we see the truth that was always present and all paths, all religions become meaningless. Let me give you some more metaphors to add to the collection!

You must have experienced an occasional nightmare. Imagine one in which you are enjoying a relaxed walk in a forest when, suddenly a lion comes out of the trees onto the path in front of you. It turns, sees you, bounds towards you with a roar and pounces. It is quite likely that you would wake up, yes?

{RJ} Very likely, yes!

{Krish} Now after you have awoken, how do you feel regarding the lion?

{RJ} How do you mean? I expect my heart would be beating quite fast and I would be somewhat annoyed at having had the nightmare.

{Krish} But what specifically about the lion?

{RJ} Well, nothing really. There never was a lion.

{Krish} Quite. But even though it didn't actually exist, it nevertheless woke you up did it not? It took you out of the dreaming state and into the waking state. Teaching such as this also functions as a 'dream lion' but now it can help to bring you to a realization of *turIya*, the reality underlying all apparent states of consciousness. When you wake up from a dream, you realize that the entire world of the dream was a construct of your mind. When you become enlightened, you realize that the entire waking world is a construct of Consciousness, including the person that you took yourself to be.

Despite his age and frailty, Doctor Minton objected vigorously and resisted strongly all attempts to persuade him to don the protective clothing. Only after the brigadier had been called in did he eventually concede to the superior belligerence of the younger man. Amidst continued mutterings and grumbling, he was helped into the suit, many sizes too large for his small frame, and, when asked if comfortable, returned a glare worthy of Trowbridge himself.

"What's this damn thing supposed to be for, anyway?" he asked ferociously. "I'm not going into a fire am I?"

"It's an NBC suit, Doctor," answered Major Allen, respectfully, "intended for use during nuclear, biological or chemical warfare. Although we don't really know the nature of the hazard out there, it should provide a good measure of protection. Please don't spend an unnecessary amount of time over the task, though, and remember to go straight to the decontamination area when you get back." He pointed again for emphasis to the place just inside the perimeter fence, where a red canvas structure had been raised on top of a small hillock. Fire tenders and other army vehicles stood nearby, outside the fence, and high-pressure hoses snaked their way through the grass. The idea was simply that anyone venturing into the site should, before returning, be thoroughly hosed down, the possibly contaminated water being flushed away, down the far side of the hill, back on to the tip. The suit, once used, would also remain on the inside.

"Now, if you don't mind, sir, would you put this helmet on, please?"

Minton opened his mouth, as if to object further but, with only a brief snort of resignation, snatched the headgear unceremoniously from the soldier and placed it over his head. Allen helped him secure the clips and switched on the built-in microphone.

"Can you hear me?" he asked, speaking into the small handheld transmitter.

"Yes, I can hear you but I can't see too damned well; this visor must be about two inches thick." The voice emanated from the speaker of the receiver cabinet, standing in the doorway to the Portakabin, and had lost little of its abrasive edge by being converted to electromagnetic waves and back again. Brigadier Trowbridge smiled at the acid tones as if he recognized a kindred spirit in its speaker.

"Well I apologize for that, Doctor," said Trowbridge, with only the slightest trace of sarcasm, "but it is intended to keep out moderate degrees of radiation you know. I think you'll find the visibility is optimum for the conditions under which it's built to operate."

"Have you brought any instruments or anything that you want to take with you?" queried Allen.

"I can't very well use a microscope with this lot on now can I, young man? If I want to examine anything I'll have to bring it back here."

Allen retreated into the cabin and returned with a flat wicker basket of the type recommended for collecting fungi. He pointed out a roll of plastic bags and wire ties, asking Minton to be sure to seal any samples he might take lest the soil be contaminated. The basket also contained pad and pencil, trowel, small spade and fork, secateurs, soil testing paper and magnifying glass.

"I think you should have most things you might need here."

"Hmm," answered Minton without committing himself as he accepted the basket but he was apparently a little surprised at the thoroughness and foresight. "Can I get on with it then?"

The incongruous, grey-suited figure turned and lumbered awkwardly off towards the tip entrance, looking like some futuristic beast out of a pantomime, with the dainty wicker basket perhaps stolen from Little Red Riding Hood and containing a spray of flowers. He left to the accompaniment of low-voiced curses and snorts from the radio, the doctor already being apparently oblivious of the fact that all of his vocalizations were being monitored.

Some minutes later, Sanderson arrived and Allen explained briefly what was happening. Sanderson, in his turn, imparted the disturbing news that one of the tip workers had just died.

"Oh, God, no! Well I hope this botanist bloke comes up with something pretty quick, then. As soon as that leaks out, we'll have the place swarming with reporters and relatives, demanding to know what the hell's going on, and quite rightly too. At the moment we can't tell them a damn thing."

"I assume this item has not been released to the press?" inquired Trowbridge, slightly threateningly.

"No, of course not, but I don't know how long we can reasonably be expected to keep it secret. No doctor would agree to lie about something like that to a relative." The implication was obvious and the Brigadier's frown deepened.

"I'm concerned about the press not knowing, Doctor. I never suggested that the relatives not be informed."

"Yes, of course, I, er... wasn't meaning to imply..." began Sanderson, lamely. Damn the man! What was it about him that so infuriated one and yet, at the same time, made one feel so inferior? He was like some Dickensian headmaster.

"Any news about the cause of death?" rescued Allen.

Sanderson shook his head. "The post-mortem showed nothing at all. We can only assume he died from some unknown type of virus. Certainly he was in a state of high fever, even delirium, just before he died; the doctor on duty said that he had the impression that all his bodily functions had been speeded up dramatically, to many times their normal rate; sort of burnt himself out, I think he said. After that dreadful affair with the boy, I was half expecting to find that his insides had dissolved away or something equally grotesque, but everything seemed normal; just as you'd expect from a natural death, in fact. We're having more detailed examinations carried out now but, somehow, I don't think they'll come up with anything useful."

Trowbridge turned and disappeared into the inside of the Portakabin, leaving the other two men alone and at least one of them visibly relieved at the fact.

"I'm afraid the condition of the other men is deteriorating too," continued Sanderson. "They don't seem to respond to even the most powerful antibiotics and antipyretics. In fact, the only good news is that, since we isolated the area, there haven't been any further cases. There are twelve men in a coma at the hospital now. Together with the man and boy dead and the three killed when the house collapsed, that makes seventeen casualties so far, and we've still no idea of the cause. What did you think of Hardwyke's spacecraft theory?"

"I'm relatively open-minded about UFOs. We all know the ministry investigates every reporting, despite its public denial of any evidence testifying to their existence but, in this instance, I'd much prefer to look for something a little more down to earth. After all, I don't think we've ever had any reports of flying saucers underground," he added with a laugh.

"Fascinating!" Their conversation was interrupted by this exclamation from the nearby radio receiver. Allen quickly moved over to the doorway to retrieve his microphone.

"Have you found something, Doctor?" he asked.

"Hmm, yes; most interesting," responded the voice, but seemed disinclined to elucidate. Its owner was apparently far too absorbed to wish to volunteer information.

"Well, what is it?" asked the major irritably, after some moments had elapsed.

"Eh? What? Oh, I've found some hemlock; not surprising, of course; it likes this type of soil, but it's really most extraordinary. You're familiar with hemlock, I suppose – white flowers in umbels – but the involucral leaves should only occur on the outside of the umbels. Here, we've got some on the inside. Not only that, either; the leaves are normally bi- to quadri-pinnate; these are much more finely toothed and – where's that magnifying glass? Yes, I thought so – the edges are doubly serrate instead of singly. It could almost be a different species but everything else points to Conium maculatum. I'm bringing this back. I can devote an entire article to this in the Journal."

"Well, that's excellent, Doctor," said Allen, though his glance at Sanderson indicated that he hadn't the slightest idea what the botanist had been talking about. "Do you think this will enable us to map the affected area?"

"Hardly; the tip's not exactly overgrown with hemlock, you know," answered the doctor, derisively. "However, I do have one suggestion. The area just around here looks particularly fertile, much greener too than one would have expected, unless that's the effect of this damned faceplate. You might try photographing the tip from above, using infrared film. Something might show up. I can't promise anything, though."

Allen waited a while and then, realizing the botanist had said all he intended, replaced the microphone on top of the cabinet and turned to Sanderson. "Well, Doctor, what did you make of that?"

"Not very much, I'm afraid; hemlock's not one of my strong points. In fact, I've only come across it in connection with Socrates. Now, if you wanted to talk about roses..."

"Yes, well. So you've no idea whether it will lead anywhere?"

"No. The old chap sounded pretty impressed by his find though, didn't he? How long do you reckon it would take him to map the area by himself?"

Major Allen looked up in slight surprise and wondered a

moment before realizing, from the half grin on Sanderson's face, that it had not been intended that he take the question seriously. "I'll go and see about getting a reconnaissance aircraft out. The sooner we get some concrete results, the better."

With this parting remark, the officer retreated into the Portakabin, leaving Sanderson to scrape out the old tobacco from his pipe prior to refilling it. He shared Mathers' unsociable habit but only indulged himself occasionally, when outside.

"What?... Good Lord...Why, I've never seen... It's fantastic."

Sanderson paused in the act of raising his lighter to the newly filled pipe as these excited exclamations burst from the nearby radio. Quickly, he replaced the implement in his pocket and, in a stride, was snatching at the microphone.

"Hello?" he enquired cautiously, unsure of whether he hadn't to press some concealed switch before communication became possible.

"Amazing. Why, I would never have believed..." continued the voice, frustratingly for the ignorant listener.

"Hello, Doctor Minton. Can you hear me?" shouted Sanderson, now also quite excited, and urgently anxious to know what was happening. When no reply was forthcoming, he leaned into the entrance and called out to Allen, who was speaking on the telephone.

"Major, quick! How do you work this damned thing?"

Allen spoke briefly into the receiver, placed the phone on the desk, and hurried over to the door, grabbing the microphone from the doctor's hand.

"Doctor, please answer. Could you explain what's happening?" He spoke clearly and decisively, having activated no switches, so far as Sanderson could see.

For what seemed an age, yet was probably no more than fifteen seconds, nothing could be heard. Then, faintly, as though a fault had occurred in either transmitter or receiver, the most distant of sounds could be heard. There was no interference and the sound was evidently that of a voice, though it was extremely difficult to discern any words. The tone of the voice indicated a continuation of the amazement already expressed. Both listeners afterwards agreed that the words 'beautiful' and 'journal' had occurred but beyond this there was no further comprehensible communication.

Allen attempted twice more to elicit a response, his voice, by now, having lost much of its original control.

"Damn the man," he pronounced vehemently, "what the hell is he playing at?"

He looked around undecided for a moment, glanced at the radio again in desperation, then threw the microphone to the ground and ran over towards the decontamination area, without any word of explanation to Sanderson.

About two minutes later, three men emerged at a run from one of the large vans. Clad in the grey protective suits, they lumbered off in the direction of the tip looking like some ungainly space-suited aliens, unused to earth's gravity. Allen appeared from the vehicle and hurried back over to Sanderson. Bending down, he adjusted the dial of the radio and picked up the microphone once more.

"Sergeant, Major Allen here. Can you hear me?"

"Davies here, major; receiving you loud and clear. Am entering tip now. Corporal, you position yourself between me and the gate. I want you to try to maintain visual contact with both the major and myself at all times. Do you understand?"

The reply could not be heard but apparently Sergeant Davies was satisfied and Sanderson deduced that the three men were on a separate circuit.

"It could just be a faulty radio link, couldn't it" asked the doctor optimistically.

"Not a chance, I'm afraid; that equipment's tested to the nth degree before we get it."

The men had, by now, entered some way into the tip and one

of them had begun to lag behind, glancing back from time to time.

"Can't see anything yet, major. Which direction did he take?"

Allen looked at Sanderson. "Left of where they are now, wasn't it?"

Sanderson furrowed his brow as he tried to recall the events. "Yes," he answered, "I'm fairly sure you're right; just slightly to the left of their current direction."

"Sergeant, head ten degrees to your left. That's the last we saw of him. Should have got him to report his heading as he went," he added as an afterthought.

The two men out in front eventually disappeared from view over the brow of a slight hill, leaving the third outlined against the sky. "That's him down there isn't it?" came the sergeant's voice at last, to the relief of Allen, who had been pacing impatiently up and down to the limits of the extension of the microphone cable.

"We've located him, major." This time, the voice was much more definite. "He seems to have fallen." A short pause followed. "Oh, Jesus! He's only gone and taken off his bleedin' 'elmet!"

Allen clapped a hand to his forehead and ran his fingers through his hair in an almost theatrical gesture of desperation. "What on earth could the man have been thinking of?" he asked, mostly to himself. "He's not an idiot, is he?" He looked up at Sanderson, imploringly.

"How does he look, sergeant," he continued, raising the microphone once again.

"Unconscious, I'm afraid, sir. Beyond that I can't tell with all this clobber on. Bringing him in now. You take his feet, Daniels."

"Another one for the isolation hospital, I'm afraid!" exclaimed Allen, with a sigh. "And I was thinking everything was going so well."

When Sanderson came back out of the Portakabin, the three men were just re-entering the decontamination area, this time with the limp figure of a fourth carried by two of them. Despite the bulk of their burden, the two men moved quickly, reminding Sanderson of the physical frailty of the old man. Perhaps his frailty had been not only physical, he thought, with an inward grimace. Whatever had possessed him to remove the protective headgear?

The military ambulance was already on site, awaiting such a contingency. Two soldiers emerged from the enclosure carrying the doctor's body on a stretcher and he was quickly transferred and removed with the minimum of explanations.

Meanwhile, the protective suits were hosed down with high-pressure water from the adjacent fire-tenders, washing away all traces of dust and mud, and, hopefully, any other contamination. The process was effective also in removing one inconspicuous blade of grass, stuck to the palm of one glove, which might have passed, had it been noticed, for a streak of blood or red dye and to which no significance could possibly have been attached.

Bradley was awoken by the muted but persistent tones of a mobile phone. It took some time for this to filter through to his discriminating intellect and trigger his dormant motor centre. His position, on the settee in Andrews' living room, was not the most comfortable he had encountered but his life was so active at the moment and times of rest so infrequent that he had been deeply asleep.

He scrambled with some difficulty to his feet, one leg partly paralyzed from lack of blood flow, and lurched across the room in the general direction of the position in which he vaguely remembered the light switch to be. Feeling tentatively but hurriedly along the wall, he eventually found it and plunged the room into a dazzling brilliance. For a long moment he could see nothing, but the caller was persistent and the phone gave no sign of ceasing its annoying sound, made even more frustrating because he could not immediately recall where it was.

He rubbed his eyes, took a deep breath and looked around for likely muffling objects. His jacket had been thrown down on a chair in the far corner of the room and, in the absence of any other obvious candidate, he moved quickly over the cold parquet flooring and lifted the jacket. The sound increased a few decibels and the phone fell noisily onto the tiles.

He picked it up and flicked the switch. There was nothing. No apparent connection had been made but at least the sound had stopped. Now being fully awake, he was sorely tempted to throw down the phone in annoyance. He looked at it with disgust, wondering who it might have been. They had not, he realized, waited for him to speak so it did not seem possible that it had been a wrong number. It would have to have meant that they had realized this at precisely the moment he had answered – most unlikely since it had been ringing for probably the best part of a minute. Just as he was about to switch it off and return to bed, he looked briefly at the display and the explanation was there. The single word 'Krish' glared back at him and told him everything.

Damn the man. Why would he not speak? Why was he so secretive? He had, Bradley recalled, once implied that he lived quite close. They could have met by now and put their relationship on a somewhat more traditional footing. The way that they communicated was more like that of spies. He decided against waking Andrews, if by some remote chance he had slept through this, he would wait and see what Krish had to say first.

{RJ} I gather you wanted to talk to me?

{Krish} Frank, yes, sorry if I disturbed your sleep but I thought you would want to know how my investigations are proceeding.

I believe I said that I would begin by looking into the background of all of the people involved with the landfill site. I began with the data held by UWD on their employees and suppliers and then continued moving outwards, checking all references on the contacts' computers and so on. I'm afraid I drew a blank; nothing 'suspicious' as you would deem it, at all.

Of course, I had appreciated from the outset that some of the relevant people just might not use their computers very frequently. After all, there are still a few reactionaries who refuse to take an interest in the web. What I had overlooked temporarily is that some of those directly involved were *unable* to use them. Obviously, the workers now in hospital (one of whom has just died incidentally, I'm sorry to have to tell you) have not been on-line for some days now, although most were regular users until their illness).

Accordingly, I looked at the council's database, where I found records of those workers who had previously been employed there. I tracked details of relatives and followed up links from there. Most led to nothing of interest but one of them looked as though it might be very relevant. The son of one of the tip workers is a co-director of a small biotechnology company, called NDA. (As far as I can tell, this is not an abbreviation. I assume it is meant to imply a proficiency in reorganizing the nucleotides of DNA!) Naturally such organizations are not very open about their work, but this one cannot easily hide the fact that it is not currently very profitable. They have recently made three of their fourteen staff redundant and there is a distinct likelihood that they will go bankrupt in the near future.

The company is privately run and has not published any details about the nature of its research. However, I have searched their electronic data and monitored their network activity over the past twenty-four hours and am able to make some reasonably definite deductions about what they have been doing. Their principal field is bioremediation. It seems they would like to find a versatile biological process for breaking down toxic materials. Very much after your own heart, Mr. Bradley?

Their basic idea is quite clever and will interest you, I am sure, although I think you will agree with me that it is also extremely dangerous. I don't know whether you will know anything about the various background details so I will describe them very briefly.

The first thread concerns a discovery made by a Canadian firm called AstraZeneca a number of years ago. They found that the bacteria that develop in rotting manure, newspapers, straw and wood chips produce enzymes called dehalogenases. As the name implies, these have the ability to break down chlorinated organic compounds such as pesticides by removing the halogen groups. What they did was to make huge compost heaps out of the contaminated soil and the rotting waste and just keep aerating them every few weeks. After a year, the DDT levels in the soil of their test site, at Tampa Florida, had been reduced by 95%. Other compounds were also reduced to below the EPA safety limits.

Another bacteria that you might have heard of is called Deinococcus radiodurans. It was discovered back in the late nineteen seventies in a can of irradiated meat. What made it interesting initially, of course, is the fact that it had survived this experience. Experiments showed that it was not destroyed by gamma radiation thousands of times greater than that which would kill humans. This astonishing property came from its ability to repair its own damaged DNA – needless to say a property very desirable and being looked into at Bethesda, Maryland. Scientists at the University of Minnesota also thought they could engineer 'improvements,' to enable the bacteria to attack certain organic pollutants such as toluene and chlorobenzene.

The third thread began at the Scottish Crop Research Institute near Dundee, Scotland. Here they are modifying the RNA of plant viruses, such as tobacco mosaic virus and potato virus, to enable the virus to carry what they call an 'overcoat' protein, fused genetically to the virus' own protein coat. When they infect a plant, the virus multiplies and the overcoat protein is manufactured at a tremendous rate, up to 20% of the total plant protein.

Now the idea which occurred to our local company is this: if they could isolate the enzyme producing factor from the AstraZeneca bacteria and the DNA correcting mechanism from Deinococcus and incorporate the former into the overcoat proteins and the latter into the virus RNA itself, then they would potentially have a phenomenally cheap and efficient process for remediation. All that you would need to do is sow some suitable plant material over the contaminated site, wait for it to grow and then infect it with the virus. The plant would spread, manufacture massive quantities of the virus (and hence the overcoat and enzyme producing protein) for you at no cost whatsoever and, over a period of perhaps a year or two, break down all of the toxic material into safe by-products.

Unfortunately, it seems that our local company might be becoming increasingly desperate to find and demonstrate a safe, workable process before their money runs out. There are exceedingly high rewards, one supposes, for something like that. Instead of the millions of dollars in cost for mechanical or chemical remediation, the costs for biological recovery might be only thousands or even less. I suspect – see Frank, now you have got me doing it! – that they may think they have a solution and the man in question may have persuaded his father to test it out on your landfill site. Obviously I have no proof of this but the known facts just might tally with my proposed scenario.

{RJ} I don't know what to say. It sounds potentially disastrous. What do you think might have happened then?

{Krish} The methods by which new genes are engineered are quite unnatural. They usually start with particularly nasty viruses – ones that cause cancers and so on – precisely because these are the most successful in inserting themselves into the target cells and slotting themselves into the host genome. In fact, several of these are often combined to make them even more active. Also, they often incorporate additional modifications to enable them to overcome any defense mechanisms that the target might have had to the original natural viruses. Of course, they supposedly 'cripple' the pathogenic function of the virus first so that they can make use of its ability to infect the target but not cause any adverse effects once there. Then they add some sort of marker gene so that they can identify the infected cells and extract them from the substrate.

When artificially constructed from several sources, they are called mosaic vectors and these are especially dangerous. Whilst naturally occurring viruses tend to be specific, only attacking particular organisms, these are able to infect a wide range of species. Results are unpredictable because the particular combination of genes that has been engineered could never have evolved naturally. Through this technique of incorporating elements from different species, they can pick up further, unforeseen modifications and create new pathogens.

These viruses are especially effective at causing something called 'horizontal gene transfer'. This occurs when genetic segments from a totally alien species are transferred into the genes of another. Although this can happen naturally, for example if one species succeeds in mating with another, it is much more likely to be caused by a virus deliberately engineered to carry new DNA into the cell. This process is one of the main reasons for the spread of resistance to antibiotics incidentally.

The techniques we are discussing here are precisely the ones that might allow this to happen. Although NDA's intention is that the virus be specific to a particular genus of plant, it could very easily spread to others and it is not beyond the realms of possibility that animals or even humans could be affected. Horizontal gene transfer is inevitably a leap into the unknown, doing things that, in nature, only occur through catastrophic events.

The arrogance of commercial science astounds me. It is rather like a schoolboy with a minor examination success in Physics being let loose in a nuclear reactor to 'improve' its efficiency. Do those making the decisions in large organizations not realize that Nature has had billions of years to try all sorts of combinations and permutations and that today's state of equilibrium is finely balanced for all? Everything is interdependent – no species exists in a vacuum. Man seems to be interested only in himself and he wants to make use of all the other resources for his own ends. All of this tinkering with the fabric of life is doomed eventually to push the system to a catastrophic event and when the new equilibrium is established, mankind just might not figure in it.

Fettered by a hundred chains of hope, dedicated to desire and anger, they seek to make their fortune by unlawful means in order to satisfy these desires. XVI.12

As Frank Bradley entered the Portakabin, the enormous color image mounted along the wall opposite the door immediately captured his attention. Momentarily, his indignation rose at the thought that, despite the serious nature of the business, the army should still find time to waste the taxpayers' money by decorating even such temporary surroundings with modern art. His mental processes were just gearing themselves up to pursue this line of reasoning with his customary enthusiasm when a glimmer of a more rational solution forced itself upon him. From the nature of the situation and the previous events and from the way in which those already present were grouped facing this thing, he decided that he must be looking at an aerial photograph. Indeed, once he had reached this conclusion, on further, more critical observation, he discerned that, in fact, it comprised many small photographs, linked together to form the whole.

Logically, the second deduction would be that it was an aerial view of the tip but try as he could, and he had lived in the area some time and also occasionally encountered these photographs in his work, he was unable to make any sense of the detail. Suddenly, he realized that the origin of his confusion and the reason for his initial erroneous impression was the color. This was no black and white, birds-eye view of a town or village, with symmetrical shapes of buildings and winding roads but a mass of abstract shapes in many shades of reds, bright blues and brown. Really quite beautiful, he thought; surely the Tate would consider it an asset. As he watched, one of the officers, who had apparently been studying a large-scale ordnance survey map, spread out on the desk to one side, moved over to the wall. With the aid of a setsquare and a ruler, and with reference to a sheet of paper in one hand, he began sticking pins into the photograph. Bradley was unable to restrain himself from thinking what desecration this was; the gallery attendant would have ejected such a vandal immediately.

The chairs, this time, had been arranged into two groups facing the wall, with a central passage left to the door. Brigadier Trowbridge was already present, Bradley noticed with a recollection of distaste, still seated behind the desk at the top, despite its poor position for seeing the photograph. Most of the other seats were already occupied too and many of the faces had changed since the previous day, at least amongst the army personnel. Sanderson, Inspector Harris and Hardwyke were there, seated to the left of the entrance at the rear and, as he looked, Andrews beckoned to him from the front right, apparently having reserved him a seat. Bradley moved over to join him.

"Morning, Frank," he said, as Bradley seated himself. "Looks like your idea paid off then."

"Really?" asked Bradley immediately interested. "Something's happened already then, has it?"

There had been no news in the evening papers the previous night, or in the dailies that morning. Bradley had presumed, nevertheless, that this could well be as a result of censorship rather than through lack of developments and was not, therefore, surprised that this did, indeed, seem to be the case.

"Only this morning; not surprising you haven't heard yet. They brought this botanist in to look round as you suggested and apparently he did find some distinct mutations; brought one back with him too, in that jar on the table."

Bradley looked over for the first time at the rather ordinary looking weed, conspicuously exhibited in a large specimen jar some feet away. He experienced a slight twinge of annoyance that he had not already noticed it but told himself that the far more impressive incongruity of the huge photograph had swamped his perception.

"I believe something more important happened, though," continued Andrews. "No one's said anything yet but Sanderson was here at the time and he looks distinctly unhappy at what ought to be quite good news."

At this moment, the assembly presumably being complete, Major Allen appeared and moved to the front to address the meeting. The other senior officer continued to mark the photo-graph, the pins combining to mark off a section of the map.

"Gentlemen," commenced Allen, "I'm afraid we have mixed news for you today. We've made a considerable step forward in mapping the extent of the contamination but the man who was most instrumental in achieving this is now in hospital and his condition is very grave."

Low murmuring arose around the room at this statement but ceased respectfully as soon as the major raised his hand. He reviewed the events of the morning and concluded by pointing out that no one could offer any explanation as to why the botanist had exposed himself to the known danger by removing his helmet.

"It doesn't make any sense," whispered Andrews to his companion.

"Quite right, Doctor," said Allen, with almost stereotyped military sharpness, "it doesn't make any sense. Nevertheless, at the present time it seems futile to pursue this question. We do have some new information and we must press on to use it at the earliest opportunity. "I would like to introduce Major Wyatt, from Reconnaissance—"

"Just a second, major," interrupted the other, who was still inserting a number of remaining pins.

"Major Wyatt's section has been extremely helpful at such very short notice, in flying over the area late this morning and producing these splendid aerial photographs. When you're ready, major." Allen seemed disinclined to improvise further and seated himself next to Bradley to wait for Wyatt to complete his task. Eventually, the latter turned to face the expectant audience and began to explain his findings. "I'll try to keep this simple; the technical details are not relevant. The composite shot you see here was taken using infrared film with an orange filter over the lens. Since we're concerned here with studying the nature of the plant life, I must tell you that the tone differentiation is caused by the varying amounts of chlorophyll present in the foliage. The higher the percentage of chlorophyll that is present in a plant, the greater the reflection of infrared light and the redder the corresponding image on the photograph. Dying plants, though they may still look perfectly healthy to the untrained observer in ordinary light, show up brown as here, and here." He pointed to the areas, using the ruler.

"I've outlined the perimeter using these mapping pins. Here's the main gate and here is where we are." He indicated three small orange rectangles, obviously the Portakabins. "Now you'll see that there's still a fair amount of vegetation despite, or perhaps because of, the amount of refuse disposed of over the years. What you won't immediately see is that this area here, of about twenty acres, is apparently more fertile than one could possibly expect. Now, Mr. Struthers," he looked around but the other was not present to confirm the statement, "assures us that this particular spot has not been used for dumping, so this can't be explained by, for example, a recent disposal of nitrogenous waste matter.

"Furthermore, this spot…" he pointed to a location just inside the area previously designated, where the depths and shades of red were just conceivably distinctive to Bradley's intense gaze, "is where Doctor Minton is said to have identified his novel variety of hemlock. And here," he said, pointing to another spot, also within the area, "is where his body was found."

Major Wyatt proceeded to insert two special pins, topped by small black flags, at the points he had indicated while the conversation sprang up again around the room. Bradley and Andrews looked at each other, wondering how best to introduce the new information revealed by Krish a few hours ago. They had still not agreed how they would explain the source of their knowledge.

"What's the scale of the photograph, major?" called out Inspector Harris.

"It's about fifty yards to the inch."

"Do you mind?" asked Harris, as he moved to the front and held out his hand for the ruler. He took it and proceeded to measure out a few points, referring then to a notebook, which he took from his pocket.

"Hmm. that's interesting," he muttered. "That means that the spot where the doctor was found must be within a few yards of the place where the boy died."

"Unlikely to be a coincidence, then, Inspector?" asked Allen.

"No," answered Harris, reluctantly. "What happened exactly? What did he see or do out there? Didn't the men who brought him back see anything unusual?"

"I'm afraid not, Inspector. I think you're wasting your time. We know that the soil, where it's contaminated, is deadly, and the map indicates that the whole of that area is affected. What happened could equally well have happened somewhere else."

One could see that Harris wished to make the obvious comment "but it didn't" but he exhibited remarkable restraint and returned thoughtfully to his seat.

Bradley looked once more at Andrews, raising his eyebrows slightly. The other nodded briefly, his expression becoming even more worried in anticipation. Bradley took another anxious breath, rose to his feet from the chair at the side of the cabin and stepped forward to make it clear to the others that he had something to say.

Major Allen, apparently on the point of continuing with his agenda, stopped and turned towards Bradley expectantly.

"Some information has come to light which you need to take into consideration before deciding any course of action."

"Really, Mr. Bradley?" Brigadier Trowbridge looked up with apparent interest for the first time that morning. "You intrigue me," he added patronizingly, "pray continue."

Bradley paused. Was it possible that people still naturally spoke like this? Pray for strength! He was tempted to make a sarcastic comment himself but would not have seriously contemplated it. The brigadier was insufferable but he probably couldn't help it. He proceeded to relate the essence of the conversation with Krish, telling them about NDA and the possible use of the tip to test out their genetically engineered virus. He did not, of course, attempt to explain the nature of the source of this intelligence.

There was a period of incredulous silence after he had finished, broken eventually by the harsh, disbelieving tone of the brigadier. "I hope you're able to substantiate all of this, Mr. Bradley. It sounds suspiciously like the sensational rumors of some left wing ecology organization."

Bradley found himself in the uncomfortable position of having to bow slightly to this disapproving and doubt-casting criticism. "I confess that I don't know the actual identity of the person who's given me this information. However, earlier discussion with him – or her," he added, as the possibility suddenly occurred to him, "does not lead me to doubt their integrity. Even without being absolutely sure as to whether it's true, I believed that we couldn't afford to take the risk of withholding it. I was hoping that you'd be able to take it from here and investigate the truth of the matter." He was reassured somewhat by several grunts of assent and murmured agreements from those assembled. Even the Brigadier seemed disinclined to argue with this.

"The main point, if it is true," he added, in case anyone had not registered this, "is that if the contamination is on the surface, in the vegetation, then it's crucial that we don't begin digging up the site and spreading the virus throughout the soil." He looked across to Andrews but the other did not seem to wish to add to what had been said.

Andrews had initially been highly skeptical. In particular he had wanted to know how the samples he had found could have exhibited unnatural combinations of isotopes of several elements. This had been one of the major factors in his extraterrestrial hypothesis. Bradley, who had not told Andrews about Krish in any detail, except to acknowledge that they had not actually met, had thought he might have to re-contact Krish for an answer to that one. Then, with sudden insight, he suggested that the technique of manipulating and extracting the relevant genetic strand from the Radiodurans bacterium could well have involved use of radioactive sources.

To his subsequent unremitting self-blame, Andrews had allowed himself to be persuaded. He told himself later that it had been because of lack of sleep and high levels of stress. What had not immediately occurred to him was that, even if this explained any abnormal proportions in the presumably minute amount of virus that had been originally introduced, it did not explain where it could have obtained those isotopes to enable these proportions to be maintained as it spread.

Outside, over the tip, the heat haze shimmered as a dry, warm breeze from the east blew gently through the grass and cluttered debris. The birds whistled and chirped unconcernedly and a rabbit pricked up its ears at the bark of a distant dog. Gone, the sickening odor of decaying refuse, dispersed after the weeks of disuse, replaced now by the faint but omnipresent tang of green fields and fainter, subtler scent of other less prolific growths. Pollination was still going strong. It was definitely going to be a bad summer for hay-fever sufferers.

It was nearly two weeks before the combined intelligence networks of Europe and America were able to track down Darren Banks, erstwhile savior, but possible destroyer, of the human race. He had gone into hiding in a small but luxuriously appointed villa in coastal Mexico, an area so remote that the nearest village boasting a name was some fifty miles away. The more decorative four-wheel drive vehicles would be most unlikely to have made it down the desperately rutted and pot-holed track that wound its way precipitously around the mountainous coastline. Even the entrance to this 'way,' for it could certainly not be called a road, was hidden from view and any tire marks had been carefully obliterated to discourage potential visitors. To any casual passer-by, if there could be such a thing in this most inhospitable of places, it was unthinkable there could be a residence several miles further on.

These same intelligence agents who had meticulously unearthed the data – from altered passports and 'lost' airline ticket data, through hotel bookings under assumed names and stolen vehicles purchased by cash with no questions asked – were truly amazed at the skills that had gone into erasing all trace of this person. It was with considerable relief and a genuine sense of real accomplishment that they finally burst into the villa with cries of 'you're nabbed' or whatever their national ergot preferred.

Banks was airlifted out by helicopter to the nearest airport and thence to Mexico City for earliest transfer back to London and on to Manchester, where a fleet of military vehicles was waiting. Several people were keenly awaiting the opportunity to ask him one or two questions, since his apparently sincere, though astonishingly naïve, partner had seemed to be entirely ignorant as to what had been going on.

This first of many interviews was intense but short. This was dictated not by Banks being somewhat tired after his enforced repatriation but by the fact that that it soon transpired that he was not, after all, the 'brains' behind the development and ill-advised testing of the virus. He readily confessed that he had spent the best part of the last eighteen months working together with one of his senior scientists at NDA. They had obtained their starting materials relatively easily, though a substantial proportion of the company's meager capital had been expended in bribes, unbeknownst to his partner. The initial stages of the engineering had progressed quickly and, after only six months, they were ready to begin to try to modify the overcoat for the Tobacco Mosaic Virus. There they ran into severe problems and it had taken another nine months before a viable product had been ready to test.

It was during a brief lull in the recounting of the story, while some strong coffee was being produced to stimulate Banks' increasingly fuzzy brain, that someone threw in the almost incidental questions, "How did you manage to get away so quickly anyway? Who organized everything for you? Who exactly tipped you off that we were on to you?"

"It was the same person for all of those," he answered, "the same one who's been helping me from the beginning. In fact, I suppose it was all really his idea in the first place. Trouble is," he added ruefully, "– and I don't suppose you're going to believe this – I don't really know who he is. You see I've never actually met him; only communicated with him via computer. It shouldn't be too difficult to track him down though; there can't be many people in the world who know as much about genetics as he does. He calls himself Mendel."

And so another week passed. With the help of Banks and Bradley, together with their computers and the archives from various servers scattered about the world, the experts were able to piece together practically nothing about Mendel-Krishna. They concluded that he must have used some very clever software that traced all of the links and followed behind the connections as they were broken down, deleting connection data, IP addresses, cookies and anything and everything that might subsequently be used to identify the source of the caller. He was like an electronic aborigine, branch brushing behind as he walked to obliterate the footprints in the sand.

So, in the end, all that they knew about him was that his computing and biological skills and expertise were unparalleled; his whereabouts, age and even 'his' sex remained a total mystery. All communications from him/her had ceased. There was no response to attempts to set up the chat group and either he had stopped monitoring web activity or he chose to ignore Bradley's searches on key words relating to their earlier discussions. None of their questions had been answered. Why had he initiated Banks' development of the virus? Why had he discussed Philosophy with Bradley and then effectively told him about the source of the contamination. Was he just playing with them? Why had he stopped now?

Whatever the reasons, they were still left with the fundamental problem of neutralizing or containing the toxic elements at the landfill. They had delayed now for nearly three weeks. In the absence of alternative viable solutions, they had to begin the excavation. Authorization was given and the work commenced… too late; the delay had been quite adequate for the intended purpose to be fulfilled.

I reveal myself whenever there is a decrease in righteousness, Arjuna, and an increase in evil-doing. IV.7

The nights were always far more pleasant than the days during these occasional heat waves; relatively cool after the oppressive heat of the afternoon sun, yet still warm enough for these temperate climes for one to sit outside until late into the evening, savoring the still, clear air and the sharp starlit sky. These were nights for relaxing with a cold lager in the beer garden of the nearest pub. There, one could indulge in a quiet, leisurely conversation instead of having to raise one's voice to rise above the ambient din around the bars.

The atmosphere, too, always seemed to feel different later in the evenings. Not any smell particularly, or, at least, none that could be identified, but a quite unmistakable freshness that made one want to breathe deeply and let out the air slowly with a deep sigh of satisfaction. The tip had been out of action for about two months now and the expected odors of dust and decay had entirely dissipated. The night held an aura of open countryside about it, despite the nearness of at least the signs of habitation. Visual signs only were they, though; no sounds of 'Coronation Street' theme music or crying babies emanated from behind darkened windows; no light from bedrooms or even illuminated doorbells to dispel the faint feeling of unease that the grey shapes, deep in shadow, created. Only the chimneystacks, sharply outlined against the moonlit sky, relieved their menacing, amorphous mass and from these came no friendly rising wisps of smoke. Empty yet not derelict; to a stranger they were enigmas awaiting the return of an explanation. To a blind man, but for possible extra information he might derive from his other senses, it would indeed seem that he were out in the middle of the countryside and he might drink in these other sensations and find nothing to detract from his enjoyment of them.

Private Daniels was not blind, however, and many were the indications that civilization was close and all was not well. The houses themselves could not form the sole source of his unease. Although it was only 10.30 p.m., it could quite easily have been that the locals had retired early and that the street lamps had being turned off to conserve electricity. But he knew that there was no one in them; that the occupants had been forced to leave, often against their will, and didn't know when they would be allowed to return. And there was no one about, except for the other soldiers who, like him, were patrolling the area. He could just see Jamieson about a quarter of a mile away, the latter having struck a match, now lifting it to his face to light a cigarette.

Daniels reached into his pocket and withdrew a pack himself. He paused, worrying childishly for a moment that the other might notice and laugh at him (for being a 'copycat' as they had said at school) then wondering further whether he really did want one himself or was merely reacting to the suggestion. Oh, what the hell, he thought; took one out and lit it unceremoniously, throwing the match away in disgust.

He inhaled and let the smoke out slowly. It did seem to be the case that cigarettes tasted better too, at night time outdoors. Yes, he could almost have enjoyed night duty like this under different circumstances. There was time to think in the heightened solitude; more of a sense of aloneness imposed by the darkness together with the open sky. The stars contributed to the isolation, enforcing a feeling of insignificance, yet at the same time reassuring that this was not all there was to the universe. There was time to forget the worries of day-to-day routine and put one's thoughts into perspective; relegating the invariable problems of life and work to a brief but relieving unimportance: good occasionally to be alive to the fact that one's life is to the immensity of the universe as a drop of water is to the ocean.

Yet the mind is so easily distracted. How difficult to concentrate on a single clear idea and exclude irrelevancies. How much more difficult to empty the mind of all thoughts and let it sit passively, accepting without selection or differentiation all sensations and impressions, neither questioning nor passing judgment, merely observing, being a sentient vehicle and receptor for external and internal events.

Daniels was distracted, constantly, by the empty houses on the horizon and, even more, by the machines. Tall and alien they stood; incongruously silent, their obvious power latent, awaiting the turn of a key to bring their terrific energy flaming into life. Huge black shadow shapes they were, springing up all over the sunken plain at the eastern end of the tip. A nearby digger stood patiently, its enormous shovel poised, half-raised, a ton of forged steel in the bucket and blade, prongs muddied and dirty, an intensity of purpose embodied in its design. A line of bulldozers stood some fifty yards away, an impregnable army of mechanized slaves frozen by its commander's orders in the midst of an inexorable advance. Two of the giant earthmovers sat massively in the near distance, big as two-storey houses, their monolithic bulk a monument to the ingenuity of man to harness the elements, to break and defeat the elements. Silently they towered above the onlooker, awe-inspiring in their power and majesty: oblivious of obstacles, all destined to fall in their path.

A temporary halt had been called to the work, now that the first phase of the plan was complete. Throughout the past fortnight, the machines had toiled without ceasing, their mere operators being replaced on a shift basis as they tired. They had now cleared an area of about one hundred by two hundred yards to a depth of about fifty feet. The intention, as far as Daniels was aware, was to concrete the bottom and sides to make a huge swimming pool and then to fill it in again with the contaminated earth, mixing it with an equal amount of chalk and covering it over with more concrete. What they were going to do then, he had no idea – presumably put up a barbed-wire fence and try to forget about it. The whole idea struck him as being quite ridiculous. His friends had told him, when he had applied to join the army, that they made you dig holes and then fill them in again. Of course, he had taken this as a joke at the time. He shook his head in disbelief. Still, it should have been pleasant enough now, the activity of the recent days having temporarily ceased, the noise of the machines silenced and the bright glare of the arc lights removed from the scene.

And yet, despite the cool, summer's night air and the mental equating of this with peace and stillness, he was unable to dispel this sense of unease and even less able to explain it. Something seemed either to be missing or present when it shouldn't have been. He was reminded of his pre-army days in the factory when, staying late, the machines were switched off and the flying belts and racing dynamos all slowed and died, leaving a strangely disquieting absence of sound quite alien to the feel of the place. The noise and the factory went together. Why, it was possible to diagnose faults in the machinery from the day-to-day variations in tone. The acoustics of the factory had not been able to cope with anything other than the incessant din of the huge machines. With these stopped, one was left with a totally unnatural silence; an unheard yet distinctly felt residual echo, as though of an emptiness of sound acting as a vacuum for noise, poised, awaiting an impulse. If you dropped a spanner, it would be certain to bang and clatter around the entire building as the empty factory made the most of the opportunity for a brief but noisy respite.

So it was now, though in a different sort of way. Possibly some sensation was present which didn't fit in with his expectations but it was certainly something unidentifiable to his normal senses. Whatever it was, its apprehension was at a subliminal level and he was at a loss to explain it. Increasingly, however, or so it seemed, now that he had chosen to recognize it, he was unable to ignore it. He looked nervously around him and towards the other soldier ahead in hope of some reassurance, which he did not receive. He thought of calling out to him or running to catch up with him but held back, his fear of ridicule still proving the stronger. Perhaps there was a certain masochistic enjoyment of such irrational fear (for this was how he now felt obliged to categorize his feeling, realizing with a distinct shock that his apprehension had grown as he had been reflecting) as when he'd used to visit so-called 'haunted,' derelict houses as a child.

The cool breeze had now subsided and one could easily imagine a sort of oppression, as if the lull presaged a storm, but the clear, starlit sky forced one to dispel any such notions. What was wrong then? Was it an effect produced simply by the machines around him, menacing shapes in the dark, carrying overtones of the unknown nature of the problem which had brought them here, together with his memories, induced by his current impressionable state of mind?

A light flared ahead of him as the other soldier lit a second cigarette. He had halted and was apparently waiting for Daniels to catch up. Did he, too, feel uneasy? They were supposed to maintain a distance of at least two hundred yards between each other whilst on guard. Obviously they would be less likely to carry out their task of observation effectively if they walked around together, engaged in conversation. Still, Daniels decided it would surely be permissible to check briefly with each other to ensure neither had noticed anything suspicious or unusual. Accordingly, he took a deep breath at the thought of the possible breach of discipline, and set off towards the other.

He stopped short again after a few yards, however, when a new and more definite impression assailed him. Again, he was not able to say that he could actually hear something but he could swear that he felt a distinct vibration at the threshold of perception, as though the very air were beginning to throb at a low steady frequency. His heart was now pounding despite his inability to put a source to his fear. Jamieson had dropped his rifle and was running towards the gate. Daniels, on the contrary, felt unable to move a muscle, though the adrenaline was now coursing through his blood. He looked to his left, across to the mechanical shovel on the edge of the excavation. Its outline shimmered, as if in a heat haze. Even as he watched, the image appeared to sway towards the brink though it may have been that he himself moved, on the point of fainting. The very ground itself now seemed to have taken up that deep resonance, almost beyond perception. Perhaps that was it, yes – an earthquake. Of course, thought Daniels, with a flash of relief, despite the seriousness that that might still imply. He found control of his limbs once more and turned to walk back to the compound. He would not drop his rifle and run in terror like that other idiot.

At this point, however, he unaccountably stumbled and fell to the ground cursing, raising himself subsequently to his knees only with difficulty. To his horror, the drumming vibration had now attained audible proportions; a regular pulsating superimposed upon a low humming sound which was itself now rising in pitch. Over towards the middle of the tip, a minor explosion drew his attention. Huge clods of earth had been thrown into the air. Even as he looked, a second and a third followed and then a whole series of eruptions as if a field of landmines had been invaded by an invisible army. A foul smell of decay, as of concentrated sewage overlaid by choice organic chemicals and hydrogen sulphide, wafted across, almost knocking him over again with its overwhelming stench. He managed to tug his handkerchief from his pocket and buried his nose and mouth in it, barely restraining himself from retching.

A final violent explosion shook the ground beneath him and threw a cloud of debris high into the air. The particles, as he looked, seemed to be glowing with a faint blue iridescence. There was a wholly abnormal lack of smoke or flames. Indeed, no apparent cause for the explosions could be discerned but the humming, however it fitted into the events, had continued rising and was now almost beyond the range of hearing at the other end of the spectrum. The dust from the last eruption was still settling down into, what must have been, by that time, a sizeable hole and from which the blue light seemed to be increasing in intensity and beginning to pulse in time with the deep throbbing which had continued throughout the spectacle. As he watched, hypnotized, the dust began to whirl in a circular motion about the hole and a wind arose blowing paper and other rubbish loosened by the blasts in all directions. The glow intensified still further and then apparently rose momentarily and hovered in a long semi-solid, semi-diffuse state, resembling a flattened sphere or cylinder about a hundred feet long. For only about two seconds had he time to examine this before, with a final gust of air of such violence that he was knocked to the ground, it rose with tremendous acceleration and vanished into the night.

Having seen you multi-colored, touching the sky, mouth open, enormous eyes blazing, I quake in my inner self, lacking courage and stillness. XI.24

Frank Bradley turned over with a barely repressed groan of frustration, aching with excitement at the nearness of her naked body yet unable to arouse a responsive spark of desire and unwilling to force unwelcome attentions upon her. The early morning sun struck the window with a forewarning of a later intensity. The flimsy curtains offered little resistance, the interior of the bedroom being suffused with a hazy light. A breeze ruffled the material from time to time, allowing a sharp beam to penetrate and reflect dazzlingly off the white surface of the drawers by the bedside. Bradley screwed up his eyes and cursed inwardly. He threw back the sheet and half rose to get up.

Brenda Houldsworth turned and sat up, reaching out to lay her hand on his arm as he was rising. "I'm sorry, love," she said, her voice miserable and inviting sympathy. Her eyes were red-rimmed and her hair disheveled. Bradley, his ardor now dispelled, looked back, the line of his mouth grim and his eyes distinctly unsympathetic. She uttered a small choked sob, turned over and buried her face in the pillow. A wave of anger rose in him and he gritted his teeth as he stood and began to dress but he managed to restrain himself from speaking until the emotion had subsided somewhat. He took a deep breath and searched for a source of rationality and persuasive argument to counter her, what was to him, irrational behavior. He felt so impotent. He moved to the other side of the bed, sat down and stroked her hair with a half-hearted attempt at tenderness.

"Brenda," he began imploringly, "it's over three months now. You shouldn't still be acting like this. Can't you understand? It's all over. We've got to begin again." He stopped. He had been about to carry on with "start afresh," but the sudden realization that he appeared to be acting out some hackneyed scene from a composite of old films, with all the standard clichés bubbling to the surface, forced him to halt. He almost felt like laughing but Brenda was not in the position to appreciate the humor of the situation. Was he being callous or was he actually deficient in some aspect of his emotional make-up? He began again, not now being able to continue in the vein in which he had started.

"Do you want to move; to a different part of the country, away from the house and this town?"

"It wouldn't make any difference," she mumbled, drying her eyes with the back of her hand. His heart softened at her pitiful appearance and he bent down to pull out a tissue from the box of Kleenex by the bed and proceeded to dab away the tears. She sat up once more, taking the tissue from him to blow her nose.

"I will try, honestly," she said. "I'll go to the grave once more this morning and then I'll try to put it all out of my mind once and for all."

Bradley stood and fought down his reaction to what he

considered to be a further relapse. He sought desperately for appropriate words of remonstration.

"I do mean it this time," she said, sensing his disappointment, "wait and see. You don't have to come. I'll take the car and I'll be back in an hour."

"Oh, you're not going now, are you, for God's sake? You haven't even had breakfast yet."

"I'm not hungry, really," she answered, now out of bed and proceeding to dress. I'll have something when I get back. There's some bacon in the fridge if you want to do yourself some."

Bradley could find no answer and left the room, going into the bathroom to set the tap running and escape the tension that further exposure to the scene held for him. He sat down on the side of the bath and tried to concentrate on the sound of the water gushing out of the tap and splashing noisily below, the sounds combining and reverberating hollowly around the confined space. After a short while, the door opened and she hesitantly looked in.

"I'll see you in about an hour then."

He nodded dumbly. She walked quickly up to him, kissed him briefly on the forehead and then left without another word.

As far as he was concerned now, the whole nasty business really was over. Even the newspapers had ceased their daily sensations over the recent incidents. Admittedly, no one actually knew the truth about the matter but they were unlikely to find out either. The army had strenuously denied all reports that a flying saucer had taken off from the site, despite hundreds of stories to the contrary, some of which were from people of undisputed integrity. It was rumored that the soldiers who had been on guard at the tip that night and who must have been eye-witnesses at close range were literally under threat of the death penalty if they revealed their knowledge to the media.

Despite the officially announced lack of further interest in the site, the area was now impenetrable except under highest security clearance and it was unofficially reported that the military were going over the ground with the thoroughness and care normally reserved for the most important archaeological discoveries. What was almost certain was that, since the 'incidents' of earlier that year, the soil had been declared suddenly miraculously free of any toxicity. Andrews had been given samples of earth from areas previously heavily contaminated with the strange and still unidentified chemical. He had later made a statement to the effect that, although some odd compounds could be found and evidence was still present of novel isotopes, all abnormal reactivity had ceased completely.

Accordingly, the estate had been declared safe once again and the occupants had returned to their houses, naturally relieved, though also in a way disappointed, that the excitement was over. Sensation seekers still flocked daily to the area but the hundreds had now dwindled to tens and would presumably soon stop altogether. After all, it was impossible to see anything; the road, which led up by the side of the tip, had been closed to traffic now for some time. A heavily guarded gate had been erected at the dirt-track entrance to the road and a barbed wire perimeter fence had been built, blocking off all other previous entrances to the site. There would never be a repetition of Mark's accident anyway, which was some small mercy, thought Bradley, with another sigh.

It was quite a common experience now for the locals of the town and, more especially, those on the estate, to be approached by complete strangers seeking first hand reports of the events of the past months. At first, a few people had responded with enthusiasm, often to excess, recounting tales more from their imagination than fact, pleased at their newly acquired notoriety. Now, however, even these had grown bored with the same questions and impatient at the stupidity of some of the enquirers. Most strangers were now met with an undisguised glare of distrust, which persuaded all but the most insensitive that their investigations were distinctly unwelcome. Those who persisted were usually simply told to 'piss off'.

Scientific research was still continuing into the nature of the substance that had been present. They must have nearly used it all up by now, thought Bradley wryly. Andrews had shown him two of the first papers to be published on the subject but, apart from being somewhat tired of the topic, Bradley had been unable to follow the technical details. It was apparent, however, that the government had been unable to dissuade the scientists from their claim that the material was of extra-terrestrial origin, even though they refused to associate themselves with that theory.

Yes, the time had definitely come to forget about it all and attempt to return to a semblance of normalcy. He turned off the tap and climbed gratefully into the bath, sinking into the hot water and relaxing completely. Perhaps he could get back to his arts centre project today. Where had he put his latest sketches?

Sometime later, as he swallowed the last of his bacon sandwich with a gulp of coffee and closed the morning paper, he glanced at the clock on the kitchen wall and realized that Brenda had now been gone somewhat longer than the hour she had promised. Her mobile had been left on the kitchen table, as though to tell him that she didn't want to be called during her vigil. Damn, he thought, as the memory of the bedroom scene cast a shadow over his relaxed mood and even temper. He looked out of the window to verify that the day was indeed developing into one of dry heat, as the early sun had portended, and decided to go for a stroll to meet her. It might well prove better for their relationship that day than if he waited at the house for her return. Perhaps they could drive out into the country later and take some sandwiches; his work would wait for another day.

He put on his jacket and set off for the cemetery, walking along the road by the route she would be most likely to take in the car. It was already hot; really more appropriate for sunbathing in the garden than walking along tarmac roads, and after he had been out for about fifteen minutes he was beginning to feel uncomfortably sticky. He removed his jacket and slung it over his shoulder, wondering if he had somehow missed her. It was now well over two hours since she had left.

Eventually, he turned the corner into the approach avenue. His car was parked outside the gate. He increased his pace now that he had confirmation that his journey had not been in vain and began to wonder what he should say when he met her. Should he complain about her taking so long or pass over it and try to comfort her yet again in her seemingly interminable sorrow of bereavement? Perhaps the best course of action would be to act as if he were meeting her at the hairdresser's or from the supermarket rather than this more somber venue, and to say nothing at all of the subject which would probably still be foremost in her mind. Certainly neither of the other two prospects held much attraction, despite the artificiality of the third option. He cursed briefly, moved his jacket to the other shoulder and pressed on through the gate and into the burial grounds.

Private cars were not allowed into the cemetery itself and, since it occupied some considerable area, there was still a quarter mile walk to the graveside. He had visited several times before so had no difficulty finding his way along the maze of inter-secting paths. These crisscrossed their way between the little plots of earth, each with its own faded headstone, most now unreadable, in memoriam of a decomposed heap of wood and bones, remembered by no one. After his discussions with Krish, he now had no problem intellectually with the idea that we are not our bodies. He would have liked to ask him about grief, to see if he had any useful suggestions that might be of help to Brenda. He had to confess that he missed their conversations. And still he could not reconcile the profound philosophical understanding of the nature of reality, with the apparently unprincipled and reckless behavior of someone who had initiated and supported the development of the virus.

He caught brief glimpses of the place where he knew Mark's grave to be, as he passed the hundreds of stones of varying sizes but no clear unobstructed view could be achieved, until he reached the last junction and turned into the final avenue. He might have left the path and walked directly over the plots but he took the indirect route, not being in a hurry now that he had almost arrived, preferring, rather, to slow his pace, to gain more time to decide on how best to behave. Eventually, he reached the turning to see the grave some thirty yards ahead. There was, however, no sign of Brenda Houldsworth.

He stopped, momentarily confused. He looked around, back the way he had come. Had anyone been walking in the area, he would doubtless have seen them but there was only a gardener or, he supposed on second thoughts, a gravedigger working some distance away. He was about to turn back, to return to see if the car was still there, when he caught a glimpse of a patch of something red by the graveside ahead, illuminated by a ray of sunlight through the branches of a nearby tree.

A sudden shock of adrenaline startled his system and he ran up to the site, his mind struggling to restrain its imagination. He could see from a distance that it was not a flower and it was too diffuse to be the color of some solid object or a handkerchief. He reached the plot and fell to his knees on the lawn by the side.

As he had feared, it appeared that the short, straggly grass now growing on the mound of earth over the grave itself was stained with blood. He tentatively stretched out his hand to touch it, fully expecting to withdraw it moist with freshness. He looked at his fingers but found nothing. Somewhat surprised, he tugged at one of the offending blades of grass and, on close examination, experienced a wave of relief as he realized that it was the grass itself – obviously some obscure variety – that was colored red.

He rose and began to retrace his steps slowly back to the

entrance. He recognized with a degree of bewilderment that, although he was making a conscious effort to decide on the next course of action to determine the whereabouts of Brenda, part of his mind seemed to be dwelling on the grass. It seemed to have some significance far beyond the apparent triviality of the incident. He stopped as some half-formed idea strove to attain sufficient clarity for perception but then caught sight of the gravedigger once again and his attention was distracted. He set off rapidly towards him, pushing the aborted thought to the back of his mind.

"Excuse me," he interrupted the man. "I don't suppose you noticed a young woman; came to visit her son's grave, just over there, about two hours ago, wearing a yellow dress.

"Good Lord, yes. 'Course I did. Are you a relative?"

"What? No, well, sort of. What do you mean? Is something the matter?"

"Yes, I'm afraid so. She was taken ill. Found her myself, I did, slumped down over the grave. I thought she was just mourning at first; they take it pretty hard at times, some of them, you know. So I left her awhile. Anyhow, I kept looking from time to time and when I saw she wasn't moving I went over. Unconscious she was; had to get the ambulance. She's been taken off to hospital. I'm very sorry, sir. I hope everything'll be all right."

Bradley turned and ran off without another word, his thoughts in turmoil as he strove to find some explanation other than the one he feared. She had seemed reasonably optimistic when she left, not really the sort of mood one would expect before a suicide attempt. Still, he thought, he hadn't been very sympathetic that morning; maybe she had finally given in to the tremendous strain that she had been under since Mark's death. What would it be – barbiturates? It would mean seeing the police again. He groaned aloud; the tip had apparently still not taken its complete toll of victims.

He was almost shaking when he reached the car, though

whether from emotion or lack of breath after running, he didn't consider. He automatically reached into his pocket for the car keys but realized at the same instant that he had, of course, given them to Brenda. At this, he seemed almost to lose control. He swore violently and kicked the wheel of the car, oblivious of the pointlessness and the time and energy that he was wasting by both activities; his body ready for action but his mind unable to find a suitable course to follow.

"Oh God, Oh God, Oh God,' he cried despairingly, and felt virtually on the point of smashing his fist through the windscreen when his unfocused vision accidentally caught sight of the open side window and the ignition key still in the lock.

"Stupid woman; I've told her before about that," he thought paradoxically, now however realizing his own stupidity and recovering some of his composure. He climbed into the car and set off immediately. He took the back way into town, round by the park, the speedometer needle touching the sixty mark despite the thirty mile per hour restriction. Fortunately, there were no police cars in the vicinity and he was forced to slow to a crawl as he neared the centre.

After what seemed to be far longer than the five minutes it had taken, he arrived at the hospital. He parked heedlessly on a double yellow line, having only reassured himself that he wasn't actually causing an obstruction, and rushed into the casualty department.

He recklessly cornered the first white-coated person he saw and badgered him for information. Realizing he would have difficulty in ignoring this earnest young man, the doctor grudgingly admitted that a woman had been brought in and politely explained that another doctor had seen her and that Bradley would have to arrange with reception to see him.

For some reason Bradley would have been hard pressed to rationalize, he felt unable to accept this statement. He was sure this doctor was withholding some vital fact. Some hesitancy in his manner, the way his eyes avoided meeting his own. He refused to allow the other to pass and, as the doctor was about to force his way by, Bradley even went so far as to grab his coat and hold him back.

"Wait," he said, surprised at his own action. "You haven't told me everything, have you? – Is she still alive?"

"Would you please let go of my coat. I'm very busy. I've told you all I know. You'll have to speak to Doctor Haworth."

Part of Bradley's mind quite rationally accepted this and was perfectly willing to follow these simple instructions, firmly believing them to be the most sensible course of action and, bearing in mind the doctor's growing impatience, almost certainly the quickest way of finding out what, precisely, had happened. Quite detached from this, however, a separate portion of his brain, seemingly outside of his conscious control, ignored all reason and pursued this relentless harassment.

"Look," he said, drawing the white coat closer to him and grabbing the other lapel to make absolutely sure the doctor didn't escape, "I know you know something. You do know, don't you?" he sobbed and strove inwardly to regain control and cease these insane remonstrations. "What do you know?" he screamed. "Tell me." He shook the doctor's shoulders but, even as a still-rational part of his consciousness began to imagine porters bringing a stretcher and straitjacket, he felt his strength ebbing and his vision blurring from tears. He must be having some sort of breakdown, he thought, as he released his grip and, instead, stumbled for support. The anger and alarm in the doctor's expression turned to concern and an arm came around Bradley's shoulders as he was plied with questions whose meaning eluded him. A feeling of giddiness assailed him, as after a night's drinking when the concentration on other activities is removed and realization dawns that one is very drunk. He felt suddenly rather sick and attempted to rise to find his way to the 'Gents' but fell instead to the floor.

At a remote, disused airfield in the North of England, a group of businessmen gathered for an unscheduled flight to an alleged urgent meeting in London. An astute observer might have registered some surprise at the fact that most were accompanied by wives and children and he might have expressed cynical disbelief at the idea that they had all arrived to see off their husbands or fathers for such an apparently routine excursion. Indeed, he might have further wondered at the seemingly clandestine nature of the undertaking, such that a private jet was deemed necessary and a secret rendezvous. As yet, he would be unaware of the difficulties currently being experienced by passengers on commercial flights. Later that day, it would be announced that an unofficial strike by airport maintenance staff was causing some delays on overseas flights but only those unfortunate people, stranded amidst growing confusion in the congested departure lounges at the main airports, would be truly aware of the magnitude of this understatement.

If this mythical spectator were to have continued his unsolicited observations, his surprise would have been greatly increased when he saw the wives and children climb into the aircraft along with the men. Also, they were carrying an altogether unjustifiable amount of luggage for a business trip – no briefcase or lunch-box but suitcases of all sizes in vast numbers. As the plane taxied across the dangerously rutted and pebble-strewn runway, he might have mentally shrugged his shoulders and concluded that the outing was, in fact, a holiday, provided by the company out of the shareholders' money or some such artificial explanation. But perhaps a nagging doubt at the unorthodox nature of the venture might have lingered on, for the rest of the day, at least.

Had our observer been further equipped with a radio receiver in the band of aircraft frequencies, he would not have expected to hear any pre-flight communication with ground control for clearance since the derelict airfield supported no flight controllers or, indeed, staff of any description. He would have been astounded, however, to find no agreement of flight path, as the jet climbed rapidly to forty-thousand feet, directly into the main intercontinental air-lanes and set course on a direction which could in no way be construed as heading towards London.

The atmosphere inside the aircraft, too, showed none of the seriousness and sober discussion, which might have maintained the illusion of a business venture, nor yet any of the eagerness and expectation normally associated with families setting off on a holiday. Instead a tenseness and uneasiness pervaded the air: children cried and no one was laughing. Conversation was virtually non-existent. Occasionally, someone would speak, but it would be merely voiced thoughts, undirected and expecting no reply; speculations (though not idle) – what would happen; what were the chances; if this, if that, if only it were over. Each had his own ideas, hopes and fears, most felt essentially the same way, unable to think of anything else but unwilling to verbalize these emotions, reluctant to have someone else confirm their own worst thoughts. Now that it was actually happening, their fears justifiable, their minds were concentrated on the reality of the moment and the ways in which Fate might manage their immediate future – it was no time for talking.

On the flight deck, the owner of the jet, company director by profession, sat in the co-pilot's seat, headphones clamped over his ears, eyes flickering nervously from side to side as he listened in frightened anticipation for some sound to emerge. Here, too, there was no conversation, though the pilot at least had ample to occupy his mind, controlling, navigating and watching out for other aircraft, feeling the cold dead weight of responsibility. He knew that, should he detect the slightest glint of light in the distance, it could signal another airplane, possibly on collision course and he would have scarcely two or three seconds to avert a disaster.

The expected warning message came as they left the coast of

England behind and headed out over the Irish Sea. "This is an emergency interruption on all wavelengths. Would the aircraft heading west along flight path red-oh-seven please identify yourself? The aircraft in red-oh-seven, leaving North England, heading due west, you do not have clearance to use this airway. This is Preston air traffic control. Please identify yourself immediately and state your destination."

Assuming his practiced air of self-assurance, and with his acquired mastery of the art of bluff, the MD flicked the radio switch to transmit, relieved that at last the silence had been broken and that he could finally do something.

"Message acknowledged, Preston. This is reconnaissance flight zebra-one-nine-two. You should have notification of our flight path from London, Preston. I am not authorized to reveal it over the radio. I suggest you contact GCHQ, Colonel Hopper. Meanwhile, would you confirm red-oh-seven clear, over."

He turned to the pilot as he switched back to receive mode. "Are we flat out now?"

"Red-oh-seven clear," stated the voice. "Please maintain your height and direction. We have no record of your existence, zebra-one-nine-two. This is most irregular. Please clarify your situation, over."

"This is a classified mission, Preston. You must contact GCHQ. They will decide what information may be divulged. Colonel Hopper may be reached on 01752 436302, repeat 01752 436302, over."

"That should keep them quiet for a few minutes at least. We've just got to hope now. With a bit of luck, that radio operator will be a complete moron and will just go off and phone Roy on that number. There's certain to be a clearly established protocol for military flights, but as for what happens when that breaks down, who knows? He'll have to go to his boss and he'll have to go to his. People will be rushing around looking in manuals and sifting through red tape. By the time they decide what the correct procedure should be, it may be too late for them to do anything. They're hardly likely to send a fighter out to shoot us down, anyway, are they?"

"I don't know, but I'll be glad when this is over," was the terse answer he received.

In the event, no more was heard from Preston. It was impossible to pretend that this was altogether encouraging but they consoled themselves in believing the worst to be over. As their distance from England increased, so their fears of being discovered and somehow being prevented from leaving decreased and their spirits rose. The high-pitched whine of the engines, reduced to a hypnotic drone by the additional sound-proofing of the executive jet, soothed their tensions and, now that drinks had been served, the atmosphere was becoming almost relaxed.

This emotional change for the better, however, plotted against time or distance, seemed to reach a maximum as they passed mid-Atlantic. When one of the sales directors remarked in a typically loud voice that they would be in America in about three hours, the precarious balance of mood was disturbed again. Though everyone intuitively felt that they had passed the most serious hurdle, it was impossible to dispel the doubts and potential fears they had at being admitted without authorization, or prior notification, into the United States. They were not, of course, worried about their personal papers, all having current passports and visas for most countries, but the knowledge that they would be entering almost illegally inevitably stirred their consciences and led to considerable unease.

They would certainly not be treated with courtesy for their action. At the very least they would probably be subjected to a degrading search of their belongings and persons for smuggled goods or drugs. At worst, they might be forced to return after re-fuelling. This, they had already agreed, they could not do. It would mean searching for another country or island to admit them.

Contact came without warning. A sudden shout from the pilot over the address system brought the MD scurrying back to the flight deck.

"What the hell?" he began.

"Look," announced the other, pointing ahead through the windscreen. "US air force jets; two of them up ahead. It can't be coincidence they're here. They must have thought we were Russians or something. We ought to have radioed ahead."

"Jesus! Can you contact them?"

"They'll be in touch soon enough!"

"They're not going to like us for this are they; wasting their time sending out strike aircraft? Why haven't they got in touch yet?"

"Probably waiting for advice on what to do about us; finding out who we are and—"

At that moment, a voice came from the hitherto silent radio, an unemotional, military voice, yet seemingly threatening in an indefinable way.

"Calling Delta-Abel Four-Oh-Seven-Six. Please state your point of departure, purpose and destination, over."

"This is Delta-Abel Four-Oh-Seven-Six. Departed Nice, France, oh-nine-hundred hours; business trip; destination Kennedy Airport, over.

"We have no data on that flight; have reason to believe you left North England by deception early this morning. Do you deny this, over?"

The MD was rapidly fastening his mouth microphone into place and motioned excitedly to the pilot that he would take over.

"Sorry, do not understand you. We have been having problems with our radio and have been unable to contact Kennedy. We apologize most sincerely for any trouble we may have caused, over."

There was silence from the radio.

"I don't know what's going to happen now. I never imagined they'd send fighters out to us. Still, at least they can see that we aren't any threat now."

"What if they check out our story though?" asked the pilot, now sounding distinctly worried.

"Look, the worst that can happen is that we'll have to refuel and look elsewhere. We can try Mexico or the West Indies or even, if the worst comes to the worst, I'm sure Cuba would have us. And anyway—"

He was interrupted again by the radio. "Delta-Abel Four-Oh-Seven-Six. Your story does not check. Unless you provide a verifiable account of yourselves, we will conclude you are the aircraft posing as military reconnaissance flight Zebra-one-nine-two, reported leaving England four hours ago, over."

"Oh no! So they didn't forget about us, after all," moaned the pilot. "What do we do now?"

"Quiet." shouted the MD desperately before switching to 'transmit' again. "OK, we concede you're right but there's nothing mysterious about the situation. Our company is in imminent danger of a take-over; we have to consult our American interests urgently. We didn't have time to organize flights routinely; it all happened overnight. You must be aware by now of the strike by airport staff in England, over."

"Sorry. We are aware of the situation just as you obviously are. You will not be permitted to land in the USA. Please turn around immediately, over."

"But we don't have sufficient fuel to return. You must allow us to land to refuel for Christ's sake." The MD's voice now indicated growing concern. Things were beginning to get out of hand. They had not foreseen the situation becoming this desperate.

There was a long pause before further communication. The fighter's pilot was presumably reporting to base for further instructions. The director and his pilot did not speak but their expressions clearly revealed their inner turmoil.

"You will turn around within the next five minutes," reiterated the voice. "If you do not, we are authorized to force you to do so, over."

There was a moment of stunned silence and the MD swallowed dryly before he could bring himself to speak.

"They're bluffing. Good God, they've got to be bluffing. What the hell do they mean 'force us to turn round,' anyway? They can hardly use weapons against us, can they?" A note of desperation was creeping unmistakably into his voice. "What's the fuel situation, Joe?"

"We've enough for about ninety minutes or seven hundred miles. No way can we return to England without refueling."

"Right, we carry on then; call their damn bluff."

The next few minutes seemed endless. The two men could feel the beads of perspiration prickling their scalps as the adrenaline speeded their heart rates, heightening their awareness and subjectively slowing time as they anticipated the deadline. Neither spoke though their thoughts argued interminably, cyclically and inconclusively as to what the outcome might be. Their eyes flickered constantly back and forth attracted against their wills, alternately by the two aircraft flying ahead and by the clock on the panel in front of them, its second hand crawling its way seemingly so slowly yet mercilessly around the dial.

There was still some thirty seconds to go by the clock when the jets ahead both suddenly accelerated and climbed away from them and from each other, out of their direct view from the cabin windows.

"Calling Delta-Abel Four-Oh-Seven-Six. You have a final warning. Turn around immediately. Acknowledge, over."

"Don't answer!" commanded the MD tensely as, since he himself had made no move towards the radio, the pilot had reached out his hand to the switch.

"We have to turn," he began to object.

"Wait!"

They didn't have to wait long. A point of light glinted high to the left of their view and quickly grew in size until the jets again became recognizable, heading seemingly on a collision course. At the last moment, they pulled away and simultaneously several loud bangs erupted the length of the plane, followed by the whistling of sudden violent depressurization as their air rushed out through the torn fuselage.

"Jesus!" gasped the pilot, flicking the address system on, reflexively.

"Oxygen masks everyone, quickly. Pull down the handle above your seat; then get strapped in tight."

The next few minutes were chaotic and serious panic was only narrowly avoided by the authoritative reassurances of several of the passengers, who coordinated the emergency procedures. Eventually, although at a much lower altitude, they stabilized their situation and had time to consider their damage and prospects.

In fact, damage was surprisingly slight. Apparently the havoc had been caused by only three small bullet holes penetrating the skin of the aircraft and, fortunately, no one had been injured at all, though many were in a state of shock and some in need of attention. The shock extended too to the control cabin, where the confidence of the director had disappeared completely and left him in no state to make the sort of decisions now necessary to plot their next move. Unfortunately, he seemed unable to want to accept the extent to which his abilities had been sapped and it was with anger that he snatched at the microphone and shouted into it, "Are you mad? Don't you realize we have women and children on this plane? You could have killed someone. We don't have enough fuel to turn back, damn you. We're continuing on to Kennedy where we'll need to refuel and carry out repairs now. Just wait 'til the British government hears about this."

"Delta-Abel Four-Oh-Seven-Six. You will turn around now. If

you do not, your aircraft will be destroyed. Acknowledge, over."

"Wh... what?" asked the MD, automatically yet quietly, puzzled, disbelieving, sanity-leaving, his mind grasping out hopelessly at the enormity of what had been said. Then, failing, he turned back to his now totally irrational belief that it was all a bluff and with a final surge of anger, shouted down the microphone, "Go to hell." and flung it away from him.

"Maintain course!" he demanded, as his pilot glanced across, open-mouthed in disbelief. "Maintain course, you bastard!" he repeated, as the pilot began to look as though he would ignore the order.

He rose from his seat and leaned over to forcibly restrain the pilot as the other fought to turn the aircraft around. The struggle was short-lived only. Neither saw the streak of vapor, outlined against the sky momentarily and rapidly approaching the aircraft. Neither saw the expression on the other's face or had time to register the fact of the event as, with a tremendous explosion, the plane disintegrated and scattered its parts, and its occupants' parts, over several square miles of the Atlantic.

I no longer know who I am. No, worse, much worse than this, I am no longer sure what I am. There are even times when I cannot, with any certainty, say "I." I believe that some short time in the past I could have said, "I am Jack Spratt, and I heat fat for a living" or some such expression of identity and purpose. But now this knowledge is gone, following into obscurity the other finer details of existence which, it seems, disappeared long ago.

I have vague recollections still, occasionally, in these brief spells of relative clarity, when impressions from some distant dark sea of memory rise momentarily to the surface. They reveal themselves in an apparent isolation, which serves to represent them to that impartial observer (who no longer seems to be the 'I' that he once was) as 'true' as opposed to all the new sensory experiences that assault me from all sides. These memories – if that is what they are and not mere imagined ideas of greater power than the others – speak of no exciting past events but of a normalcy; of a time when one could know, from one minute to the next, that the situation would not change in an unexpected and unfathomable fashion. Indeed, the impression is of a stable or even humdrum existence; tedium – day following day without any real change; working manually without thought, without question, yet feeling sure of where and why; a continual reassurance of the maintenance of the status quo. Other, fleeting sensory data arise periodically but I can no longer connect them. I worry incessantly.

Let not the integrity of the Life Force be degraded, nor the purity of the Spirit be defiled. For even as the material universe plunges irreversibly into dark anarchic disorder so must the spiritual ascend to Truth and Light and Knowledge absolute. This is the aim and purpose. Pursue it unceasingly.

"Much worse I'm afraid; acute renal failure now. We'll have to put him on dialysis."

Earlier – again I have no feel for time, it may be minutes or months – there was much pain. I'm sure there was not always pain. A sudden onslaught; something happened. I don't know. I seem to think I slept. Yes, a long period of unconsciousness followed by an awakening to an agony of acute pain and local, general aching and body-wrenching torture. I passed out many times only to awaken to renewed suffering. The agony was such that I could only imagine that every organ in my body, every muscle and bone, was uprooting itself and rearranging the whole into some ghastly impossible configuration.

Though there was no associated pain in my head itself, I can easily believe that some similar activity was taking place in my brain, too. Despite any real knowledge to that effect, I somehow conceive that my mental activity and intellectual potential were far below the level they have now attained, and for which they are still reaching out. Yet I find a complete lack of an ability to communicate. My thoughts and cognitive processes continue to grow, seemingly out of control, but my command over what was my body and its associated sensory apparatus grow less in direct proportion. I can only assume I am dying. I am being prepared for heaven – or for hell.

In the void, in the silence, in the timelessness divorced from sentient experience of time, it moved. It had moved. It would continue to move. Journey was an inappropriate word, implying, as it does, a beginning and an end. Purpose was not in question, for the beginning was so rooted in the dimness of the past, and the end, as yet unforeseeable, that the conceptions of start and finish were all but meaningless. Motion was its perpetual state. Motion not only of its physical body through space, but incredible, unceasing motion of its parts within parts; gathering, collating, filing, retrieving, analyzing and making decisions.

In the stillness of time, in the emptiness of space, the movement registered as an infinitely slow but inexorable change of conditions, monitored, recorded, assimilated, each datum accruing to determine future action.

"Blood pressure still dropping; intense brain activity, despite the low oxygen intake. I don't understand; it just doesn't make sense."

The surroundings are quite alien. I feel sure this is outside any prior experience. I see a rugged mountain landscape set in a deep red valley. Yet the red is not of sand or rock; ferrous material eroded by successive ice ages and scorched by a desert sun. It is foliage, grass perhaps. Waves move gently across its surface, guided by a warm thick breeze carrying a faint scent of aromatic spices and something... indefinable.

A placid lake of a translucent pink lies half-hidden by larger clumps of the omnipresent dark red vegetation. Heat beats down out of a leaden steel blue-grey sky from two unequal spheres, one of intense yellow-white and the other a dull golden-orange, positioned at a thirty-degree angle to one another, each some fifteen degrees from the mid-heavens. Some winged monstrosity flashes past, as though caught only out of the corner of an eye in the midst of a blink; a sense of disproportion about its outline, huge yet inexplicably fast. The anticipated blast from the super-heated air, as the sound wave crashes past, fails to materialize – another dream image conjured from a diseased and failing mind. Angular growths of flowering shrubs tower in the immediate vicinity, their tops lost to view in the heat haze. A vague irregular buzzing or susurration, suggestive (yet not quite right) of insects, pervades the heavy air and alerts the senses.

And then there is a period of disorientation. The scene around me changes, yet does not change; my perception of it changes. My mind is betraying me; it is undergoing some wild hallucino-genic misinterpretation, temporarily lost to any form of conscious control. My senses disintegrate and rearrange in a novel form; diverge again into separate entities without meaningful relationships, only to merge yet again into a single, all feeling, seeing, smelling, hearing unity, and more.

I rise up high into the grey, grey void, far above the swaying, moving crimson fields, aloft alongside one of these ptero-dactylian shapes, whose actual outline still evades direct perception. Higher, still higher, faster, out towards the glaring ball of orange.

The patterns of stars in the blackness of nothingness altered fractionally as it sped ever onwards to its unknown destinations while they pursued their predestined paths through the heavens. It saw; measured changes of intensity and Doppler shifts; analyzed spectra: gamma, X-ray, UV, visible IR, microwave and radio emission;

computed probable origins and destinations and deduced the internal constituents, temperatures and life spans.

Radiation superimposed itself over and modulated the background noise of space. Radio waves, wavelengths spanning solar systems, originating from the centre of galaxies, strode across the universe, oblivious of obstacles. High energy X-rays from distant quasars slammed their way through the scattered atoms of matter. It heard; constantly collected data, calculated periodic fluctuations, pinpointing the positions of twinned neutron stars and deducing the locations of black holes.

Stray particles, some with half-lives of millions of years and some short-lived ones, born out of recent random events, impinged upon its surface, giving birth to hosts of new ones. It felt; counted numbers; determined energy and directions and inferred the nature of the original radiation and its likely origin.

"Emergency, nurse; oxygen for number four."

Higher now, higher; far above this oneirodynian landscape, reds differentiating themselves into crimsons, rust and vermilion. Some pattern here which yet eludes precise definition; no orderly segmentation into fields of various crop, nor demarcation of ditch or fence, rather a natural congregation of minds of like thought; a continental, vegetative cocktail party. And changing! Even in the moment of my observation, colors drift slowly, slowly, swaying in the heavy scented atmosphere. Here, scarlet merges along an edge with an adjacent deeper red; there a ripple of cadmium spreads outwards, introducing its own clear tone into the surrounding coral hues. The vast orchestration of color moves below me, playing out some complex, yet achingly beautiful symphony of light to the direction of an unseen conductor.

Then, suddenly, all is lost to view; vision reduced to almost nil. A soft yellow light bathes my aching body; the sound of rushing air combines with the shifting streams of flowing cloud-like substance to suggest an ever increasing rate of ascent, though with the disappearance of the scene below has gone all sense of my speed relative to it. When the train leaves the station, the scene outside the window appears momentarily to move away, but one can't maintain this deception for long. Here, however, the complete lack of any objects of familiarity would have convinced me that I was now stationary in a wind of dense yellow smoke, had I not believed myself to be ascending previously. I drift for an eternity; must now be close to death.

It drank deeply from the cold swift streams of radiation. It fed ravenously on the ultramicroscopic particles that were its fellow swimmers in this sea of night. It breathed freely in the clean near vacuum, tasting the delicate flavor of atoms and savoring the pungent smell of ions. It reveled in the play of the neutrinos as they passed through unheeding, unfeeling, at the speed of light.

The whole mass of data, endlessly accumulating, was broken down, correlated and, out of it, the quintessential facts and deductions stored away in its memory, atomic configurations linking up where information was interrelated or dependent, neuronal pathways growing and merging as data assumed a meaningful interpretation.

Occasionally, out of the immense influx of radiation, a spectrum would speak of intelligence. This was no random fluctuation or even the regular pulses of a natural phenomenon but a complex overlay of pattern and form. Rare indeed was a coherent directed beam of intelligible information, which could be analyzed and deciphered, but from the fragments, a source could often be postulated and it would alter course accordingly and move towards it to collect more data.

"I doubt if he'll last 'til morning Mrs. Bradley. I'm sorry. He does seem to be sleeping peacefully now and we don't think there's any pain."

I think I awoke because of lack of air. Out of the clouds now; clear, washed-out sky and atmosphere thinning fast. One of the suns has sunk below the horizon whilst I slept; the other looms larger now, seemingly, intense orange balloon of nuclear activity drawing me ever upwards while the undulating layers of yellow and brown recede beneath me, and time is withdrawn.

An infinity of blackness, unrelieved by the faintest twinkling reassurance of a distant star – this is the one half of my vision. The other is now unseen because unseeable, but its presence is felt increasingly. Its light alone would be sufficient to overload my retinas beyond repair a thousand times over, were I able to force my head to turn to look. Its ultra violet radiation has turned my skin to a blackened onion shell; its infrared bakes my body and has left it now almost without moisture. Why I still live, I cannot tell. The pain is almost beyond endurance. I am going to scream. A tortured cry of frustration and impotence would rise from my throat, were there any water to lubricate it. An agonized shout of despair would fly unbidden from my lungs, were there any air to fill them. I scream, long and silently.

Silent, watching and waiting as thoughts and actions filtered through time laying down the sediments of history and building towards an ever more predictable future.

"I'm sure he's dead now, Doctor. He's been on the respirator for over an hour with no response at all. And yet his body temperature is still increasing, over 150 now. It seems impossible, but there it is."

Another re-awakening. No, not that, a re-birth, a new life. i am still me, yet i am more; we are more. i do not understand.

i sense the landscape of my original vision; a feeling of redness, which concept though has no further meaning, for i see beyond this. Peace, serenity, a gentle, warm breeze blows through our stems. Quiet, yes, but i hear much more, a replacement of its nature and purpose by something far subtler, and at the same time far more powerful. i do not use it yet, fearing its latent energy but i am aware of its presence all around, reassuring, but awesome.

The smell that i detected previously is here again now, far stronger though, transposed into something more intimate. i, we, bend and sway in the thickly scented air, knowing a peace never before experienced. The pain was a refining fire to prepare me for such bliss.

i must now, however, cross the final barrier. The force around me knows no impatience, but gently prods my individual consciousness from time to time, to remind me of the step to be taken. i realize what must be done and no longer feel the trepidation which the initial idea caused me. Soon, all will be understood. Already, i believe i know the truth; now it will be revealed.

i open out my consciousness and let the force flood in. i let go my attachments to the body, to the past, now all seen to have been illusion – delusion. i surrender my mind to the unity. i become one with the red grass. I am one; I am free; I rejoice and exult that all is good. All is existence, consciousness and bliss. i am nothing; I am everything.

I bow to you from in front and from behind – indeed from all sides. Your energy is limitless; your power infinite. You are everywhere; therefore you are everything. XI.40

"There will shortly be a nation-wide broadcast by the Prime Minister on the present crisis. The broadcast will be transmitted on all BBC and ITV television channels and on all national radio stations. It is possible that someone in your neighborhood does not have access to a TV or radio or is unaware that the broadcast is to take place. It is imperative that everyone be acquainted with the details of the bulletin. Therefore, it is requested that each person check with his immediate neighbors that they are watching or listening. If they have no receiver of their own, invite them into your home. This is an emergency. Do not, however, use your landline to contact relatives or friends; their neighbors will be notifying them in a similar manner and trunk lines must be reserved for urgent calls only. The exception to the use of telephones in this way is if you live in a remote area and need to use it to contact your neighbor. You may use your mobiles but you can expect congestion and delays; this also applies to internet communications and access. The broadcast will begin in thirty-five minutes.

"There will shortly be a nation-wide...

"As most of you are only too well aware, the nation is in the grip of an epidemic more serious than any since the middle ages. It is deadly, let there be no doubt about this. But I believe that our scientists, who are working with all the single-mindedness and dedication which has made British scientists renowned and respected throughout the world, will very soon now find a cure, vaccination or treatment for the illness, if only they can be given time. It is our duty to give them that time by preventing the spread of the disease. It is to this end that I am speaking to you now. Please listen carefully and obey our instructions to the letter.

"First of all, we know the source of the infection to be contained in the pollen of the new species of grass recently observed about the countryside. This is readily identifiable by its characteristic red coloration, though this may vary from copper through to dark crimson.

"If you see any, do not approach it. Note its position and report it immediately to your nearest emergency station. The location of these will be sign-posted at all major road junctions and a map showing the route to your local centre will be delivered to all households. You may also inform them via the Internet. Full details, a transcript of this announcement and all of the latest information will be posted to this site: www.gov.uk/red-grass/.

"Secondly, because the infection is carried by air-borne pollen, you are at risk whenever you are out of doors; city dwellers are no less vulnerable than those who live in the country. Avoid going outside if you can. If you must, wear a scarf or handkerchief around your nose and mouth at all times. Those of you who volunteer for emergency service, as I am sure many of you will, will be issued with a mask. When inside, keep all doors and windows closed. Avoid unnecessary contact with other people. The disease is not believed to be communicable in its early stages but after death the organs generate spores which will transmit the illness.

"The initial symptoms are dizziness, accompanied by periodic blackouts or hallucinations. If you believe you may have become infected, do not contact others in person. Return home, if not already there. If you have a telephone, phone your emergency centre, not, repeat, not, your doctor or hospital. Do not call for an ambulance – these have been requisitioned and will be used and coordinated by the centers. Having notified them, you will eventually be transferred to the nearest available treatment area, which may be a hospital, school, church or alternative accommodation, as appropriate and available at the time. If you do not have a telephone, hang a white sheet or garment out of the window. Police cars will be patrolling constantly and your situation will be reported within a very short space of time.

"Do not attempt to leave your locality. Roadblocks will be installed to prevent movement between towns. It is essential that we try to contain the spread of any infection. Even less will you be able to leave the country. The rest of the world has been informed of our situation and Britain is now effectively in quarantine.

"Above all, do not panic. Assist the authorities in every possible way, and follow any official instructions you may be given. If you wish to provide more positive help in this, your country's gravest hour of need, report to your nearest police station where further details will be made available or visit the website. I believe that together, as a nation, we are capable of dealing with this situation, however serious it may be, provided that we all act in a reasonable and responsible manner and do not deviate from the simple rules that I have outlined.

"Colonel Adamson of the British Army will now describe in greater detail how the emergency centers will be organized and how the army intends to administrate during the crisis."

I am Time, destroyer of worlds, come forth to annihilate this world. Even without any help from you, all of these warriors arranged here in battle will cease to exist. XI.32

"Did you hear about the Centrepoint take-over yesterday?" Doctor Meredith Wilson leaned back, lifting the front legs of his chair from the ground and resting his knees against the desk. He rotated the pencil carefully but pointlessly between the middle finger and thumb of his right hand.

"No," answered his assistant, Ruth Maxwell, without obvious interest, not even looking up from the figures which she was studying intently.

"No, I don't suppose you would have really; they're suppressing all that sort of information now. Anyway, I have it on good authority that about a hundred louts from the country suddenly appeared in Tottenham Court Road, armed with spades and pickaxes, and forced their way into Centrepoint. They unloaded canned food and other stuff from several vans and barricaded themselves in. Closed all the windows, switched the air-conditioning on full and settled in for the summer, so to speak. 'Course, it didn't last very long. After the police had failed to persuade them that they were being rather unreasonable about it all, they switched off the electricity.

"Funny, really, isn't it? After all this time, with so many people moaning about life in the cities, pollution, noise and what have you; unable to wait to get out to the country away from it all; now they're all going back again. Do you know you can hardly get on to the platform in the Underground? So many people are camping out down there, the police can't do a thing about it. It's worse than the Blitz, I hear.

"Ironic, isn't it, all the silly things people are doing, trying to get away from something they've probably never even seen and, for them, nowhere is really safe. Yet here, we're only about ten feet away from that very same source of horror and fear; that apocalyptic horse straight out of Pandora's Box, to mix a few metaphors, and yet we're safer than anybody. Good Grief, I hope it doesn't enter into anyone's head to break into this place."

"I wouldn't have thought so. They're running away from that thing. They're hardly likely to want to sit in the same room staring at it, even if it is behind three inches of armor-plated glass."

"Yes, they'd probably try to break the glass and set about it with a blowtorch." Wilson's exceedingly low opinion of the intelligence of the 'man-in-the-street' was notorious.

"In any case, it's not public knowledge that we have any of the grass here," added Ruth.

"True, I doubt that anyone's likely to think of a biological research station as a refuge, far too clever. Yet, of course, it's ideal. Complete isolation; comfortable living quarters," he glanced around, his expression matching the sarcastic tone with which he had uttered the comment, "air perfectly clean, cycled and filtered, oxygenated and de-ionized; own generators; endless supply of filthy coffee. We don't know how lucky we are! As far as the GP knows, this place is stocked with a variety of the nastiest nasties known to man, from obsolete smallpox virus to the very latest models of Gamma-Di, though on second thoughts, perhaps they don't know anything about that – at least I hope not. Anyway, they won't come banging on our door very readily. Unless, that is, it leaks out that, in fact, we have the best biological nuts in the country, concentrating their tiny minds on just one nasty; the one to end them all apparently, the red grass itself."

"Have you had any ideas yet then?" asked Ruth, now looking earnestly up from her work.

"I never cease to have ideas, my dear girl; it's merely a question of waiting for the right one. After all, everyone else is looking at the obvious, collecting facts and figures, taking photographs, weighing and measuring. What we want is inspiration. Perhaps they'll find the solution via the obvious but, if they don't, the answer, if there is one, will be found by the devious.

"In the meantime, however, until something original occurs to me, I think we'll just have to see if we can communicate with it. Will you get on to it? We'll probably want some equipment that's not in stock."

"Sorry, Merry, I don't know what you're talking about."

"Good grief, woman, don't you ever read any interesting scientific literature? There were lots of fascinating articles back in the nineteen seventies, in Psychic News and other such journals, about connecting plants up to some sort of lie detector.

"Apparently it all started more or less by accident. They had a plant wired up, to detect changes in surface characteristics of the leaf, under the effects of light and temperature. Anyhow, it occurred to the sadistic character that was conducting the experiments to put a lighted match under one of the leaves. He didn't actually do it, mind you, just thought about it. And, so the story goes, the pen that was tracing the voltage changes shot off the graph paper at precisely the moment that the idea had entered his head.

"From there, the stories got more and more preposterous. They had plants testifying against people who had mown their lawns that day. 'Course, they claimed that there was a 'rational' explanation behind it: the resonance effect of a basic Life Force, possessed by all living things but not yet scientifically quantified. Pseudo-scientific mumbo-jumbo; you know, Kirlian photographs and all that."

"No, I'm afraid I don't. It all sounds rather farfetched to me. We have a very serious problem here, possibly the most serious ever faced by the human race, and all you can do is think about some humbug article in Psychic News."

"My dear young lady, *I* may patronize and sneer; *you* may not. Anyway, that was all well over a quarter of a century ago. They call it 'DMILS' these days, 'Direct Mental Action with Living Systems'; sounds impressive, don't you think? In these more enlightened times, they've demonstrated that the experimental conditions back then were somewhat suspect, to say the least. Not surprising really, the sort of person who got involved in those things tended not to be the most rigorous of scientific practitioners; sloppy technique, poor calibration of instruments, inadequate preparation of samples, no controls, etc. etc. When a group of 'proper' scientists attempted to repeat the same experiments they found nothing at all. Nowadays, they're more interested in trying to make bowls of blood go off by staring at them, although where they got that idea from, I can't imagine.

"Still, one can't help wondering at how frequently scientists find what they expect to find. They start off with some vague theory or other and think of a test that they can do to prove it. And, surprise surprise, if they ignore one or two spurious bits of data, they can often confirm the theory. Yes, OK," he held up his hands as if to ward off an attack from his assistant, "I know I'm being overly cynical. I apologize.

"Now, I'm not interested in repeating those particular experiments. After all, they were fairly crude back in those days. No, I want to use the very latest equipment. There's something called a 'plethysmograph' I believe. It's used for measuring pressure and flow of blood in the arteries and veins in the body, to monitor congestion and so on. It's extremely sensitive and can be used on small capillaries as well as larger vessels. The best models come with computer interfaces and Windows Software. I want you to get on the phone and start making enquiries. We want the best that money can buy and we want it by this afternoon. If that stuff really is from another planet, it may just prove to be more intelligent than you are."

Pure knowledge is that by which one sees the one limitless being in all creatures, undivided in the apparently separate. XVIII.20

The summer had been long and hot. It was still hot, though it was now August. And it had been dry. Many areas were now under enforced drought conditions, with some reservoirs showing only cracked earth for the top few feet. Forest fires were rife and the fire services were strained to their limit, with one rather odd difference – many were now not quite so eager to put out the fires. They were willing to contain them, yes; keep them away from habitation, yes, but extinguish them out in the dried up countryside, where the grass was straggly and sickly yellow and occasionally red and very sickly – no. And not all the fires were started naturally, either – a piece of broken glass catching the searing rays of the midday sun and concentrating them on to the parched tinder of dried vegetation was the least likely of causes. The carelessly dropped match was often in reality very carefully positioned, with paper or even paraffin or petrol added, just to make sure. Arson had become a national pastime out in the country. Even in the town, green lawns, beckoning on a lazy Sunday afternoon, were rare indeed. And the sun had not yellowed them, either. If the conscientious owner did not remove the 'health hazard' himself, his neighbor or local GVG (Grass Vigilante Group) was sure to oblige.

So far, most trees and many flowers remained unscathed,

though the days of such unfortunate specimens as Copper Beech and the many varieties of Acer were definitely numbered, as the more botanically ignorant of the populace indulged in a little overkill.

The government had made available some of the more noxious of the defoliants, used with such devastating effectiveness decades ago in Vietnam. Although initially only the armed forces and police had been given access to them, it was only a short time before virtually anyone could, and did, obtain a supply. Their effectiveness against the grass turned out to be doubtful but that did not prevent their widespread use. Whatever the outcome of the crisis, Britain had been changed disastrously. Whole areas of productive land had been laid waste. If only ten per cent of the population survived the plague, they would find it difficult to produce sufficient food. Grain and vegetables would not grow for years, or would at least be inedible. Livestock would find no grass to graze. It was the start of a fight for survival of epic proportions but one thing was sure – Britain was finished as a country significant in world affairs. Its economy was being systematically reduced to that of a third world nation.

The British Isles was under the strictest quarantine. The combined navies of the world patrolled the seas, while satellites watched for the slightest sign of movement in the air.

But the most advanced of technologies could not prevent the movement of dust and pollen in the higher atmosphere nor the migration of bird and insect...

It was the most embarrassing week for the security services since the summer of 1998. Back then, teenage hackers from Cloverdale California had instigated what Deputy Defense Secretary John Hamre had called 'the most organized and systematic attack the Pentagon has seen to date.' This was the week in which the special group set up to track down Adi-Mendel, announced their findings, or lack of them, to Government and asked for permission to abandon their attempts. The investigation had been headed by a unit at GCHQ, working in conjunction with the Air Force Information Warfare Center (AFIWC) at Kelly Air Force Base, near San Antonio, Texas. Together they constituted the elite of the world's hackers and crackers. Nothing relating to computers and networks was beyond their capability – until now. They had failed and this was keenly felt. But it was not their blackest day – that was to be on the day immediately following the acknowledgement of their failure by their masters.

In England, it was a junior minister in the Foreign Office, rejoicing in the improbable name of Auberon Oxtoby-Ffitch, who had the honor to inform his superiors about the news. He had never wanted to change his name, and did not suffer the handicap of a domineering father, so his nature was readily deducible as self-confident in the extreme, egotistical and extravert. He was also physically tough and above average height and build. Accordingly he was not at all perturbed at the prospect of having to upset many and cause consternation throughout the higher reaches of government and military circles.

It was an email on the secure network that brought the news, routed from a friend of his in the US senate, someone who had the free time, and inclination to waste it surfing the Internet. *Hi, Berry*, it began, this being the nickname he had suffered amongst his closest friends since his days at public school. *I see your lot have had a change of heart, then. I am impressed. I think it's very laudable that you should inform the people about what's happening. Who's the guy that's producing these pages? The design and presentation is out of this world! But have you really authorized him to put out all that philosophy shit as well? I would have thought most people would be more interested in how to get off with as many women as possible, as safely as possible, before the end comes so to speak. To get to the point, though, are you sure that we have been told officially that you were going to do this? I can't find anyone around here that knew anything about it. There's going to be hell to pay if you haven't gone through appropriate clearance channels first. Be seeing you (or then again, perhaps I won't. Damn!) Harrison.*

Oxtoby-Ffitch was momentarily at a loss. He had no idea what Harrison was talking about. And obviously he could not ask for details, since that would announce his ignorance and, much worse, make the government look as though it was not in control of events. He was thinking through the likely routes by which his friend might have found something revealing and re-reading the message for clues when the light on his keyboard winked again to indicate another incoming email. He opened the relevant window and found a second message on the external secure link.

Just in case you don't know the address, it's www.gov.uk/red-grass/– Harrison. Trust him! He had obviously guessed that Auberon had not known about this release of information. But it made it doubly embarrassing that Harrison was sarcastically pointing him to their own site!

Quickly, he clicked on the address. The browser window appeared and a new index web page loaded immediately. Auberon, too, was impressed. This had not been produced by anyone within the department, of that he was certain – far too professional. Whoever it was could certainly get a job as a web designer any time, even in the competitive and oversubscribed field that this had become in the past twenty years. The intro-ductory screen captured the viewer immediately, yet without any of the unsubtle elements of 3D animations or pulsating, color-shifting text. The title, in simple, heavy bold, sans-serif capitals, was blood red, raised above the background to show a cutout effect of the same letters beneath. 'Red Grass Roots' it announced simply. The central logo in an oval frame, fading and merging into the background at the edges, showed a swathe of red grass moving across an attractive rural landscape, with a couple picnicking by a stream, the hanging branches of a willow providing shade from a hot summer sun. As the grass passed by, the figures were transformed into skeletons, with the trunk of the tree turning into a gravestone and the branches dissolving into falling snowflakes, turning the sun into a cold, full moon. At the same rate, the title changed color until it was a deep midnight blue with a faint twinkling of stars in the depths of the letters. He shivered as he watched it.

He clicked on the picture, expecting the next screen to be loaded. Instead, the whole picture faded and a number of new ones gradually assembled themselves as links to the various parts of the site. There was a view of what he assumed to be strands of genetic material. Cross-links formed as the picture completed itself. He moved the cursor over the image and, instead of a simple description associated as straight text in the HTML code, a heading appeared, floating above the image and casting a very real looking shadow. The other links included a recognizable view of the electron microscope scan of the plague virus, several links to sites such as the EVA in America and one to Frank Bradley's homepage, the guy who had been involved at the start of all this. There was also a conspicuous link to a site with the intriguing, if seemingly irrelevant heading 'What do you want?' This must be the aspect to which Harrison had been referring. He jabbed his pen at the corresponding location on the graphics tablet to activate the link.

An index to the key locations remained on display as icons surrounding the main window, which was irregular in shape with the tattered edges and texture of a rich vellum scroll. He read quickly through this introductory text.

What do you want?

Ever since mankind attained self-consciousness, this is perhaps the question that has been of most relevance to the individual.

'What do I want (now, from life, work, partner etc.?)' Following closely upon this was the question 'How can I get it (more easily, quickly, cheaply etc.?)'

Whenever he analyzed this more carefully, he probably told himself that, whatever the immediate answer might be, what he was **really** looking for was happiness. If asked what is meant by that word, most people might have some difficulty formulating a reply but they usually believe that getting what they want at this particular moment is the first step along the way towards that end.

Once upon a time, the desires of the typical human were simple, if not always so easily satisfied – somewhere to live (safe from saber-tooth tigers,) a ready supply of water and access to food, a mate. Civilization has made these available to most people so that their lack is no longer such a concern. Does this mean that people are now generally happier than they used to be? Or is it the case that, as society has developed and satisfied the basic needs, it has simultaneously generated desires for other objects, so that happiness remains elusive and imagined to be dependent upon increasingly sophisticated acquisitions?

This egotistical demand for something 'for me,' to make me happy, regardless of how it might affect others, or other life on the planet, has burgeoned with time instead of decreasing, even though people have become more intelligent, educated, and aware of the ecosystem. Once upon a time, the most that a person might do was to pollute his own immediate environment, make his home dirty and his garden or field unproductive. Since the industrial revolution, it has become increasingly possible for him to pollute and destroy on a grand scale, eliminating species and making the environment unable to sustain others as well as himself. Being able to do this, of course, does not mean that it has to happen. Responsibly used, technologies can optimize conditions for man without upsetting the balance. Unfortunately, the continual striving for profit (in order to gain more money for 'me' and hence more material possessions and supposed ultimate happiness) has meant that responsibility has taken second place to expedience. 'If something can be done and the result is something we want, what the hell – let's do it!'

Inevitably, the growing capability of technology, and the insatiable demands of the consumer, have meant that research in all areas of science has continued without thought of morality or potential consequences for life on this planet. As soon as new techniques become possible, governments and companies begin calculating how to use them to their advantage and/or to the detriment of competitors or enemies. And hardly anyone ever gives thought to long term effects on themselves, other species or the environment. Even with the hindsight of earlier disasters such as DDT or CFCs, universities and private companies rushed to join the genetic engineering race, lured by dreams of cures for everything and food for nothing. Yet no one could have failed to realize, in his or her occasional moments of reflection, that the potential for disaster in this field exceeded everything that had gone before, even the splitting of the atom.

And so we come to pollution from toxic waste, the possibilities of bioremediation and the red grass..."

Oxtoby-Ffitch could understand Harrison's reaction to this and, probably better than he could, imagine how his masters would respond. This was the tone of activists, not of a government organization, even if Auberon privately agreed with the sentiments being expressed. He clicked on one of the more technical links. The actions of NDA and their consequences were spelled out in unambiguous terms, full of details to which no private individual should have had access. Clearly someone must have leaked classified documents. Auberon read on in horrified fascination, all of this data being quite new to him and telling of a situation far worse than he had imagined.

He wasn't altogether sure that this 'philosophical content' deserved the opprobrium of his American friend. It certainly seemed worthy of consideration and he would be very interested to read the rest of the material. Unfortunately, he realized that he had to contact his minister as soon as possible to inform him about the hacking into the government site, so that some remedial action could be taken if it were not already too late. He would have to return to read the rest at a later time if he had the opportunity. He picked up the phone and keyed in the digits to make a direct call to the minister's private mobile, something he had never before had cause to do. It was answered quickly, since instructions were that it should only be used in an emergency.

"Sorry to bother you, sir but…"

To say that his superiors were not amused was far more of a clichéd understatement than usual. They were embarrassingly appalled; everyone was looking for a scapegoat, whilst simultaneously doing their utmost to ensure that this did not turn out to be themselves. The news reached the Prime Minister within minutes, interrupting a cabinet meeting and bringing proceedings to a temporary halt. The instructions were clear and to the point – 'find out who was responsible, wherever he might be, and bring them into the Presence. Meanwhile, get rid of all trace of this material.'

Needless to say, this was less easily complied with than commanded. This was on two counts. The first of these was the more obvious, inevitable because of the delay before the ministry had been informed. Quite simply, various people around the world had found the site, recognized that, in all likelihood, it contained material that the government had not intended should be made public, and they had copied it. As soon as the site was closed down, they would re-instate it on other servers – and there was not a lot that anyone could do about this. The other reason was much more surprising and alarming. The web master for the Environment Agency, which was responsible for the government site, naturally denied all knowledge of it; this was to be expected. However, having been instructed to remove it from the server, he was unable to locate it. He continued to claim that it was not there, showing his boss a printout of the relevant directories, whilst at the same time admitting that he was able to call it up from his PC via the web. He was totally unable to offer any explanation, other than that the operating system had been corrupted in some fiendishly clever manner, such that normal functionality was apparently retained, yet incorrect information was given to the operator.

It was at this point that the task was handed over to the specialist group who, still in shock from the failure of their prior assignment, had not yet decamped to the pub, there to get pissed and forget, for a while, their tarnished self-image. They set to it with a renewed enthusiasm, seeing this as an opportunity to redeem themselves. With their abundance of skills and experience, if *they* could not understand and unravel this mysterious skein of computing illogic then no one could. They emerged much later in the day subdued and more frustrated than ever. 'What's happening is not possible' was the most informative comment that they could offer. Even closing down the server in question – an extreme measure – had not prevented the website from being returned using the same URL. Clearly the addresses must have been picked up and amended by other servers en route, in order to point to pages replicated at other locations. This in itself was not particularly clever but they had been unable to find any evidence that this was actually taking place; furthermore, they had failed to locate any computer that was actually holding the information. Attempts to follow the route of the data back to source had failed, with addresses becoming invalid beyond the first few links. The perpetrator had to have direct hardware access to many of the servers in each country or 'hidden instructions' in the switching centers – something that seemed extremely improbable. Without a doubt, it was the most embarrassing week for the security services.

"Well, it looks impressive doesn't it? You'd better get on and read all the manuals – find out how to set up the computer interface and…" he paused. "In fact, no, the first thing we must do is find out how to wire the detectors up to the grass. We may well need to acquire some more hardware. I don't suppose the designers gave any thought to our unique requirements!"

"Are you positive there's not something more useful we could be doing?" asked Ruth, not wanting to be overly critical of this, admittedly, extremely clever scientist, but unable to stop the skeptical outburst.

"Look, Ruth, there are brilliant scientists all over the world doing all of the obvious, 'useful' things. I doubt there's any logical area of study that isn't being replicated several times over. If any of those approaches are going to lead anywhere, they'll find them. Having us repeat the same tests will not further those objectives; our experimental techniques are no better. Anyway, I've always fancied doing some experiments in the fringe areas of science and parapsychology.

"There's an awful lot of bigotry on both sides. You know, it may seem that the so-called psychical researcher will believe anything and refuse to be convinced of the silliness of some of the ideas perpetrated under the guise of psychic phenomena. But, conversely, the more reactionary of the scientists won't believe anything unless it has a rock-solid foundation in physics and mathematics. I'm damn sure that the former is the healthier attitude, even if it does leave the way open for cranks and charlatans. The scientist's mind just seems to switch off immediately anyone mentions ESP or PK. Even things like life fields, which have a fair bit of bona fide scientific research behind them, are derided by your average scientist, who almost certainly hasn't even made any effort to look at the literature on the subject. We're supposed to be so impartial, judging results purely on their merit, without any emotional or subjective bias but how many do?

"Take black holes, for example. How many scientists understand the mathematics involved in their postulation? How many astronomers know what really happens beyond the event horizon? How many people have seen a black hole? Even the nearest contender is tens of light years away, yet no one really considers them with total disbelief, or regards the astronomers involved in their study with contempt. Most scientists are perfectly prepared to accept their existence without the slightest shred of first-hand evidence.

"And then, on the other hand, consider something like those experiments carried out by that German chap years ago – Herschel, Heinkel or something. No, Schmidt, that was it, Helmut Schmidt. He built this device whereby radioactive decay caused rows of lights to be lit one at a time in a totally random manner. Now, if you ask any scientist whether it's possible to affect physically the rate of radioactive decay of an element, he'll answer quite categorically that it is not.

"Anyway, this chap carried out two types of tests with various people, who in no way claimed to have any special powers, mind you. In the first set of experiments, the subject had to try to guess which light would come on next, i.e. to test for precognition. In the second set, the subject actually had to try to make one specific lamp light more frequently i.e. to look for evidence of psychokinesis. Thousands and thousands of results were collected and analyzed and proved statistically, beyond any possibility of doubt, that people could a) predict and b) affect random external events.

"Yet what's happened to this work? Nothing – ignored, as were all the Rhine experiments before it, though admittedly, Rhine's methods have been largely discredited now. Even though they'll admit that the circumstances of the experiments allowed no room for fraud, they're still not interested. You know, I read somewhere the other day that someone had stated that, rather than believe some of the conclusions logically deducible from the results of experiments like this, he would rather conclude that the science of statistics itself was in error.

"Part of the problem, I suppose, was the abandoning of Bayes' Theorem in favor of Fisher's 'p-values' as the method for determining whether results were statistically significant. All Fisher does is tell us how likely the observed result would be, assuming it was due to chance. What we really want to know is how likely it is that chance is actually *responsible* for the observed effect. Bayes may initially allow the believer to prove that something he believes is true and allow the skeptic to prove it false but, as data accumulate, everyone gets driven to the same conclusion."

Karma – the lawful consequence of Action

You will probably have asked yourself how it can be that such a thing as this can happen. It all seems rather like some sort of biblical plague sent by God as punishment for the moral decline of society. AIDS didn't work so He decided to try something a bit stronger.

Under the heading of *karma yoga*, we talked briefly about how we should act in a way which 'leaves no trace' in our subtle body. *Karman* itself means 'action'. When people talk about *karma* as a sort of principle, in relation to reincarnation for example, they are really referring to *karmaphala*, the 'fruit of action.' Everyone in the modern world is happy with the idea of cause and effect in a physical sense. If you are clumsy and knock over a cup of coffee, you are not surprised at having a mess to clean up afterwards. Yet when someone tries to relate this to the things we do that are not obviously physical, we have difficulty. We think it unreasonable to suppose there will be some sort of repercussion if we go around being rude to everyone. Or on second thoughts, perhaps this is not so unbelievable. If, one time, someone turns round and thumps us, perhaps we might see that this was inevitable sooner or later! But if, on the other hand, we always went around being nice to everyone, out of a desire to be liked by them, we would find it hard to believe that this was building up some kind of reaction for the future. But the concept of *karma* tells us that this is indeed the case.

If we have **any** motive for our action, rather than just responding to a need in front of us, then the action will not be 'clean' or 'pure;' it will have a consequence for us in the future. Good motives will reap good consequences, called *puNya*. This will bring comfort, wealth, position and so on. Bad motives will reap undesirable consequences, called *papa*. These bring discomforts, poverty, disease etc. And these consequences stay with us until they have been played out, so to speak. If they are not exhausted in this life, they will carry forward to a future reincarnation. So the story goes. This is another aspect of *mAyA* i.e. it is ultimately illusory. As stated earlier, we are not our body and do not die when it dies. Since we are really one Self, present everywhere and always, who is there to be reincarnated? In this apparent creation, however, the causes have their effects and at the level of the individual, there appears to be rebirth.

Karma, you see, has rather a lot to do with what is happening in the world today. We are living in what will probably be the most significant moment in the history of humanity. Cause and effect operates at the level of nations and, indeed, the universe, as well as at the individual level. It cannot reasonably be expected that you can carry on in total oblivion, or at least complete disregard of your planet without, eventually, some of the *papa*, resulting from all of your past actions, coming to maturity. Even scientists have come to realize this over the past few decades, though they have been having a hard time convincing the politicians to pay attention. Even in respect of the discovery of the depletion of the ozone layer and the dire consequences of carrying on polluting the atmosphere, scientists quickly recognized the causes and identified the remedies but did anyone do anything? It took years before any real changes were being implemented. Even now some of the developing nations carry on regardless. No, I'm afraid that profit and popularity continue to motivate the policy makers.

Well, I'm afraid it is time for the debts to be called in, time for the wind to blow away the dust of indifference and procrastination. This is the metaphor at the gross level. At the subtle level we can use it in a different way – time for the wind of wisdom to blow away the dust of ignorance. Again let me emphasize, there must be no sense of 'punishment' here. Consciousness is quite indifferent to the outcome – it is all part of the enjoyment of the play. It is simply a matter of *karma*.

What about free will? Free will and *karma* go together really. If there is none of the former, there is none of the latter either, and so it is in reality! (In fact, of course, even your Theory of Relativity says as much. Since time exists only as an integral part of a four-dimensional space-time continuum, all of our past and future as well as the present moment must be laid out in a single, already-existing pattern. What will happen already exists in another part of the continuum. Nothing we do could change this; we must be bound to do whatever is the necessary consequence of our past actions. Free will is an illusion. You do still have the Uncertainty Principle at the quantum level to give you a potential get-out for all of this but let's face it, so-called 'modern' science doesn't really understand any of this!)

This philosophy acknowledges that the world seems to be real – in the darkness of our ignorance, we see a snake, even though there is only a rope. While we continue to live in this state of delusion, believing that we act, we will appear to have free will and there will appear to be *karma*. Indeed, while we believe in the world and duality, we must play by the rules and those rules include free will, cause and effect, *karma* and all of the happiness and pain that go with these. It is all quite lawful and intrinsic to the relative world in which we believe ourselves to be. But we create our own heaven and hell because of our failure to see the unity of all things.

"Now, we need those leads and contacts fed in through the airlock. There should be more than enough connections available in the cabinet; all of the terminals have matching letters inside and out so you shouldn't have any difficulty wiring everything up. Make sure the capillaries aren't trapped anywhere. Can I leave that to you, Ruth?

"I'll scan through these articles to refresh my memory on the original procedures. We'll have to adapt them quite a bit. This equipment's rather more sophisticated than the stuff that was used before. A bit like using the latest multi-processor PCs instead of a slide rule, in fact."

The purpose of the leaves was, as yet, not clearly understood. The plant was effectively saprophytic (or at least this was the nearest descriptive term for any similar terrestrial plant) and thus the leaves were not used for photosynthesis and had none of the corresponding cells for this purpose. Nevertheless, nutrients were collected by the root system and passed via a central core of vascular tissue, corresponding to the xylem, up to the aerial parts of the plant. Thus there was a system present which was amenable to monitoring using the plethysmograph.

"Right," said Wilson, sometime later, rubbing his hands in anticipation. Are we ready then?"

"Well, I don't know about these contacts. They were obviously not designed even for large-leafed plants, let alone blades of grass. Where are you supposed to put them for goodness sake? That poor strand of grass is completely flattened by those two probes. It'll be a wonder if there's any life left in it."

"Stop complaining, woman and switch on the current! There, now adjust the meter 'til we get a reading – it's the one in the top left-hand corner of the screen. Start on the finest resolution – we don't want to electrocute it. OK, now start the plotter-file recording and make sure the file size is increasing. It'd be terrible to have something happen and not be able to play it back. Perhaps we should be video-recording this as well, as a backup?"

The graph being drawn in the plotter window of the monitor showed a moderately straight line, wavering but slightly from time to time, and closely following the baseline to which it had been initially adjusted.

He bent to look at the trace. "Not much happening at the moment, is there? Right, how about a lighted match, then?"

Ruth did not move. Meredith continued to stare intently at the image on the screen. Nothing happened. The trace continued its slightly uneven but persistent adherence to the middle of the plot.

"Did you just think of doing this or was it at the back of your mind all the time?" asked Ruth, now beginning to gain interest herself after digesting Wilson's impassioned plea on behalf of fringe science.

"I don't know, to be quite truthful. I'm fairly sure I did only just bring it to the front of my mind, so to speak. I suppose it might have remembered that we said we were going to do that, though, in which case it wouldn't have come as any surprise."

Ruth looked over at him incredulously but quickly moderated the expression on her face when she saw that he was only being facetious.

She had noted before that he could argue quite vociferously on a particular subject, giving the impression that he felt most strongly on the matter and then, only minutes later, make jokes about it as though he felt almost embarrassed about having committed himself so outspokenly.

Wilson smiled slightly, as though having read her thoughts, though he had not looked at her. "I know, go over to the window and glare at it; you know, the way you glare at me when I refuse to take your remarks seriously. That's right, just like that."

"Oh, this is silly. How can I do that? It's only a clump of grass for goodness sake and it's really quite attractive; certainly a very pretty shade of red."

"You know, that last comment of mine might not be quite so stupid as it first appears. No, I'm not suggesting it has a memory," he added, as he caught her look again. "I mean, we haven't even got a match inside the chamber, have we, so we can scarcely apply it to a leaf. Can we rig up a Bunsen burner or something in there? No? No. There are no gas taps, are there. Anyway, we don't want to incinerate it, do we? What about a heated filament or just a small, powerful light bulb – that would do it, just enough to singe it slightly. Take the bulb out of that desk lamp, will you? No, wait; put the whole damn thing in through the lock! Yes, do it now."

Ruth reluctantly unplugged the lamp and carried it over to the airlock, carefully locking the outside door after placing it inside. She pushed up the sleeves of her lab coat and plunged her arms deep into the gloved recesses of the isolation chamber to manipulate the locks to the inner compartment. Wilson watched the computer trace eagerly.

"I do believe there's the slightest of jumps just there. Perhaps we haven't got the scale set correctly. I know you checked in the journals to find out the pressures but those would have referred to common terrestrial plants wouldn't they? If this is a completely alien life form, the pressures might be substantially different. If it were an order of magnitude lower or higher in response, we might not be able to see anything. Mind you, the program and equipment ought to be able to calibrate itself automatically for the price we paid. And document all the results and produce a report," he added. "How are you doing?"

"Shall I plug it in?"

"Yes, that's what we put it in there for, isn't it? Plug in and switch on. Now, select a blade and hold the bulb against it. That should raise the temperature a bit.

"No, it's not having any effect that I can see. Switch it off before you burn it to a crisp. What next then? Shall we adjust the range to a higher sensitivity manually?"

"It seems to have become much steadier than it was at the beginning," said Ruth, having moved to look over Wilson's shoulder. Indeed, now that he specifically looked for this characteristic, it was indeed apparent that the traced line was remarkably steady when compared to its initial jerkiness.

"Are you sure the contacts haven't come loose?" he asked.

"No, I don't think so. Well, in fact, they can't have, can they, otherwise the output would have stopped and the pen returned to the zero line."

"True, very true. I wonder if there's any significance in that, then. Perhaps it's settled down now that we've decided not to torture it. Or, more likely I suppose, it simply means that the electrical circuits have warmed up now and the resistance has steadied. Any suggestions as to what we should try next?"

"No, I presumed you had all the ideas about where this was leading," answered Ruth, with more than a hint of sarcasm.

"I do have an idea actually, come to think of it," said Wilson, suddenly becoming more active. He lifted one of the chairs from beside the desk and carried it over to face the plant behind the toughened glass. "Just sit here a minute or two and look at the grass, will you."

"Oh, come on, Merry. What good can that possibly do? It hasn't got eyes has it and I'm certainly not going to touch it."

"Argue not! Merely sit down and shut up, please! Make your mind a blank! Shouldn't be too demanding…"

She sat down and attempted to make herself comfortable, a task made difficult both by the hardness of the chair and the somewhat embarrassing silliness of the situation. Wilson continued to stand behind her, watching the graph output and resting a hand lightly on the back of the chair. She succeeded in relaxing somewhat, however, after a moment or two, even beginning to daydream slightly, content to wait until Wilson decided to divulge the nature of his next experiment. She was just contemplating what she should wear that evening when Richard came to see her, when a sudden sharp pain brought her violently back to the present. Wilson had had the nerve to take hold of a strand of her shoulder length hair and tug it out at the roots.

"What the hell do you think you're playing at?" she shouted, hand raised to rub her scalp at the still sore area, though, admittedly, she realized, it had not been quite as bad as all that.

"Very interesting," said Wilson, apparently ignoring her completely. "Just take a look at that."

He pointed significantly and, she thought, somewhat smugly, at the previously steady penned output. It was now broken by a sharp peak, followed by several smaller fluctuations, before returning to its linear progression.

The situation was now becoming desperate. Hospitals had long been filled to overflowing and other public places, schools and churches, had been opened to the sick. But it was hopeless. So hopeless was it that people living on their own had been advised that, should they contract the sickness, they should call the special emergency number, leave their name and address, and then go to bed with a hot drink and a bottle of spirits and rest. They should then wait for someone to collect them – after they were dead – though of course this last phrase was never actually communicated.

For families or groups of people, the situation was rather better. They were encouraged to take their sick to one of the special centers rather than to try to care for them themselves. Indeed the authorities made it very clear that any attempt to withhold sick or dead would be treated 'very seriously indeed,' though quite what the penalty might be was never stated. In general, people were only too pleased to get rid of even their closest relatives. A reversion to basic interests of self-preservation was taking place and altruistic acts were limited to those few of the highest moral caliber or the deepest religious beliefs.

The military had adopted what amounted to a 'bring out your dead' policy, using open trucks and soldiers wearing heavily protective clothing. Naturally any overt reference to the similarity with the Black Death plague of the 17th century was most carefully avoided, but not a soul had failed to note the resemblance.

The symptoms of the sickness had now been very well established and everyone was continually on the lookout for them, both in themselves and in others, with a perverseness and inner terror that verged on, and often actually became, paranoid. Asylums also were filling with people driven mad by the suspense and perpetual fear. The first signs were but a slight dizziness and disorientation. Mild hallucination with feelings of persecution followed, with an increasing fever and clamminess of flesh.

People could no longer act in any way 'strangely' or unpredictably in company without bringing cries of 'PV' down upon their heads. A man could find himself suddenly alone when, only moments ago in the midst of a crowd. Unless he then moved very quickly indeed, he would soon find himself pursued by the ghouls in their protective clothing, the faceless fiends who could spirit people away in the middle of the day, never to be seen again.

Within hours of the initial symptoms, the plague victim succumbed to ever more frequent attacks of nausea; became unable to walk or talk coherently and soon lost consciousness. If receiving medical attention, though few now did, he might struggle through as long as a fortnight of continued decline, during which more and more ailments would besiege him. Organs failed; usually the kidneys first, followed later by the liver and pancreas and, finally, the heart itself. Those autopsies carried out in the early days had discovered a total cessation of all organic functions. The cell structure itself had altered drastically and continued to change until the physical form and makeup bore no resemblance to the original. For those very few early cadavers that had been left to decay, it was noted that the cell walls broke down, DNA rearranged and totally new cells were formed. Eventually, spores developed which, as had been noted from those initial unfortunates who had been buried, would eventually disperse and, taking root, grow into the blades of attractive, totally innocuous looking grass, some six to nine inches tall and a variety of reds in color.

The explanations were only now, too late, forthcoming for some of the recent events. All had been misled into thinking that the novel chemical, whose nature was still beyond current scientific understanding, was the only consideration as far as the casualties were concerned. It was assumed that it had caused the undermining of the road and later the estate – this much was clearly true. It was known to have been responsible for the mutilation of the boy and assumed to have been the cause, thereby, of his death.

The mechanism whereby it had affected the council workers at the tip and on the road maintenance was not easily explicable but again it had been assumed that the chemical was to blame. Theories varied from the production of toxic gases to interference with bodily defense mechanisms, resulting in simultaneous attack by many diseases.

It was not until the appearance of the grass that the experts realized how badly they had allowed themselves to be misguided.

The authorities were ultimately forced to concede that a 'craft, presumed of extra-terrestrial origin' had been involved. Andrews' theory of a sophisticated refueling system accounted for the existence of the chemical, and its disappearance along with the flying saucer. And the red grass, with its disease-laden spores, was its deadly legacy and the true explanation for the plague which followed in its wake.

Crowds were rarely seen these days; groups of three even were uncommon. Corpses were invariably cremated, sometimes, it was claimed, even before they were quite dead.

"Will you sit still, please? How do you expect me to get you wired up properly if you keep fidgeting?"

"I know this is all in a good cause, but—"

"There are no 'buts' are there? Sit still! Now let's switch on and see what's happening."

The array of instruments in the room was impressive. Ruth wondered that even Wilson could just lift a phone and have hundreds of thousands of pounds worth of equipment at his disposal within just a couple of hours, especially for such a scheme as this, with no firm scientific foundation whatsoever.

But, she realized, the government was now so desperate that it would clutch at the most tenuous holds it could find. Virtually anything would be given a try if it had the remotest possibility of providing an opening to any sort of solution. Wilson's whims were more than adequate to persuade the authorities into acceding and supplying anything if it could be obtained, transported and assembled inside the building. Cost was no object any more. Manpower was available free of charge, non-essential work having ceased totally weeks ago. Accordingly, there had been no difficulty in acquiring the electroencephalograph and electrocardiograph machines with their associated power units and computers. In fact, Ruth believed that much of the data now being produced at the centre by the other, important, labs was being beamed via satellite to several huge 'number crunchers' in the United States. Computer operators and software experts were, after the emergency services, amongst the most overworked people in history.

Ruth sat in the same uncomfortable chair as before, now

connected, via what looked like hundreds of fine wires festooned and fastened by sticky pads to various parts of her anatomy. The attached arrays of machines and computers almost prevented entry and exit from the room. The hospital technicians who operated the systems sat in front of consoles, adjusting figures in displays, clicking mice to bring up one impressive graphical output after another. One assumed they knew what they were doing but it appeared a black art to the uninitiated onlooker. Certainly Ruth doubted that Wilson would be able to make anything whatsoever of them but she was also certain that this would in no way deter him.

"You've started the program which analyses all this stuff, have you?" he asked one of the technicians. "Good! Right then, Ruth. Now, you go in for this meditation thing, don't you?"

"Yes, I took up TM three years ago. You ought to try it yourself."

"I don't have the time or the neuroses for it, I'm afraid. Now, would you mind going into a trance or whatever it is you do?"

"I do not go 'into a trance.' I'm sure you know a lot more about it than you're admitting anyway, if you're so interested in this set-up. TM has been scientifically studied whereas this hasn't."

"Sorry. OK, I do know that meditation relaxes the body and mind and reduces tensions. Brain activity becomes dominant in alpha rhythms, while betas and thetas are suppressed. Now would you get on with it, please? I know these are probably not the easiest of conditions under which to relax at the moment but I'll give you a few minutes."

He walked over to the glass and looked intently through to check that the grass was still wired up satisfactorily. He then switched on the plethysmograph and its sensors and adjusted the output as before. This time, it settled down immediately to a steady, straight-line trace. He moved over to check the outputs from the other machines. The cardiograph indicated a regular heartbeat now, and the encephalographic output, in so far as he could make out with his limited knowledge, at least seemed less complicated than it had a few minutes earlier. The third of the lines had flattened out almost completely, while the upper was now showing a series of smooth undulating curves, even suggestive of relaxation and peace. Clearly they had a good subject.

"Now, Ruth, if you'll bear with me a while, I'd just like to try to stimulate a little reaction in that brain of yours. Just stay relaxed and keep your mind empty but try to make it receptive to suggestion if you can do that. I know meditation is in no way similar to a hypnotic trance but do the best you can. I somehow don't think a hypnotic trance is what we want anyway. I'd like you to think of something pleasurable. What's this boyfriend of yours called? Richard, isn't it? Are you sleeping with him tonight?"

"Now look here, Doctor," began Ruth, angrily.

"OK, sorry," interrupted Wilson. "We got some reaction anyway. Whether it was excited anticipation, embarrassment or repressed violence I won't go into, but the heart rate's increased – added adrenaline, no doubt – and your betas have come back with a vengeance. I thought your meditation was supposed to reject trivial input from the outside."

"I don't consider invasion of my private life to be trivial, if you don't mind," retorted Ruth, the initial anger now having subsided however.

"And just look here! Our empathic grass over there shares your outrage apparently. It seems that its feelings are not limited to the most basic ones of pain after all. Well, well, well, who would have believed it?

"Now I'm really sorry to have to do this, Ruth, especially in this way. You've no idea how much I hate myself even now and I'm sure you'll hate me too, after, but there's so much more at stake than individual feelings, as you yourself pointed out this morning." He looked carefully at the now somewhat unsteady graphic output from the plant, as though waiting for an indication to continue. "I'm afraid the director received a telegram a few hours ago. Both your parents died of the plague yesterday."

"Oh my God!" Ruth raised her hands, formed into fists, to her mouth; her composure lost completely, eyes becoming wild as tears broke and began to course down her cheeks. Her shoulders hunched and began to shake uncontrollably. It was almost beyond possibility for Wilson to restrain himself from going to comfort her. He knew his behavior was callous to the extreme, but some small core of his intellect remained un-swayed by emotion and called the rest of his powers to attention. Perverse though he still believed himself to be, he concentrated on the various graphic displays. The pen on the plant's plotter appeared to have gone berserk, as if the single line output were attempting to reproduce all the combined peaks and troughs from the dozen or more representing the brain and heart activity of his assistant.

Wars and terrorism were, one had to admit, already at an end. While, yet, only Britain was affected, the other nations knew full well that it was only a matter of time before the plague spread, unless a cure could be found. Co-operation was unprecedented. Those countries which had officially shunned the Internet up until now, opened their electronic frontiers wide and a true global network was formed. All of the major universities and research centers of the world, whether privately or government funded, had free access to each other's data. All red tape and political intrigue had been by-passed completely. The governments had become administrators and assistants to the scientists, who now called the tune. All of the resources at CERN in Switzerland had been turned over to the endeavors and their massive computing facilities were now coordinating the collection and collation of the data. It was important that studies should be duplicated to some degree for corroboration but, once a particular aspect of study had been verified, and results agreed, further repetition had to be avoided. Conclusions, if any, and pointers to further avenues of research, had to be decided and forwarded to those institutions in the best position to follow them up.

Within a few months of world recognition of the outbreak, and its threat to all nations, more information had been collected on the grass than on any other species save man himself. Its structure had been examined minutely, from the macroscopic to the subatomic. It would have been stated by any reputable geneticist to be impossible to analyze the cell structure in such detail, down even to the level of its RNA structure, in anything less than several years. Yet with the combined efforts of the world's best equipment and technicians, directed by the experts in each of the various disciplines, all this was achieved in just over eight weeks.

Unfortunately, it had gained little. They had dissected the plant down to its constituent parts but some of these parts had totally unknown functions and quite how these parts interacted or why they should affect man in the way they did was beyond even the most imaginative of the scientists. They would have had to understand all of the mechanisms of man's physical functions and brain chemistry to the same degree, in order to fathom the interactions. This had not been achieved by science to date and another eight weeks could not make much difference.

Some argued that the task was doomed to failure. It was a life form from beyond the earth – that, now, was accepted without question by all but the most obstinate. Its biochemistry was based on an alien ecosystem about which we knew nothing. We could never gain sufficient understanding unless we knew the conditions to which it had had to adapt on the planet from which it had originated. Some claimed it was so fiendishly obscure that it could not be natural in any imaginable conditions and must have been genetically engineered by some diabolical super-scientists at the other end of the galaxy for their own inconceivable purposes. It was generally agreed, however, that the fundamental make-up of atmosphere and soil was probably similar but the plant needed no light to develop, no photosynthesis being involved. It grew under almost any conditions of simulated climate and on the poorest quality earth, only pure sand stunting its growth, and even that not actually killing it.

While not growing without water, none of the samples totally deprived of it had yet died and its ability to extract water from the most noxious of chemical solutions was truly remarkable. The defoliants had had no effect on the species, other than to reveal the smallest patch of it in an area devastated of any other life. Extreme heat appeared to destroy it, but some of the more paranoid believed that pyrophilic spores would survive ordinary fire and would be able to regenerate when conditions improved.

Of course, even these skeptics were prepared to admit that a high radiation bombardment would completely destroy them and, for some time, amongst the politicians, there was serious discussion as to whether Britain should be subjected to a saturation nuclear strike. Even the fact that Britain had anticipated this and made it quite clear that any such attempt would result in reprisals on European and American cities was insufficient to deter them. After all, they reasoned, it seemed better that one or two cities should be wiped out by a relatively clean atomic blast than that the entire world should slowly be eaten away by the inexorable advance of a slow but certain and very unclean death.

The decision was imminent and it was widely believed, amongst those who knew it had even been considered, that it would be in favor of this solution. Then, to everyone's surprise, Russia announced that it would not accept this as an answer and would retaliate if such an attempt were made. It was not until much later that it was realized that Russia had just developed a far more fundamental rather than merely moral reason for objection.

Doctor Meredith Wilson watched the monitor intently. The display showed two constantly moving points of light. The upper trace recorded the minute changes in osmotic pressure in the capillaries in the body of the main leaf. The lower trace, meanwhile, showed a computer-simulated synthesis of the more significant aspects of the electroencephalograph and cardiograph outputs from the machines that had been attached to Ruth. The recordings of the completed session of about two minutes duration had been set up to match the initial start times and the two displays now marched along at the same rate, recycling when they reached the end.

By keying in various commands, Wilson was able to select different aspects of the girl's output to compare with that of the plant. Statistics from the program that had been run indicated no significant correlation in the size or positions of the peaks and troughs but Wilson felt convinced that he ought to be able to find some correspondence. Even after slowing down or stopping the procession of curves on the screen however, it was difficult to suggest any matches. He believed that the lower line was being confused by the incorporation of too many aspects. He called over to Ruth who, disregarding his injunction to the contrary, had insisted on staying, despite the now inevitably cold atmosphere between them. He would have ordered her away to avoid the friction, which could scarcely aid his concentration, but he couldn't bring himself to add further ignominy to his actions.

"Could you see if you can find Alan for me, please? I want him to tell me how I can use this damn machine to selectively display single inputs, instead of letting the computer decide what I ought to see."

She had been sitting, facing the plant, staring as if unseeing, through the glass for some considerable time but tore herself away and, without speaking, went out through the door. Wilson, idly glancing over to the plant's current graphic output, which was still being displayed on another monitor, noted with momentary surprise that in fact the pen had, for the last visible section of output, been tracing many ups and downs, no longer keeping to its original central steadiness. Now, however, it had settled down again and was remaining flat. He paused and reflected for a moment upon whether there should be some significance in this. Certainly it seemed to be reacting, in some way, sympathetically with Ruth's mental and emotional brain activity. Most curious, but he decided that a continued study of the recording was most likely to provide the connection and turned back to the main screen.

The software engineer arrived and, after some consultation, sat down at the terminal and began to key in amendments to the analysis program. The original discrete outputs from the various electrodes that had been attached to Ruth had all been stored and were available for direct access from disc, in digital form. It was a simplification of the program to provide the features that Wilson wanted.

"Can this program of yours also try for matches with a time discrepancy?" asked Wilson. "You know, it's conceivable that the plant isn't reacting immediately to whatever it's reacting to. There could certainly be a few microseconds delay."

"Well, yes, it can actually. It's not designed quite for this sort of application of course but it already has a built-in capability to shift one or other input in time by any amount you care to name. Shall we say one second, to allow for a very slow reaction?"

"Yes, fine. Take each input in turn and let your program play with it. When… correction, if it comes up with anything, put it on the screen and let's have a look at it.

"Is it doing anything?" asked Wilson when, some ten minutes after starting the program running, nothing had apparently happened.

"I think so. I suppose I ought to have put some message out

every so often, just to make sure, but you'd certainly get an error notification if it crashed.

Another five minutes passed and even the engineer was looking nervously at his watch and wondering whether he shouldn't abort and find out what was happening, when a row of cryptic figures appeared along the top line of the VDU followed by a display of two graphs. The upper trace – that of the plant – looked much as before: complex, with frequent and irregular variations in slope. The lower was much simpler with only minor undulations, very smooth by comparison.

"It looks like a very significant correlation," said the engineer, after studying the figures for a moment."

"You could have fooled me," muttered Wilson who, having no key for the figures, had been looking intently at the traces for any correspondences.

"That's the theta output isn't it?" he asked, indicating the lower graph.

"Wouldn't know, I'm afraid; not my field. I must admit I can't see much similarity."

"The trouble is, of course, that the plant trace is too complicated. What we want is to extract just that part which relates to the theta transactions."

"I think I can see some slight matches, just here and here." The engineer pointed out several minor perturbations of the steeper maxima. "Hold on, I'll see if I can't get the other data suppressed."

For the next ten minutes, he studied listings of the program modules and keyed in further amendments. After a further delay, while the program was recompiled, he set it running again with the new instructions. Also, taking Wilson's assumption to be correct, he began analysis with the theta output. In under a minute this time, another, much simpler display replaced the first, and now the correspondences were unmistakable. It looked almost too good to be true and Wilson was compelled to question it.

"I don't think I've made any mistakes," answered the programmer, after checking through his penciled amendments. "Mind you," he added, after looking at the figures displayed above the graphs, "there is one thing distinctly odd. I really don't understand that at all."

"Well, what is it, Alan?" queried Wilson, impatiently.

"You know how I programmed in a time shift allowance for comparison?"

"Yes, yes," came the snapped reply.

"Well, I didn't specify that it should only allow for a positive one, so naturally it didn't assume any such limitations. Anyway," he concluded almost guiltily, "it seems as though the output that we're looking at from the grass occurred before that of the girl's; almost a millisecond before to be precise."

Wilson stood transfixed, glaring with disbelief at the display, trying to find words to suggest that the engineer was an idiot and must be wrong, but failing. After seeing the rapidity with which he had found his way through the program, Wilson knew the other was good and unlikely to make such a stupid mistake. On glancing across at him, Wilson realized anyway that Alan was probably thinking the same of himself.

Suddenly, his attention was drawn to the monitor recording the plant's current output and he saw, with what almost amounted to horror, that the graphic output from the plant had gone wild. It was registering what would have been sharp peaks way off the extremities of the scale of the graph, as though it were a seismograph responding to a direct hit by a bomb.

Wilson, who had already made a mental leap to attempt to accommodate the assorted items of data, looked over immediately to where Ruth was again sitting, in her chair, facing the isolation chamber. A cry caught in his throat as he saw, but was powerless to prevent, that she had the key in the lock below it and was pressing the button, which caused the armor plated glass to rise to reveal the interior. With a shock that carried with it a multiplicity of overtones of emotions, he realized, and then accepted, that he was a dead man.

Though existing as undivided, he appears as if separated into different beings. He should be known as the sustainer of all but also as their creator and destroyer. XIII.16

Hot sun, blue sky, tranquil sea; everything seemed at peace. It was still difficult to appreciate that the situation could be as grave as rumor had implied. There should have been a sense of urgency as he donned his suit, adjusted his mask and checked his oxygen supply but all he could claim truthfully to feel was a vague sense of unease. This was almost drowned by an overwhelmingly pleasant sensation and desire to relax. But he was unable to allow his mind to be soothed by the warmth of the late autumn sun and the gentle lapping of the almost abnormally calm sea against the sides of the aircraft carrier, anchored about fifty miles off the coast of Cornwall.

The sudden and increasing roar, as the engine started up and the rotors beat the air with force sufficient to deafen everyone within a twenty yards radius, disturbed him not one iota. The acoustic generator built into his helmet cancelled the sound with an efficiency that never ceased to amaze him and all he could hear was the composed voice of the radio operator clearing him for take-off. His instruments already thoroughly checked out, he glanced over to his passenger to ensure he was correctly belted in and then took the helicopter into a smooth, slow, vertical ascent before opening up the throttle and setting course for England.

Conditions aloft were equally serene. Visibility was superb and the anti-cyclonic conditions over Western Europe gave rise to very stable air movements and the gentlest of flights. For the next twenty minutes they headed northeast, gazing out through the panoramic cockpit windows over what seemed to be an endless millpond, canopied by a uniformly blue sky. Not a speck of movement blotted the scene – neither cloud in sky nor ship in sea. This latter at least was notably unusual – what was normally the busiest shipping channel in the world devoid of movement. Yet, apart from this fact, it seemed in no way incongruous. The peacefulness of the scene seemed to demand that the seaway not be littered by hundreds of vessels, so many specks of dirt from the air, destroying the simplicity of the composition and reminding of man's more mundane concerns of commerce. It would have seemed more natural for the vista to continue without end, regardless of the direction in which they travelled or how far.

Soon, however, the line of Cornwall and the white line of surf against the land's edge came into view and a discontinuity in both panorama and mood was introduced. Their attention and awareness became immediately heightened as they began to prepare for the job ahead. The passenger swung around in his seat and busied himself setting up the cameras and electronic surveillance apparatus in readiness for their approach.

"Hey, there's a boat down there, see? About three miles off coast, sixty degrees west."

"Check – do we go take a look?"

"I'll report back." The pilot relayed the information back to the ship and they were advised to investigate and observe but to take no further action until they had reported again.

It took only a few moments to reach the boat, a medium sized fishing vessel. Its nets were still cast and, at first sight, all seemed normal but, after descending to about a hundred feet, they could discern no movement. The nets were in fact trailing aimlessly behind the boat, which itself appeared to be drifting. There was no sign of any life.

"Do we go down to investigate?" radioed the pilot after passing on the details.

"Negative. Proceed back to course after you've got all the

details on video."

They followed the line of the shore until they came to a small fishing village. As they hovered low over the harbor, the sense of unease, which had been slowly dawning, now began to make itself distinctly discernible amongst their emotions. The harbor was packed with boats of all sizes, from commercial fishing vessels, down to dozens of privately owned boats, yachts, dinghies and motor cruisers. It being a high tide, all the boats were rising and falling, straining at their ropes on the gentle swell of the waves.

It was a picturesque old village with narrow streets filled, no doubt, with places of photogenic interest: ancient churches and 'olde worlde' corner shops with windows of distorting glass. But it ought to be alive with late holidaymakers on a day like this; the yacht enthusiasts with their ostentatious captain's peaked hats; the children with their ice-creams, looking in the souvenir shops, deciding what to ask for next and their patience-almost-exhausted mothers trying to drag them away. But nothing. The streets were empty save for the numerous parked cars, also stationary and empty. It was almost like a film set, deserted while the actors had gone for lunch; only the cameras and micro-phone booms were absent.

They were about to fly on when something caught his eye. Descending lower, he saw it was a dog, head raised in the air and muzzle vibrating as it presumably barked and howled. It was standing outside a house, the door of which was partly open. Swinging the helicopter over a few feet, he saw the reason – the top half of a body protruded slightly through the opening, as though it had been crawling out to get fresh air when it expired. The irrepressible creeping of gooseflesh caused an equally invol-untary shudder. He swallowed to attempt to dispel the sudden feeling of tightness that had developed in his throat. What had before only been a disaster inferred from the deserted aspect of the village, was now a disaster confirmed by more positive and inescapable evidence.

He felt as though he ought to stand up and shake himself. He was a war-hardened soldier and ought not to feel such chills of fear as those that still threatened to rise within him; it was an alien emotion and it was, perhaps, by that very fact, that he managed to avoid succumbing to it. He had had experience of car-bombs in Iraq, when he had been younger and impressionable, and those were many times more graphically horrific than the scene beneath them. Arguably, he ought to be able to ignore this. Yet that thrill of the unknown refused him the ease of mind he sought. No solid, scientifically understood and tried, honest-to-goodness bomb had wrought this devastation without material destruction. It was uncanny and very disturbing.

"Interesting that the dog hasn't been affected," he said to attempt to break the spell, which seemed to have struck them both at the sight of the body.

"Yes, and look at those birds on the telegraph wires down there."

Indeed, a line of several dozen huge, black crows were visible where the other had pointed, adding a Hitchcockian touch of menace to the already chilling picture. Now they had realized that there was, in fact, life of inferior varieties present, he had little difficulty in picking out a second dog and a pack of four cats roaming along the quay looking for scraps. He also noticed the flock of gulls wheeling around the boats very low down near the water. Surprising he hadn't noticed before, but then, they were so common in these surroundings that they would probably become conspicuous only if absent.

As he reflected upon the gulls, he suddenly saw, with a new shock of fear, a black figure standing on the cabin of one of the boats waving vigorously. So unexpected was it that it was some moments before he realized that it was a frogman, with two large oxygen tanks strapped to his back. Flying lower, he saw that the deck was piled high with spare tanks and with mingled amazement and pity, he understood what must have happened. How long had this poor guy, or even girl possibly, been trapped like this? He must have been in the wet suit, breathing from air cylinders for weeks. It seemed impossible. God, he thought, he must have been taking food underwater, perhaps opening cans of food and feeding himself under such awkward conditions to avoid exposure to the air. He didn't know whether to feel relieved that someone had found a way of beating this thing or dismayed that man had been brought down to such a pitiful state.

He radioed back the information and listened to the reply. He nodded his head slowly as the answer came back and, without acknowledging it, as if having already accepted the fact but not wanting to admit it, turned the helicopter around and accelerated off to the north-east, leaving the figure gesticulating desperately but futilely and vanishing rapidly behind them.

There was only one option left. Many had concluded this in the early days. It had been easy to deceive oneself then, in the growing optimism; the irrepressible glow of good feeling in the quite novel atmosphere – nations working together with lifelong enemies towards a common goal. It was unprecedented. Politicians proved quite unable to calculate beforehand the extent to which co-operation and goodwill continued to increase, as humanity pooled all its talent and knowledge to try to comprehend and combat this new and so much more deadly foe.

But even in the beginning, while everyone else was still uplifted by this positive and hitherto unfamiliar emotion, and most were convinced that such a force could defeat the devil himself, a few believed otherwise. They recognized in the havoc that was being wrought upon the Earth a force that was not *of* the Earth and knew that mankind had not yet developed to the stage where such an alien life form could be understood and dominated. Fortunately, they were in such a position as not to have to keep their opinions to themselves and merely lament the inconceivable amounts of effort and materials being lavished on the study of the grass. They believed the attempts to find a cure or prevention for the disease to be in vain. Instead, they launched a second, equally ambitious project, also on a vast scale and involving all the nations of the world.

The idea had been discussed before, as a necessary contingency when there was an ever-present threat of extinction from global nuclear war but until now, nothing had provided sufficient impetus to initiate anything other than the wishful thinking of a few far-sighted individuals. There was an abundance of material bordering on, or actually in, the realm of science fiction but nothing in the way of seriously formulated plans. Now there was motivation and manpower, available on a scale not achieved since the age of the pyramids, and vastly exceeding that because no coercion was needed here. The only commodity lacking was time. On the evidence of the spread of the disease throughout Britain, from the moment of the first identified case, it had been estimated that the world could hope for no more than about six months before the plague became ubiquitous. If humanity were to be saved, its only chance seemed to be to send a number of its members far away from the source of infection, and that meant outside of the atmosphere itself. Thus were the world's leaders successfully convinced and thus was the 'Island Project' begun in earnest.

Various authors, a number of them respected scientists in their own rights, had considered the question of sustaining life outside of the Earth, whether in relation to the tantalizing possibilities of extra-terrestrial civilizations or to the more germane aspects of constructing interstellar space craft or stationary space cities. All who were still alive were now assembled to contribute their hitherto mainly ignored ideas to their more practically minded colleagues.

It was known that no other planet in the solar system was

habitable without resorting to extreme artificial measures. Over a long period of time, large habitations could undoubtedly be established on the Moon or Mars. This would have been the preferred solution, providing several crucial advantages over orbiting space stations. Foremost amongst these were the proximity of planetary resources and the capability for expansion of the colony. Unfortunately, not having initiated plans for such an endeavor several decades ago, this solution was beyond the capability of even the combined world efforts in such a short time.

The only sensible and plausible solution was to transport a number of people to an orbiting installation. They would have nowhere to go nor even very much to do other than, hopefully and eventually, to return to Earth. Initially, it was thought that the aim must be to isolate a cross-section of scientists, away from the diseased world, in order to give them time to find an antidote or cure. Also, both men and women should be sent so that, if the inconceivable really did happen, and all of humanity was eliminated from the surface of the Earth, then re-population might eventually begin.

However, nothing could ever be quite so simple. The scientists quickly foresaw difficulties as the investigations advanced. It was realized, too late for many, that the grass exerted some totally unknown and unforeseen influence over people in its proximity, quite apart from its spreading of the infection by spores. No protection had been found against what had become known as the 'Double-F Effect,' a fatal fascination which surpassed that of any spider or scorpion over its prey. Accordingly, they found themselves in a dilemma with no apparent solution. If the space travelers took some of the grass with them in order to carry out the months or possibly years of further research that might be needed, they would inevitably succumb to the double-F themselves, even if they avoided the more obvious accidents. It was a recipe that could only produce an orbiting mortuary. If, on the other hand, they did not take any, they would be severely limited in their work and would be quite unable to prove the effectiveness of any remedy before submitting themselves to the test.

Politicians, too, had their problems. Who should go: Presidents and Prime Ministers: Nobel prize-winning scientists? And should art, music, literature be represented? Should men be sent without their wives or should only married couples be allowed? Should any children be included? And, the biggest problem of all, must all races, all nationalities be represented? Which nation would accept self-imposed genocide?

It was fortunate (if fortune could be considered to have played a part in recent events) that a potential facility actually existed. At any other time in the history of man, such a course would have been totally impossible. As it was, the International Space Station was available, albeit in a form presently unsuited to such a purpose.

The ISS had had a checkered history to say the least. The idea of a space station had been around since the early days of space exploration; long before then if you counted science fiction. Reagan had first committed the American people to actually building one, when he allocated $8 billion of the budget to Space Station Freedom. Bush continued the initiative, in support of his dream of using it as a necessary staging post in a manned mission to Mars. By the time Clinton came to power in '93, it was six years behind schedule and costing $8 million per day. The estimate to put a man on Mars had risen to $400 billion and the program was dropped.

The project was simply too ambitious and too different from anything which had been done before. There was no shortage of ideas and NASA happily spent the original $8 billion allocation researching, designing, scrapping and re-designing, without ever getting round to actually producing any hardware. But the idea was clearly not untenable. After all, there was Space Station Mir, which had been accusingly staring them in the face since 1986. Cramped and smelly it might be, low-tech certainly, but it worked and was a constant, unpleasant reminder of something at which the Russians had beaten them.

When the Soviet Union collapsed, it paved the way for a wonderful face saving and dollar saving opportunity. A combined international endeavor would be established. All countries could contribute money and equipment and share in the benefits. In particular, Russia could contribute her life support technology, developed and proven during many years of actual use, while the more sophisticated US equivalent was still on the drawing board. They could truthfully claim that the same air was being breathed aboard Mir after ten years (and even provocatively suggest that it smelled cleaner than that in Los Angeles).

The recycling of perspiration and urine was an equally important aspect conquered by the Russians. Since each person was estimated to consume about 10,000 pounds of water per year, this was vital. The alternative, of shipping water up to the station, would cost $100 million per person, per year but this was clearly not an option anyway, if there were no one left on earth to send it.

Needless to say, the program had not maintained its schedule but it was largely in place and it was manned and powered. In fact, it was a bonus that the final laboratory and research modules had not yet been added. This meant that they could be refitted here on earth for more mundane functions. Of the eleven major, pressurized modules, three had been intended to serve as crew habitats, with life support functions, and seven had been dedicated to research. Now, all but one had to be converted into accommodation and supporting functions. It had originally been intended to house no more than seven personnel. Facilities had been planned for scientific research, to expand the frontiers of human knowledge in areas involving micro-gravity or the vacuum of outer space. All of the long thought out plans had to be dropped and turned to imagining all that might be required to help the crew survive for an indefinite period. This might be as long as, or longer than, the thirty years originally specified in the design requirement for Freedom, rather than the ten-year operational requirement for the ISS.

It was a mammoth exercise simply to think of all the things that they might need, for what would be an indefinitely long stay in space. Essentials had obviously to be considered first and, ultimately, relative luxuries such as entertainment would have to be discarded if there were insufficient room. Fortunately, things did not come to this pass, since entire libraries of books and films could now be accommodated on portable hard drives and if these were not essential for entertainment, they might become so for education.

And there was a multitude of tasks to be done here on Earth. Acknowledging that a large proportion of the populace would perish, the remaining facilities had to be rationalized. Arrangements had to be made to optimize the infrastructure for their purposes. Energy would no longer be derived from city-sized power stations – these had to be progressively closed down and made safe. Similarly with all other processes – chemical factories would not be needed for a long time; farms would need to be geared to produce food for a village-sized market, not for export. Many manufacturing industries would be able to supply the world for many years to come from existing stock. Museums and galleries had to store away their valuables for a potential future society. Libraries coordinated the systematic organizing of knowledge and technology, with priceless books and special 'long life' optical media being locked away in underground vaults at various sites around the world, to guard against possible civil unrest. The list went on and on, though perhaps this was just as well, since it kept peoples' minds off their own likely future.

Tickets for the mission were severely limited and it was not possible for just a few leaders from the main participating countries to make the decisions about who should go. Intercommunication between the scientists involved in the study of the plague was so widespread and all embracing that to keep any such details secret was a total impossibility. That this had to be a truly multi-national venture was quickly, if reluctantly, accepted by the major powers. But this did not ease the difficulties. The schedule for the US Space Shuttle and Russian Soyuz rockets to complete the ISS had been specified years before and there was little scope for making more available. It was eventually agreed that, by judicious redesign of the various modules, cannibalizing of other parts and taking into account turnaround of shuttle trips and remaining Soyuz ships, that a total crew of around twenty people was possible, or slightly more if some children were included. Even this small number would produce somewhat cramped conditions and would fall far short of the hundreds considered by the psychologists to be ideally needed for a viable community in isolation.

The difficulties of selection were formidable. The decision was quickly made not to send children. The day to day maintenance, and the very business of existence under such circumstances, would be a full-time activity for intelligent and capable adults. It would be unfair to submit a child to such conditions and would impose a concomitant strain on the rest. If it should transpire that their stay was to be a prolonged one, there might be some limited scope to expand their accommodation, using the material from the last shuttle that had brought them there. They must then proceed to have children of their own who would be completely at home in their surroundings, not having known anything different.

And so the requirements for the personnel were for ten men and ten women, who should be compatible and multiracial as the fundamental criteria. Since it could not be anticipated that stable pair bonding could occur, all needed to be exceptionally, if not abnormally, emotionally stable and naturally inclined towards promiscuous behavior. It was decided that all should be between the ages of twenty-five and thirty-five and, together, should comprise the most comprehensive selection of disciplines ever assembled in so small a community. One person had to serve as medical practitioner, geneticist, writer, cook, while another must be electronics engineer, computer scientist, chemist and musician. All needed to be fluent in several languages and be tolerant, sociable non-smokers. The list of requirements seemed endless, such that it began to appear inconceivable that so few could have so many talents and virtues.

The selection was further limited by the fact that an absolute minimum of three persons had to be skilled in piloting the shuttle and the US and Soyuz Crew Return Vehicles. These would remain docked to the station to provide their return capability and additional storage facilities.

So it was that the arguments about who should go never matured. The stringency of the demands dictated the choice. Candidates were put forward by the thousands but swiftly whittled away until the conditions themselves had to be reduced in order that as many as twenty people could actually be assembled.

It had been agreed that those who had passed a certain point in the selection process, but who failed the final stages of qualification, would be the principal candidates for the special gene banks that were being established. Sperm, together with both fertilized and unfertilized eggs and embryos in various later stages of development, would be frozen using the most sophisticated cryogenic techniques. This would provide a much more varied genetic base for the castaways when they eventually returned to earth. It also gave those remaining behind an impression of purpose and a feeling that they too might contribute to the future of mankind in the more traditional sense, albeit in a somewhat unconventional manner.

The Island Project became mankind's hope for the future. Those masses of individuals whose ambitions now looked no further than a painless death (chemist shops had long since sold out, or been looted, of all stocks of barbiturates or any other drugs which might provide an easy way out if the need arose) identified themselves with the chosen ones. Newspapers were no longer in existence – no one would deliver them and very few people ventured outdoors these days except to collect essential food items, which were becoming increasingly scarce. The average person now spent anything up to twelve hours per day watching television and the progress of the Project occupied a considerable percentage of this time. The detailed biographies of the travelers were known to everyone and their day-to-day activities as they prepared for launch were followed with a profound avidity. Even had it been merely a fictional activity, designed to distract people from the anti-social behavior which might easily have resulted from a belief that their own death was imminent, it would have achieved something positive. The world hung on every word the media could offer.

And the countdown began...

The 'Person' and the Self

There is no purpose to life. If the intellect needs some sort of explanation for this, regard it as simply *lllA*, the play of creation. It's a bit like writing a novel with yourself as one of the characters and then becoming so involved in the story that you forget that it is only fiction and begin to act as though the events in the book are really happening. In Sanskrit, it is called lIla, *lllA* and means 'play,' in the sense of a diversion or amusement; an 'appearance,' 'pretence' or 'disguise.'

This is what we are doing all the time, playing roles; like an actor on the stage 'one man in his time plays many parts.' This is what it means to be a 'person.' We forget the true meaning of this word, from the Latin *'persona,'* referring to the megaphone-mask worn by actors when they performed in the amphitheater so that the audience could hear them. We are not the 'person' – that is only a mask covering our true nature – yet most of us live out our entire lives believing that we are 'John Smith,' a 'husband,' a 'father,' a 'chemist' and so on. We think we are the roles we play, as though Kenneth Branagh went through his life believing himself to be Hamlet! So many things are the opposite of the way we have always thought them to be. This is another example. Because we are so caught up in the play we have really come to believe that we are the person, the role, instead of the actor just playing a part – to the extent that the very word 'person' has come to mean the opposite of what it originally meant!

We speak of ourselves and others as having particular 'personalities.' It is *because* we cling to 'our' ideas and opinions and identify with our bodies and roles and religions and family and country and... you name it, that all our problems arise.

There is not *literally* any such thing as Self-realization. To realize something means to make it real. The Self already is the only reality – what is there to realize? You cannot make something that is false real nor vice versa. What needs to happen is for the mind to gain the self-knowledge to recognize this as true. Enlightenment is the bringing of this light to the mind so that the darkness of ignorance is dispelled.

So what do you have to do? Recognize (= know again what you have forgotten) that this is so and that is all. If you want to learn lots more about this philosophy, you can visit Dennis Waite's website at www.advaita.org.uk.

My legs give way; my mouth goes dry; my body trembles; my hair stands on end. I.29

The helicopter landed in the square of what had once been carefully mown grass at Westminster. Now it was a blackened ruin with not a sign of green, or red, present. The place was deserted, not a tourist or taxi in sight. The Abbey and the Houses of Parliament stood, for once, alone, without admirers. The fingers of Big Ben stood at half-past the hour but no chime rang to break the uncanny silence. The mechanism had not been re-set now for several weeks and time had come to a halt. It was as if the clock knew that there was no one left to alert; no one to care; its measured time now serving no purpose in a world devoid of rush-hours and appointments.

The bridge was barricaded at each end, all traffic between north and south having been curtailed, resurrecting the role of the river as a frontier. The barrier itself, together with a pre-fabricated hut for the guards, further emphasized the impression of a border with another country, resembling as it did a customs post with the bridge a no-man's-land, watched warily by the two sides. It, too, was now deserted.

The two men looked at each other and, as though a hidden signal had passed between them, though neither had spoken, simultaneously turned to open their doors and climb down to stand on the scorched earth. Opening the storage locker, they began to unpack the equipment they would need.

Davidson, the pilot, strapped the bulky transmitter to his back and plugged it into his helmet, disconnecting the conventional radio and switching over to the new mode.

"Davidson to base. Switched to TETRA system now. Do you read me, over?"

The acknowledgement was received and they set off towards the entrance to Westminster tube station.

"Going underground now," radioed Davidson.

"OK, good luck," replied the base operator, traditionally though, without conviction. Knowing the seriousness of the situation, no one involved could converse with any degree of normality. Whilst convention was still maintained, anything said, which was not directly related to the business in hand, appeared unnatural and strained. Furthermore, Davidson, his companion Captain Howard, the men back on the aircraft carrier and the men who had sent them were all aware that there was a strong possibility that they would not return.

They carried weapons, though they did not anticipate encountering any opposition against which they would prove effective. It was argued that they might, for example, meet a starving dog and to have no means of defense against such an enemy would be irony indeed. They slung the guns across their backs as they switched on the powerful LED lights on their helmets and, without thought for the almost obligatory glance over their shoulder, at the world that they might never see again, entered the subway.

They located the escalators easily enough; light filtering in from the outside would have allowed adequate visibility up to this point. As they descended, however, the ambient darkness became total and they became entirely reliant upon their lamps. This condition required some adaptation, since the field of view demarcated by the beams was controlled by movement of their heads as opposed to the more usual hand-held movement of a torch. Neither man had ever been inclined towards mining or pot holing so that this mode of illumination was unfamiliar.

Davidson had never been able to walk naturally down stationary escalators, so this presented him with additional problems. Walking while the stairs moved created no difficulty; it was possible to develop a smooth rhythm of movement, as though in harmony with that of the conveyor itself. Yet, as soon as the motion stopped and it reverted to a simple staircase, with metal treads and a rubber banister, a strange psychological quirk resulted and brought forth a sudden tendency to stumble as though he had actually forgotten how to walk downstairs. Though now surrounded by darkness, at least at foot level, unless he consciously looked down at his feet, this same feeling struck him again and he grasped desperately for the handrail as he failed to make the necessary movements of his legs and missed a step. He swore aloud before remembering that the radio was still transmitting and pulled himself back to a standing position with some embarrassment at his momentary loss of balance.

As they resumed their now more consciously careful descent, the sound of their boots clanging on the stair-case rang hollowly through the empty tunnel, clearly audible even through the metal of their space-suit-like headgear. The atmosphere itself was distinctly eerie. The lamps glared back at them from the glossy coating of the posters lining the walls on the way down, the frequent, scantily-clad female forms in the adverts seeming now incongruous since the station was not functioning in its intended manner. It felt, indeed, more like a deserted art gallery in the darkness, exerting neither the impression of hinted intimacy as at rush-hour with many bodies closely packed as they descended, nor the empty withdrawn isolation of the brightly lit but deserted station of late winter evening.

The journey along the white-bricked tunnel down towards the platform was worse than they had anticipated. This was not because of any problem of navigation – they had memorized the basic plan before leaving. The Underground had been a final desperate source of refuge for hundreds of thousands fleeing the plague. But it had proven no safer for them than their own homes, and sharing their fate with so many others had given little consolation. Now the floors of the corridors and the platforms themselves were strewn with bodies in varying stages of decay. As if this were not bad enough, packs of rats roamed freely. Unaffected by the plague and provided with this sudden, apparently unending source of food, they had themselves now reached plague proportions. With such plentiful supplies available, they had no interest in anything other than eating and mating. Accordingly, they ignored the two intruders to their nightmare world, but it was impossible for this attitude to be mutual. It was as well that they had their own source of oxygen; the stench must otherwise have been unbearable. It took the most intense effort of will power to avoid retching at some of the scenes they witnessed. To react in that way would almost certainly have been fatal. Since the authorities were now aware that the two men might very well experience an intense desire to remove their helmets at some stage, these had been sealed before they left base. If they were to vomit inside them, they would probably suffocate or choke.

Eventually, after a journey whose memory they would live with to the end of their days, they reached the end of the platform. Though both feeling some initial reluctance about stepping down on to the rails, it offered a more than welcome escape and they exhibited no visible hesitation to each other as they left the platform and headed east on the Central line towards Charing Cross.

After some twenty yards, an opening was discernible on the left that might have been presumed by the casual observer to be intended for a new extension that had never materialized. They took the turning and, within a further fifty yards reached an apparent dead end. The walls were black; no white glimmer of the original glazed brick surface was visible after the many years of fumes, smoke and dirt, never cleaned away. It was some minutes before they located the grill of the air vent high on the left-hand wall. With considerable effort and the help of a crowbar brought for this precise purpose, Davidson eventually succeeded in prizing the grill away. Reaching in, he managed to find the switch only with difficulty, since he was unable to remove the protective gloves he was wearing. He pressed it down and was immediately rewarded by a bright glow of light from the interior of the aperture. This was soon accompanied by an almost inaudible hum, which grew steadily louder. After about fifteen seconds, though knowing full well what to expect, he was unable to suppress a start of surprise when a whole section of the wall suddenly swung open to reveal the dimly lit interior of what was clearly a lift.

They entered quickly and Howard keyed the six-digit code, with which they had been supplied, into the keypad that was affixed to the wall, in lieu of the column of floor numbers found in more conventional lifts. There was a momentary pause and then the lift began to descend. The section of wall closed above them again, like the entrance to some secret passage in a mediaeval castle.

After what appeared to be much longer than the time measured by mere clocks, the background whine of the motors ceased and they came to a halt opposite a brightly lit passage still similar in style to the Underground station they had recently left. The end of the corridor was clearly visible however, only yards away, blocked by a heavy metal door with a central wheel resembling a large bank vault. To the right of the door stood what appeared to be an automatic Oyster-card validation machine, of precisely the same type as was found throughout the London Transport system. It was incredible to think that someone might still be attempting to maintain the pretence that this was a part of the station complex, for the benefit of any visitor who had succeeded in coming this far but wasn't actually meant to be here. The mechanism really did look as though it were genuine, perhaps left lying casually around as though for repair. Even in the tense atmosphere that was reality, the observers were aware of a sense of the farcical about the arrangements.

On closer inspection, the machine was obviously connected to a power supply and the slot was standardized for the SMART London Transport tickets. Davidson reached into his pocket, pulled out a definitely non-standard card and inserted it into the slot. There was a brief pause as a remote computer checked the data and then the card was returned.

Howard and Davidson simultaneously set their watches to

stopwatch mode and the lieutenant began to turn the wheel of the vault-like door clockwise. After fifteen seconds had elapsed, Howard inserted a second, similar ID card which was also checked and returned, upon which Davidson pulled the door open and they both entered, much relieved that this ritual had been accepted without incident. They carefully closed the door behind them and sealed it with a similar wheel on the inside. As the bolt locked home, a loud whining sound began as the air in the compartment was extracted, purified and recycled. Simultaneously, the two men were bathed in a dazzling blue light, which persisted, together with other not entirely sensed radiation, for some time. Eventually, both noise and light ceased abruptly and a section of wall opposite their original entrance slid open.

Stumbling through, they found themselves in an empty, curving passageway, dimly lit by small emergency lamps fitted to one side of each of the strip-fluorescent lights, which were not functioning. Dismayed though not surprised by the fact that no reception committee was there to meet them, they set off, one in each direction, towards the central computer room and control area.

The complex was arranged in very much the same sort of way as was depicted by traditional science fiction for a Space Station. It was designed in the form of a wheel with the centre of activity at the literal hub and the degree of supportive work radially organized about it. All the multifarious and nefarious activities of a military intelligence, dedicated to planning and coordinating the defense and counter-attacking capabilities of a nation were centralized here, in closest proximity to the vast computer network and communications area. Beyond these, one graduated to the conference rooms and lecture theatres, out to the kitchens, dining and leisure areas, on to the rim of the wheel, where the bedrooms were located. One could almost imagine the gravity decreasing as one approached the hub.

The two men appeared almost simultaneously on opposite sides of the computer area. It was apparent that neither had encountered any of the personnel. This room was also conspicuously empty. Here, at the very heart of this enormously expensive and sophisticated construction, where the effective government of the entire country ought to have been taking place, several hundred persons should have been engaged in processing the masses of data and feeding them to the decision makers for consideration and planning. Yet not a soul was in sight. It was uncanny.

They approached each other past the rows of silent and motionless computers and storage devices. At the very middle, a circular bank of monitors, keyboards, input and output devices were arrayed but unattended. Messages flashed up periodically to inform or alert the missing operators:

'RAS operative – D & RM all check OK'
'Condition all green'
'Backing store overwritten. Please assign new area.'
'Malfunction in cameras DS03 and CT14'

But, for the most part, the machine continued to play out its preprogrammed war-game role as it had been intended to do – without human intervention. Monitoring and calculating at unimaginable speed, it required no administrative support to maintain its function. Without further commands to the contrary, it would run and re-run through its fixed series of instructions, complex though these were. It would respond in its limited way to the changing data input, until several of its critical duplicated components failed irrecoverably or until the power failed, which could be for a very long time indeed. And all to no avail, for there was no one left to care; no one to react to the information and force a response. No battle had been fought but it seemed that everything had already been lost.

Even while the process of selection of the 'castaways,' as the media had dubbed them, was taking place, preparation for the launch of the first shuttle had been in hand. The intention was that trained astronauts would make upwards of a dozen missions over the following six weeks, to transport the parts for the extension of and enhancements to the ISS, to enable it to support the twenty chosen ones.

The area around Cape Canaveral had been sealed off for a radius of one hundred miles. Armed soldiers patrolled the entire circumference, with electrified fences erected for several miles either side of access roads. Everyone and everything entering the site was subjected to the most rigorous process of decontamination. Fortunately, a test was now available to detect the disease in advance of its outward manifestation so that there was no need for a quarantine buffer zone. Instead, those who could prove that they had good reason for being there were forced to submit to the necessary tests at one of several, separate, advance border posts, long before they reached the main perimeter. As the very last line of defense for humanity, no measures were too strict. All were happy to be subjected to whatever safeguards could be thought of. At all costs, the area had to be kept free of the grass and the plague until the last shuttle had departed. Even subsequently, it was intended that research into a cure should continue at the site for as long as possible.

The investigations and experimentation had continued unabated but there had been no breakthrough and there were now few ideas for new avenues of research. As optimism for a cure waned, the masses turned to the Island Project as the final hope for mankind and the force of popular opinion on this scale was an awesome power indeed. The vast scientific apparatus that had been set up to organize those previous efforts was now forced to swing desperately to these. The worldwide network of computers switched to processing the millions of calculations that had to be made to design, construct, launch and assemble.

The events leading up to the first shuttle launch were followed avidly by virtually the entire population, only those remaining unfortunates in the backwaters of developing countries being excluded. At least one channel on the television of every country was devoted to the proceedings at any given hour of day or night. The fact that very little new information was available from these continuous broadcasts deterred no one. It was the ultimate in escapism for a humanity who now had every justification and emotional need for total escapism.

And thus it transpired that, as the final countdown began, it was reckoned that some 98 percent of all those with access to radio or television were tuned in to the transmissions. The preparations, rushed though they had been forced to be, had been thorough and flawless. The shuttle, atop its twin boosters, rose with its now familiar gush of flame and smoke, which had, in the early days, engulfed the towers and exacted significant damage at each launch. Up it soared with fearsome acceleration, though lacking some of the magic of the old Apollo rockets, and vanished from view of the naked eye.

The sound began within minutes. Initially almost below the threshold of hearing, a faint electronic buzz in the radio or TV receivers of those millions of remote observers, it grew imperceptibly, acquiring discernible intensity, pitch and the quality of a low organ note. It was nevertheless some considerable time longer before those scientists involved on the project concluded that there was no fault in the equipment and began to look elsewhere. Although no source could be imagined, concern began to grow rapidly as it was realized that the disturbance was affecting all electronic devices and was increasing in volume and frequency. Reports back from the shuttle also complained of interference in radio reception.

The NASA operators were becoming frantic. No one had any ideas and such an inexplicable event occurring at such an instant was almost too much for some, working as they had been under such psychological and physical stress. It was the observatory at Arecibo in Puerto Rico, linked in by satellite, which first noted the movement of an unidentifiable body amongst the scores of known and charted hardware orbiting the earth. A later replay of the recorded data showed quite unarguably that, impossible though it seemed, this object had appeared as if from nowhere and was now moving on a course which had been plotted to intercept that of the shuttle.

The Mission Control computers at NASA quickly confirmed this. Despite the virtual pandemonium which followed, as conjecture, speculation and arguments saturated the communication channels around the world, it was not long before someone concluded that the sound interference was apparently increasing in proportion to the narrowing distance between the UFO and the shuttle. Once this had been noted and voiced, it was but moments before someone suggested it might be some sort of warning.

For a time, there was talk of using one of the orbiting defense systems. Both major powers had launched laser-armed satellites, capable of destroying enemy craft, before the end of the cold war. But there now remained so little time to the anticipated interception, that there was virtually no possibility of programming the appropriate computers to calculate the complex maneuvers necessary to bring these into action, even assuming they were within range. They had, after all, been designed with an earth-originated target in mind.

So it was that the scientists and other observers at Mission Control, together with the rest of the world at their receivers, waited with varying degrees of consternation and dread as the seconds ticked by. The sound continued to grow in intensity and the pitch was now approaching a scream. A huge overhead screen at the control centre displayed a computer-generated image of the two dots as they converged. The scale above indicated a separation of only some hundred miles. The noise was becoming unbearable. Many were already covering their ears and some had even lost consciousness from the effect on their auditory system in combination with the intense strain of the situation in general. That some climax was impending seemed inevitable and the tension of incomprehension and unpredictability was almost beyond human endurance.

The separation reduced to only tens of miles and suddenly, without warning, the sound ceased abruptly and the silence, which followed in its wake, was profound indeed. The UFO had stopped; an achievement which itself provoked new dismay amongst the onlookers. Whereas previously it had been a mere orbiting object, albeit from an unknown origin, its movement had implied intelligence at source only, as of a guided missile, even if that source was still inconceivable. Now, however, its ability to stop dead in such a situation pushed it into quite new fields of technology. No simple missile this – it clearly contained within itself a level of sophistication quite beyond our capabilities.

Even while people were contemplating the implications of this new phenomenon, however, the shuttle was continuing along its inexorable pre-programmed trajectory to take it into the orbit of the space lab. Then, just as suddenly as the noise had ceased, there was a meteoric eruption of sound which deafened everyone for some time and, upon recovering sufficiently to concentrate once again upon the monitor, it could be seen that both shuttle and UFO had vanished without trace.

The brightness of the sun, which illumines the world, and the brightness of the moon and in the fire – know this brilliance to be mine. XV.12

For Howard and Davidson, enthusiasm and hope had now been transmuted into depression and despair. They exited via the main lift and passageway out into Whitehall, encountering no sign of life and only open doors and airlocks on the way. The missing personnel must have evacuated totally, with apparently no thought of returning, and their destination remained a mystery. They walked back down to Westminster, their steps echoing eerily in the vastness of the empty and silent thoroughfare of this once so busy road.

Howard reported back the cold facts of their discoveries in a dull monotone, scarcely aware of the sound of his own voice. They dumped their equipment back into the storage space at the rear of the helicopter and prepared for the return journey, executing the checking procedures without conscious thought or concern. Neither felt like making conversation.

Both men were alone with their tormented thoughts and questions to which no answer seemed satisfactory. The rotors whirled into life and only the dust of the scarred earth rose with them into semblance of activity. The helicopter lifted gracelessly into the air and headed south to the coast.

Though both still scanned the empty roads and fields below them half-heartedly for sign of life or movement, they found none and, as the sea came into sight in the distance, their spirits reached down into an abyss of hopelessness. The fields of red grass waved gently in the downdraft as they flew low over the coast. Such beauty to an innocent eye, such fears and dread for these observers. And, as they flew on and out over the breaking waves on the beach, their horror rose yet one more intolerable octave. The helicopter jerked as controls were relinquished, the pilots no longer able to maintain sanity and, after a brief moment of apparent suspension in mid-air, plummeted down and smashed into the sea to be swallowed up without ceremony.

And the dull red waves washed over the drifting wreckage.

Just as a man abandons his worn-out clothes and takes new ones so, after abandoning worn-out bodies, the Self finds other, new ones. II.22

Bradley let out a sigh of relief as he finished the typing and backed up the file to his USB key. He rose wearily from the chair and went to look out of the rear window. There was no one to be seen. In the distance, the sounds of the voracious seagulls at the tip were clearly audible. There was no noticeable smell but the dust, raised by the occasional miniature cyclone forming in the exceptional late autumn heat, drifted lazily and joined with the shimmering haze above the baked ground to destroy the sharpness of distant objects. Little vegetation of any sort remained visible in the parched landscape, apart from the occasional tufts of hardy grass in the baked lawns of front gardens.

What, he wondered, would Krish have to say now? He thought a moment and then smiled as the obvious answer occurred to him. He sat down in front of the computer and typed the following brief interchange:

{RJ} So how do we bring this to some sort of meaningful conclusion?

{Krish} I think there is a very suitable ending from the same source with which we began, isn't there?
    Dust in the air suspended
    Marks the place where a story ended.

Indeed only the infinite consciousness, which alone exists even after the cosmic dissolution, exists even now, utterly devoid of objectivity. All these mountains, the whole world, the firmament, the self, the jIva or the individuality and all the elements of which this world is constituted – all these are naught but pure consciousness. Before the so-called creation, when only this pure consciousness existed, where were all these? Space, creation, consciousness are mere words and they indicate the same truth even as synonyms do. Even as the duality experienced in dream is illusory, the duality implied in the creation of the world is illusory. Even as the objects seem to exist and function in the inner world of consciousness in a dream, objects seem to exist and function in the outer world of consciousness during the wakeful state. Nothing really happens in both these states. Even as consciousness alone is the reality of the dream state, consciousness alone is the substance of the wakeful state too. That is the Lord, that is the supreme truth, that you are, that am I and that is all.

Now, I have explained to you that knowledge which is more secret than secret. After considering it in its entirety, do whatever you want. XVIII.63

Acknowledgements

The prologue is based on actual events reported in the 'Guardian' February 11, 2000 – http://www.guardian.co.uk /theguardian/2000/feb/11/features11.g2.

The quotations scattered throughout the book which are followed by Roman numeral references are from the Bhagavad Gita, translation from the Sanskrit by the author. The references are to chapter and verse, e.g. II.17 is chapter 2, verse 17.

The third version of this novel (this is the fifth!) utilized quotations from T. S. Eliot throughout, as opposed to Gita quotations. These were principally from 'Four Quartets,' which I consider to be perhaps the most profound poetry ever written (though I concede that I am a long way from being an expert). But I also tried to use a few quotations from this in my first book ('Book of One') and I discovered, when I attempted to obtain copyright permission, that there was no possibility of ever being able to afford to pay for all these, even if Eliot's estate gave permission. Accordingly, the only remaining ones are very brief, the longest of these being the short extract at the beginning (from which the title of the book derives) and a brief quotation from 'The Hollow Men.' Four Quartets, T. S. Eliot, Faber and Faber, 1944. ISBN 0-571-04994-X. The Hollow Men, from Selected Poems, T. S. Eliot, Faber and Faber, 1944, ISBN 0-571-057063.

The long quotation at the end of the book, about only Consciousness existing, is from 'The Supreme Yoga (Yoga Vasishtha)' translated by Swami Venkatesananda, Motilal Banarsidass Publishers (Private) Ltd., Delhi 2003. ISBN 81-208-1964-0. © Chiltern Yoga Trust, Australia.

Some of the material in the philosophical parts of the dialogs between Krish and RJ has previously been published in 'The Book of One: The Spiritual Path of Advaita,' Dennis Waite, O-Books, 2003, ISBN 1-903816-41-6 and some will be published in

'A-U-M: Awakening to Reality,' by Dennis Waite, O-Books, 2015, ISBN 978-1-78279-996-2.

Most of the information relating to landfill sites was obtained from papers on the Internet but an excellent book, containing all that you might want to know is 'Waste Treatment and Disposal,' Paul T. Williams, James Wiley & Sons Ltd., 2005. ISBN-13 978-0470-84913-2 (paperback).

Most of the information relating to hazardous waste disposal was obtained from the website of the Environmental Research Foundation – http://www.rachel.org/.

Information on specific toxic chemicals was obtained principally from the website of the Agency for Toxic Substances and Disease Registry – http://www.atsdr.cdc.gov/.